I0674913

SELAI

BY

J.D. BELL

An ACOA Publication
www.aconspiracyofauthors.com
ISBN: 978-1-936507-86-3

Selai

A Conspiracy of Authors Publication

www.aconspiracyofauthors.com

Copyright © 2019 by J.D. Bell

ISBN: 978-1-936507-86-3

Cover Art Copyright © 2019 by Lazette Gifford

First Print Edition: June 2019

Dedication:

This is dedicated to Carol Bell; who taught me Bears could talk, Cars needed names and that she had a bag of holding full of quarters to buy a story from me.

Table of Contents

TALLEN 1

It was end of summer and I was back at the Memorial Union. I'd made a delivery run from Windsor to Chicago and took the long way home through Iowa. Spent the night at a motel on the outskirts of Ames then I drifted through Dogtown and the parts of the campus I could still drive through, before parking the Chevy close to the student union.

I was just looking for ghosts.

I found them, in the Union's North entrance, Gold Star Hall. The hall where the names are chiseled deep into the granite. Abbott. Barnes. Evans. Franks, Ronald T.

I pulled a cheaply bound booklet from my leather dispatch case and opened the now ancient twenty-fifth anniversary pamphlet to the "F's".

Under Franks, Ronald T. there was a small black and white photo of a young man in a dark blazer; white shirt, high collar and a thin black tie with a straw boater in his hands. His eyes were dark shadows in the low-quality photo, his smile only hinted at. But he was there in that photo. Came from Yates Center down in Kansas to attend Iowa State as a Pre-Veterinary major. He joined the American Army in 1917and died late in 1918 from the 'Spanish Lady'. He was in the 1st Division AEF.

There was Pasaschof, Calvin M. There was no photo of him in the booklet. Calvin was an Engineering major, he died at Belleau Wood with the 23rd battalion, Sixth Marines.

Ripley, Donald Lee. College of Veterinary Science; 33 Division, Army. AEF.

Ratzlaff, Jacob. USN, Faculty member College of Engineering. No explanation given as to how an Iowa teacher ended up with a Gold Star from the Navy, but there he was.

I found the name I was looking for. Tallen, Royal A., College of Agronomy; BEF, DSO.

In the old and battered book there was a very blurry studio photo of RA Tallen, in a Canadian uniform and wearing the name of Ray Tallen. The United States disapproved of its citizens serving in anyone else's army. Thus, all of the Yanks that went to Canada for that war carried new names. When Lance Corporal Tallen went missing in 1919 it took a while for the Canadian army to sort out the subterfuge and send a letter of condolences to his American family, along with a medal. Part of the confusion was that he went missing and was declared dead after the official end of the war to end all wars. But he was on active duty and under arms, so, the Commonwealth considered him a casualty of the war. While the ISU Memorial Union committee were more rigid in their awarding a Gold Star, he had a medal from the Crown and a scroll of honor from the French. So, they let Roy Tallen into the hall.

When the Alumni Association got the Memorial Union rolling in 1922, Royal A. Tallen was listed as being among the lost students and suitably remembered on Armistice Day.

Which was odd, considering I was Tallen, Royal A.

I placed my hand against the cold stone. Rubbed my palm along the inscription. I wondered, not for the first time, if I shouldn't be struck dead. Here in the hall, under the stained-glass windows. I remembered the first time I had come here, at the Bicentennial, to look over the landscape and found my name cut into the granite. It's a queer thing to come upon your own grave marker. Particularly, while you are still among the quick.

That thought brought a chill and the stench of things long dead in black mud. But the odor was part of the here and now.

I casually turned towards the stench. At the south end, in the central hall by the desk for the Alumni Hotel on the upper floors, stood two men with stick-on badges and a map of the campus. They were tall and well-trimmed, their suits hung by bespoke tailors and their hair was strictly GQ. They'd been consulting that map for a quarter hour, folding and refolding it. Stepping back out of the general path and then wandering back into the gangway. All the while they kept watch across the central hall and down the Memorial Hall towards me. I hadn't paid too much attention to them before but, talking to the Lance Corporal tends to focus the Subtle mind.

They had no auras.

This is like having no shadow on a sunny day.

Their eyes kept shifting off me, towards the revolving doors and the bench in the other corner. I looked up and another pair was having a friendly conversation in the open arches of the second-floor landing, which overlooked the Memorial Hall. They'd got their suits from the same tailor and their tradecraft from the same cereal box.

They had no auras.

They were ghost walking.

You can suppress your aura. Sometimes this comes as the unhappy side effect of attempting to master a Subtle art quickly, without a proper grounding. The student learns all the katas and masters the throws, but it is just mechanical. Rote learning. There are several paths that seek to hide the aura, place it deep in the Overt body. The benefits from a suppressed aura lie mostly in the discipline it takes to maintain it and the lack of a wake as you move through the world.

Everyone can see auras. They just don't see them consciously. It is a quarter of the way we communicate; verbally, non-verbal cues, pheromones and auras. Auras function beneath our normal awareness, along with but stronger than, pheromones. Auras can tell us when the person facing us is friendly, intent on taking our cash, or cutting our throat.

The Adept that suppresses his auras distorts that communication. A subtler poker face as it were. You blend into the woodwork. Refuse to stand out. Wear clothing that blends in. Don't talk much. And suppress your auras. You aren't remarked upon. The suppressed aura makes you even less memorable to the casual, overt, observer. The "he was too ordinary" description. Again, useful in certain habits.

I checked out the hot corner. On the polished granite bench there was a woman with a backpack on her lap and a pair of crutches. She was reading a book or leafing through it. One hand never far from a slit pocket in the pack, her eyes drifting up to focus on the revolving doors to her left but, keeping the four suits in the corner of her vision. Her left ankle was in an air cast. Her jeans were dirtier than fashion demanded, and I could see a long scrape under a tear in her buttoned-down left sleeve. Her auras were bright and rolling in the semi-darkness of the hall. Her fear and her resolve plain if you had the eyes to see and the experience to understand.

I turned my back on her for a second to look at Lance Cpl. Tallen in the mirror of the granite wall. Then I tucked my handbook away, picked up my overnighter and turned towards the girl on the bench.

"Hello." I said, moving my body to block her from the suits.

She looked up from the book, her hand drifting towards the slit in her bag, her face pale under her coal black hair.

"Been waiting long?" I extended my hand to her and winked. "Ready to get some lunch at Hanratty's?"

She hesitated for a breath, her nostrils flaring as she gathered her good leg under her, and then she read me. Whoever the hell I was, I was not with the gents in the suits, and that was enough for her.

"Long enough," she said. Her voice a pleasant alto, crisp and clean with nothing of the public-school slop in it. She contrived to drop her book and while we both bent to retrieve, she whispered. "Two above, three outside. Where is Del?"

I just nodded and handed her back the book. She muscled herself up on one leg and positioned the crutches under her arms. I walked her past the concierge, nodding at the two suits by the desk. Then I sidestepped her through a door marked Staff Only and into a dim service corridor running to the parking garage. It had bricked up windows from when it was an entry hall in the '30s, tile floors with rough concrete patches and naked light bulbs at the midpoint and each end of the hall.

"Don't stop, I'll catch up."

And I knocked the light out, just over her head, with my overnight bag. She didn't flinch, just kept swinging on down the passage.

ALENA 2

I was waiting for the teams to close in. I hoped for one or
two clear shots before they darted me. If the darts were
lethal or stunners, it did not matter. The safe house was
burned, literally, and I was on my last legs. I had a Lethe
capsule tucked into my cheek. I would not be taken.

"Hello."

I looked up from the book I had been pretending to
read. The man that stood before me was not one of the
hunters. He did not have that sleek, satisfied look of a well
fed Medji. His hair was dusted with gray. His skin was
tanned and creased with outdoor living. The suit he wore
hung well over his shoulders, cut to make motion easy, cut
to blend.

He smiled and winked. Held out his hand for mine.
"Been waiting long?" He spoke English with the local
accent. His hand dry and callused. He was not Mihaly, but

he did not smell of enemy. I dropped my book as I took his hand and tried to warn him but, he just levered me onto my crutches and escorted me away talking about some 'place' to have lunch.

He walked me through the lobby of the Union, past two of my hunters, who dropped their maps, flustered by a new player on the field. Past the desk clerk and down a dark passageway behind the desk.

He patted me on my bum, said, "Go on. I'll catch up." then knocked out the only light in the that end of the passage with his luggage. I put my head down and worked the crutches as fast as I was able. Hoping to get to the door at the far end before the pursuit came. As I got to the door, I heard a scuffle and two heavy blows, like a maul crushing bones for the grinder. Then the pop of another light bulb breaking.

When I turned my head, he was looming out of the dark, his small suitcase in his hand, his eyes hidden behind sunglasses and his face blank. The next thing I knew he was handing me into a large ground car and tucking my crutches in under my legs, while stowing my pack where I could have my hand on it. In the excitement I swallowed the Lethe capsule.

Fortunately, it does not work taken orally.

TALLEN 3

I walked her through the Union car park and out a pedestrian entrance, then down the long hill to my car. My back itched all the way down. The overnight bag in my left hand, swinging gently as we walked, and I told her about the history of Lake Laverne and the Swans.

She smelled like musk, patchouli, grubby clothes and scared girl. She was breathing hard and wincing at each step by the time we got to where the Suburban was parked. The late afternoon sunlight poured over us like snowmelt over rock. I beeped the remote door locks and handed her in, settled her crutches in beside her, patted her backpack, and the hard, angular lump within it. "Okay?" I asked. She nodded. Her face, if anything, paler than before.

I got in my side and fired up the diesel. By the time I powered out of the parking lot, three of the suits were just crossing the street from the Union. I turned east on

Lincoln Way and rumbled on into Ames proper. When we got past the Highway Commission's complex I turned right again and took a street that I knew turned into a country dirt road. Keeping the big Suburban at a comfortable thirty. When I went over the hill the chill went away.

She was breathing easier, but her hand was in the backpack and holding the gun on me. I'd left the radio on, but it was soft and low, and I let the silence do the interrogation.

"Why?" She finally asked.

"Why not."

"Whose are you?"

"Believe the proper form is `Who are you?' or is it 'Whom'?"

"Where is Del?"

"Don't know him."

She slumped. "She. Del Minor."

She turned her face to the front. Took her hand from the pack. Closed her eyes, like a child waiting for a blow. Leaning her head against the window with tears beginning to wet her face.

She was tired, bone tired to the point that I could feel it from where I sat. So, I started to ramble.

"The name is Ray. Ray Tallen. Short for R period A period. Won't answer to my real first name so I won't tell you."

By now the suits were in their cars, burning down the four-lane casting about for the Suburban or Hanratty's. "Good luck to them on Hanratty's" I thought. Since they'd paved it over just after the first Kennedy died.

"I went to college here, Iowa State. Didn't finish. A war got in the way. But I had maybe the best time of my life here. When I get time, from time to time, I come back and see how the memories are."

I flipped the radio over to the scanner I had a friend install. Selected the digital cellular mode and also set the decoder module to detect and decode. Wouldn't likely come to squat but, lucky is as lucky does.

"I hate to see the changes but, I just can't resist. Like

scratching stitches or poison ivy, sometimes I just keep digging."

She rubbed at her runny nose with her hands. Briskly shook her head. Dark black hair, brown eyes so dark they were almost black. Indian looking. Grubby but smooth, light brown skin. She might be five, five and a half feet, when she wasn't stumping around on crutches.

I pitched her a packet of wipes. She grabbed a handful, scrubbing at her face and then at her hands. I kept her in the corner of my eye, watching her shake off the pain.

She'd quit waiting for the punch, the ice pick, or the .22 short to the base of the skull. She patted the backpack again, looked to the rear and around, checking out the interior. Snapped her belt about her and settled in her crutches where they wouldn't likely impale us if we rolled the big wagon. She did not have her second wind but, she was getting close. She took a deep breath and faced me to speak.

I pulled to a stop at the crossroads, where the pavement turned to sand road. "When I looked up from my memories and saw those goons tracking shit through them, it did not please me. So now I'm asking. Who are you and why would they be after you?"

"They will kill you." She worked hard at warning me off. "They have killed Del. I live only because I am worth more alive." She reached out a hand to touch me.

I looked down at her hand. "Really." I nodded, looked her in the eyes. I let her see what face I showed the gunmen at the hall. "And, again, who are you?"

She backed slightly away. "I am Mihaly. Alena Constance Mihaly of the House Mihaly."

"Mihaly, that's a Magyar name. Hungary?"

"Once. You do not know the House?"

"No," I said, looking to the mirror to see if we had any traffic. "I've fair knocked about the world, but I never met the Mihaly's of Hungary? You lose your chateau when the Russians rolled over Hungary in '45?"

She blinked, all but insulted that I didn't 'know' the House. "No, somewhat earlier than that. You are a professional soldier, a mercenary?"

I winced. My turn to be insulted. "I am not. I am a trouble shooter, bodyguard, security consultant. Not a merc." Not in this incarnation.

"I see." She fumbled at her shirtfront, trying to unbutton her shirt with one hand, keeping her other still on my wrist. "Are you at leisure now?"

"You hiring?" I hadn't quite bought it before this. Yes, they were wet work teams. That stink was about them. But I figured that her father was in the background. Sending them to pick up Missy and bring her back. The signs were really all wrong for that sort of situation, auras were never as well suppressed in your garden market wet team but, I was never the brightest Tallen. Just the meanest.

Alena nodded and pulled a small chamois bag from between her breasts. Out of it she poured six gold coins into my hand. Krugerrands they were. Each worth a good four hundred US for the gold.

I whistled softly, forgetting her hand on my wrist. They were near mint with just enough wear on them to give them a history. "And what would you be hiring with this?"

"Safe passage. To Canon City."

"And what are you running from, or to."

"To friends. Good friends, I hope."

That first day we just ran south at a steady thirty miles to the hour. I had a full tank of diesel and no particular reason to go fast. The suits would be covering the interstate, smothering the airports and hanging out at the bus stations. But the back roads of Iowa are a big place. Now if they had the cops helping out, things could get chancy. But I figured they didn't. My fancy radio system would have picked up any traffic looking for us.

I didn't ask her any questions. She flicked down the lock on her door and turned her head to watch the road go by. Soon enough she went to sleep. I put my brain in low gear and just let the car take us south.

I stopped twice, once to change plates on the car and tap a kidney and once to let her powder her nose at a McDonald's close to the Missouri border. She turned up

her nose at a quick hamburger. I didn't. Never turn down a
chance to sleep or a bite to eat.

When I got out to change the plates, I changed my ID
as well. Shucked my suit coat and slipped on a worn, leather
bomber jacket. I combed my hair forward and slipped in a
set of colored lenses to match the ID. I put a set of
magnetic signs on the doors, advertising McCoul's stud
farms and ran the car down a dusty dirt road just to set the
image. She woke up when I stopped and gravely watched
me change. Then went quickly back to sleep.

It was dark when I pulled up at the gate.

"Where?"

"Missouri. Northeast of St. Joseph." I got out and
eased my back. I walked over to the chain looped over the
fence post, swung the gate open, got back in the car and
drove over the threshold. When I shut the gate, I armed the
alarms. "Safe place."

On the other side of the hill was a large white wooden
barn, a stock tank, a feed rack in a paddock and a singlewide trailer. The grass was ankle high in the paddock and
around the trailer. But the yard light was still on and a little
red LED telltale, glowing on the telephone pole, told me
that no one had broken in and Nigel was still paying the
bills.

I got out and helped her out of the big car. Then I
escorted her to the barn.

"The barn-?

"Um, the trailer is a lure."

She looked at the trailer, then at the rough wood slats
of the barn. "A lure." She hitched her backpack around to a
more comfortable hang and shook her head. "Alena
Constance," I heard her mutter. "what have you gotten
yourself into now."

She let me walk her into the barn. I closed the sliding
door behind us and walked her through the dark to another
door. When I had her and her crutches through that door, I
stepped in close behind her and closed the outer. We were
in a light tight, sound proofed, vapor tight airlock. I turned
on the light and opened the last door into the hidey hole.

The air was musty, but it was clean enough. Built on the old CD bomb shelter design, with low noise ventilation fans powered by Ni-Cads on a solar cell charger loop. The lights were battery, less mission critical. There were two beds, a water cooler, a food locker, a low-flow stool and a shower stall behind a curtain. I opened a cupboard and dug out a medical kit, opened another and pulled out a set of linens sealed in a bag. Then I handed her a small radio.

"I'll be wearing an earbud. You click the transmit button on that and a tone will sound on it. I'm going out to get some food and tell some people that I'm here. If I don't touch base with them, they'll come looking."

"That would not be good."

"I gathered that. You need anything?"

"Clean clothes would be nice. A shower."

"Behind that curtain. Thirty-two waist, thirty-three inseam, medium T-shirt?"

"Thirty-inch waist. You were a tailor in a past life?"

"No. I'll call before I come through the door. If anyone else comes on the place, that light will come on and stay on."

She nodded. "Be careful, R.A. Tallen." She shucked her gun from the bag and laid it close to hand as she sat on the bed to undo the aircast.

Outside I got in the SUV. Started to punch Nigel's number into the set, then got second thoughts. It was eight o'clock. I looked at the house trailer. It was more than a lure, but I hadn't wanted to put her in it. The shelter walls in the barn were proof against anything short of a twenty millimeter. The trailer wouldn't stop a fast-pitch softball.

I needed to age a little. Forward to a comfortable fifty or so. I got out of the Suburban and high stepped through the weeds to the trailer's stoop, making lots of noise to encourage any wildlife to go elsewhere. Didn't need a close quarter dose of skunk to add to my problems. I opened the door with the key I kept in the mailbox bolted to the aluminum shell. It was mustier inside than the barn but, the roof was still solid, and no one had broken in to party. In the back room I had a platform bed and a dresser full of makeup. Fifteen minutes later I was a grizzled middle fifties.

Town wasn't much. Had a 24hr Walmart and a Kwick Shop just north of the old crossroads. A hundred yards south of the crossroads there was the dying farm market town. I'd bought a quarter section of land in the late seventies and dug me a little hide out. Established it as a breeding farm for quarter horses. I could launder a little cash, have a fair reason for traveling about the lower 48, even a good explanation for being banged up once in a while. Horses being what they are. Almost as good a dodge as import/export. Without the bother of customs.

Nigel came a bit later. I needed a helper like I needed a second set of legs, but he was a promise made to a dead woman. Promises made to the dead are the most binding of them all. I called his answering machine on the way into the town and told him to call me.

I stopped at the Walmart and picked up enough clothing to get her through a week, plus a half-dozen new jeans and shirts for me. Paid cash for the clothing and the two bags of groceries, since I didn't want to be in their database. I stopped at the Kwick shop and bought a twelve pack of beer, topped off the Suburban's fuel tank and bought a Des Moines Register as well as a KC Star. Didn't see anyone I knew but, I knew both places ran video monitors 24/7. So, I was just a tired old dude in jeans and a feed cap, pulled down low. I caught myself scratching my neck for the fourth time while I was paying the bill. I smiled at the clerk and muttered something about bailing hay. She took my fifty with two fingers. Placed my change on the counter.

I pulled the truck off the blacktop into a school bus turnaround, to watch my back trail for a while with a folding carbine in my lap. Her chamois bag was in the lock console between the front seats. I pulled it out and weighed the coins in my hands. Gold.

It's funny. Some people, mainly players on the fringes, think more of gold than greenbacks. Two Krugerrands will buy you out of trouble faster than a wad of cash, even a handful of dead presidents. It didn't make much sense to me. American or English paper bought just as much as gold and didn't weigh anywhere near as much. I hadn't touched gold since I left Macao.

So why did I sign on with Alena.

And why did my neck itch.

My phone buzzed, the number was unfamiliar, but it was Nigel.

"Yeah."

"You're back early."

"Smooth run. Anything I need to see you about?"

"No." He said, drawing it out. "Not really. Tomorrow would be fine."

"I'm on the road again tomorrow."

"Oh. That's a problem."

"You'll handle it, won't you?" Dead silence on his end of the phone.

"We really need to talk."

I grinned in the dark. He was about due for another try at my cushy chair. When I signed him on, not too long after I came home from the Pacific Rim, he had been a hustler with the bad sense to try to roll one of the very last mob connected casinos in Las Vegas. He fumbled the con and only a well-tuned sense of danger saved his ass. That sense of danger and a willingness to leave his inside people hung out to dry kept him alive. Then the dead called in their marker and I managed to buy him a pass.

He was so very grateful. For about a year. Then he tried to run a game between me and a client. I did not take a finger from him, deliberately. I am not Yakuza and that sort of drama-queen apology doesn't cut it with me. But he got the message well enough. After he got to where he could eat solid food again, I treated him to a fish fry. Farm bred catfish. Then I told him how his buddies in the scam ended up feeding the catfish. Being a partner with Nigel was not the way to grow old.

That kept him on the straight and narrow, for the most part. But, like certain horses I have come across, every so often he would try a little crow hop or just casually rub up against a fence post. Just to see if I was paying attention.

"Mac..."

"I'm out of the office. Still." And thumbed the phone off. He called back once, but I didn't answer. I tucked the phone into a pocket in my jacket and headed for the horse farm.

Back at the safe house I brought the groceries and the dry goods into the barn. I used a crank phone in the barn's tack room to give her a heads up. When I came through the door, she was off to the weak side with her gun at the ready. She lit up at the clothing, placed her gun on the bed and unconcernedly shucked the blanket she'd draped over herself. She was naked as a jaybird.

"You thought of under things, thank the god." She ripped open the packages and pulled out a pair of briefs. "I can get by with just a tank top."

"I scored a medium sports top, might do."

Her breasts were high and firm, brown as her neck without a tan line, the skin flawless. The scent of musk and patchouli made my head spin and her nakedness made my ears burn. Between her breasts was a shiny medallion, about the size of a cartwheel silver dollar.

"I..." I started to make my excuse and step outside. Casual and nudity being words I wouldn't use in the same sentence. Then her pendant caught the light.

She reached out a hand and grabbed my shoulder so she could step into the briefs. I gently stretched out my hand and took her medallion, warm from her skin. Turned it in my fingers like a poker chip. It was outsized, say the thickness of two of the old silver dollars stacked and half again the diameter of those dollars and heavier. On one side there was a tau cross deeply struck, like an exaggerated capital T, and on the other side there was a delicately engraved profile of Alena. Alena, or someone very much like her. She froze. Her bad leg tangled in the briefs, her hand trembling on my shoulder. She let go of the briefs letting them drop to the floor and brought her hand up to cup my hand about the medallion. I felt her other hand smooth back my hair and trail her scent over my face. A cat marking territory.

Around the tau cross there was an inscription. Greek letters. Under the profile on the obverse was a date. Sixteenth century in faint Roman numerals. It was heavy, heavier than it looked. Inside it would be a wafer of steel, the rest of the medallion would be either a very hard nickel silver or electrum. It marked her. Like extra nipples below her breasts on the milk line or the blue patch I would have found at the base of her spine. It marked her.

I knew what she was supposed to be. Only the Holder or the Heir Designate carried one of those talismans. But it should be the size of a sand dollar, better than four inches in diameter. The inscription should be in Kana. The obverse a family badge like a chrysanthemum or a tiger's mask. And finally, it should be pierced through the middle to receive a sword tang. I had never seen one like hers. And I had four others buried in a trunk, in Kansas.

I looked from the engraving to her face, not a foot from mine, her breath soft and rapid on my cheeks. My head was starting to spin, the edges of the room graying out. I breathed deeper, sucking down her scent, like the first hot drag off a pipe of black poppy. Her eyes widened. The pupils dilated until there was only a thin rim of color between their black depths and the white.

I could feel the heat uncoiling up my spine, hear her heart beating and see the blood pulsing under the skin of her face. Her auras appeared, faint in the dim room and then growing brighter with each pulse.

It was then that the light came on beside the door.

"Your people?" She husked.

"No." And if it was, they weren't my people any longer.

I turned my back on her. Breathing deeply, slowly, paced by a drumming surf only I could hear. The room brightened still more as my eyes dilated. The thirty-watt bulb glinting off her medallion.

"Get packed. Pull up on the stool and it swivels to the right. There's a tunnel under and out. I'll follow after-"

"After?"

"After I do what you impressed me for."

She extended the gun to me. "You will need this."

I laughed. "You're mistaken. Guns don't kill people." I flicked off the light and as I went out the door I said. "I do."

ALENA 4

He laughed and said "You're mistaken. Guns don't kill people. I do." And he slipped out the door.
My ankle hurt. I needed another shower. I stank, again. I hobbled to the door and listened. Nothing. I flicked the light back on and cursed in my mother's low Nagi and hobbled into the shower. Damn him for not remembering my leg, damn them but I will go cleanly to my death and damn me for not having more care.

The Bloodseal nestled hot between my breasts. An Avar, by the god, and by what I sensed when I pushed him unpressed, a belted warrior at that! I had thrown the seven coins and all showed heads, an unpressed Avar!

It was twenty minutes of silence by the clock in my head when I heard the single ring of the land line and then the tap at the door. I knew it was him.

"Enter." I said, holding the gun on the door.

"You didn't try the tunnel?" He slipped through the door, not bothering with the light this time.

"My leg..."

He nodded. "My fault, I forgot about your ankle. They had a gizmo."

"Gizmo?"

He showed me a small device, not much bigger than a paperback book. "It tracked you. A bug in your clothing, your backpack, those crutches, worst case, in you."

"Can you tell?"

"No," He shrugged. "It got damaged when I took it away from its operator." He smiled slightly, threw the device on the bed. "And we can't ask the operator. He got damaged as well."

"They'll track us again."

"Only if their bug is in you. Lose the backpack, the crutches, the aircast. Anything that could incorporate it."

"I've changed clothing from the skin out." I opened my pack, emptied it on the bed.

I sorted through the items I'd salvaged from the hospital after the wreck of the car. After Del and I separated. A wallet of traveler's checks, some toiletries, worry beads, a set of identity papers that matched the checks, hair brush, mirror, a Sony Walkman. My pistol and a spare magazine.

"The checks, and the papers..."

"Both likely compromised." He said. "Ditch it all here. Leave your shoes as well."

"And the pistol?"

He grinned. "Yes. It's French Para issue, isn't it?"

I nodded. "It suits me."

"Well, leave it. I'll see if I can scrounge you another."

He knelt and undid my shoelaces, then the aircast. He was close, so close and so fresh was the impress that my head swam. I smelled blood and cordite. Cordite and something more. Burnt copper and a corrupt low tide. Blood and death.

"Now where?"

"Away, before the next set of hunters come belling on

your trail." He looked up at me, his eyes were so very dark. "I'll carry you to the car."

"I could walk."

"There's a lot of crap on the ground; wood splinters, broken glass and the like. I'll carry you."

"All right."

He scooped me up, as if I were a child, and carried me through the darkness of the barn out into the moonlight. The moon was low on the horizon. Large and bright even to my unadapted eyes, throwing deep shadows darker than the ones thrown by the sun at noon. There were bright scars on the side of his truck, the passenger side window starred but, not punctured from bullets. Another truck, much like Tallen's, sat in the yard next to the trailer. Its tires were flat on the trailer side, all the windows shattered, and the driver's door hung open. From the open door a body spilled out onto the grass. Two more were huddled by the rear tires. Their clothing dark and shiny wet in the moon's cool light.

"Can you open the door." Tallen asked me.

"Yes." I pulled up the latch and swung the driver's side door open. He slid me in, being cautious of my ankle.

"Start the motor. You know how to start a diesel?"

"Ignition switch on, wait for the light, and crank the starter."

"Okay." He reached under the seat, pulled something loose with a solid click. Then he handed me a heavy canvas holster. "Colt three eighty on a forty-five frame. Shoots dead on at ten yards. Alternating ball and hollow points. I'll be back in a minute." He walked back into the barn.

I unsnapped the holster's flap, drew the pistol, ejected the magazine, cleared and locked the slide, then slipped the magazine back into the grip. I let the slide rack forward and put the safety on. I felt better.

When he came out of the barn, he had a large backpack and an even larger sea bag. I had the truck idling. He opened the back and slung the pack and the bag into the cargo area. I watched him in the rear-view mirror as he dug through a toolbox. He pulled out a roll of dark tape.

He went around the truck taping the bullet scars in the metal.

"Shouldn't we be on the road?"

"Hm?" He looked up from the tape. "We have a while. Might as well make the damage look less memorable."

"What if they..." I nodded at the bodies by the other truck, meaning others of their kind. "come back?"

He grunted. "Unlikely." And tucking the tape between the dashboard and the windshield he walked back into the barn.

I was glaring at his back when I noticed dark forms huddled in the corner of the barn and the paddock fence. My heart pounding, I flicked the headlamps on, the unfamiliar gun awkward in my off hand.

After a long look, I shut the lights off. I closed my eyes and willed away the images on the back of my eyelids. I didn't open them again until he touched my arm.

TALLEN 5

The barn was alight when we pulled out of the drive. I knew the trailer and the other truck would be burning soon. Alena was huddling in the passenger's seat, nursing the antique Colt I'd gifted her and letting the night air blow her hair back.

I'd rolled all the windows down. Bullet scars on black glass are cop magnets and we were lucky enough not to have taken any rounds in the windshield or any of the rear windows. The hundred knot tape on the dings made the Suburban look rust shot and not gut shot. I'd changed the plate and ditched the magnetic signs that linked us to the McCoul place. The three cans of leak stop I poured into the radiator helped as well. Someone had used really small flechettes, almost as small as needles, in a shotgun round and pumped one into the radiator, two into the side of the Suburban.

It hadn't been too hard. They had eight. When I came around the corner four were in the cab and bed of a big dually truck, covering four gunmen assaulting the single wide trailer. The assault team had silenced submachine guns, flashbang, body armor, coal scuttle helmets and all the other SWAT toys. Swarming through the front door and lighting up the empty rooms with gunfire by the book.

Like I said, the trailer was not much more than aluminum painted cardboard. The SWAT subsonic rounds buzzed right through the sides, losing a bit more velocity in exchange for some inspired tumbling and ricochets. The covering party dove off the truck and groveled on the driveway while they tried to get the happy cowboys in the trailer to cease fire.

I dropped to my belly and crawled through the wet grass, my shovel on a lanyard looped over my shoulder. Could have used the gun she tried to force on me but, I wanted one to live long enough for a bit of conversation. So, I scooped up one of my old reliables; a trench shovel with one edge sharpened. It made a nice short coupled axe, without the nasty tendency of axes to stick.

I crawled towards them while bullets thudded into their dually and my Suburban, punching holes in my paintwork which pissed me off more than the way they were shooting up the trailer. I stopped crawling at the base of the yard light. Stood up slowly and rested my hand on the main power switch. When the guns quit hammering in the trailer, I pulled the switch and the yard went dark. Then I took the four in the covering party down. One got off a shot but, that was all. I threw the last one towards the light pole and rolled under the dually.

The fire team came out the backside of the single wide and tried to assault where they thought I was. The light pole.

It was easier than drowning ducklings. Shovels don't have muzzle flashes and make less noise than even the best silencers. Only the last one caught on and danced in a circle, firing his shotgun on full auto. He dropped it when it rattled empty and then dropped two heavy flash grenades behind him as he ran for the paddock.

I caught him just the other side of the fence, high diving from the top of the gate with my spade whistling through the dark. I scythed his legs out from under him using the dull edge so as not to let him bleed out too quick. He hit the ground hard, with that wet crunch that tells you broken bones are the best you can hope for. I landed close by and parachute rolled to my feet, then a silent glide to the left. I figured he'd had a side arm and would empty it where he'd last heard a sound from. Then while he tried to reload, I'd step in and disarm him for a chat.

He just sobbed once and tucked it under his chin. I saw the flash light up his mouth, heard the round bust his head open, just like a melon dropped on a rock. No field interrogation for him. I purely hate it when they do that.

I collected and checked the others, but they were dead as well. Couldn't use any sort of stun reliably because of the SWAT armor they were wearing, couldn't just bash them on the knot between the shoulder blades and pick them up later for a bit of 'conversation'. I had to crunch them at the base of the skull with the dull side of the spade or use the sharp side like a broadaxe across the throat. Messy.

After I got her in the Suburban, I dragged the bodies into the barn. Scattered incendiary packets over them after a bit of judicious butchery with a corn knife. Mixing up the number of the dead. The fires would muddy the evidence. If the 'bug' was in her castoffs and the fire killed it, our trail died there. If it didn't ruin the bug, they'd be confused for a while. I threw one of the smaller bodies on the bed in the hidey hole with a thermite grenade on a timer tossed under the bed. I peeled down to skin and stepped through a hazmat flood shower to rinse the blood away. Fifteen minutes until the grenade went off.

I'd pulled my emergency cash and three clean ID from the plug safe in the trailer's foundation. Changed into a fresh set of clothing, tucked my new ID away in my front pocket. I dropped another grenade on a shorter timer in the safe with my entire old set of 'Mac McCoul' identity and my cell phone then locked the safe. Not a chance in hell they could retrieve that. I didn't call Nigel. If he was lucky, they'd overlook him. If he was smart, he'd pull up stakes and leg it.

Knowing Nigel, he'd try to sell me to them and get his throat cut for his payment. That thought made me pause. Promises to the dead. But I scooped a bag full of clothing off the couch and left the trailer as the floor safe began to whistle like a teakettle from the heat. McCoul had made the promise and he had just died.

"I went through the pockets, looked over their gear." I looked out of the corner of my eye at Alena. She had her good leg tucked under her. "Plain vanilla cop identification, some cheap stuff you could almost do on the computers at Kinko's." The guns had been nothing special; nine millimeters, shotguns and HK assault guns.

"But the shotgun rounds were odd, flechettes mixed with a funny slug round."

I pulled onto the state road running to the Kansas border. "So, in the words of Butch and Sundance, 'Who are these guys?' "

"Butch?"

Her tone said it all. As one of Nigel's playmates used to say, 'swoosh' right over her head. "Who is chasing you." And me, now.

She sighed. "Those were hirelings. Medji, in the Nagi." She had popped her tongue against her front teeth before the word Nagi. "Catsfeet."

"Cat's paws?"

"Yes."

"How long have you been in the states?" She was tired, her English slipping. A tired child, a very tired child.

"Since the winter. Your winter." Not mine was the implication. Southern Hemisphere?

"Why?"

"A present," She yawned. "a trip before I must choose."

"Okay. So why are these 'Medjays' after us." I could see flashing lights ahead of us, coming fast.

"My cousin died." She dug the oversized coin out of

her shirt. Watching it twirl on the chain. "She died and sent me this."

I pulled off the road and let the sirens scream by. Volunteer Fire department. I looked in the mirror, in the distance there was a glow over the hilltop. Better than twenty years I'd stayed there. I felt almost nothing, not for the trailer. I was sorrier about losing the barn, burning out a family of owls.

I pulled back out onto the blacktop and turned my head to check her out. She was asleep. Her head between the window pillar and the seat back. The gun was tucked between her legs. I pulled it from her hand, gingerly. The safety was on but what little I knew of her told me there was a round up the spout. I did not particularly trust her reflexes. I wore a few faded scars from reflexes I knew she had to carry. She carried the coin. The reflexes came with it.

I let her sleep through the dark, her auras swirling around her. The slow drift of silt in a deep pool.

The Suburban got us to where I had another vehicle cached but the over temp lights were flickering when we pulled into the Self Store. I punched the identification code into the box and the gates opened. It was coming on four in the morning, but these things ran 24/7, that was part of the package. Nobody checking you in or out, just a video camera that fed to a backroom VCR.

A back room that I had a key to.

I'd bought into the place about the same time I bought the horse farm in Missouri. Different name, different source of financing and the income went to a bank in Wichita, not KCMO. I needed someplace to securely store items I was uneasy with keeping at the farm. Someplace to stash the occasional human contraband and a place to park my other rides. It was also a good place to launder cash. It was always about 70 percent full. Imagine that.

I tucked the suburban around the corner from the big rollup storage locker and left it idling. When I had the door open, I flicked on the light and opened the hood of the truck that nearly filled the locker. I had a trickle charger on the battery, running off a tap on the light circuit. But I'd had the old beast out and running about just a month ago. It was a 1969 International Harvester with saddle tanks, a flatbed big enough to haul a VW even with the armored lock box on the bed. I checked the battery, unplugged the charger and crawled into the cab. It started on the first crank. I let it warm up for a minute, then pulled it out into the alley and set the parking brake.

Alena was awake, sitting behind the wheel of the Suburban, the .38 auto in her lap.

"And?"

"We change vehicles here."

"How long did I sleep."

"A while."

"Is there any sign of pursuit?"

"No. How is the leg?"

She grimaced. "It hurts."

"What happened to it?"

"A car wreck, severe bruising and some twisted ligaments."

"Not good, but not as bad as it might have been."

"Do you have any aspirin?"

I opened the door and lifted her out. "Maybe. Maybe something better." She nestled her head on my shoulder, her left hand cradling the gun while the right hung on to my neck. I carried her to the old truck and boosted her into the driver's side. She felt the cracked oilcloth seats and looked at the crud on the floor.

"I should hazard a guess, camouflage?"

"No. Just dirt. I'll throw down some paper for you to put your feet on."

The overhead liner was long gone. The only radio was an AM mono which hadn't worked since I bought the truck. It smelled like any other working vehicle, of oil and mildew and too much sun on old paint.

"Not as up to date as the Suburban but it will get us there, when you tell me where there is."

"I will need a map, of Colorado." Her accent was off slightly, the photocopy effect. She had learned English at second or third hand.

"We can do that."

She looked at me. Her eyes shadows in the dark cab. "What did you use on the men by the barn?"

I hadn't thought she had seen them.

ALENA 6

He paused, and then gently tucked something into the storage space behind the seat.

"A shovel. Or more precisely, an entrenching spade."

"A tool?" I asked, remembering the long glistening splash of fresh blood against the barn wall, higher than a man should reach. "A weapon."

"Like any other tool."

I nodded.

He took that for a dismissal. Closed the door with a solid chunk and walked quickly away. While he brought the other car around and drove it into the open bay, I found a heavy leather jacket stuffed between the passenger door and the seat back. I rolled it up into a fair pillow and cushioned my leg with it, then rolled down the window on my side of the cab. I dozed.

What sleep I had got made me hungry for more but,

my dreams were not ones I would welcome.

Ten days. Ten days since Del Minor appeared at my door with two Medji and the token I hoarded against my breastbone. The Medji were soon dead, almost before we left the tidewater zone. Del had said little, slept little. At first, after the Medji fell, we used buses. Then she bought a car.

Twice they almost had us. Once in a river valley west of the mountains. Then we wrecked the car in an ambush, east of the college where Tallen found me. Both times the attackers had focused on Del and not me, as if they didn't know who held the token. When she fled the hospital, they were on her trail.

After I lost the car and Del, I bought a Bus pass with my last packet of local money. When I got off the bus, I hitched a ride to the closest thing the Americans had to the old kirk, an Episcopalian church. All of the Houses kept factors in the larger cities, but by then I knew I could not rely on any agent not to sell me to the coup. I did know of one organization that might not betray me.

They were a shadowy net of Footlocker Houses, Avars and Unchurched Dai living in exile here in the Broken Lands, in AngTerra. Enough of them were Wolfs Heads or Runners that they kept a lance length clear from the factors and the headhunters. They left tokens in the churches, little notes on the bulletin boards or a chalk sketch on a southeast corner. Most of the Manifested but Unchurched knew about this, mouth to ear and never set to paper. When or if you became 'of' a House and not simply within a House, you put this knowledge aside.

It was an escape that no one House wished to seal off. And I found what I needed. They took me in, no questions asked, nor tale offered. I got a little sleep and some food.

I woke to silence. And when I ventured from the safe room over the garage, I found the household dead, down to the last child. And a note. It said that anyone who sheltered me, fed me or offered me any aid, would die. That was when I quit hiding. When I readied the Lethe capsule and resolved to sell my skin as high as I could, in public and as notoriously as I could.

They had taken the household I had sheltered at, flushing me into the open. And they waited. I was a lure, not the quarry, in their eyes. I intended to be a lure that bit.

Who fed them, I could not tell. Only that they intended to expose me until someone stretched out a hand.

I do not think they expected Tallen. I certainly did not. With a shovel. And I had bound him, if lightly yet.

TALLEN 7

I pulled the suburban around and up into the storage bay. Under the bays unforgiving light, it really looked hammered, some of the tape had peeled away from the bullet holes along with a swatch of paint. There was a steady dribble of coolant from the radiator and one of the tires was well on its way to flat. There were blotches on the paint and bodywork that drew my eye. Shotgun patterns about the size of my hand that had all the paint stripped from the metal and the metal was severely eroded. In one place it was eaten away completely. The plastic bumpers hadn't fared any better. I puzzled over this for a minute or so then set it aside.

I pulled the radio element from the dashboard, it being too good an item to leave behind. And opened up the back to pull the transformer/inverter package. That's when I found a splice to the DC power lead. The bootleg power lead went through a small hole in the flooring. I didn't touch the package. I did position a work light where it shone through the hole. Then I slid under the rear end.

The wire ran to a black box strapped to the frame on the passenger side of the car about six inches long by an inch and a half wide. There was a long, maybe three-foot long, ribbon antenna running along the frame from where the box was tacked on. I'd been wrong about the gizmo and about the prey the awkward squad back at the trailer was interested in. I ran my finger gently across the rough surface of the box, roughened to avoid reflecting light and to attract dirt. Found ideograms where I had expected serial numbers. The ideograms for Kunaicho.

This made a difference.

I owed Alena a pistol. And remembering the conversation I almost had with Nigel, I owed him a death. If the Imperials hadn't saved me the bother.

The ideograms for Kunaicho. Kunaicho, the Japanese Imperial Household Agency, officially watched over the Japanese Imperial Household. The Agency was an odd mix of archaeological janitors, gardeners with Uzi's and butlers with a portfolio in protocol and diplomacy. They maintained the residences and tombs of all the one hundred and twenty-five Emperors. They held the Great Seal of the Emperor. They arranged his day and kept all the records touching upon the dynasty and all the collateral family lines. They also maintained the official fiction that the Emperor of Japan descended directly from Amaterasu, with a determined vengeance.

Before the war its name was Kunaisho, the Imperial Household Ministry. And it was a full member of the Imperial Cabinet, with its minister equivalent in rank to the Justice Minister. They had their own paramilitary police forces protecting the honor and persons of the Imperial House and a very heavy mob of agents who hunted alongside of the Kempetai, the Japanese version of the Gestapo. But, the Kunaisho's concern wasn't war or politics. Politics and war were of the Kempetai domain. The Kunaisho wanted no taint of any impurity in the linage of the Emperor or a hint of any lesser scandals touching his sacred person. One of the first things MacArthur did after his military government got a firm hold on the throat of the Japanese was to disband the Imperial Household Ministry. The ever-accommodating officials of the Japanese occupation government changed the name and the new Imperial Household Agency was placed under the close scrutiny of the Justice Minister. Oh, and they used American issue .45 autos instead of Nambus. Big change.

That awkward squad at the ranch was not looking for Alena. They were looking for me.

That meant that Nigel had likely sold me to the giddy Imperials. I'd come home early, before the real wet team had come on the scene and looked to be moving on. So, the surveillance tried to get lucky. Murphy's administrative decree number 128, 'Don't do the other guy's job.' That explained all the blue on blue mayhem.

It sounded right; none of them had been Orientals. If they were working for the Kunaicho, they were working through a cutout. Nigel again. Or maybe not. They were slightly more competent than his usual bunch of gun bunnies, as bad as they were. So, they were hired through a Keiretsu, a corporate front? Someone tasked them to 'engage if possible' as well as 'watch for the old fool'? But they had tapped me before I collected Alena. Why jump me now? And there was the fool who ate his own gun. Surely, he hadn't gotten a detailed briefing from the Kunaicho. They needed to pretend I never existed and the less people they had to clean up the better.

And now I'd drawn them to one of my dens. Bright, real bright.

Fire wouldn't work twice. Besides there were real people storing things here, not just me. Hot enough to cover my tracks and the fire would wipe the entire storage site.

Snipping the wire would probably send out a squeal, telling them where and when I spotted the thing. But I dragged a mini-arc wielder over and fired it up. They'd used a pair of nylon cable ties, where I would have spot welded

the transponder. Maybe it wasn't really fond of amperages.
I might be able to fry the "I got found." transmitter,
confusing the issue. I drew a dozen beads across the casing
and touched off on the wire. Then I snipped it clear of the
frame and the antenna. If I hustled, I could make a FedEx
drop box. I was going to send it to the Chinese Communist
Embassy in DC. Working or not, the homing beacon
would set the cats among the pigeons at that address.

But I also needed to clean out this cache and add a few
items to the care package. I wouldn't be coming back and
there were things here that the Kunaicho had wanted back
in their hands since '42.

I'd moved my China baggage into a new locker unit
about a year ago, so I knew just where all of it was. The
majority of it was nothing exceptional; clothing, mess kits,
the odd poster or sets of identity papers. I had a dozen
bibles from a missionary station in South China. All
hollowed out and ready to be a hideout for a .32 Colt.
Bamboo tubes filled with silk maps that detailed the
dispositions and strengths of three Japanese army Corps in
Manchuria as of June 1944. There was a broom handled
Chinese Mauser Model 97chambered in .45 Colt and still in
its wooden holster, bearing the proof marks from the
Shansi armory. Ammunition and spare magazines for the
gun. A flat box with IJA munitions stencils on it. Heavier
than sin and holding enough silver Shansi Taels to finance a
battalion of irregulars for a year. Another set of boxes, not
as big and stenciled in French and Chinese, held thirty
pounds of mid-sixties proof Krugerrands. Gold for the folk
of the rim.

Alongside of the box there was a Japanese long sword
in an elaborate scabbard and three broken arrows. A heavy
dispatch bag next to a small pouch, the pouch was sealed
shut with wire and a lead crimp. The dispatch bag was
weighted in lead, sewn of waxed double leather and had the
Kanji characters for 'Unit 731, Kwantung Army' stamped
into it.

I hauled an empty footlocker down from the shelves
and made a load. One of the bibles with a .32 inside on a

layer of moth-eaten woolens. A layer of blankets. The Mauser and its accessories, then the silver and the Krugerrands. Another layer of moth-eaten woolens. Then I packed the sealed pouch and the dispatch bag and the sword. The sword I had wrapped in a plastic drop cloth and then a blanket. I packed some more woolens over the lot and closed the footlocker. The rest of the stuff I abandoned. It meant things to me but, nothing I couldn't leave behind. Ghosts.

I had a floor safe in the bay where I'd stored the old flatbed. In it I had two more sets of identification and a clean plate for the truck. It also had a three-inch roll of fifties and a very old leather bag. The bag had a hundred dollars in silver cartwheels. All struck before 1918 at the San Francisco Mint. I shook it in my hand and had to laugh. She bought me with gold. Once before I was bought and sold for silver. Inflation.

I hauled the two footlockers back to the truck after locking the battered suburban away. I had enough medical gear in the one footlocker to outfit a young hospital. With what was already on the truck I figured we were set. All I had left to do was stop at the office on the way out, zero out the security cameras and the sheet counter on the Xerox machine in the front office. I had photocopies of the front and back of the dispatch bag tucked in around the tracking bug, along with the crimped seal from the bag. All ready for the FedEx drop.

Alena had been sleeping the two times I had passed the truck before. This time she was bolt upright in the cab, her left hand rubbing the medallion between her index finger and her thumb, staring off into space. She didn't flinch when I horsed the footlockers up onto the bed, or when I jumped up after them to tie them off to the pad eyes. She just barely noticed when I got behind the wheel and drove off the storage center after I wiped the security tape. There was a FedEx drop box I knew about near Manhattan, Kansas. I'd send the bug and the photocopies off from there.

I stopped at a Kwick Shop outside of Salina to call

Dodge City from the pay telephone. There was a campsite at Dodge, almost downtown, where you could park a fifth wheel camper or a one-man pup tent. It had showers, swimming beach, mini mart and a pool table, a laundry and it was quiet. I reserved us a campsite with a clean credit card. Told them we'd be in about sunup.

"You thirsty?"

"Hm?" She blinked. Then looked at me. "Thirsty?" She said.

"You want a coke or something?"

"Bottled tea, unsweetened and no lemon if they have it?"

"I think they might. Want something for the leg?"

She rubbed at it. "I think just aspirin, until we get to somewhere safer."

"Okay."

When I brought back the tea, she took it from me in a languid daze. We were back on the road, cutting southwest through the Kansas darkness when she woke up, like she had been asleep with her eyes open.

"Tallen."

"Yeah."

"They weren't the same men."

"Oh?"

"The ones in that college, the men you shook off. They were not the same men that came for me, for us, at the trailer."

"Okay." I considered telling her about the Imperials, but she did have the gun back in her hands. "How do you figure that?"

"They could have taken me any time in Ames. They forced me into the open once while I was there."

"Forced?"

"Some innocents offered me a place to stay until my 'friends' found me. They..."

"I follow you. They wanted you 'found', but by someone else."

"Yes. They do not know." She said. "They do not know."

"What don't they know?"

She stroked the coin with her left hand. "That I hold this.

"That changes things?"

"Yes."

She was quiet for a mile or so. "In the normal run of things," She said. "I would not be holding this. I was well out of the path. Far enough that I could run free, without minders or agendas. Something happened-"

"Your cousin?" She stilled, like a deer about to bolt. "You talk freely when you're half asleep."

She shook her head. "A habit my Amah tried to break me of. But at any hand, my cousin should not have had it to send me. She was nearly as far from the critical path as I am, or as I was." She looked around at the landscape, blue in the false dawn. "Where are we going again?"

"Dodge City."

"Of the television show?"

"Uh-hunh." Sort of. "We'll do tourist things when we get there, after we set up. We got about another three hours, get a little sleep."

"All right. Thank you, Tallen."

"S'welcome, but for what." But she was asleep.

The lake site was six blocks south of the main drag of Dodge City proper. It was an old gravel pit that had developed haphazardly through the years. Growing neighborhoods and settling out the classes like silt in a water glass. There were expensive houses fronting on the east side of the lake in a gated community, reachable only by two causeways and a guarded road. The Club. Then there was a clump of old single wide trailers lining the road to the lake. Their front yards mostly sand and sticker burrs, and the children played games in Spanish or Lao. Between the two, hard by the swimming beach and the utility buildings, were the campsites.

I backed the truck into the site and killed the engine. She was still sleeping hard, her hand tight about the medallion. We were way slow getting in, could have been in the camp just after first light if I had stayed on the main roads. But I'd doubled back, fox dragged and lay to until I was sure that we didn't have any ground pursuit. Air trackers would have been a different story but, I hunkered down in a dry creek bed, just before dawn and quartered the sky with a 2x wide angle scope. You see at daybreak you're still in shadow on the ground but, any airborne trackers would be in sun with bright light glinting off their aircraft. The only thing I saw was a hawk.

I had the tents set up and the first air mattress filling before she stirred.

"Tallen?"

"Yo."

"I need the facilities."

"Okay. "I duck walked out of the tent and zipped it shut. Drove her down to the bathhouse and helped her to the door, giving her a cane I'd picked up at the grocery superstore up the highway. She took long enough that I was getting nervous when she hobbled out of the bathrooms.

"Everything all right?"

"My ankle hurts, my neck is stiff, I could eat an ox with the hair singed off and my mouth tastes like an ox with the hair still on."

"Fresh doughnuts instead of singed oxen and fork coffee coming up."

"I know doughnuts. Fork coffee?"

"Thick enough to stand a fork up in."

"Joy." She allowed me to put her in the cab. "And for afters?"

"I wrap your ankle, we go find a WalMart and get you some shoes. Then we see Dodge."

"Shoes are nice, but..."

"We are going to linger here for a day, maybe three."

ALENA 8

He drove us back down the sand road to the campsite. It was under a large tree, maybe ten meters from the lake. There was a water spigot and a power outlet by the concrete pad he parked the truck on. The tents, two of them, were small dome tents, four-person tents if you were on very intimate terms with your three partners. He had a cold box with ice on a tabletop and some folding chairs by the tents. The lake was full of boats with waterboards and one-man skimmers charging across the wakes. A breeze from the lake lifted my hair off my shoulders and dried the sweat from my forehead.

The pastries were good, I couldn't remember when I had eaten last, and the coffee was tolerable with cream and sugar. Then he slipped a pair of rubber sandals on me, bundled me into the truck and off we went.

"Are you concerned about the tents?"

"Not much. Everything worth stealing is in the lock box behind us and if some jasper tries to steal the tents one of the fifth-wheelers behind us would rain on their parade."

"That is good, I think."

"The large trailers or mobile homes camped behind us?"

I nodded.

"They are mostly retired or on vacation, and very, very nosy."

"Oh. And would take great pleasure in interfering?

"That's right. But the bad thing about using them as watchers is..."

"That they will watch us just as closely."

He smiled. When he smiled, he didn't look as old as he felt to me. "On the whole," I said, dragging my hair out of my face. "I'd rather had a murder of crows keeping watch."

"Hmm."

He pulled out onto the macadam, to the north, and we drove through the town. It did not resemble the television show. It looked much like every other town I had ridden through in the Americas. Sandwich shops interspersed with car lots and retail plazas. They lined the main road like fortified berms. Past them I could see older houses and structures, not quite as uniform as the retailers' holdings. Nor as bland. It had not quite been that bland in the tidewater, what I had seen of it, but I could see the monotonous stylist behind the commercial architecture. It was not a place where I would reside by choice, but with care I could den up in it for a season or four.

We pulled into a plaza and he parked the truck close to the entrance to one of the great mercantiles, WalMart. He switched off the motor and took off his gun, stashing it in a box under the seat, he held his hand out for mine.

"Disarm?"

"Contrary to what they think in the loopy east, nobody goes armed to the teeth in Kansas as a matter of course. And the folks who might be carrying take notice of anyone armed in their vicinity, you know that."

Drape, walk, carry and clear.

'The Drape of the jacket, the Walk of the armed, the Carry of their manner and the gun hand held Clear.' I chanted under my breath as I handed over my pistol.

I was just past my first red month when Ilona Starets came to the stake with a sword stave slung over her shoulder, for livery mostly, much like a song smith would carry a lutein. And a long canvas duffel in her left hand, full of the real tools of her trade. She came to teach me survival and I was ecstatic. My very first arms master. I had daydreams of becoming a bandit with a wild war band behind me. No holding but my saddlebags and no flock but my warhorses. Or sometimes for a change up, I would walk the broken highlands of the old country as a free Herr, my enemies, the staked lords of the Confederated who bound themselves to cold icons and not to blood.

Ilona thumped the daydreams out of me. For the first full turn of the wheel she taught me how to watch and listen. When to run and when to den up. When to stroll openly down the crowded way and when to creep through the alleys. Only after I had those lessons mastered, then she opened her tool bag to teach me weapons...

"You all right?"

I opened my eyes. I did not recall closing them. I was cold suddenly, so cold. I rubbed my hands over my arms and looked away from his face. Ilona was long on her road, alone she came and alone she left, declaring herself modestly satisfied that I could stand against the cull.

"Yes." I said. "Yes." I shook off the chill and the fugue. And swung my aching leg over the door sill. He backed off, looking away from me but leaving his arm available if I should need it.

"Shoes first I think." He said. "I got a pair of socks in my pocket so we can try them on without distressing the clerks."

TALLEN 9

We got her a solid pair of runners and a light set of sandals as well. She chose to wear the runners. I let her browse through the clothing until she had about a hundred dollars' worth of stuff then headed us for the check out. On the way out of the door she saw a unisex barbershop, every chair empty.

"May I have some money, please."

"For what?"

She pulled at her long hair. "This. It is driving me wild."

I pulled a bill out of the roll and passed it to her. "This should cover it. I'm going out to the truck to drop this off. Be back soon. Okay?"

"Yes." She said and limped into the hair shop.

The truck hadn't been messed with, that I could see on a casual once over. I unlocked the box and stashed her clothing then relocked it. I took a long walk through the parking lot, sniffing the wind. Watching the colors stream past me.

Since Missouri I'd been looking hard down my back trail. I was still trying to figure out where and when they slipped that tagger into my Suburban. But there were other ways to track. Ways that didn't rely on microchips and radios. I should know, it was part of my stock in trade.

Out in the lot were a hundred people, coming and going. Each one of them trailed ribbons of light. Auras, the happy little New Agers named them. They trailed behind their owners like banners on parade. Curled slowly into the air above like cigarette smoke or burned around them like a flare off at an oil refinery. Each banner, flame or curl of smoke carried a thumbnail of its owner.

I could read them like thumbing through a passport, trailing my fingers through the aura. Hate and fear and lust were hot primary colors, envy was green while depression was a deep oceanic blue. Murder could be black as crude oil, shot through with veins of red and yellow fire. Could be. I'd seen murder as cold and clear as blue glacier ice and worse yet with no color at all.

This was part of what I am. What I had been since 19 and 18. That I could thread my fingers through a man's aura and know if he was a traitor, a liar or a fool. That I could lay my hand upon his forehead, peel back the layers of his Subtle aura and know his life from birth to the moment I touched him. Turn him inside out, like skinning a rabbit, if need be. Crack him like an egg and let his life drip through my fingers. I jingled the leather bag in my pocket, watching the light change about me, watching the lives stream by like so many banners on parade.

"A gift from the immortal gods." Kluge had said in his version of Mandarin, separating me from the rest. "Young Dragons are not often to be found among the pi-dogs." And he brought me away.

I had been sent East to Vladivostok. Seconded to serve with an exploring Officer, a Colonel of The Great Game, straight from Kipling's stories. Myself and five other ranks.

The Foreign Office wanted to put some pry bars in the mysteries of Revolutionary Russia and Vladivostok and Northeast China seemed to be a good place to start. My Captain was eager to be shut of me. I was a Lance Corporal with a sorry attitude and an absolutely unnerving talent for mayhem. So, he sold me to a dog robber of a Major, who then delivered me and the other shites to Larkin. And we all took the low road to Manchuria.

Larkin and I took a shine to each other. He was a very old hand, preserved from the hell of the Western Front by the fact that he had a knack for dealing with the peoples of the Northwest frontier. Truth be told, he was too old. He knew he could trust me but, we had at least two political officers wished on us by the Foreign Office and the Army. Besides the other ranks from the Regular Army, there was a couple of low caste Indians, a cashiered Lancer, two Yankee deserters from the China Marines, several ex-Boxers, some White Cossacks and all the confused sweepings you get at the end of an Imperial era. We set out to 'explore' the situation along the border between China and Russia, on tartar ponies, draped with bandoliers and drums for the Lewis Guns.

It would have made for a helluva cover for Argosy, or a grand role for Barrymore the elder. We lasted most of a fighting season. That was when I got my grounding in Cavalry action and irregular fighting. Neither side wanted us there. Eventually they cooperated and butchered us.

Larkin was killed outright. Shot in the back. Half of us turned and ambushed the rest of us in a classic betrayal. Between the traitors and a troop of Red Cossacks there were only three survivors. One of the political officers (a 'cashiered' Buff), an American Marine deserter and me.

The Cossacks sold us to a bandit troop operating in Mongolia, along with two Lewis guns and a crate of ammo. I think the idea was that we would instruct in the care and feeding of the guns. The Reds thought it was amusing, since the ammo was not the right caliber for the guns and all the drums had their winding springs broken. 'Broken goods' they called us all.

Ten days after Larkin was shot in the back, the bandits stopped over at a caravanserai. They cut us loose from our mules and fed us, then staked us out in the courtyard like new caught horses and ignored us. The Marine was in a bad way, like to die from the beatings he provoked at almost every stop. Conal, the Ex-Buff and political stoolie, was nursing broken ribs. And I had a split scalp from a Cossack saber, the only reason I hadn't a split skull was that I'd stuffed a steel pot under my wool cap. We figured we were dead men; the Marine was just trying to hurry the process along. Conal and I were eager to take a few more with us when we went down. I had a bottle shard hidden in the rags I was wearing, and I'd been sawing at my thongs for a while when Conal whistled to me.

I looked up and saw a big man watching us from across the courtyard. He was muffled up to his ears in a blue quilted horse coat, what the cowboys used to call a slicker only padded against the cold and not rain proofed. He had a long pig sticker of a lance over his shoulder and a German broom handled Mauser hanging from a lanyard about his neck. He just stood there in the shadows by the entrance to the stables and stared at us, his head lowered against the cold winds of October.

Then he walked across the courtyard and entered the common room of the caravanserai. I started sawing even faster at my bonds. Conal kicked the Marine awake and huddled closer to me, so I might slash at his bonds with the shard.

The big man came out of the common room again, dragging one of the bandit leaders by his arm and pushing the other one ahead of him with the Mauser. The one he was dragging was out cold, blood running down his face and dripping to freeze on the stones of the courtyard. The gunman dropped the wounded bandit, spun the other one around to face him. He produced a leather bag from inside his long blue coat and backhanded the bandit with the bag. Splitting his face open and dropping him like a poleaxed steer. He opened the bag and poured a good double handful of silver cartwheels onto the bandit's chest.

He turned his back on us and faced the crowd that was drifting out of the common room. They froze. For a long moment they stared at him and then they turned and drifted back into the smoky doorway, slow and careful like. I'd seen dogs fade away from a Wolverine like that.

Then he came over to me. He wasn't oriental. That was the first shock. His face was greased against the wind and his hat pulled low, but I could tell he was Northern European by the pink glow of his skin and the red stubble under the grease. He stuffed the empty bag into his coat pocket and slipped the Mauser into a flap in its breast. Then he bent down and squinted at me with ice blue eyes.

"Вы советские?" I knew enough Russian to get a beer and a whore, so I shook my head.

"Deutsch?" I knew more German than I wanted to let on, so I shook my head again and sawed harder.

He nodded. "English, then?" And he said it in better English than any of us possessed. "Yes, you must be English, or worse yet, Yankee. Pig ignorant, goat stubborn and hardy as a Mongolian pony. You smell like a pony. Mongol pony and too much fat. Oh, be a good chap and quit sawing at that, eh?"

That was Kluge Willm. He loaded us into his caravan and headed back into Manchuria. Deep into the mountains. In the winter after the Armistice. The winter I was awakened.

ALENA 10

I found him in a dusty copse of stunted trees, by the entrance to the car lot. Sitting cross legged in the shade on some very thin grass. His eyes open but unseeing. I was angry.

Angry, hungry and footsore. I had been honing the words I was going to flay him with for the last quarter hour. No references to his sadly subhuman parentage nor a rude comment on his lack of the sense the god gave a goose but, a good rain of broken glass drenched in acid.

Then I saw his eyes. They were brown when I first saw him. Dark and warm last night when I pressed him and saw him rise hard and strong to my call. Now they were almost black, with only a thin ring of color between the pupil and the whites. He was sitting in a half-lotus, his back rigid, his breath slow and measured. Four to the minute.

I stepped back and looked about. No one was paying

much attention. I got up sun of him and gently rattled my cane on the kerb. He blinked, swung his eyes on me like he was swinging a gun mount in my direction and blinked again. I did not move until I saw something more human in his face.

"Are you alright?"

He took a deep breath and stood. The unfolding of a waking lion. "Finished?" He said.

"An hour ago."

"Truly?" He took a closer look at me and nodded. "Beyond doubt. I am sorry, but I got comfortable and drifted..."

"Comfortable?"

"Comparatively. The truck is over that way."

"I know. Perhaps I may have a set of keys, sometime?"

"Maybe." He rolled his neck on his shoulders and led the way back to the truck. "Let's get something to eat. To Go and go for a drive."

"I thought we were going to 'do' Dodge City?"

"Tomorrow will be soon enough." He turned and looked at me again. His eyes still gun bores under his brows. His face the smile of the Buddha, all bronze and weathered stone. "We have things to speak of, under four eyes."

TALLEN 11

I took pity on her and bought two box lunches from a good TexMex restaurant, instead of MickyD's. Then we drove out into the country. The meals were on the seat between us and a big jug of ice tea in the back of the truck.

Alena was changed. With her hair cut short it made her age difficult to call. She kept jumping from fifteen to forty in ten words or less. I wondered if she grew up in France, or in Australia. 'Your winter', she had said. She had a guilty attraction to American junk. Junk food, pop culture. Wanting to go through the Front Street tour so bad, but not wanting to ask. She just about fell out of the truck when she saw the stagecoach go by with a four-horse hitch, then pumping me for details on the harness.

"I don't know that much about tack for coach driving."

"You sold horses."

"Quarter horses, saddle horses. Not dray horses.

Different all together."

"I would think that you would need to have..." She waved her hand about, the left hand, trying to swat down the term she wanted. "Expertise about everything of horse."

"I'm not a fox."

"Excuse?"

"A fox knows a little about many things, a badger knows much about one thing."

She picked at the seam of her jeans. "I thought that it was a hedgehog, that knew 'one big thing'? "

I grinned at her. "Depends on who's telling the fable, doesn't it?" I signaled and turned off the blacktop onto a dirt road. "Ask any dog, that's hunted them both, and they'll tell you they'd rather chase a fox than catch a badger."

"If I get the chance, I'll make a point of asking after their preferences. Are we there, yet?"

"Over the hill. If it's still there."

It was. When they drove a spur line through the hills west of the city, back about 19 and 10, they had built a little cattle pen facing on the track right of way. When they pulled up the line, about twenty years ago, they tore down the pen but left the turnaround looking out over the cut and the valley down towards the Arkansas River. It was a popular spot after dark, for both teenagers and cops, but in the afternoon, it was usually quiet. I pulled the truck around and backed it towards the view. I pulled an old quilt out of a lock box and spread it over the grass, then spread the food and poured us ice tea.

She inhaled her food, then ate half of mine, her head down and intent on the enchiladas. But every time something called out in the grass or a puff of wind rattled the cottonwoods, she froze for a second, her gun hand always close to where the .38 auto was. "It is thin here." She said, once when a quiet had swept over the draw. Her food forgotten in her hand, her eyes on the valley.

I looked around at the late grasses and wildflowers, barely beaten back by the nighttime traffic. "Well, it's not the coast or Kentucky, but I wouldn't call it thin?"

She jumped and peered at me through the fringe of her hair. Then she smiled and shrugged. "I grew up where the grass was much more, lush. Even this late in the year." And applied herself to my enchiladas.

I got up and went to the lockbox at the back of the cab, hauled out a sleeping bag. The sleeping bag I rolled up and stuffed behind her back, while I palmed her .38. Then I sat across the quilt from her, with my back to the sun.

I watched her finish the food. Her hair had feathered in the wind, just the hint of a curl and she had highlights in it like the sheen on a blackbird's wing. Her medallion glinted in the sun, swinging in and out of her shirt as she finished.

When she put the empty plate aside, she grabbed a napkin and cleaned her hands before checking her gun. It wasn't there. She turned to see it in my hands.

"Careless." I said.

She extended her hand. "May I..."

"No."

"I insist."

She turned her hand in the air, her palm up. Suddenly her scent filled the air about us, as if someone had spilled a flask. I smiled and shook my head. "You bound me. Or tried to."

"What makes you..."

"Pull up your shirt."

She pulled her right hand back and made as if to stand. I snapped off the safety and centered the gun on her. She froze, sweat starting on her brow.

"Tallen?"

"Pull up your shirt, please." And I held my breath.

She slowly rolled her shirt up, then stripped it over her head. "Is this what you wanted?" And she clicked something that would have blistered my skin if I could have understood it.

Underneath both breasts were small scars, on the ribcage beneath and inboard of the swell of her breasts. Scars, where a wart or a mole had been burned off, or something else. Something else gently removed. Like a nipple.

"Kitsune." I said "Kitsune, fox woman!"

Her nostrils flared and she threw herself at me heedless of the gun, giving me a solid butt to the head and a knee to the chest. I fell back, dropping the automatic, my left hand twisting her right arm up behind her back and blocked her left with my right as she swiped at my face with clawed nails. Then her face darted forward, and she kissed me, her mouth swimming suddenly with blood and her teeth slashing at my lips. A mouthful of hot peppers mixed with raw alcohol and chased by a spoonful of oil of cinnamon. The dirt swung under me like a hammock, the back of my head ice cold while my face was burning. Her eyes were open, all pupils. Her auras bloomed. Sheets of colors running over her skin, like animated tattoos. Bright swirls of sky blue, ribbons of green and crimson, gilt words that hovered in the air between us like smears of smoke or fog.

My talent woke, answering hers. Black lace shimmered into being around us, lace that fed on her auric streams, like sparks among ribbons. Silver threads crawled up her neck from my hand on her back; nestling into her hair, her ears and following the facial nerves under the skin. She savaged my lips until my blood came. Until her blood mixed with mine in our mouths.

Once I had made the mistake of sheltering under a tree in a summer thunderstorm. I was thinking more of how the rain would stain my Sunday go to meeting suit than what precedes the thunder. The bolt split the tree almost to the root, knocked me out of my shoes and burnt my suit to Polish lace. But all I remember of the strike was a great light that washed every color out of the day and an awful silence. I lay in the rain, with my eyes blind to the sky, digging my fingers into the wet earth, screaming at the rain and not hearing my own voice. For days after that I saw halos and ribbons in the air, auras. I did not know what they were, then. Intermixed with the auras were mirages and wobbly hallucinations, not quite pink elephants and blue snakes, but fever dreams, nonetheless.

That blood tinged kiss was ten of those bolts. I arched my back and flung us up, my hands locked on her body, her mouth locked on mine. We tumbled in midair, so I landed uppermost, crushing her beneath me. She gasped into my mouth, her breath searing away all the cobwebs that a hundred years had left. Leaving nothing behind of thought or opinion, just need and drive and demand. Then the rain soaked my clothes, pelting us, rain mixed with hail. I couldn't see, but I knew we were in about three or four inches of very cold water, in one hell of a freezing storm. A storm that had blown up from nowhere. I was half blind, my ears ringing with thunderclaps. I closed my useless eyes and opened my other senses. I could see no more with them. I was as blind with my Subtle body as I was with the Overt senses.

She was pinned beneath me, coughing up her lunch and hanging on to my chest with both hands. I scooped her up and started crawling up the side of the ditch we were in. Her auras were faint, her hands weak. At the edge of the ditch there was a fence and I pulled us to our feet by it, feeling the wood planks splintering under my hands. I wiped at my eyes, clearing them. The fence was part of a corral, all but rotted away and crumbling to punk under my fingers. In the lightening I could see a shed at the far side of the corral. I swung her up into my arms, cradling her face against my armpit so the hail would not strip the skin away. Then I kicked the fence apart and staggered across the corral to the shed.

ALENA 12

I was sick. So very sick. I felt the rain pounding at my back, numbing cold. Sick with the transition, I wanted to void everything I had eaten and more. My head ached, pounded, every heartbeat threatened to blow my forehead off. Nothing helped, none of the thirteen slights eased the pain. I could feel his blood scalding me, feel his heartbeat matching mine.

I turned my head to the side and vomited one last time, then nothing.

TALLEN 13

I felt her go limp just as we got in the lee of the shed. I tried the door. It would not open, locked with age and neglect. I ripped it from the hinges. I had to stoop a bit to get inside but, once through the door I could stand upright.

It was dark, the only illumination the bolts lighting up the entire sky. I could smell old horse apples, mildew and animal musk, rotting wood and wet earth. I shifted her to my shoulder in a feed sack carry, to free my right hand. Then I fished out a penlight and scanned the place. In one corner there was a wooden manger, where they'd fed the horse hay. It was clean and drier than the dirt floor, under a part of the roof still whole. I laid her down on the trough and began to gather wood for a fire. We were soaked to the bone and she was shaking with the chill, I could ignore it, but it was killing her.

I got the fire going, then stripped our wet clothes off

of us and arranged them where the fire might dry them. I
sat close to the fire and cradled her in my naked arms, while
I summoned the Lesser Dragon. I slowly stoked the fire
within me even as I fed the fire before us, raising my body
temperature to what was a killing fever for a man. Until I
was wreathed in vapor, as if I had just come from a sauna,
the steam rolling from me. A Dragon.

I wiped her face with a corner of my shirt, cleaning her
mouth and nostrils, brushing her hair back from her closed
eyes. Then I awoke the Greater Dragon, carefully bringing
the auras swirling close about us. I slowly let my Subtle
body embrace hers, knitting up the sectors of her auras that
were laced with holes and burns. Her heartbeat slowed to
match mine. She breathed easier, no longer chilled. She
slept then, snoring gently. Her head cradled in the crook of
my arm, her hair reddish in the firelight.

The downpour slowed to a steady drenching then
stopped in that deadly hush that can come behind a
flatlands storm. The hush that promises more to come. I
watched the sky crackle just beyond the horizon.
Remembered other times, laying up in a broken manger,
waiting out the rain and watching drumfire just at the
horizon. I counted faces in the shadows, faces that only I
still had names to give. I slowed my heartbeat. Let go the
present. Then I tasted bully beef and smelled rotten wool
over rank bodies and listened to singers dried to dust eighty
years past.

An hour later I heard horses and the rattle of tack. I
summoned the Greater Dragon again, the thing that made
me worth the price of a hundred lances.

ALENA 14

Gunshots woke me. I came from a deep sleep to wakefulness and standing by the edge of the door without any space between. There had been a fire, now smothered. There had been a door, now it lay in the mire of the corral. I held my breath and listened. A horse nickered, snorted in protest. I heard voices, muffled by rain and distance. Then volleyed shots and screams, horse and man. Binders instruments; we bind with blood and sweat, and the subtle chemicals embedded in them. Like a musician picking apart a song we can 'read' scents. Anger and fear came on the wind and then terror. Terror overwhelming all the other messages. I heard a horse galloping away into silence. Then for a long time nothing.

In the silence Tallen appeared at the door.

"Alena?"

"Here."

He stepped through the door, mother naked and dressed in mud, leaves and blood. He carried a bundle of clothing in his left hand, a weapon in his right.

"Dry goods. Try these on for size."

I took the bundle. He nodded at the fire. "Start the fire back up. I'll be back."

He left again. Left the weapon leaning against the wall of the shed. I picked it up as well. Brought them both to the low manger behind the fire. When I had the fire well lit, I opened the bundle. Wool tunic, felt hat, leather leggings, linen breechclout and a pair of double thickness moccasins, moccasins with split toes. I picked up the weapon, broke it open. It was a double-barreled shotgun with a single rifled barrel mounted over the pair. It had a round in the upper barrel, two in the lower. All three unfired. I left it open, the safety on this gun looked chancy. The dark wood stock had an ownership chop burned into it. A stylized double-bladed axe. The clan mark I thought. There were other marks carved into the stock and forearm that looked more personal.

I slipped on the tunic, having lost the shirt in the hurly-burly. Then I checked on my jeans. Wet, muddy and burned here and there. Gate corona effects, I'd feel it tomorrow. If I had a tomorrow.

What the hell was he? And who under the god's sky fed him. A manifested Avar that strong, that...I rubbed my hand over the wool tunic and knew we had crossed. It was wrong, the tunic and the weapon and the byre and...and I felt the worlds shift left hand and arse over and I threw up over the byre what slops I had left to me.

"Oh god and all your bright daughters. Oh, She who shows the Way."

I started the morningsong. The fear would have made me piss my britches save I was not wearing any.

"Meg be under me! Meg be over me!
Bright Lady well beside,
On the fore hand leading and on the
left hand guarding!
Ladies, before me, behind me, about me be;

This day, An every night
Be thou within and without me!"

I had not sung that plainsong since, since, since I left 'Zeme for the Hanse. And now I had crossed, crossed blind and unmindful and only the god and his daughters might know where in the book of worlds we were.

TALLEN 15

When I came back to the shed, she was dressed and sitting tailor fashion on the manger. The drilling across her lap and her medallion glinting in the firelight. I had a bundle of clothing and another drilling, as well as a sack of round bread and some pemmican in wax paper twists.

"The riders?"

"One escaped." I put the gun down softly, the things had hair triggers.

Then I got dressed. Breechclout first, then the rest. "It was maybe two hours after I lit the fire that they appeared." I ran my thumbnail along the seams of the tunic, leaving a long light blue streak that faded slowly in my Subtle vision. I purely hate greybacks. "I figure that gives us between two and four hours to get clear." I pulled the tunic over my head. "On foot. Between us, we killed or stampeded all the horses."

"We will not need them. Three hours since...?" She gestured with her left hand.

I used my ragged shirt to clean off my feet. Slipped one moccasin and then the other on, then pulled the leggings on. I tried to tie the leggings to the band around my waist, but the laces wouldn't reach.

"Tie them to the tunic, at the leather reinforcements."

I pulled the heavy wool tunic over my head, fastened the leggings to the tunic. "Okay. These were spares."

"Tallen." Her voice was changed. Deeper, stronger. Like an actor assuming a role, or an orator stepping up to the podium. "Come here."

It was a summons, not a request. A part of me wanted to leap across the fire and kneel at her feet, a larger part wanted nothing more than to walk out into the storm and keep walking. She had set deep hooks in me with that last kiss. Bindings that I had not felt for nearly eighty years. Stronger than any I had ever felt.

When last I was bound, it was a slow and voluntary thing. Candles and sand mandalas along with mushroom teas. Each step had opened another door within me, explained things that I had known but not understood. At the last I had given my free assent. To be adopted into the people and to be made into a weapon. When I had knelt at Eldest Brother's feet, when he had drawn the ideogram on my forehead and handed me the crooked knife, I did so willingly, a groom to the wedding.

What she had done was not that sort of binding, it was more like rape. And it was maybe closer to the root of the thing. I now knew something more, when it was done in that rude fashion, it set hooks deep in the soul of the Binder as well as the Bound.

I stepped around the fire, to stand close to her.

"I am spoiled." She began. "That is one reason I stood so far from the critical path of descent." She caressed the medallion. "This should have come to someone stronger. Older, certainly wiser. I was bred for this, to be a Heart Binder. And to rule."

"And."

"I should have been culled in my first, before my menses. I carried not the talent of the Binding only, I also carried the talent for Walking. Being a Ferryman."

"This means?"

"If the conditions are right; if I am strong enough, the web thin enough and the need great enough, I can step from World to World." She tilted the drilling up to let the fire light glint on its stock. "We are here."

"That explains a hurricane in Kansas, and raiders in breechclouts." I reached out and traced with my fingertip the brand in the wood. "Can we go home?"

"I do not know." She laughed. She unfolded her legs and stood up, handing me the drilling. "Perhaps. If you can lend me your strength. If we can find the thin place, we came through. If..."

"We need to police the shed in any case. Are you hungry?"

She made a face, like a child presented stewed greens. "No, but if I am to be sick, it should be on a full stomach." She rubbed her mouth with the back of her hand. "It makes the transition easier."

"It wasn't just the enchiladas?"

She said a rude word, by the tone, in her clicking language. I turned away to gather up the rags we had blown into this world with. She was sorting through her side of the fire as well, muttering under her breath and since my ears were burning, muttering about my rude behavior. I was calm.

I shouldn't have been. I'd been presented with more impossible things since breakfast than Alice could have handled and dumped on the other side of the looking glass as well. But I was calm. One thing I knew from nearly a century of trooping, was when to follow and when to lead. I had no clue how we got here, or if we could go 'home' and stewing about it would do no good. My job was to get her from here to there. Keep the locals off our backs and not distract the Lady.

As for being bound.

I was an orphan when the war came. My father was six months dead and my mother had died birthing me. One sister was long dead and the other moved to Oregon. All that was left in Missouri were a gaggle of half-sisters, a worthless half-brother the apple of his mother's eye, and a god's plenty of step-cousins. When I came back from the Rim close to sixty years later, it was as if I had never been. I found a great-grand Nephew with a trunk full of pictures and other small treasures, eager to sell out the farm and retire to Florida. That was in Missouri. The farm in Oregon was gone without a trace. I bought the farm from him and all the goods in the house but, I never opened the trunk. It was stored away, along with everything else that I might have touched before that war.

Kluge Willm's people became my family. Made me a place by the hearth and a pallet on the floor. Then the Chrysanthemum, the House that leased the Imperial Japanese Army as casual labor, came and broke us. Well, they gave me something almost as good as family. God knows a blood feud can keep you as warm and motivated.

I lived fifty years past the end of the feud, mainly out of habit and being just mule stubborn. I might have lived another fifty but, I hadn't woke the Dragon in ten years. I was getting careless. About got mugged last year in KCMO before I woke up and slipped away from the hunters. Twenty years before I would never have come to their attention. Sloppy. Disgrace to the unit, pack drill for the next fortnight.

Then I stumble into her. Well enough.

ALENA 16

He smiled at me, across the smoky fire, and tossed the remnants of the clothing we were wearing when I forced the passage on the flames. He slipped his watch on, tucked his wallet into the breechclout.

"I'm going back out, to see if we dragged anything across with us. I was thinking about the .38, the sea bag and the blanket."

"Perhaps."

"I'll look." He carefully picked up the drilling by the door. "And if it should be there, that will mark the place where we came through right?"

I nodded and he slipped out into the rain.

I picked up the bag of round bread, cut one of the buns open with a knife that had been in the bundle of clothing. The outer crust was tough enough to loosen teeth, but inside it was still somewhat moist. I started methodically eating the bread. I would need it and the pemmican.

TALLEN 17

The gun and the sea bag were gone. They were ether in Kansas or under a foot of quickly rising creek. Either way they were gone. I did find the blanket and some of the trash from the taco shop. I thought it could mark within about ten yards where we came through her 'soft spot'. I drove the drilling I carried barrel down about four inches into the mud.

If time ran here as it did where we'd come from, it was close to midnight. But here, even through the drizzle, I could see dawn coming. I did not want to face those horsemen's messmates in daylight, not without better guns than three-barrel drillings.

I rolled the blanket up, picked up the trash and stalked back up the slope. We had maybe a half hour before the creek rose over Alena's soft spot, ninety minutes or so at a guess until we could expect more raiders in breechclouts.

The creek was narrow but rising. If we could get clear of the ambush site and den up along the creek…it would force them to come one at a time. And this time I would collect some horses.

ALENA 18

I met him in the corral. I'd eaten all he'd left me, including
the pemmican. What clothing we had left was wrapped
up in my jeans and slung over my shoulder with a belt.
Smoke rolled past me and I heard a rising crackle of flames.
I had laid a fire in the dryer end of the shed, fire being a
trail break.

He had the blanket draped over his left shoulder, water
dripping from it. He paused at the sight of the fire, then
nodded and waved me along with his free hand.

"Water's rising. It will be over the 'soft spot' soon."

We half walked, half slipped down the hill towards the
creek.

TALLEN 19

It took three tries to find the soft spot. We came through with much less fanfare than before, though just as wet. It was raining on my side of the gap now but, it was a late summer thunderstorm and not a Chinook hurricane. We landed about halfway down the slope to the old railway cut. Smack in a tangle of blackberry bushes. She landed on me, nearly spitting me on the drilling she brought across. I took a deep breath and shifted her off my chest. She coughed and hacked like a cat throwing hairballs. I had a hangover. The first I'd had in ninety years. As a method of transportation, Walking Between was the second worst experience I'd come across. The first being the short-coupled, leaking, unclean cattle boat I crossed the North Atlantic on in '15.

It was dark, just after sunset, here in the cut. I crawled up the slope, listening through the rain and thunder with both my ears and my other senses. We were alone.

The truck hadn't been touched, as far as I could tell. The locker on the bed was still intact and there was just a little rain on the seat in the cab. Alena was tapped out again. Her auras grayed out and her steps wobbly as she lugged the bag and her drilling to the truck. I bundled her into the cab, rolled her window up, dug a dry blanket out of the lockbox and wrapped her up in it. I stashed the drilling under the seat. I recovered the sea bag just down slope from where we came in. There was no sign of the pistol, which was a worry. All the way back to the campsite she was shivering, slumped over into my side.

At the camp I parked the truck and left the engine running, the heater finally warming up the cab. I got out to dig a can of stew out of the camp box and start it warming on a steno candle, then I changed out of my exotics into a dry set of sweatpants and a sweatshirt and trotted over to the little store on the campgrounds. I bought a loaf of French bread, a pound of real butter and a couple of chocolate bars. I also drew a mug of coffee from the big percolator by the soda fountain. While the canned stew was coming to a slow bubble, I got Alena out of the truck and into the big tent. I stripped her, rubbed her dry and wrapped her head in another towel. She smelled like rising sourdough, her skin loose and chilled, shock and starvation/dehydration too. I stirred a tablespoon of sugar into the coffee and helped her down a mouthful, followed by a small chunk of buttered bread. She leaned into me, wrapped up in the blanket and warming her hands on the mug, slowly chewing the bread.

She swallowed and rubbed her nose with the back of her hand. "We returned." She said.

"Yes." I tucked the blanket in around her.

"`most got lost. Did you know you could get lost in a single step?"

"Not surprising." I leaned out and picked up the pan of stew. I dipped another piece of the bread into the stew and offered it to her. The first bite was unenthusiastic. The second bite nearly took my fingertips off. In short order she finished the stew, the bread and one of the candy bars. She curled up in my lap, tucked her head under my chin and gave a big sigh.

"Much trouble." She mumbled, taking my freehand in both of hers, clasping it to her breast, to the Bloodseal. "Aludjon jol." And she started to snore.

I gently unwound the towel about her head, laid her on the pallet in the middle of the tent and threw one of the sleeping bags over the top of her. I snuffed the steno can, wiped up the last of the stew in the pot and ate the other candy bar for my supper. Then I stretched out beside her, my head to the tent door and one of my nines to hand. I brought the Dragon to the middle distance, over watching but not fully awake or ready for combat. With his scales enveloping me, I drifted into sleep. "Much trouble…"

I awoke just after dawn local time, birdsong and someone trying to start an outboard motor. I didn't open my eyes. I just let my other senses sweep the campgrounds, like a beast with its nose to the wind.

There were people all around us, their auras all within a normal range of passions. Bright and dark and all the tones between. The children were the brightest, but they were weak, unfocused. Think of gauze net, glowing like molten glass but giving no heat. This aura could interlace with yours all day long and leave little trace. Beautiful primary colors; rage, joy, love, fear, delight, envy, desire. All the colors of the kindergarten pallets, swirling about the children.

They darkened as they grew older, the colors muting as the gauze grew stronger. Then at the change, and its onset varied for each child, their auras suddenly jelled about them. After the change the auras became more tightly linked to the Subtle and the Worldly body. No longer harmless, or immune to harm. The auras wound around them like sheets. Or a sari. Or a monk's robe. If they stood still, usually, the aura would veil them like the candle flame veils the wick. On some, the aura was so strong as to dance above them, like the flame of a Bunsen burner. Others smoldered beneath dark shawls, Subtle energies winking like banked coals under a shoal of ash. Some were nothing more than a hint of hot copper or iron drifting on the air or auras black as lamp smuts without a single gleam of light within.

When it was done, I knew there was no one within my range that I should worry about. This did not mean there was not a brigade of rifles two li to the northwest or a hand of assassins enjoying the tourist traps up on Front Street.

'The eyes of the Dragon were exceedingly short,' Kluge used to say. 'and more suited to Subtle work under the new moon than glorious charges in the blaze of noon, so use the ruddy eyeglass.'

I sat up in the tent and checked on Alena. She was asleep on her belly, one hand clasped about the medallion. The skin of her neck white against the obsidian of her hair. I slipped out of the tent, got a towel and a change of clothing from the supplies and went for a shower, a shave, and a thought.

When I came back, she was awake, sitting cross legged on the pallet and knuckling the sleep out of her eyes. She was naked as a jaybird, her skin mottled with bruises and traceries of sunburn like she'd slept raw in a hammock and woke up in a hailstorm.

"Hungry?" I asked, averting my eyes from her and resolving to discuss courtesy, clothing, and tribal mores with her real soon.

"Always." She said. "More rations or real food?"

"Depends." I retrieved the 9mm from her lap and stowed it in a fanny pack holster. "Tell me more about 'Walking between Worlds'."

"More." She pulled her injured foot up into her lap to make a half lotus and began to massage and flex the joint. "Why?"

"I need to know. I need to know how well you shoot, if you can throw a knife, can you run on that ankle now and how far? I should know just how your 'House' is organized and how your enemies are arrayed. What their names are and their numbers. I should know your allies, if any." I handed her a fresh packet of clothing, along with the sandals. The new shoes we'd purchased yesterday were plumb shot. Water soaked and caked in mud.

"If we have to Walk again, will you be throwing up your toenails on the far side?"

She looked down at her foot and smiled. "Perhaps. The softer the crossing, the easier. That spot was not ideal. Each time I force a particular crossing, it will get easier but..." She waved her hand about. "Walking thusly, is art and breeding, more breeding than anything else. Once a suitable breach is marked and mapped it is possible to force it reliably and mechanically."

"Mechanically?" Art and breeding. The last time I had someone tell me that, he was trying to explain to me that I could never be an officer, lacking good breeding and Knowledge of the Art of command. Art and breeding my ass.

She frowned, muttered in the clicking tongue and rubbed her thumb along her nose. "Technical aids. To enlarge and add on to the Walker's natural ability." She brushed her hair back from her face with both hands, static ruffling it up on the top of her head in an ebony crest. "You felt the energy we carried across?"

"Yes." I still felt it, like too much fun in the sun on the day after.

"A Walker can tap into stored energies, batteries and the like, to open the way."

"So that was why we were trying for Canon City?"

She nodded. "There is a major concourse there, wide enough to bring six abreast and deep enough for ten ranks at a time."

"That's a major?"

"Yes. Even with technical aids we are limited to what can be controlled by the Walker. Limited by the human element."

I nodded. "All right. I assume that someone, call him a Watcher, can tell when one of your crossings are forced or opened?"

She nodded.

"That was why the riders with the leggings and

elephant guns came calling. Some one knew we had come in the back door?"

"Perhaps." She said. "I do not know that World, or rather I can only speculate. It might have been a random encounter."

"They were loaded for bear. Only thing that kept me out of the kimchi was my usual mix of good luck and dirty tricks. Get dressed, we need to replenish the clothes locker and get another set of shoes." I snorted another handful of blood clots out of my nose, she hadn't quite broken it when she tried to bind me.

I should have known it was a setup.

We stayed in Kansas two more days, doing Dodge City and resting up from the visit across the shadow we made when she tried to seal the deal with blood and pheromones. What I got out of her, slowly, was that she had personally Walked to three other 'Combs' or 'Sheafs' in her lifetime. "AngTerra" or what I was pleased to call Earth, "Hanse" and a place her linage kept as a House secret. Each time, she had gone through a version of a bus station and rode a jitney through the gate. No fireworks and she didn't upchuck.

Where we had stumbled into was none of these. And we had almost not come back. She hadn't mentioned that staying lost was a high possibility. More than I was cleared to know, I suppose. Well, we made it back and thinking back on it she allowed as the place we tumbled into might have been "The Anarchies", or a shadow of that particular 'Sheaf'. Not that it mattered, but we now had a bolt hole if needs must. She could walk across it and likely it was not a well-known ford.

From the description she gave me, "The Anarchies", even in the best of times was a last-ditch bolt hole.

Anarchies:

Something happened in Europe that dropped Rome like a rotten tree. Just after Augustus, from what Alena remembered reading in what passed for her middle school, a pandemic-maybe a flu-swept through the Mediterranean, Asia Minor and Europe.

Barbarian horsemen flooded into the ravaged lands and held them. Vikings-or their analogs-ventured across the North Atlantic and settled among the Skraelings of North America. The Vikings also brought the pandemic with them, along with smallpox and measles. This allowed the invaders more than a foothold among the natives. A second wave of diseases then destroyed what was left of the GrecoRomans, but it was virulent enough that it did not spread across the ocean.

The ships being slow enough that their crews perished before landfall, and primitive enough that an unmanned ship foundered quickly.

I asked her about the weapons.

"I don't know." She said. "The Eisenring are supposed to stop that sort of thing. Stop Walkers from bringing technology or other contraband across the veil." She stroked her hand across the Damascus barrels of the drilling. "This is not native to the Anarchies. It was made in Little England, or even 'Zeme. The Pika have guns like this, but bigger."

That was the first I heard of the Eisenring.

I didn't like the way we got to the 'Anarchies', and when I got a close look at the welcome committee, I had liked the destination even less. Mummified hands dangled from their horses' tack. Scalp locks and threaded finger bones were woven into their tunics. Made me feel a little less guilty about scything through their ranks like a McCormick reaper. And they knew just what I was all about. One of them carried a silver inlaid lance and two of them had silver shot in their big bore guns. Silver being one of the simpler ways of laying a Dragon down.

That I thought about for a couple of sleepless hours, not the silver but that they knew they were about to swap insults with a Dragon.

After one last pass at the horses on Front Street, I broke camp at the lake and loaded everything into the truck. This was mid-morning on the fifth day since I collected her.

We hadn't been idle. She worked the kinks out of her

ankle, with a little lay chiropracty on the sly from me. We did more shopping. I got her a hard side suitcase and more clothing for both of us. I also did a little snooping on the internet.

Nigel was dead and wanted for questioning. So was I. Dead and wanted for questioning that is. Maybe as many as twelve more were dead at the crime scene in Missouri according to two separate news stories I scooped up at the Dodge City Library.

I evidently had been supplanting my meager income as a rancher by brewing meth, then fell out with my biker accomplices and was killed in an early morning drive-by shoot out.

Nigel had "died" in a botched carjacking on Troost in Kansas City. Although knowing him, it just might well have been a random act of violence brought on by his dreams of being a player.

These were the KC Star's versions. They went into more detail on the scourge of meth and played down the problems of carjacking, tourists are so skittish, but that was basically the play-by-play.

Now the St. Joseph's News-Press didn't mention Nigel, understandable since he seemed to have died in Kansas City "and you know about that place", but I was thought to have died in a fire of suspicious origin. Two horses died in the fire as well, which was an outright lie as I had no horses on the place when I torched it. No mention was made of any other casualties.

And the Lawrence Kansas Journal World had an account of a Federal raid on a storage facility, uncovering a meth lab and detailing the arrest warrants for Franklin McCoul, so recently deceased in Missouri, on Federal and State drug charges. You have to wonder if these people ever paid attention to each other's press releases.

It took us about seven hours to make the outskirts of Canon City. She slept most of the way. I idled along at 45 and let the Dragon knit up the thin spots in my Subtle body while I went through about a pound of beef jerky and chocolate. There was a hefty price for wearing the Dragon.

If you pressed the issue too far you could starve to death in a long night's work.

Near as I could make out, Alena thought I was some sort of double stitched hero for hire, or for binding, if she got the right tip on the harpoon. I was handy with a shovel and handier yet with a gun. She didn't mention the fact that I blew her clothes to rags and gave her a sunburn under her jeans the one time she tried to bind me with blood and musk. She lectured me about how a forced crossing like that tended to cause all sorts of local phenomena. Ball lightening, hallucinations and the like. What she went on about, when she wasn't drooling over horseflesh or trying to educate me, was 'Whose' line I came from. The closer the linage, the more resistant the subject to a proper binding. Since I was not trotting at her heel…I had to be a cousin or something.

She got insulted when I gave her the old Irish joke about coming from a long line of dead men.

We rolled into Canon City just after sunset. I had a decent pair of jeans on and a western yoked shirt. I planned on getting a haircut after I settled her into the safe house she was aiming for. If the Feds or any state police were looking for Franklin McCoul, just getting the gray out of my hair and shedding a little more time would help confuse the issue.

The place was nestled into the mountains just outside the town. Up a well-kept gravel road to a trophy house with a four-car garage attached to the house, a barn and a corral just down the slope on about six acres of level pasture. No outside lights to speak of and nothing moving that I could see with my eyes or my night scope.

"We are going to just walk up on them? Like we were invited?"

"Yes. We walk up, or rather, we drive to their door."

"Think you'd call first. Nothing else, to keep the rabble out."

"If you know to come here, then you are past the first barrier."

"A blind pig."

"Excuse me?"

"If you want a truly exclusive establishment, like a Gentlemen's club, a bordello, a tailor or an illegal bar, the blind pig, there will be no sign at the door. Just a solid door and an even more solid doorman. You have to know which door to knock at, then get by the doorman."

"A blind pig. Exactly."

I stowed my night glasses away and walked back to the truck. We were parked about a quarter mile uphill from the place on a county road.

"Are you coming with me?" She was watching the end of the sunset, the sky going that cold purple.

"Walking across worlds again?"

She nodded.

"Wouldn't miss it."

I opened the arms trunk and took out a four-shot derringer, long .22. I slipped it into a Velcro holster and strapped it around my ankle. I figured when the doorman found the .22 and my 9mm, they'd be happy. I had a fiberglass knife and thirty-six inches of monofilament fishing leader tucked away in the belt of my jeans. Just because.

She leaned against the bed of the truck and watched me adjusting the lie of the .22. "Why are you coming along?"

"You bound me."

"It was a botched binding, Tallen. I think you could simply walk away."

"I suppose. But then I'd be missing out on the fun, wouldn't I?"

"You have a large chip on your shoulder."

I smiled up at her. "You have no idea." I emptied my pockets into the arms trunk and locked it with a combination padlock. Wouldn't keep a Cub Scout out for ten minutes, but the mail order ID I replaced it with to carry was worthless

"I would almost rather not have you at my table."

"Uncomfortable, is it?"

"Most uncomfortable."

"My apologies. If it matters, I am of two minds about this."

"It can be quite the shock, if you have not been Churched before."

Churched. Odd way to put it. "So how do we get past the next barrier?"

She fished her Bloodseal out from between her breasts. "This will serve." She looked at my ankle again. "They will find that."

I nodded. "I know."

ALENA 20

I should have known better. I hoped to simply stroll into the gatehouse, make my needs known and my place confirmed and, La! I would be the Mihaly. No worries. I was still young.

We drove up the graveled lane and cleared the truck cab. Tallen had insisted on my using crutches. "Misdirection." He had said. "They'll be looking at your crutches and your injuries and not necessarily me."

"The gatehouse is neutral territory."

"Yeah. Best place for a hit. Somebody else has to clean up the mess."

He resisted. Which confirmed my notion that he had to be at least a double cousin in the generation before his birth. I just did not fathom why he showed so little interest in his linage. Even if he was an Unchurched Avar, he must have known some of his kindred. I puzzled over this as we slowly made our way up the walk and the stairs to the door. A double flood light came on and I heard deadbolts, then the door swung inwards a double hand span.

"Can I help you?" The warden was wearing a house dress, dark grey and with the sheen of an engineered silk. Bullet resistant I thought. Her body blocked the gap, one hand was on the door frame and the other hidden by the door. She was neither young nor old.

"I am come." I said in the Nagi. "To walk the unseen paths, I am come."

Her eyes widened, she breathed deeper and quickly. She called over her shoulder in a liquid burst of Spanish that I could not follow. I heard people coming at the run.

"Welcome traveler." She said. And stepped back from the door with both of her hands open, fingertips to the earth and her palms towards me.

I stumped through on my crutches, Tallen close behind with a hand on my off elbow. I could smell him on the breeze blowing past my shoulder. Then I was in the lee of the door and I could smell the warden. I smelled treachery and death.

TALLEN 21

I saw the grab team out of the corner of my eye. One of them hit her with a cattle prod and she dropped like she'd been killed. Another one tried to socket a gun into my ear. Bad move that. I'd brought the Dragon from a restless sleep to swirling hunger as we walked up the path to the door. I had not expected anything, if I had been expecting a takedown, I'd been the first through the door and I wouldn't have been lugging a 9mm. More like a 10gauge pump and grenades for doorknockers.

Bad move indeed, for the fool with the gun. The black lace took him apart. Like shoving his arm into a wood chipper, the lace dissected out his nerves, flayed off his skin and then turned his spinal column off at the base of his skull before I took another step inside the house.

Then I let the Dragon fully loose. In a dark haze I danced through them.

ALENA 22

I tried to turn. They hit me with a stun baton, knocking me to the floor. I hit hard, flattened my nose and the pain cut through the stun. I had a knife in one hand and my gun in the other. I emptied the gun down the hall. Somehow the knife cut the Warden by itself. Cut the ankle to drop her then a short thrust to the kidney and a shorter slash across the side of her neck. I saw the blood. Felt it splash from my knife but, I did not will the cutting. No more than I willed the gun cycling at the end of my other arm. I was the knife. I was the gun.

Then the gun locked open, empty. I rolled to reload in the blood and the shelter of the warden.

I saw. I saw what I tried to bind to me. What followed me into this ambush. He glowed in the doorway against the dark. A soft white light, ghost wood in the rain forest. Around and through the glow swirled a black Host. Now big as crows, now shattered into a storm of wasps, now pelting obsidian drops with oily slicks trailing behind. All tumbling in a rolling boil about him. His hands were wreathed in black glass scythes, blades as long as my forearm. Blades that cut through any one that stood against him.

The smallholders fell, cut down like rye or broken like stalks of Indian corn. Their stun guns and truncheons clattering on the inlay floor. A handful of Medji in half-armor poured into the hall, pistols and shotguns at the ready. The Host formed as birds, striking like hawks then mobbing their prey like a murder of crows or crawling on their armor like a hive of bees at swarm. Blood started under the armor and streamed from their helmets. The cut glass heads of the avian forms worrying through Medji bulletproofs with crackling arcs and pops of light. When the stricken troopers slapped and clawed at the Host the forms morphed to scorpions or simply melted to blackly iridescent sheets that peeled skin and flesh and burned lacy shadows into pink bone.

They shot Tallen. They shot everything and everyone around him too. Their own falling in the crossfire. Through and through they shot him. And the Host flowed over his wounds leaving thin smears of blood and extruding spent bullets that rattled on the wood floors like cracked nutshells. They clubbed and hacked and stabbed. Raw bone and acid washed flesh gleaming behind their matte grey battledress. Oozing through their gloves and slicking the grips. He cut them down. Their chests burst under the bulletproofs, their legs folding up under them like rice stalks in a fire, their hands drying to bone and black lace.

Every last Sworn Medji died at the narrows. The last two brought needle guns of an antique make and mark and stood in the doorway to the gate, their guns rattling like clockwork sewing machines. He took the needles in his chest and face. Open sores burned where the needles sprayed. The Host closed over the sores and glittering needles washed from them. Then the Host burst outwards like a great wave and took the last Sworn men. Left nothing of them. Nothing but dulled gunmetal, smoldering rags and dust.

When the Sworn fell, the rest fled deeper into the hall. I felt them open a gate and flee this world.

Tallen started after. Then he stopped and stood over me, the black Host wrapping about him like a buffalo robe or a living shawl. Stood over me with his sightless eyes, weighing me. The glow softened, faded and the Host faded away. Until he stood there in ragged clothing, a gun in one hand. Scars whealed and rayed across his chest, puckered his legs and his abdomen. Scars that faded as I watched, fading to nothing.

"Best be going, I think." He said and held his hand out to me.

"Selai." I named him. Then I fainted.

TALLEN 23

She called me a name "shee-li", then passed out. Well who wouldn't have.

The silly bastards had poured in from both sides and from behind as well, cramming themselves into the entry hall. Half of the dead were shot to doll rags by their own side. She made her bones in the hall, if I had rightly understood her before. She'd been in two firefights on the road to Ames, but she hadn't put anyone down that she could have stepped on. Just banging away at silhouettes, not anything like getting up close and bloody. She dropped two on top of her after they hit her with the cattle prod. One with a tuck-away knife and the other with her pistol.

Then she got to watch the Greater Dragon dance. She likely fainted from being left alone with me. I would have fair pissed myself at the thought of being left alone with me.

I squatted down and ran my hands over her. She'd had a nasty shock and bloodied her nose. She was covered in blood, but it wasn't hers on the most part. Someone had shot her in the calf. Small wound, through and through. I had a sudden thought and checked my hideaway gun. It was gone and its make had a reputation for firing on being dropped. Damn. I scooped up her gun and knife. Made sure she still had her Bloodseal. Then picked her up into a fireman's carry and walked down the hall. We needed a bathroom or a hazmat shower. Blood does attract attention.

They had a kitchen near big enough to mess a company and at one end of the kitchen was a place to wash out full carcasses from a hook over a drain. I kicked on the water and stood her under the shower head. She sputtered and cussed in all the colors of the rainbow. When she was well rinsed, I pulled her out and laid her on a butcher's block. I stripped off my shirt and wet it and used it to scrub the worst off my jeans. Then I spun back under the spray. As for my skin and hair, blood never stuck to me when I wore the Dragon. It soaked in. I did not like thinking about that.

I doused her again rinsing her leg and looking for other wounds. There were none, just welts from the stun baton. Then we left. I did a quick pass through the cooler as we left the kitchen and got a two-pound chub of hamburger and a gallon of milk. I drained the milk before we got out the door. I'd make hamburger tartar on the road. The Dragon had cost me a good fifty pounds. Even with the kills I'd left as soup bones on the floor, I was eating my own flesh just walking down the hall. The bones of my hand were stark under my skin, my fingertips raw and oozing sera.

The lights were on everywhere outside, but even with my Subtle senses at full draw I didn't pick up any humans close. In these weak, whining, days of rifles that shot two thousand yards, it did not mean we were safe. I found a kill switch that dropped the inside and yard lights, just inside the door along with an alarm pad and an empty gun rack.

Some of the survivors had fled outside, stampeding

past the truck and up into the brush or down the road towards the town. I looked to the right and left along the house front. Then I frog marched her over to the truck. We didn't draw any fire, but anytime soon this place would be crawling. Cops, State police, Guard helicopters, the News of the World and the Men in Black.

I got her in the cab, then jumped onto the flatbed and opened the armory locker. Pulled out a short carbine. Pistols are for when you don't expect trouble, long guns are when you count on trouble, tac-air is when you want no trouble at all.

We actually got away from there without a single hitch. It helped that there was a demolition protocol in place, though I did not know this at the time. Something went boom deep underground and then the house and the main outbuildings started burning with a deep whoomph and a Hollywood flash. I got us the hell off the property and in a southern direction.

Where we were going was a good question. About a mile from the house I saw a gravel turn off that led down into a valley. At the bottom of the gravel road there was a two-lane asphalt road that followed a river. I headed south with my headlights off. When we got out of sight of the burning house I pulled over. I needed water. Water, salt and a pound of the beef just to back off on the headache I was cranking. I knew there was a creek close by, draining into the river through a culvert under the road.

I took the beef with me along with a shaker of salt and a bottle of Worcestershire sauce. I stripped my jeans off, let them trail in the creek weighted down by rocks while I wolfed down the beef mixed with the sauce and the salt. Then I drank my fill upstream of the jeans to give my body a chance to bulk a little. I knew I'd have to be drinking a lot of water in the next week to flush all the poisons I likely picked up from the creek.

When I got back from the creek, she was standing nude by the truck, shivering in the cold. One of the guns in her hands, watching down our back trail. Her clothes were kicked aside, including her sandals.

I didn't ghost up on her, I made enough racket to wake the dead. She was not tightly wrapped. She looked over her shoulder at me, her eyes dark pits in the starlight. Then she turned back to face her enemies. I picked up her sandals, left the rest at the side of the road.

"Getting a chill in the air." I remarked.

"I could smell the blood. Everywhere."

"Ah." I stepped around her and opened the truck cab, pulled a jacket out from behind the seat. Draped it over her shoulders. I jumped onto the truck bed. Over the running water and the wind, I could hear sirens high up on the ridgeline. I pulled a set of sweats and a t-shirt for her out of the footlocker. Then I pulled a long-sleeved shirt out for me, a light pair of cotton gloves to protect my ragged fingertips and nail beds. My jeans were ragged but dry and still covering most of me. Blessings of the Dragon, I'm my own dryer. I dressed her like I was dressing a doll. A doll armed with a gun. Her eyes were measuring distance in thousand-yard increments. All the way to hell.

I picked her up and put her back in the truck, knelt and put the sandals on her.

"What are you?"

I looked up from wrapping a bandage around her calf, it was hard work with gloves on. "You named me. Sealer. Something like that."

"Selai. See-li."

"And?"

"You are a myth. Something to hang operas on."

"Thought I'd been insulted every way possible, now this. I'm quite real."

"You did not tell me."

"Well you don't walk up and just introduce yourself as an Operatic Plot Device. You have to ease into the subject."

"A Selai is more than that. Some of the Pelagic Houses call them Walking Razors."

"Pelagic?"

"Oceanic, pirates with..."

"I get the picture. Walking Razor, eh. My House called

me, Ji'long, the Young Dragon. Gave me a nice brocaded nightshirt, two handmaids that carried swords mounted on spear shafts and a tea set." And a regiment of dragoons. Well on paper I had a regiment. On ponies I had a heavy company.

"Your House?"

"Yeah, my House. Any one pass by us? On this road? While I was down at the creek?"

"No. I thought you were Unsworn."

"No, just orphaned. Death breaks most vows."

"Some vows."

"Point to The Mihaly. Time to get on the road."

I took the gun from her hands. Cycled the slide open, ejected the empty magazine. I slipped a fresh magazine in and let the slide snap forward. Put the gun on safe and pressed it back into her hands. "Ready to go."

She just shivered inside my coat, the gun clasped between her legs like a stick pony.

About four hours later I found a small town with an off-brand convenience store by the county blacktop we were on. I'd kept an eye on her with the Dragon, brushing my aura through hers every so often. She was still bleeding. Couldn't get her leg up to let it clot and couldn't stop long enough to do a little Subtle fixing.

"We are going to pull off here and let me have a look at the leg."

"The bullet went through, I think."

"You think. Let me know." I peeled the bandages back, did a little rough and ready patching with the auras, stopped the bleeding. "Nice clean hole, small caliber." My goddamn bullet.

"It bled quite a lot, that was fortunate."

"How so?"

"We so often poison bullets."

"Not many rules in your Manuals, are there?"

"Just the one. Win."

"So where do we stand now?"

"I still hold the Bloodseal. And for the next ten days I hold the purse strings."

"We get to the bankers; the coup is stymied?"

"Not entirely. But it means I can mount a counterstroke."

"Okay. Where to next?"

"I am not certain."

"South by southeast then. And put your gun away."

I lost the gloves in the bathroom Pissed blood, then rinsed my hands, my nails were regrowing almost as I watched. I bought three tubes of chocolate chip cookie dough and three big packets of jerky. I looked like death warmed over. The clerk looked much worse than I did.

I tore a cookie tube open as we pulled out of the convenience store parking lot. I had a lot of calories to make up. She was asleep before we were a hundred yards from the store, her gun still in her left hand under her left leg.

I pulled the truck around at the back of the motel. We were just outside of Trinidad, Colorado. Maybe a hundred and forty miles south from the ambush. I needed to eat, sleep and scrounge us some more clothing. And eat. I looked like I'd been dragged through a coil of barbwire backwards and she looked like she'd been dressed in the middle of a concrete mixer. The hotel folk had been a little chary of us until I mentioned having a helluva time mountain bike racing up around Cripple Creek. Then they had us pigeonholed as 'idiots, athletic' with more money than sense. I got directions to the nearest Wal-Mart and went to put Alena to bed.

She was having none of it, of course. Rather than argue, I stacked the three footlockers from the truck in the room and took her with me. It took me twenty minutes to spend another hundred dollars on clothing, beef jerky, random supplements and Gatorade. Then we drove back to the hotel. I took what was needed from the footlockers and put them back on the truck. If I quit being an Operatic Plot Device, I had a future as a stevedore.

"Tell me about being a Selai". She was sitting on the bed across from me, uncertainly wrapped in a very small towel and drying her hair with another.

"Hunh?" I was skimming the cable. Slim pickings this hour of the morning but I was looking for news about Canon City. Nada.

"Is... Are the legends true?"

"Let me guess. Selai fly through the air, turn into smoke and command mice?" I purely hate Stoker and all his kith.

"You are being condescending."

"Yeah, I am. You picked the name, you tell me what a Selai is."

I shut off the TV and opened another packet of beef jerky. I had wolfed two of them down along with another tube of chocolate chip cookie dough and a box of prunes while I surfed the channels. I'd devoured a barn buster at the Country Kitchen we had found after I'd settled on the hotel. with an order of a chicken fried steak and a second short stack of pancakes on the side. I was just beginning to feel full. She'd had a cheese omelet, tea and toast and some of my pancakes.

"A Selai is hard to kill, hard to control and worst of all, hard to bind."

"I'd have to agree with that triplet. Anything else you know?"

"You kill with a touch."

"More than a touch. You aren't going to let this go? Are you?'

"Would you?"

I thought about it. "No. I wouldn't. You comfortable?"

"Yessss, why?"

"It is not a simple story. But we won't use 'Selai'. I am the Elder Dragon of the Three-Legged House. I don't know anything about Selai, but I am somewhat familiar with the Dragons of the Three-Legged House."

She smiled and worked herself into a full lotus and out of her towel. Damn.

"I'd say sitting in a full lotus is ostentatious, not comfortable."

"The flexibility of youth..."

"Is greatly oversold."

I took a long drink of the Gatorade and tried to ignore the taste. I've eaten sheep's head stew. I've drunk Hmong beer. I can take almost anything the food demons throw at me. But Gatorade is rough stuff.

"The Dragon is born, and the Dragon is formed. You cannot make a Dragon. You can awaken the Dragon within, if the Dragon is there to begin with."

"I understand. Much like a 'Walker' cannot be trained up from any odd sod you find in the street."

I looked at her with my best "who is telling this lie" gaze. "Yeah. In my case, I was a dead man walking. And a Sniffer crossed my trail."

"Sniffer?"

"You ever had people who could look at a colt and see a three-year-old cutting horse?"

"Ah. He saw a Dragon in you."

"Truly. And he bought me."

"Bought!"

"For a large bag of silver coins. Funny old world, isn't it? Nowadays the style is gold, of course."

She did not favor me with a reply, just ran her fingers through her hair to fluff it.

"It was kindness, really. Much like buying an abused dog from an abusive cretin. Although, Kluge did break most of their teeth out sealing the purchase."

"Kluge?"

"I think his personal title was Esteemed Discover of Diamonds in Night Soil. He was forever bringing home starveling mongrels and making them flourish."

"You must have been a disappointment."

"Clever. McDonald's for breakfast then?"

"I withdraw the comment."

"He bought three of us with his silver and his subtle charms. He only killed one of our former owners. For insolence, I think. Though I never quite knew if it was for showing insolence or to demonstrate it. Then he lugged us home to the Three-Legged House. The other two were as near dead as I but, they fed them well and splinted their bones after they deloused them. One went back to the

Ruperts and marked me dead along with the rest of the unit. The other just vanished into China."

"Ruperts?"

I nodded. "That was what we called the intelligence officers wished on us by GHQ" I continued on. "It was in the last summer of that war and in the Foreign Office eyes were turning from Imperial Germany to Revolutionary Russia. Vladivostok and Northeast China seemed to be a good place to insert a pry bar. So late in that summer, they plucked a Colonel out of a posting in India, pulled myself and six others from the Western Front. My Captain was eager to be shut of me. And when we arrived at Vladivostok we hired on as advisers to the Whites. Nudge, nudge, wink. Not an official British Imperial among us."

I finished that bottle and fished another out of the ice bucket. Terrible stuff, but it balanced out the fluids. After that mess in Canon City, I was sadly out of balance. Yin and Yang. Blood mist hanging in the air. It had been a long while since I'd let the Dragon dance so freely and for so long.

"The Whites liked us only a bit more than the Reds and gave us a dog's breakfast of mounted infantry and unfrocked bandits then sent us along the Chinese border. We lasted most of a season. Then we were sold like cattle and butchered."

"And Kluge rescued you?"

"Hated to see good stock wasted. When the other survivors were slipped out of Manchuria, I stayed behind. Becoming the Dragon."

I took another drink of the Gatorade. Ate some more jerky.

"Kluge spent good silver on me and dumped my sorry ass on the tiles in the House kitchen. They burned my rags and boiled my sins away. Fed me pork rolls and egg soup. Adjusted my elements and popped my back. While Kluge smoked in the corner by the fireplace. Odder than hell, the Three-Legged House was sort of a cross between a Dutch townhouse, a Chinese palace and a sod hut. Ceramic tile in one room, inlay wood and red trim in another section, dirt floors in the others."

"This relates to you becoming a Selai?"

"Dragon, if you please. Told you it was not simple. Some things were never said, not where I could hear them. I never saw the other two after I arrived. Someone took them off in a cart while I was frog marched into the kitchen. From the beginning, to the end. I was singled out."

"How do you know about the others, then?"

"Conal, our political officer. Read his original reports, during one of my other lives."

"Oh."

"After I got healthy enough to piss standing, they put the question to me. Stay here or take out on my own. I knew what it was like outside the House, didn't have anything to go back to and they were offering me a family and a role to play."

"Medji."

"Söldner, was what Kluge called me. When he wasn't going on about 'de jongedrakke'. The shilling I took and I kissed the book. This was early fall, 19 and 19. They put me through the short course in mayhem and meditation, horseback and on foot and with every weapon known to man at that time. I got to train them with Lewis guns and Maxims. They taught me to use swords and halberds. I thought I was shaping up fine as frog hair. Then they let me brush up against the Ältestes Drache of the Household. The Old Dragon."

"Selai."

"Yeah, tomato, tomahto. I got swatted down hard, elegantly and with grace, but hard enough to rattle my teeth. And by a granny old enough to be my grandmother's grandmother. Then they told me I could be a Drakke."

"Why did you accept."

"I was young and dumb. Wanted to 'earn' my place at the table. Knew from what was not being said and not being done, that the Old Drakke was in her last days. I also got the idea, from the couple of skirmishes I had gone on after the short course, that we were holding off a pack of enemies with just her reputation."

"And they didn't mention the changes? The risks?"

"No. They needed me just as much as I needed them."

"How long did it take to change you."

"They didn't have to change me, just open my eyes as it were."

And my channels, and my Chakras. They cleaned out my sinuses with hot mustard on spring rolls, opened my lungs with mustard packs and balanced my ley lines with mustard and henna wrapped in wet towels. If mustard couldn't cure you, it wasn't a disease but a curse. Curses they cured with enemas. Gott straf all German grandmothers. Especially Chinese grandmothers who thought they were German.

"And..."

"I did more meditation. Ate my own weight in mushrooms and Drachebrot. Learned to breathe from a Tibetan Rinpoche, medicine from some Chinese herbalist, German card games from Kluge or his kinfolk."

"Card games?"

" 'Gambling sharpens the mind. It will teach your Yankee mouth more Chinese than a pillow book and cheaper too.' That's a direct quote from Kluge. All the while the Old Dragon held my hand and I sipped mushroom tea. When I started seeing black lace floating through the air things sped up. They started really pushing my limits."

"Hmm?"

She draped her small towel across her lap, to draw my attention there. I thought longingly of handing her off to one of my handmaidens, now long dust and ashes. Li Na had a gift for the long willow switch, a true patent medicine for the condition of being a smartass. Better than mustard cookies. "Some of the martial arts have followed that path."

"I suspect martial arts had their roots in this transformation. And as I became able to See Auras without having to be stoked up on mushrooms or Drachebrot..."

"Drachebrot?"

"A bread made from sprouted rye and likely just chock full of ergot toxins. It'd kill anyone who wasn't born a drache."

"Not so much different from Walking."

"Really. I'll see if I can recall the recipe. After I learned to See Auras then I learned to manipulate them. Simple things. Expand them out in a thin cloud then contract them until they simply skimmed my skin like a smear of oil. Fade them. Strengthen them."

I sipped at the damn stuff. Much worse than the mushroom tea. Ate some more cookie dough for the grease and the sugars. Finished off a summer sausage I'd picked up at Wal-Mart, grease and protein. Prunes, to keep me regular.

"And after that?"

"She changed me."

Sharp intake of breath. I could see goosebumps on her arms from where I sat.

"Yeah. Taught me to See my form and See the pattern I carried and then to 'shape' my form. First to match the pattern and then to match her forms. To carry two patterns in my center, one human, one 'other'."

I drank some more Gatorade. "When I wear the Dragon, the Greater Dragon. I am very hard to kill."

"Sever the head," She said in a low voice. "dismember the body, burn the scraps and sift the ashes into a running stream. And say your prayers."

"You have the gist of it." I finished the drink. "More propaganda than truth, but there is a large kernel of fact in the legend." I pulled down my bedclothes and swung my legs under the sheets. I tucked the pillow gun away and stretched to turn out the light. She still sat in a full lotus, massaging thoughtfully the place where I had shot her. It was a flat scar now, the size of my thumbprint. Auric flows. "More questions?"

"I watched you, you know?"

"I am sorry."

"Why?"

"Some things are not to be seen."

She looked up and met my eyes fully for the first time since Canon City. "If I have my sums correct, you are close to a hundred years old."

"More than that. Does that matter?"

"You are a noted monster."

Now that took me aback. "Do tell."

ALENA 24

"Do tell." He said, in that damn flat accent. He settled himself into bed, one hand tucked under his pillow and with his left hand pulled his bed clothes up over his shoulder. "How many more days do you have."

"Nine."

"Since the gates seem to be out of the question, who's going to smuggle us over?"

"You know about the Grey trade?"

"Smuggling is just about as universal as murder and fooling around. If you have a locked border, someone is going to cross it with some sort of contraband."

"Much of the smuggling is done with the aid and connivance of the authorities."

"The same authorities that just tried to wrap you up?'

"It would seem so."

"But there are others?"

"It is possible. No, it is certain. But, the possibility of my being able to make contact and achieve a crossing is unlikely at best."

"Gotta touch them, promote a crossing without much in the way of front money and then go across in the right spot?"

"Yes."

"Why don't you just open a gate yourself?"

"There are many reasons not to try that, not the least among them is the very real likelihood of not going to the right place. Getting there is a function of talent, strength and discernment. You have to have the talent to open a soft spot, the strength to hold it open and the discernment of where/when to go." She shifted slightly on the bed. "Location governs your destination. One crossing point will take you to the Hanse for example. Not a mile away, the next crossing point will only take you to the 'Zeme. Unless you have traveled those roads, you will not know which is which."

"No maps?"

"Closely held maps exist. Most of the ones you find outside of a gatehouse are traps."

"And so, we need access to true outlaws, not the mildly corrupt functionaries at the official gates." He smiled at me. "Outlaws like the ones you found at Ames."

"I did not tell you that they were outlaws, as I remember."

"Your hunters killed them as a sideshow. You needed to be staked for the true player to find."

"So, I think."

"They think that the true players deftly removed you from Ames, then ever so clumsily tried to cross over in Canon City? And..."

"Confusion, uncertainty if not panic. I am being escorted by a fully manifested Selai, or so the survivors would have averred. There are reasons you inspire operas and nightmares."

He nodded. "Could we have forced a crossing there?"

"Um, it would not have been wise. Going forth from

the 'Zeme can be a simple thing. Coming to the 'Zeme through a known gate you will face rigorous defenses and humorless defenders. At last resort, defenders may broach the gate." I shivered. "What happens then, to the assaulting force, no one knows."

"I see. You got a list of possible, covert, crossings?"

"Why?"

"See if any are in reach. If I have sussed out the set up rightly, forcing a smugglers crossing is slightly easier than slipping through an official one."

I got up from the bed.

TALLEN 25

S he produced a scrap of paper, from somewhere in her clothing, no bigger than an unfolded gum wrapper, pulled a note pad from the desk. She tore off the top sheet of the pad and staring intently at the gum wrapper began to write. She'd lost the towel, again.

I thought about the talk I'd been meaning to have with her. Somehow it had stopped being a priority. I didn't know if she was traipsing around buck naked to try and set the bond, because I was a servant, or just because everyone around her just wore enough clothing to suit the climate.

She had the blue patch at the base of her spine.

"Why'd you remove the extra nipples?"

She stopped writing. Looked over her shoulder at me. "It is vulgar to…retain those tokens." She started writing again.

My. This is something she is tetchy about. "I see. Or to

remark upon them?"

She ignored me.

Just as well. I put my head down and watched her decoding or translating her note. My hands hurt still, but they were almost healed. My ribs were not showing as much. Cookie dough and hamburger tatar had helped. Riding the Greater Dragon wears holes in your hide, Subtle and Overt.

Been a long time since I danced like that.

The trick was to not have to use your own flesh as the weapon, but all of the old blades that would carry the aura were lost. And I never got the urge for a research program to duplicate them. I'd spent four years hiding in Macao once to get shut of a very determined OSS section that specialized in oddities.

If I'd had a bit of warning, or a lick of sense, I could have used less 'Operatic' methods, stopping hearts or causing a stroke at the brush of a hand. Dead is dead and much less taxing when it is simple. But you play the hand you're dealt, no whining about it. I closed my eyes and let go of the memories. Practiced my breathing, focused my mind, and let go the memories. Let go.

I let go the memories I carried and the memories I had taken. And somewhere in there Tallen, Royal A., went to sleep.

ALENA 26

He was asleep when I finished the list. His face softened in the half light, not the blood drenched bronze statue that had danced through the hallway. The pits the needle guns had burned in his face were mosquito bites. The toxins and acids they had carried should have stripped the flesh to the bone and through it. They should have dropped him to the tiles like the executioner's coup de grace.

He lived. I shuddered. I feared for my enemies and for me.

TALLEN 27

I woke up when she closed the door to the hotel room. The Dragon came swirling awake. The room suddenly filled with black snowflakes that swirled and danced in patterns then faded through the walls as they hunted. Right out to the fifty feet or so that was my limit. I rolled off the bed and with my gun in hand, padded over to the window, looked out. She was climbing onto the bed of the truck with my keys in her hands.

I had a fair idea what she was doing, but the details were lacking. She didn't open the armory box, nor the medical. She opened the locker I had placed the Kwantung Army items in, peeled the woolens back and ran her hands over the items in the locker. She took the Army dispatch bag out and the smaller pouch as well. She took the blanket wrapped sword out and gently laid it on the tops of the other footlockers. Then she put the rest of the folded wool blankets back in the footlocker and locked it. She picked up the dispatch bag, the wrapped sword and the smaller pouch and headed back to our room.

I stepped back from the window and slid back into bed, with my back to her. The Dragon watched her all the way back.

I perceive auras two ways. One is visual. I Saw auras that behaved much like banners or flames or smoke. Sometimes the auras crawled along their skins like moving tattoos, changing shapes or forming words as they moved. I could See these auras at respectable distances, depending on the strength of the aura and the light conditions. The maximum distance was about two hundred feet. At that distance it was more of a nimbus of light than a legible aura. I could not use optics to enhance my Seeing the auras. Looking through a telescope or a pair of binoculars suppressed the aura no matter what distance.

The other way was much more than seeing. If you were within my nimbus, which varied from skin on skin to about fifty feet-optimal being fifteen feet, I could do more than just See your aura. I could kill you. Simply stop your heart or burn you to a cinder depending on how much energy I wanted to use. The more flamboyant the method the more it cost me. I could also unravel your mind or sense your emotions through the auras. Depending on how much time I had, I could slowly but thoroughly extract everything you had ever seen or done and be able to recover it in a usable memory. I could, with much less effort, Read your emotions and basic intentions. Which made me a world class poker cheat. Or I could simply, metaphorically, rip off the top of your head and run your mind through a sieve for the information I thought I wanted. The second method was distressing to me, since it had unhappy side effects of a mental hangover and occasional cross contamination. It was more stressful to the subject since it usually killed him or her. This trait of the Dragon was really more useful than the flashy combat moves, particularly after gunpowder had become readily available. Being able to See around a corner or through a wall is handy in any case. It made room to room fighting simply a tedious chore rather than grimly murderous.

When Alena came back in the room she walked through a net of my aura, a net that gradually meshed with her own fields. She was cold and scared and determined and terribly angry.

But not at me.

She opened the Imperial Japanese Army dispatch bag first.

In the bag was an Imperial rescript documenting the provision of the long sword I had brought from the storage in the footlocker and who it was going to and why. The sword was old, likely dating from just after the 1500's. It was longer than most of the Samurai swords that surfaced in the west. And it was death to have or even know about. It was a presentation weapon. A token of how much the recipient, Colonel Dr. Shiro Ishii, was esteemed by the Imperial House of Japan. It also was half of the proof that the Imperial House knew all along what Shiro Ishii was doing in Unit 731 at Pingfan. Human bio war experiments with one hundred percent mortality among the test subjects.

The papers would have been more than enough for the West, but the Kunaicho could turn up their noses at the 'blatant forgeries' and go on. But the sword combined with the documentation; well the number of suicides in the prefecture of Tokyo would have just skyrocketed. This was why they had never quite believed I was dead. It's why I still owed Alena a pistol.

I felt' her place the two bags and the sword on the bed and bend her legs back into the lotus. And then she opened the dispatch bag. I slowly rolled over and watched her sort through the mix of late '30s operational orders and hand-written scrolls in elegant formal Japanese. She could make no sense of any of the paperwork, although she knew it was important from the presentation.

Then she went to pick up the smaller leather bag.

"I'd rather you not open that."

She did not jump off the bed, but her auras damn near

washed out my Subtle sight. I let that part of the Dragon go
dark and the room lost its shoals of auric forms.

"I thought you were asleep."

"Thought I was deaf as well?"

She blushed and waved her hand in search of a proper
explanation.

"How'd you know it was in there?" I asked.

"It was the only locker you had not gone through, item
by item, the contents for me."

"I am a noted monster?"

Chin up and eyes bore into mine. "Yes."

"All right then, open the bag."

She bent her head and unwound the wire holding the
leather pouch closed. She opened it and froze. I could see
the fine hairs on her arms erect and her nostrils flare.
Goosebumps. She slowly reached into the bag and just as
slowly brought a dusty honor into the light. On the struck
side was an eight spoke wheel, on the engraved obverse, an
onyx inlaid tiger mask. Through the middle was a hole, just
big enough for a .455 slug. She gently laid the medallion on
the quilt. Then reached into the bag again.

When she was done there were four. One was white
enameled with a Triskelion on the struck side and a crane in
flight engraved on the obverse. Another was only barely
recognizable as a medallion. It was crushed to the size of a
walnut and the chain running through it was caked in cold
lead. The third was cut in two. It was marked with the
Chrysanthemum talisman, with obverse a Tau cross.

She sat back on her buttocks, back straight, hands
gently brushing at the medallions. "These are graves." She
said.

"Truly." I said. "You could see how I was a bit startled
when I first saw your seal. I had thought these were the
last."

"Then, you are the one." She was looking me over for
horns, or at least for buds on my forehead.

"The one?"

"The Breaker of Houses." Her free hand waved at the
medallions. "Of these four."

"Three." I corrected her.

"There are four, I know the crests…"

I slowly reached out my hand and touched the medallion caked in lead. "This was the honor of my adopted people. The House of my Eldest Brother, Kluge Willm. Ächtet Zirkus. He found me hungry in the darkness and fed me, naked in the winds and clothed me, bladeless in the face of my enemies and armed me. I was given a new name. A true name and he forged a knife for me from bright iron. I became The Ji'long of The People. The Young Dragon.

I drew my hand back from the lump of lead and iron. "Then there came the House Koshitsu." I touched the Chrysanthemum. "Twice they sent raiders to us. Twice I and my Dragons crucified their survivors at our borders."

"And the end was…"

"We were sold, by these." I waved at the other medallions.

She hissed between her teeth. "Betrayal."

I nodded. "Gold, weapons and our land. A good price."

"And you turned bandit."

"Not that easy, not quite that easy, but yes."

"You did not know, that you were of the Dai?"

"Don't you want to know the ending?"

She smiled, grimly. "Tallen, they have made a novel, a play, two very bad cinema plays, one excellent telenovela and that excellently terrible Grand Opera about you. All lacking the part about you avenging the betrayal of the fourth House."

Opera. I shook my head. I had thought she was pulling the one that had bells on it. "So, who lived to tell the tale?"

"Uzumasa Jirobee?"

I shook my head. I didn't know the name, but that didn't signify. "Koshitsu?"

She nodded. "After the doors opened, in '48, the Nihon found them."

Doors. '48. "And?"

"There was less than fifty of them, hiding in the north

of Hokkaido. None were... whole. None could carry the line. So, it fell to Koshitsu the Greater to replenish the House. They culled a double banner from their cadets and Fain and came across to hold the House in Edo."

"And I became a monster?"

"They had broken Koshitsu to kill you."

"Did they now?" Dead twice over, three times if you count Laos in '59 or is that four times with the Yucatan. Or five now with the business in Missouri. Damn, it's a sign of age when you start forgetting things like that.

"So, it ended."

I grunted. "I hunted the Koshitsu and their hirelings, later the Keta Ichii and the Kempetai through Manchuria and down the coast to Shanghai and the mudflats of Hong Kong. My war started in '24 and it didn't end until I left the mainland. When I wasn't hunting Koshitsu or the Imperial Japanese, I was re-educating Bolsheviks or cutting down Gongzuodai, bandits with badges."

"And then?"

"I left China proper, in 1949. Oh, I stayed on the rim, Hong Kong and Macau then Vietnam, Laos and all that, until 1975. But I never went back to Manchuria or the coast of the Yellow sea." I sighed and leaned back on my elbows. "I came back to the lower forty-eight in '75. Washed my money through Brazil and the Caymans. Bought several good identities and settled in to retire. Found out that retirement cost a bit more than I could safely wash through the banks, so I did a little work."

"You didn't know?"

"About Houses? And what I was? Oh, I learned more of what I was all right, in bits and pieces. Found some of my kind working for the Koshitsu in Manchuria. Found a few more knocking around in South China and Malaysia. Freelance Monsters. Unbonded and uncontrolled for the main part. It wasn't that they were hard to kill but, they seemed to be damn hard to find. I thought the Houses ended when Mao took the mainland. He had a Monster hunting directorate staffed with old Bolsheviks and forward-looking Heroes of the Revolution. They burned out more Houses than I ever knew existed. There hadn't been more than seven when I became the Dragon. After Nanking and Shanghai, I didn't see a trace of anyone other than the Koshitsu and their puppets. After Mao, well even the memory was purged."

"There was maybe a score of Houses still existent in Europe and fifty more in the Americas. They were thinned terribly by the White Death after your first war, but, when the doors were opened again, they were still in place."

"Twenty in Europe, eh?" I was surprised. I sort of figured that the Houses were part and parcel of the East, like Triads and opium. I should have known better.

Things happen at the fringes that you never believe in when you are sitting at the diner back in Polk City, or even a strip joint on the Vieux Carrie. I wasn't one when Kluge bought me, but he could see the 'sleeping' Dragon in my sorry hide. Said he could smell it, like a dead mammoth. Never asked him how he knew how a dead mammoth smelled. Kluge called me a Dragon. That was good enough. Said I had several gifts. A good eye for ground and a good sense for where my enemies might be standing. A sure hand with a gun or a blade and an understanding of horse. But what was sleeping under those gifts was what made me worth thirty cartwheels of silver.

"The House name was Ächtet Zirkus?"

"We thought of it more the banner name. The House was just the 'House'. The joke was that we started out as a traveling show. A circus of Outlaws."

"That is not the name used in the novel, or anything else ever spun about the four Houses." She held up a hand with four fingers wide spread. "Koshitsu Tachibana," She folded one down. "Mutsurensen, Kyogoku and the last House, Hattori."

"All the House names are Japanese?"

"The Chrysanthemum Throne." She shrugged. "The Takamikura Throne, the Linage of the Peacock and the Horsetail Banner all are fed by the Kikuza. The only Houses that still stand clear of them in that quarter of the world are the Pelagic Houses. The Chrysanthemum led the way back to AngTerra-the Gunpowder World. The Houses you broke were Nihon of course."

"Victor's fiction." Only the Americans landed on Overlord's D-Day, only the French took Paris, and no one ever mentioned the Chinese fighting the Japanese since '31 in Manchuria.

"Pardon?"

"Only Koshitsu Tachibana I recognize. One of the Houses was Lei, Manchurian they were. Now the other was called Tey-sha-rah, spelled T-e-i-x-e-r-i-a. They claimed to be Portuguese, but all of the household I saw were Northern Han. They had a twitch about revealing their true names and so went by common Chinese names."

"I recognize only the Tachibana."

"So, now that you know who used to feed me, can we get some sleep."

ALENA 28

❙❙...can we get some sleep?"

I nodded. I left the Bloodseals on the bed's counterpane. Then I stripped again. I flipped back the comforter of his bed and slipped between the sheets. He was shocked. I snuggled into the furnace of his body, my back to his chest and my head forcing a pillow of his arm. "You can turn out the light."

"Is this wise?'

"I am still chilled to my center. Should anyone force the door I will be in the center of your pattern, in the center of your strength. You need sleep as much as I do, but will your Dragon let you rest if I am not within your aura?"

"Within this room, Mihaly, you are within my aura."

"That is comforting, but I prefer the warmth as well. Good night, Tallen, Dragon of the Mihaly in Shadow." And I slowed my breathing and let my tensions drift away.

Come morning I still lay in his warmth, feeling hunger rumbling though him. He had not moved and perhaps he had not slept. A night embraced by his aura and I did not feel the wounds of yesterday, I was quite recovered. I rubbed my head along his arm until his face nestled in my hair.

"I am already bound, Mihaly." He rumbled at the back of my neck.

"Lightly."

"Bound, but lightly. Agreed."

"We never had the conversation about House Mihaly." I said.

"The House."

TALLEN 29

"We order the House in this manner." She said. "There is an inner hearth and an outer yard. The Yard is open. There we wear 'masks without laces' There is a Master and a Mistress of the House who walk openly through the Yard to set the courses of the day. Manifested Dai, Holders Small and Great, those who might have a Seat at Table and the Sworn Medji; all look to the two who sit at the Head of the Table in the Yard." I could hear the capital letters in every word.

"And where do I sit?'

"Under open sky, in the Yard, you are a Bound-by-blood Retainer. You sit above the Medji, below the Holders and the Manifested Dai. Within the Hearth, you are more." She nuzzled me again. "You stand only second to me."

"Quit with the pheromones."

"I bind you thusly. I may bind a score more. They

form the inner circle. The Hearth. They will not necessarily correspond to the hierarchy of the Yard."

"Misdirection."

"I would likely be the Mistress when we recover the House only because the adversaries were so thorough when they purged the Manifested."

"And the adversary is...?"

"We broke cousins once, Mihaly but not Mihaly. Madgji are the lineage. Close kin of a sort. You killed six of them at Canon City. They have to be the ones. When we finished with them, they had no Manifested Dai and only Small Holders and Fain to carry their lines."

"How did you know what I killed at Canon City?"

"I just knew, they are kin. Kin speaks to kin."

"And now?"

I shrugged. "It has been long enough for the wheel to turn. Del said I was not the first choice. That Long Knives had been very thorough among Dai and Fain, Yard and Hearth." She shivered. "I should not be holding this." Her hand was clasping the Bloodseal on its chain.

"But you hold it now."

"I hold it now."

I got her up and shoved her in to the shower, then policed the other bed. I trailed my fingers over the emblems, but there was nothing for me. I laid out on the unused bed a new set of clothing for us both, from the skin out. Then I took a good look at myself in the mirror by the TV.

I'd picked up enough food to take the starved prisoner look off my ribs. Most of the wounds were cleared up, leaving just faint scars and pock marks. I had a boil coming up, at the side of my neck. Inside it was a speck of metal or glass, I could see it just under the surface of the skin. I dug at it a bit with my fingernails, but all that accomplished was to push it deeper.

"Leave it until after you shower."

I hadn't noticed her. "One of the things they used at the last?"

Her dark eyes met mine in the mirror. "Yes. The guns

were of the oldest mark, but they were specifically developed for threats such as you." She slipped into her underwear, her eyes still on mine. "You should be dead."

I waited until she was half into her t-shirt. "In dog years I am."

She made an indeterminate noise, somewhere between a laugh and a cough. Fluffed her hair after wrestling the shirt on and muttered something under her breath. "In dog years. And a dog's year is what?"

I looked at her and for the first time, in a very long while, I truly felt my age. Or maybe it was the gap between us. I'd felt it, the gap, when I closed the books on the farm in Iowa. Understanding just beyond my fingertips.

"Seven years for every one of ours, Mihaly. And really, I suppose, I am the age of a dog's civilization."

"That is an interesting concept, that your lifetime spans their civilization."

"The concept doesn't bear much examination."

"More than one might think."

I let that go and took a safety razor into the shower with me. I still used the old double-edged razors like I had in college, the traditional ones that opened like a clamshell. Given a choice I liked to be clean shaven and, well, clean. I'd spent my time in filth, thank you. When I finished the shave and shower, she was sitting on the stool with a towel in hand.

"Is the concept of privacy new to the Dai?"

She smiled and handed me the towel. "No, but you need me to extract the needle. The boil is about the size of your thumb pad now and it will get messy."

"I could do it myself."

"In a mirror and cack-handed? Let us not do that. Wrap the towel about your modesty and I'll take the razor."

I let her have the razor while I wrapped the towel about me. She opened the razor and flicked the blade to the countertop, drenched it in Listerine and with her fingernails picked it up. Alena folded it in a washcloth with one corner exposed. She had me sit on the stool. Then she stepped between my legs and gently pushed my head back. "Take this towel and hold it under the boil."

I rolled the towel up and made a loose collar under the boil. "Like so?"

"That will do nicely." Her scent filled the room, washing over me like a sudden shower of rain.

"Pheromones."

"Sorry, nerves. Stick and a burn, now." She made a small motion and seemed to light a fire on the side of my neck. I felt something squirm and then burst through my skin, run down my neck into the toweling. "You are very resistant to the load in this needle, else wise you would not be breathing. But our armorers fabricated this little devil with silver and beryllium. The silver was machined to encourage your body chemistry to corrode it; the beryllium just helps matters along. And you start to abscess with all sorts of toxins brewing."

"You know a lot about an Operatic Plot Device?"

"Selai, pardon me, Dragons are a fascination for Dai of a certain age and inclination. Much like the American popular culture's fascination with the Vampire." She patted at the wound with a washcloth drenched in Listerine. "Stands to reason, since the Vampire and the Operatic Plot Device have the same source."

Damn Stoker. "Are we done?"

"Yes, I believe so." She stepped back and wiped at a trickle that was running down my chest. "You do heal quickly."

"Right. Could I..." And I motioned at the folded clothing on the countertop.

"Certainly. I will go and check the news."

I checked the boil in the mirror, and it was a fading blister, the skin flaking away in short black strips. I took another shower, just to be sure.

There had been a mention of a major methamphetamine operation broken in Fremont County, Canon City, on the television. Many arrests, several killed in the operation, details sketchy. I asked her what the Dai would do about the dust up.

"Little or nothing." She shivered. "After that massacre

there would be only casual hirelings, likely given only a cover story for what security they provided. Maybe they were the source for the drug story."

"And any Dai survivors?"

"In this case, in this world, they do not break cover. If they must, they go to jail as a drug lord or a murderer. They might escape your law dogs, but if they break faith with the Dai...!" She shivered again.

"We have the death penalty. They could face that. Does that make a difference?"

"If they have a House connection, an extraction might be attempted. But most of the Dai who work the gates are orphans, without a place at anyone's Table and without kindred to bring their ashes to the Garden. Once the connection is broken, once you lose your place at the Table, you are alone. An Avar has nothing but memories." She was shivering more now, pulling the blanket from the bed we shared last night around her shoulders.

"Cold?" I sat next to her and added my warmth and my aura to her.

"There are whole Houses who were turned out, into the Comb of Worlds with their Table broken and their Hearth shattered. We call them sacd'eritage you might call them Footlocker Houses. All they can carry of their House within a saddlebag. Their crests sable on charcoal to mark the end of a House."

"And you fear this."

"Madgji breaks Mihaly and then who circles around the winner? Yes, I fear this. We had just begun to recover completely from the White Death, your flu. Recover enough that I could be...set aside. Now I am The Mihaly."

"And I am the Dragon."

"I bound you lightly."

"I know."

She started to speak. I touched her lips with my finger.

"No." I said. "I have been lightly bound, but well and truly bought." And I hustled her out of the room.

We checked out of the motel and went back to the Country Kitchen. I was still hungry. She perked up when the waitress offered a cup of tea and ordered a side of pancakes, then went to organizing her purse.

"You asked last night about smugglers gates, true smugglers?"

"Mmm?"

"Here." She handed me a list of names and places. Mostly in the US, a few in Mexico and Western Canada. They had notes beside them; obsolete, unknown, uncertain, small, dangerous. That sort of notation. They were all over the country west of the Mississippi, thinning out in the Sierra Nevada. Then I saw a name towards the end of the list, north of Amarillo. In the panhandle.

Barbara Nagle.

I'd done some 'work' in this part of the country about eight years back. I had contracted to pass a load of ammunition into Mexico, I would land it on the Yucatan coast just west of the tourist complexes there. We had planned to stage the shipments in Texas, embark them under cover of the spring break madness around Galveston and sail them the seven hundred or so miles to the buyers.

It didn't happen. Between buyers trying to hijack the shipment, sellers trying to stiff the buyers and the brokers shopping the whole damn gig to every single government agency that had a slush fund for informers, the project became a huge clusterfuck. Half of the dickheads became fish food scattered across the Gulf deeps, the other half are growing old in prison. I got out just ahead of the come-apart.

I did get to know a lot of people in the Panhandle of Texas. Most were standup folks, and a few wanted killing in the worst way. One of the standup folks was an old Jarhead named Harry Nagle.

He wasn't one of the people who'd hired me, but in the end, I was working 'longside Harry. When I got out, I burned a lot of son-of-a-bitches, but I made sure that nothing led back to Harry. And at the end of it all, I died. Officially. Again.

Now Alena conjures out of the thin air a name I knew. Harry's wife. Barbara.

ALENA 30

He took my list and skimmed through it while we were waiting for our drinks. I saw him stop skimming, almost stop breathing. Then the waitress was there, and he folded the paper away.

After she took our food order and left, we sat in silence. I was still coming to grips with the notion that I had bound and bought the Breaker of Nations. A feat something on the order of throwing a halter about the Sun. If I lived through this, even if I did not live through this, there would be operas and telenovelas commissioned about my place in his myth.

My place. I arranged the silverware on the table top and thought about my place, then arranged the silverware again. Ten days ago, my place was…negotiable. "Alena Mihaly; Binder, and disappointingly, an erratic Walker." I could hear my great-aunt Pearl grumbling around her hookah. "Fair shot though, fair shot but unbloodied. Sent the girl to the Hanse did they, for seasoning?" I had expected Del or any of the other Sworn to show up at my door. But with the hiltless knife of the Avar in a rosewood box. Exile not heir.

I would have not minded getting the rosewood box, truly. The Mihaly are, were, lax in their observation of the codes. You do not manifest a known gift, or you are not quite what the House needed or what you wanted to be, you take the Hilt Less Knife and leave the House. That was by the code. But most of our Avars did not drop the connection to the House. Some became Consul Covert on Worlds we had an interest in. Some ventured out into the Comb of Worlds and then came back to the House to settle in the Fain or oath as a Sworn Avar. Many brought home new blood and new ways to consider. I would have taken the knife cheerfully.

That path was closed now. More than closed, it had never been.

If I failed. If we failed. The Mihaly would disappear. Some might survive in the far corners of the Comb, but the Madgji had been…thorough. I wondered at that.

Madgji, they had flash and a delight in breaking things; windows, pottery or lives. As long as it made a lot of noise or a splash of blood to the transoms, it entertained them. Mihaly had kept them on a short leash and shorter numbers. When it was needful to fix an enemy's attention to his front, we would unleash the Mad Madgji. If they overran the enemy, so much the better. If they died with their faces to the front, then our steadier Sworn Avars would have rolled up the flanks of the Madgji's killers.

Del had mentioned that some of the victims of the Long Knives were Fain. I had not believed it. Even when one house overran and adsorbed another, no one willingly killed Fain. My parents were Dai, but they came from the Fain. Any children I might have would have likely fostered into the Fain and my heirs would have come from the Fain. That was the way it had stood for the last six thousand years, Fain beget Dai, whose children become Fain. Only the Houses changed.

One constellation of Houses extirpated Fain lineages. One constellation only. One philosophy made a point of establishing a pure lineage. Koshitsu, the Chrysanthemum Throne.

And that gave a name to the hunters using me as a staked lure. The Jurchen.

They were one of the Confed Houses war band. One of the seven Rootless Houses. All had suffered the worst thing that could befall a House and yet not be utterly destroyed. Their Fain, their wellsprings, were exterminated. Given time and lands they could have slowly regained their strength. But each of the seven had been forced to balance on a spear tip, then offered mercy that was no mercy.

They did not expand. They did not recover. They existed on the tithe the Confederated Houses granted them for each generation. Hoped that their scant children bred true and manifested. If the child did not manifest, it was lost. Abandoned into the Comb of worlds, like a babe exposed on a hillside in a dark old custom.

Jurchen was one of the seven in the last long generation. The House that had fed their children to the crows was the Miyake House, Takamatsu. Takamatsu the unsheathed sword of the Nihon. And the Jurchen would gladly stake a minor Dai of a middling House out in the sun to take a Nihon Miyake all unawares.

"Are you going to eat, or just wear holes in the tabletop?"

I looked up and found his dark eyes on me. My tea was cold, the food just warm to the touch. I pushed the plate away. I caught the eye of the waitress. "Could you bring me another tea?"

TALLEN 31

She mopped at her eyes with a napkin and sat mum until the new pot of tea and a fresh cup of coffee for me appeared.

"I have had an, an enlightening moment,"

"It was more like a half hour."

"The Madgji are but a front."

"And..."

"Koshitsu."

"Truly?"

"Yes."

I sat back in the chair and waited out her making tea. She'd given me a thumbnail tour of her world and the spheres of interests. The Commonality was a thoroughly competent and thoroughly frightening version of my European Union. All of the Commonality Dai manifested right into the loving arms of the State. Civil service was their lot in life. They were constrained by a parliament and ministries populated by Fain. No Houses on the old, Feudal, plan. They had done away with all of that and now was the golden age acclaimed. The Commonality were very interested in welcoming the Confederated Houses into their more rational system of governance, even if they had to kill all of the Confederated Dai and Avars to achieve this laudable end.

The Nihon on the other hand were followers of the old ways to a theme park T. All of their ruling class were Dai and belted Dai who came from Fain plantations of documented provenance and descent. If you manifested and did not have the approved stud book entry, the best you could hope for was a quick procedure to keep you from polluting the gene pool and a long career on a short, brutal, leash. If you had the phenomenally bad taste to manifest from a forbidden remnant population, crucifixion and a thorough purging of your tainted bloodlines from the populace.

"And." She continued. "I know who fed the hunters at Ames. House Jurchen."

I don't think I breathed for a good half hour after she said that. I wanted to reach across the table and peel back her Subtle mind, just peeling it like peeling a tangerine with your thumbnail.

I stumble across her, in the one place still fixed in my life's wanderings. In a flurry of close action, I discover that she holds the Bloodseal of a House's heir. A House much like the House I had buried in China. Coincidence. It happens, good or bad. One of the people I had to kill in Hong Kong in 1947 was the son of Conal, the East Kent Buff I'd rode across Manchuria with in 1919. But twice was no coincidence and thrice was…forcing the play along. Ächtet Zirkus. That was what we called our House. The Outlaw Circus. It was a regimental nickname, like Cherry Pickers or Carlson's Raiders. The House name was something else, hidden.

Jurchen.

All of the tradecraft I'd learned told me she was a plant

and a delay for the Kunaicho. The ambushes at Canon city and in Missouri, the 'inadvertent' crossing, all an elaborate move to fix my attention away from the Imperial Household Agency. The fact that not one of the ambushes even came close to succeeding, Canon City being a simple minded clusterfuck on both sides of the ledger, did not ease my paranoia. Too many coincidences.

"Why is it, every time I turn over a rock or a leaf, I find scat from the merry land of Dai?"

She blinked at me over her cup of tea. "Do you?"

"Your list had an old acquaintance on it, which strained at my trust and then you bring up 'Jurchen' as a casual reference."

She sipped at her tea. "Leaving the list aside, Jurchen is not a casual reference. They are a rather important and aggressive apparat within the Confederated Dai. The Jurchen are one of the seven Rootless Houses that Croton-upon-Hudson House maintain as a standing force within the Confederated. The Seven have no Fain, they cannot intermarry with any of the Established Houses and their children who do not manifest are fostered into the Comb of Worlds without standing. Much like dumping kittens at the side of a road."

"How did they come to be one of the Seven?"

"They were one of the last independent Houses in the Nihon sphere of influence on Mize or 'zeme. After the gates closed to your world..."

"About seventy years ago?"

She frowned. "I think it was just less than eighty years past. After the gates closed, Nihon sent a Miyake House to crush the last House on the mainland in the 'Zeme. The Jurchen." She sipped at her tea. "Outnumbered and stripped of allies, they retreated into the interior. Guerilla war."

"The enemy advances, we retreat. The enemy camps, we harass. The enemy tires, we attack. The enemy retreats, we pursue." Sun Tzu by way of Mao."

"Yes. With variations and grace notes, but that is the whole of it."

"What made this passage at arms different?"

"House Takamatsu, the Miyake. They were indifferent to the pinprick raids of the Jurchen Dai. They simply burned and butchered their way through the Fain of the Jurchen."

"They drained the lake."

"Pardon?"

"Guerrillas swim in the civilian population like fish in water. So, you drain the lake. Sometimes you drain the lake by making the civilians support your side. Usually you drain the lake by disposing of the population."

"I see. This is not an accepted stratagem among the Dai, to drain the lake."

"Any Jurchen raids against the Kikuza lately?"

"Point taken. In any case, they are very interested in thwarting any designs of the Nihon, either the Koshitsu Tachibana or any of the Miyake Houses. Faction Madgji has been very rough in its handling of the Mihaly Fain, hinting at Koshitsu involvement. I propose that the hand behind the Madgji is that of the Kikuza and that the Jurchen having discovered that used me as a lure to expose the Koshitsu."

"Mistake on all their parts I'd say."

Jurchen.

"Let's be on our way. We got about three hours on back roads to find you a smuggler."

We'd picked up a tub of chicken and cold fixings and a throwaway cooler on the way out of Trinidad. That meant lunch was settled. I had a cooler full of water up front with us and we started sloping south by east.

"You know someone on the list, truly?"

"Yeah. Barbara Nagle."

"How?"

"I was intending to ask you that. It struck me odd that I'd shaken hands with one of the Dai, all unknowing like?"

"We breed like cats."

"Do tell?"

"The Fain tend to run fraternal twins, and healthy ones at that. Not every pregnancy, but often enough to be remarked on. We also start our family's young. Fain women keep their fertility for about thirty years. Our men will often marry a second wife if the living is good. If the living is not so good, a Fain woman might marry a second provider. Dai are harder to gage, being as they don't form conventional families. They, the Manifested Dai, will have children for fifty years or more and while they don't often occasion twins, the children will be just as healthy as the Fain."

"And you aren't armpit deep in kinfolk?"

"No. We are only a quarter of your world population, perhaps less. Dai and Fain are not particularly fond of census takers. Next of kin to taxmen they are."

"What happens?"

"To the census men, tar and feathers as a rule...oh, to the myriads of children we bring into the universes? Wars, duels, hunting bears with spears and foxhunting with fools. Many are the ones who don't Manifest or settle into a trade, who go through the gates and don't come back. For the best part of five thousand years we have sent our restless ones through gates." She put down her cup. "This is only our experience in the Confederated lands of course. The Commonality, the Unity, only allow licensed children and the Nihon reportedly cull seven of ten of their Manifested Dai."

"And why aren't we..." I waved my hand at the Colorado ranches surrounding us." armpit deep in Dai?"

"Recessive gene constellations and being restless is not indicative of success. I have been told that some milieus are more dangerous than others. The Gunpowder ones for example. And..."

"Yes?"

"In the last short generation, research indicated that population density and pheromones had a role. Fain settlements that did not Manifest one of the higher forms of Dai, a Binder form to be exact, drifted rather quickly towards a normal birth rate and a normal incidence of multiple births."

"If you don't live in snug little 'villes', with a bit of the gentry rubbing elbows with the local boys of a Saturday night at the pub, you quit being Dai?"

"That is a simplification worthy of talk radio. Possibly."

The idea I had was make contact with Harry and then give Barbara a side look. I couldn't figure Harry not knowing she was of the giddy Dai, but he might not know what that entailed. Or maybe he did. Of the two, she'd been the harder case. The old Fleet Marine used to wince at the thought of her coming home before we'd settled the clusterfuck out. 'She is just so damn casual, Risley' He said. 'I had to rescue some big old boy once, she'd taken a dislike to. Never did find out why, but she was going to dress him out like a mule deer using a broken Lone Star longneck for a blade. I had to cold cock her with a pool cue and sleep in the stable for the next month, but it kept her out of Gatesville. She come home to find these jackasses cutting up and we'd be digging graves with that there Caterpillar. I'd swear her favorite song was Deguello.' And she still got her boots wet at the bitter end of that clusterfuck.

The place had changed. You could tell it right from the road. The ranch house was boarded up, with black streaks running up the siding from the boarded over windows. The roof was burnt out, the shingles melted like candy under a blowtorch. The front door was off the hinges, leaning against the front of the house with fist size holes punched through it.

There were only a handful of cattle in the feedlot. Beside the ranch house there was an Airstream trailer, one of the new big ones. It had an electrical drop running to it, a mini-satellite dish and a hundred-gallon propane tank hooked up at the back. There was a new Ford 350 diesel pickup parked in the driveway. I saw an older pickup rusting away on the far side of the house. It had no windows and all the paint was burnt off. A couple of dogs appeared out of the high weeds next to the house and announced our arrival. I took my time getting out of the truck. "Lock and load, then stay put."

She looked at the dogs barking just outside her

window. "Any rules of engagement?"

"I start shooting, you shoot anything that moves and isn't me. Otherwise, you're an ornament."

"Your mission tasking leaves something to be desired."

"I was poorly trained as a child. Stay sharp."

She slipped one of my 9mm out from under the horse blanket on the seat and checked the load indicator.

I got out of the cab and stepped to the back of the lock box. I ignored the dogs and after a startled moment, they backed off and watched me. One of them looked like a Jack Russell terrier. The other was a mutt about six hands high at the shoulder, a light brown mix of a German shepherd and a Boxer. The half-pint was the dominant one of the two, every time I made a move the bigger dog would check to see what the smaller dog was doing. I didn't fear them, and I wasn't behaving like an aggressor, so maybe I was not fair game. Like most MP's they bucked it up the chain of command.

I shrugged out of my jacket and walked towards the trailer, slowly with my hands clear and empty. I could feel a gun or two on me. There was a long silence and my mouth dried up. Then.

"Risley, goddamn! George Risley?"

"Afternoon, Barbara Ann."

"Well hot goddamn!"

There was a grunt and a rattle of metal. She walked out into the noon light with a handgun in her right hand, shading her eyes with her left. She wore a light blue shirt, very fresh and unwrinkled, silver bracelets with turquoise inlay and a matching silver medaled leather belt with a large buckle. The loops of her trousers had been modified to let the belt pass through. It was wider than three of my fingers, tanned to about the color of bread. The belt had recently been taken in to allow her to wear it.

"Wonders never cease, so they tell me. Thought you were doing a thousand years in Leavenworth, one of the living dead. You roll over?"

"I cut a deal. They needed some things done down in the Yucatan. I make things happen in Mar Muereto, my records go missing."

"Surprised they didn't renege." She de-cocked her gun and slipped it into a holster at her back.

"They did, but I died."

She laughed. "Ghost, that's what I'll call you, Ghost Risley. You and your gunner want t'come in the Airstream, get out of the sun?"

"I'm not running under Risley anymore," I started to lie to her, give her one of my new legends. Then. "I'm Ray Tallen now." I found myself telling her my real name. "And what about..." I nodded towards the burnt-out truck.

"Braugham's crew."

"That pissant?"

"Yeah he grew a pair. 'Bout six months back."

Braugham had been on the distant fringes of the clusterfuck, being an informer with a small part of the local meth trade. Working both sides of the street he was. Harry would have cut him off at the ankles if he'd looked sideways at him, let alone torch his truck. I had a sad feeling.

"I'd like to see Harry, Barbara Ann."

She grimaced. "You're a little late. Tallen."

"How late?"

"About six months. Stroke."

"Son of a bitch." Stroke induced by a Molotov. Braugham just moved up on the list. "Sorry."

"Not half as sorry as I am. What did you want to see Harry about?"

I nodded at the flatbed. "We're in the wind."

She lifted her eyes. "And?"

"Told me a lot of lies about you, while we were staking out the pole barn that night."

"I can only imagine."

"One of them was that you ran fugitives, out from under the collective noses of the Zetas, the Outfit, the Rangers and the Federales on both sides of the border."

"I haven't heard 'Outfit' in a while."

"Yeah, it's about as out of fashion as 'Black Hand', but us old folks are kinda set in our ways."

"Who you got in the International, Tallen?"

"Mihaly."

She sucked air like she'd been sucker punched.

"Who feeds you, Roy Tallen?"

I spit on the ground. "Don't you start that shit. The last three days she's been going on about 'whose table' I had my boots under. I keep telling her I'm just a happy little gun bunny. I make one mistake, picking up a stray, and Shazam! She wants my papers, a rubbing of my birth mark, and a blood test."

"Thinks you're Avar?"

"Yeah."

"You don't look like your usual Avar. You kinda scruffy and all. Little thin."

"Uh hunh, and I dress to the right. You want to talk to the Lady, or you want to discuss hygiene and high fashion?"

"Call her out. I want to see what has the Eisenring in a lather."

Eisenring again.

I waved at Alena. I could hear her de-cocking her gun, then she stumped around the hood of the car with her piece down by her leg. They stared each other down for a long minute. Then Barbara said. "I'm dammed, she does take after them. And you know enough to call her 'chief of the name'."

"She pouts and gets the sulks if I don't."

Barbara laughed. "Come on into the Airstream, out of the heat and we'll have a talk."

Barbara Ann and Alena went ahead of me to the Airstream, Alena holstered her gun and casually slipped her weak hand through the crook of Barbara Ann's arm. Minx. I hoped she wasn't trying on Barbara Ann.

Three steps later they were passing for old acquaintances, I left them to it and went back to the truck. I wanted my side arm and I wanted to pull the truck around to the side, close to the barn. Keep it out of sight from the road. They went into the trailer and closed the door.

I brought the Dragon up and kept an eye on them, as it was. Alena's auras were surging, no fear but avid interest predominated. Barbara Ann was very focused. Some of the difference was maturity, from what I could tell she had fifty years on Alena, and it had not been an idle fifty years. Now that I had two samples, I could tell the difference between Dai and the standard run of humans. They matched what I could dimly recall of The Three-Legged House and our enemies. It was interesting that I hadn't run into a Dai in the wild-then I recalled that Barbara Ann was a Dai and I had not picked up on that. Maybe the successful Dai had a knack for hiding under a bushel basket.

I got out of the truck and the dogs started up again with the barking and threat displays. The Jack Russel even essayed a tug at the cuff of my jeans while the big mutt tried to hold my attention. I didn't kick the terrier so much as lofted him over a fence into a paddock, the mutt I just bowled over on my way to the trailer. It cost me about a three-inch strip off of the cuff of my right leg, the terrier had it when he was flying over the fence. I knew I was going to have to visit a WalMart in my near future, that was the last intact pair of jeans I had.

I got up the steps into the trailer, the big mutt slunk in with me and I shut the door firmly in the muzzle of the aggrieved terrier. Barbara Ann yelled at the terrier to 'shut the hell up' and he quit barking and scratching at the door. The big mutt tried to make himself invisible in his proper corner, a pile of old horse blankets by the door.

Alena and Barbara Ann had their heads together over a topographic map, covering from just north of Amarillo to southern Colorado. There were two cups of tea and a bottle of beer on the table. The beer was Barbara's. I sat down and drank some tea and accepted the big dog's apologies. The terrier, a Jack Russell, was sulking under the trailer. The women, with occasional lapses into the King's English or Texican, were speaking in tongues. I got to thinking and realized that Alena's English was liberally salted with French, German and some things that sounded Russian but weren't. The almost Russian struck me like listening to Dutch in the middle of a spiel of English; almost, you felt like if you listened hard enough it would make sense. The whole damn thing almost made sense, if you listened long enough.

"Most of the roads between here and there are worthless, not even graveled. You might be better off using horses, even over a four by four." Barbara killed the beer. "But given a choice I'd use an ATV or a real Jeep-not one of those worthless Chrysler's they slapped a Jeep logo on. Those things travel in pairs, because they can't go muddin' all by their lonesome."

"Alena gave me the impression that all of you were still horse happy."

"They're cheaper on the whole," Barbara Ann said. "they will merrily reproduce using very unskilled labor and no more resources than good grass and good water. We imported almost everything more complicated than a bicycle when I was a cadet." Barbara twisted off the top of the bottle. "God, I love these, no more trying to find the church key. I like horses, but I'd rather coax a diesel to life on a cold morning than saddle a..."

"Barbara's told me something extremely important." Alena, tapped at the topo map with a spoon's handle, indicating a small draw that the USGS had marked with labels for seasonal water and flash flooding. "There is a ford here, a very soft spot."

Leaning over. I looked at the map. "And we are?"

"Sixty miles, by road. Forty miles across country." Barbara said, carefully putting the beer down. "And it's often used."

"Meaning?"

"It's a black crossing. The locals on both sides of the Veil know about it. The seasonal flooding wash away any tracks and it's soft enough that a watcher would have to be right on top of it to sense the opening. A smuggler's ford."

"Thought you said only the non-talented went for an exile?"

"Lots of folk turn out." Barbara said. "Your side goes under in a coup, or you don't want to marry or breed by the book, or your talent is so common in your House that you end up being one of fifty with that twist. Or you are so weak that it's not worth having." She took a drink from the bottle. "And you hear all the stories about how you can live like a Holder on the other side of the Veil, you can bond a hundred Medji with a smile or-" She broke off. "Ah the hell with it, my twist was Gates, Walking. They found out that I was weak for the particular uses of the House I was born into, but they thought that crossing me with another Gate-Walker might produce a better line."

"That's a filthy practice!" Alena was almost sputtering.

"It was a filthy time." Barbara grinned at her, entertained. "Just after they closed all the passages, both high roads and the low, to AngTerra. Put a lot of Houses in the shade, that did."

"And so, you pulled up stakes and came over."

"Not here, they'd closed them all when the White Death surfaced hereabouts." She turned and faced Alena. "You know the Book?" I could hear the capitals in the word. Alena nodded. "I found passage to the Little Englanders, carried about ten pounds of silver and a proscribed set of blueprints, steam locomotive improvements I think it was, and went across in the black."

"Did they send the Eisenring after you?" Alena's eyes were dark and large above the rim of her cup.

Eisenring. I was going to have to ask Alena, about just who the Eisenring were and how they figured into the churn.

"Not then. Later, when I had settled in and began a family. They sent a reckoning team. How they located me, I don't know. I had fifteen good years before they came." Barbara rolled her bottle across her forehead, her eyes closed. "My husband, Geoffrey, he died at the threshold along with three of them. I killed the other two in the dark, it was my house they were in after all." She drank from her beer. "I knew they'd send more."

"Did you open a black ford there and then?"

"No. Not until much later. I was on the wing from that tidy little house with my babe in my arms and her brother on the donkey behind me. I fostered them with the manager of the arms manufactory I did a bit of tinkering for. Told him I was a refugee from the Terror-over-the-Water, and they had found me, killed my husband and were after the kits and me. He took the children in, gave me a new carbine, a hundred rounds and his best horse." She rubbed the top of her bottle. "Never went back. Never. All of a lifetime ago, it was." She looked me in the eyes. "Just about the time things came to a boil in Spain with their Civil War."

"How did you link up with Harry?" I asked.

She smiled. "Met him at a Rodeo, right after he came back from Korea. Told him I was a refugee, he thought I'd come out of Eastern Europe. Damn but was he flabbergasted when I took him through the Veil. He was a lovely man in a duster, ahorse or on a great rumbling Harley." Her beers were catching up to her.

"You started running folk through about then?"

"Yeah. What got me to thinking about that was Harry mistaking me for a displaced person. So, I ran folks from here, mostly DP's that had lost their argument with the immigration suits or natives on the run for one thing or another. Then I brought Avar exiles, who were not approved by the Confederated or the Eisenring to come over"

"How the hell did the DP's settle in… never mind." I leaned over the map. "I assume you got horses?"

She nodded. "Not here, but over at the neighbors."

I ran a fingernail along a dirt road on the map. "This is your sixty miles by road?"

"Yeah. Road goes around this coulee, but you can get a horse up and down the walls. Brougham bought himself some friends. When Harry died, his connections faded into the woods. Harry left me some water rights, some minerals as well. Brougham would like to round out his rights in this county."

"He knows you?" I wondered if she'd lost more than a husband.

"No. Harry did most of the dealing with him."

"What are you thinking?" Alena asked me.

"That's been a long time since lunch."

ALENA 32

❙❚Lunch?" Barbara, who still had not given me her true name, blinked like an owl and nodded. "I got some brisket in the box, already cooked, we could just microwave it." She started to stand and wobbled. Tallen sat her back down.

"We'll forage and after we get some food into Alena, she gets downright mean without regular meals, we'll talk outfitting."

I did not get mean and I was not particularly hungry, but I was not the slowest of my cohort either. I organized some iced tea and sliced tomatoes while Tallen produced a cold cut lunch. At one point, Barbara excused herself to the restroom and then disappeared into the bedroom at the rear of the trailer.

I missed her when I went to set the table and roll up the map. "Tallen."

"I know." He brought over only two plates. "She's asleep. I checked on her when I washed up."

"Three beers, perhaps four?"

"Look in the butter compartment of the refrigerator."

Muttering under my breath I did. There were four ampoules of an unlabeled medication and a very old, reusable, hypodermic set. I got a jar of pickles out and placed it on the table. "And what do you think of that?"

He shrugged, started assembling a sandwich. "I think we go across at her ford. With or without her, on horseback. We are Barbara's usual refugees, or fleeing felons, and we don't speak the language worth a damn. Then the question is do we go south and east towards the coast to get you to the bankers, or straight into the Lion's mouth to clip his tonsils?"

I considered that while doing justice to the brisket. I was hungry, I found. "I can cross to the Hanse going north into the Sunset Range. There is an established gallery at Manitou Springs." I told him.

"How far is that into Colorado?"

"I think it is just north of your Pueblo city."

"How much will it cost and in what coin."

"A little more than three of these," I held up my medallion. "or at least three ordinary coins and not Bloodseals."

"Gold."

"Preferably Gold, yes. Silver will do. Only the noble metals. Silver, electrum, platinum or gold." I stirred some sugar into my tea. "Tallen, they will be looking for me. Or at least someone like me, crossing from 'Zeme to the Hanse."

"And if they see you crossing."

"They would try to take me or kill me. As they did at Canon city."

"What happens if, instead, we kill them?"

"I don't understand."

"Would they pursue us into the Hanse?"

I thought I knew what he was about. I put down the tea. "There is a latent time, a lag between one opening of the Gate and the next."

"A minimum time for the door to cycle?"

"Yes. When we cycle through, we might have ten or fifteen minutes before someone could follow."

"Would they engage us in the gallery?"

"No. It is a safe haven, it and everything within a three-hundred-foot radius of the gallery. A haven enforced by law, custom and a half company of dragoons. In the 'Zeme."

"Not over here I take it?"

I nodded. "Gates on a covert world are guarded lightly if at all but guarded closely on 'Zeme."

"And the 'Gater' is immune from attack?"

"Nominally. Within the gallery, they are immune and covered by maybe a hand of guards. Killing or attacking a Walker can cause a Gate to open or close erratically. Not a good idea. Outside, they are protected by their patrons or employers."

"We walk up, slip the cashier the required gold, the Gater rips open the Gate and we walk through. Could our enemies be waiting on the far side?"

"Yes. They would be very discreet, by necessity in the Hanse. The Hanse are very unhappy about promiscuous bloodletting, they show this unhappiness by deploying heavy infantry around our ports to their world and shutting them down."

"They know about the Dai?"

"Yes. They are in trade. They provide negotiators, they maintain banks for us, they sell technology and people across the Veil -within certain strict limits-and they trust us not one bit. I spent four years there. I was going to choose exile among them. It would have been a benign exile since they are cognizant of the Dai. The Hanse are a people of Law and not equity. A written contract will be followed to the letter and only to the letter. Treaties are never to be bent, only honored or broken. If we bring our private wars into their lands, they will return the remains of both sides along with an Itemized Bill of damages and the costs of suppressing the combatants."

"Swiss."

"Pardon?"

"They bank for you. Can you hire troops there?"

"No. Treaties forbid the Dai bringing Hanse mercenaries into 'Zeme. It is bad for the Dai and generally bad for the Hanse."

"How about non-Hanse?"

"It is discouraged, strangled by red tape. That is one reason we have used AngTerran mercenaries in the past. We did not have to route through the Hanse."

"Yeah. We barbarians are always up for a fight."

"She does not know about you."

"I gathered that. She was explaining things to me like I just fell off the turnip wagon."

"If we take her, she will likely die."

He turned his head to look at where Barbara slept. "I think she will be likely soon dead in any case."

I considered the hypodermic in the refrigerator and nodded.

TALLEN 33

I had parked the flatbed around the back. When I'd found the first tag, on the suburban of blessed memory, I'd done a quick check on the flatbed truck. I did another check now, just in case I had missed something or the giddy Kunaicho had resurrected the ninja. Then I really emptied the lock boxes with an eye to travel and war.

I hadn't gotten it clear in my mind why, with all the lovely iron available in the States, why the horsemen I rubbed up against were using breech loading drillings or pump action carbines. The carbines had not functioned well in the skirmish. I saw two misfires and a jam from up close and personal. And a drilling is just a shotgun with two extra barrels and pretensions to nobility in its background. More a gun for gamekeepers than dragoons.

I'd brought the drilling out to the lockbox. I didn't trust Barbara too far, so I had scooped up all the ironmongery I could find about the trailer. She had two more pistols than the one I'd scoped out earlier, a shorty pump shotgun and an uncut AK74. She had enough thirty-round magazines for the 74 to keep it rocking and rolling for about twenty minutes. Serious stuff, but just about normal for Nagle's household.

I knew Nagle had a private stock of munitions besides what he'd kept in the house. Kept it in an underground bunker he'd dug alongside of the septic tank. The one time I'd been invited into it I'd seen several M60 variant machine guns, a rack of Mattel-16s, as well as a couple stands of M14 rifles. I intended to cherry pick that stock before we went across the Veil. I wanted what the drill instructors called force multipliers and I didn't give a rat's scabby ass if the local Regulators permitted it or not.

ALENA 34

Tallen sorted and resorted the load he intended to carry across into the 'Zeme, while we were waiting on Barbara to wake up. He went through her meager closet, selected all the rough trail outfits and had me inventorying her pantry, when she came out of her bedroom.

She eyed the heaps of clothing on her kitchen floor and the stack of canned goods. "You are one busy fellow."

"Ready for a cup of java?'

"I could do with something to cut the crud."

He poured all three of us a cup and after we sat down, he unrolled the map again. "We're going to come across here, just south of Black Mesa?"

"Most near." Barbara nodded.

Tallen turned to me. "And the first place you can cross over into the Hanse domain is up here around Pueblo?"

"Unless I double back towards your Missouri, yes."

He turned towards Barbara. "Where do you place your clients on the 'Zeme?"

"There's an Overlander laager at a ford over the north fork of the Cimarron. I keep a cache there. Clothes, papers, currency and the like. Usually I put them on the Liner Overlander going east, they have enough money to last about three months and the freetons on the rivers down to the Gulf are always needing workers."

"No questions about language?"

"I tell them to flash their documents around. The identity documents say they're war refugees down from the Maritimes, nobody cares about eurotrash. In time they learn one of the trade languages. Anglenord, Trade Manchu, even Simple Nihon. A lot of the freeton use your Spanglish as a lingua franca now."

"Could you outfit her as one of those." He nodded towards me.

"Dirty her up a little and keep her quiet, no problem. If she opens her yap, the accent will tell."

"What accent?" I asked.

"You are, I think, what the Brits used to call 'of the quality'." Tallen poured himself another cup of coffee. "You are educated, you speak several languages that I know of and you think you don't stink at the end of a long day's ride."

"You got her pegged Tallen." Barbara looked at me over the rim of her cup. "That means I'm along for the show."

"I make it a day, maybe two days through the short grass. We bring over your horses and a string of pack horses. I get you into eyeball of this laager. Now from there, you both take the Overlander to..."

"Manitou Springs, in my milk tongue."

"Manitou springs." He almost had it right. "Take the Overlander to Manitou Springs and then go through to the Hanse. Both of you."

He looked at Barbara. "What's killing you?"

She blushed, stark against her pale skin. "Cancer."

He turned and looked me in the eyes. "Take her to the

Hanse and have them work on her?"

"It'd cost." Barbara said.

"You ride for the Brand, the Brand provides."

"That is so." I said.

"You're going up against the Kikuza, you know that?" She looked to Tallen. "Does he know?"

"The Kikuza?" Tallen said. "You mean the Chrysanthemum? Yeah I know."

"They come at you, they won't back off."

"They have come at me before." He said, stirring his coffee with his thumb. "I wasn't too impressed." He drank it off and smiled at Barbara. "Well this makes it easier, all I got to do is pack for three days and such. You got a key to the storehouse by the septic tank?"

She nodded. "By the door, second hook." She looked like someone had struck her with a large hammer. He nodded his thanks and scooping the keys off the hook left. "Not too impressed." She said. "He either thinks he is the left hand of god or he reads too many romances like 'Breaker O'Houses.'"

I choked on my tea and made a solemn vow not to tell Barbara who Tallen was, or to tell him that she had all the versions of the Legend existent on a hidden shelf in her pantry.

Tallen was late. Barbara and I were at the crossing. It was close to local dawn, but Tallen wasn't back from an "errand" he said he had to run.

Barbara was sitting cross-legged on the ground with her dogs. There was a spare horse blanket thrown over her back, the terrier glaring at me from under the fringes and the big one curled with his head under the blanket. There was heavy dew on the grass, chilling the air. We had three saddle horses and one pack horse with us, all loaded and ready to go. Tallen had dropped us off at a crossroads about ten miles out, helped load and saddle the horses then drove off in the truck with the trailer.

"How long?" Barbara asked.

"Four hours." There was a wind coming up. I wrapped

the poncho about my shoulders tighter and huddled against my horse.

"I don't want to make the crossing in daylight."

"We should not."

"You really going to go up against the Kikuza?"

"Yes."

"He must be even more of a hard case than I thought, or maybe just a nutcase."

"He is...unique." I wiped moisture off the saddle. "I should likely be in a Kikuza cage right now, but for him." One of the horses brought his head around, ears pricked forward and stared off into the night. The other two grew restless and shifted to bring their heads about.

"Jaeger, guard." Barbara whispered from the ground and loosed her larger dog who bounded off into the night. "Prince, watch." The terrier sprang past my ear and crouched in the center of the saddle.

I could hear Barbara's joints crackling as she came to her feet beside me. I pulled my assault rifle from the saddle scabbard, eased the bolt open to confirm a round was ready, then eased it home and took the safety off. From under the poncho Barbara produced a carbine with a banana magazine, unfolded the stock and cycled the bolt in one easy motion. There was movement on the rise above the draw. The terrier danced on the saddle, his ears pricked towards something only he could hear. I rested my rifle on the cantle pack and aimed the gun in the general direction of the dog's concern.

We heard a yelp and a thud, followed by a string of curses and the sound of someone rolling through the brush and down the rise. The terrier snorted and looked at Barbara, then turned around twice on the saddle and tucked his nose under his tail.

"You certain about him being a hard case?"

"Tell me again about how Jaeger is a war dog, absent without leave from the Marine forces?"

"It's Marine Corps..."

Tallen limped to where we could see him, holding the dog by a scruff of its hide. "I guess we're taking the mutts across?"

"My crossing, I choose who goes. And who stays." Barbara snapped her safety on.

"Are you alright?" I set my safety and stowed my rifle. "And where have you been?"

"Cleaning up behind Barbara."

"What'd you mean?" Barbara scooped up the terrier from my saddle and clicked her tongue at the bigger dog. It whined and rolled onto its back in front of Tallen.

"Brougham." He bent over and rubbed Jaeger's belly. "Go. Off with you." And Jaeger sat up, licked Tallen's face and trotted off into the dark.

"Where does he come into it?" Barbara turned and looked after the dog.

Tallen stepped over to his horse, looped the stirrup up to where he could check the cinch and the saddle rigging. Checked his rifle where it rode in the scabbard and tugged at the cantle pack. Opened it and took out a large wooden holster with shoulder straps. He took off his duster, strapped on the holster. Then he placed his automatic into the cantle pack and strapped it closed. His new gun peeped out of the top of the holster. He shrugged his shoulders to settle the rigging. Then put his duster back on.

"Mauser?" Barbara had watched the change out as closely as I did.

"Shansi, .45 ACP."

She hummed. "You got more damn antique iron hanging about you, that half-breed gun and that sword Alena showed me."

"You find something that works, you want to keep it around."

"Must be a guy thing, Harry was always tinkering about with a BAR he'd smuggled back from Korea." She walked over towards her horse. "Go on about Brougham."

Tallen dropped the stirrup and stepped into the saddle. "He would be sniffing around our back door. Things go to hell, we can at least rally hereabouts, if we don't have a busy Mister Brougham in the background."

"What'd you do?"

"A little of this, a little of that. Got lucky. Mister Brougham now has a company of Texas Rangers wishing to make his acquaintance, as well as a shit load of pissed off meth cookers who think that Brougham ratted them out to the Rangers." He leaned precariously out of the saddle and snagged the reins to the pack horse. "It's amazing how much chaos several well intentioned telephone calls can produce. I left the truck and all in the stables, put the envelope on the tack box like you said. We done here?"

"Near as dammit." Barbara mounted up and I did likewise. "I need to be in the lead. You and the pack horse, then Alena. Prince will ride with me, Jaeger will stay close to my horse." She turned and glared at Tallen and me, her face gaunt in the growing light. "We go at a walk until I tell you to bring them to a trot. Stay within a length of each other and you damn well better not stray off the path. You'll vanish like a bubble. Once I open the way you've got less than three minutes to cross."

"I take it," He said. "that being slow to transit is not recommended."

"I wouldn't know. "She said. "No one's ever reported back."

TALLEN 35

One moment we're trotting down a draw between two sticks with a white ribbon tied to them, the next second we're going down a slightly different draw, no sticks. No lightshow, no nausea, no fuss. The horse I was getting acquainted with didn't even twitch an ear. The only way I knew we were coming across was when I saw Barbara's crop tailed paint trot into a wave in midair. Like a standing ripple of water, only in air. I had enough time to take a deep breath and I was through it. All the time I could see Barbara's horse trotting down the draw. Must be the difference between professionals and hobbyists.

We'd also gained a couple of hours. Local dawn looked to be about three hours off. I made a mental note to ask if time always slipped in the same direction.

About a quarter hour later we came up out of the draw and Barbara kicked her paint into a canter. The grass was up to my stirrups, drenching the cuffs of my jeans with the dew. We kicked up birds and clouds of hoppers, startled a deer out of a small thicket that the big dog really wanted to chase. We put a quick quarter mile between the draw and us, then Barbara motioned a halt.

"Take a rest and listen."

"What for?"

"Motors if anything. I've only had two over flights in the last twenty years, but..."

"Okay. They use night vision?"

"Not that I'd know."

I swung off the horse and walked a wide circle from them. The dawn was coming on fast, lots of birds waking up in the knee-high grass. I woke the Lesser Dragon, taking in the wind and the sounds that rode on it, extending my senses beyond what humans could normally reach. We walk about in a gray fog, well trained in not-hearing or not-smelling. Lose your vision and soon enough you will grow phantom ears as sharp as foxes or a nose to match a bloodhound to compensate. One of the disciplines of the Lesser Dragon was to sharpen all the senses in turn, without slighting any of them. You learned to process all the information coming into your eyes, your ears and even the subtle vibrations through the ground, instead of ignoring them. And you learned to dull the senses as well. It would not do to have to shovel manure with a bloodhound's nose.

That's how I knew we had truly crossed over. Everything was different.

I went to visit a friend one time when I was about ten. He and I had become friends at the local school the year I was nine, but his family lived a good day's travel away on the other side of the county. Jan was boarding at the principal's house during the term, and then going home for holidays and summers. After they built a school closer to him, we kept in touch by writing letters. I know it seems odd, but forty-five miles then was just as far as two hundred now. I was not the only correspondent he had. The other half-dozen in the school wrote letters as well at the direction of the teacher. One time, before school was to take up again in the fall, I got permission to spend a week with him on his family's farm. I rode over there on the back of the US Mail wagon, which was an adventure in itself, with a bundle of clothes and a ham from one of my pigs as a gift. It was a good visit, though we were a little awkward at the start of it. Jan met me at the lane and hustled me and the mail up to the house and through the back door.

The place smelled wrong. Not bad, not dirty or any such thing, just wrong. Different. It only lasted for a minute, maybe two. Then I couldn't smell anything other than the chops and cottage fries that were cooking. It wasn't the food, though Jan's folk came from Czechoslovakia, and they were as clean as any of us then and there. But they were not my folk. Not bad folk, but not mine.

Everything was different on that prairie. The dew, the grass, the wind coming down out of the mountains. The air was alive in the pre-dawn with insects and birds and I heard a coyote mocking Jaeger for being a kept dog. I bent down and scooped a handful of the unplowed earth, grass and all, and crumbled it in my hands. Its odor like the wort from a brewery. I changed, and the earth turned under my boots.

We reached the Overlander laager just as the sun was dropping into the mountains. It was the first structure I'd seen since we crossed over. It was a story and a half, pressed earth building with an above ground fuel tank farm and a big corral of horses and mules. There was a courtyard marked by a low brick wall, just enough to sit on, in the front of the station. The doors were open, and people were milling in and out with bags and such. From three hundred yards away, I could hear music from the common room over the low rumbling of the two Overlanders idling in the courtyard. On top of the building were two sandbagged strong points. I could see three more just inside the wall. All were manned, ready.

"This normal." I marked with my hat the strong points.

"Nope." Barbara was riding beside me, her rifle in a fringed case across her lap and both of her dogs trotting at her stirrups. "The square mile around the station is usually neutral territory."

"Usually."

"Uh-hunh. You can roll an Overlander, if you got the guevos, and the only folks that'd get twisted about it are the master and owners. Maybe the insurance mob would come looking for you. But you fuck with a station and they whistle up a company of Confederated Dragoons and a stick of Pika Aknepteh. Stations are Confed House property."

I looked the vehicles over. Each one was composed of three segments linked by a heavy articulated limber. Their wheels were about ten-foot-tall, ground clearance was such that you could kneel under them and work. The hatches to the interior were better than two inches thick.

"I can figure Dragoons, what's a Pika AwkNepTeh?"

"Harry called them Gurkas on a pony." She leaned over and hawked a gobbet of mucus out of her throat.

I guessed that the overall length was about twice that of a Greyhound across the Veil, with the lead segment being half the size of the trailing two. They were wider than a Greyhound as well, maybe eighteen to twenty feet at the wheels. I swung up my glasses and took a good look at the working parties. "Gurkhas on a pony? Helluva note."

"He was impressed with them. Said they made the Turks look slack."

The Overlander was being armed. One team was on top of the rear segment of the closest one, using an air wrench to close access hatches on a gun turret.

"They always go armed?"

"Mostly, but just enough to discourage those occasional Pika or wandering Dai with more testosterone than brains. They don't mount those turrets unless there is some serious shit coming down. Costs money." She pulled her paint closer to me. "Did you see the banner?"

"No." I swung the glasses towards the Laager again. "Where?"

"At the head of the far Overlander."

It was a white square of canvas fixed to an L-shaped

guerdon in such a way as to keep it from furling if there was no wind. Screen printed or stenciled to it was a stylized flower, a Chrysanthemum.

"Well now." I turned and looked to the rear, slipping the glasses into their case. Alena was about twenty yards down the reverse of the rise we were skylining. She was afoot, leading her horse. It'd picked up a stone in its hoof and she had to lead it for the last couple of hours. No complaints and no suggestion of remounting her on one of the other horses. No one was after us and we didn't want to hit the laager too soon. Now I wondered if that was a mistake. I whistled at her. Her head came up and her hand rested on the carbine slung across her chest. She came on at a trot, dragging the sore-footed horse after her. "Stay off the crest."

"What's wrong?"

Barbara backed her paint slightly off the crestline. "Kikuza in the station. Looks like they've either chartered or commandeered an Overlander."

"What's the odds they got wanted posters out for you?"

Alena looked at me, shrugged. "Not unlikely, but I am stuck across the Veil, in AngTerra. There is more of a chance that I might look very much like one of my cousins and attract their attentions that way."

"Either way is bad news. Any way in that does not trail Alena past the bannerette?" I asked Barbara.

"Maybe. Nobody likes Kikuza, the operators might open up the door on the other side of the station, by the corral, to keep the trade flowing in."

I watched the bustle about the Overlanders for ten minutes or so. Long enough that the guards in the strong points were beginning to take notice of us.

"Change of plan. We all go down to the corral. You check into the hostel and get your passage to the Springs arranged. I'll settle up with the hostler for the horses and your tack, then get a drink and leave."

"You stand out like a pink dress at a funeral."

"This whole setup is like cat shit on linoleum, you can't

cover it up, you just have to pretend you don't see it." I nudged my horse into a slow walk down the rise towards the back of the station. "We're smuggling saddles, not horses."

"I do not understand." Alena.

"Everyone knows Barbara is one of the local Coyotes, right?" I looked at Alena, still walking her lame horse. "They don't know how or where, precisely, she comes across, but she is the escort."

"Yes."

"If she is escorting you, then you are the refugee and I am the hired hand. She's taking you on through to the city. I'm leaving her horse and a lame one with the hostler and taking the remuda back to wherever we crossed over. If I get asked, two clients backed out and we had a storm warning." I turned to Barbara. "Think that will stand up?"

"It's got enough truth mixed in the lies." She looked grim suddenly. "I brought Harry across a couple of times as a drag rider, when I had a dozen Greeners coming over to AngTerra. Once we brought a bus load of jackleg Mormon polygamists from the backside of Glen Canyon, thought they were going to establish a New Jerusalem over here. They were in a hurry as both the LDS and the FBI were on their case. Came over in the last snowstorm of that season and we had a helluva time getting them across in one piece."

"Alright. You got any problems with that?" I looked at Alena again.

"No. You still intend to make contact with our people in the foothills?"

"That's the plan."

"You are going to need a name."

"And?"

"FitzMurran."

"One name?"

"They have…connections with the command lineage."

Barbara snorted. "She means they're the Fain they settle the culls onto. Better and better. Tell them that Barbara el Corredor vouches for you. You might live long enough to tell them about Herself here."

"You came from the Mihaly?"

There was dead silence from both of them. The music was louder, and I could hear someone working a forge now, smell food and hot metal on the wind.

"Not quite." Barbara's accent was gone. She had the same lilt, the same crispness to her voice, as Alena. "We were allies once, in the old lands, more than allies. Time was we married pretty closely into each other, cousins with cousins as it were. We were maritime where Alena's kin were fools for horses. When they came across the big water, the Mihaly's rode in the merchantmen of my House. Mihaly settled at the edge of the sea of grass, eventually my folk sailed around to the Western ocean and settled there."

"The 'Runner', eh? I suppose you've been playing at Coyote across the mountains as well, under the Kikuza? No problem, I'll use any name to get my cloven hooves in the tent. Suck it up ladies, here is the gate."

They both wanted to explain things to me that I didn't need to know. Wasn't in the briefing. Though maybe I should have listened.

We'd marked a rally point near one of the southern passes into the Rockies, down in the Reserves. There was a sheltered canyon there with a campsite under the north wall, big enough for a dozen hearths, hard to see from the air. Alena had told me she'd be at least six weeks my time in the Hanse, maybe more if someone got crazy and invited lawyers. Less if they tried to shoot their way to a compromise. Then there was Barbara. She might be in therapy six or seven months. I'd swing by the rally point, north of where we crossed over, every thirty or forty local days. Just a snooping and a pooping, looking for Alena. I wasn't to expect them before the first snows closed the passes. But they'd come through down on the flats and work their way up in to the canyon from the east.

I really didn't expect them before the spring. And given how bad Barbara looked, I didn't expect her at all.

"You're keeping the dogs." She'd said at the rear gate when we were dismounting.

"I figured."

"She's going to try and raise a cadre in the Hanse. Smuggle them across."

I unstrapped the cantle pack with half the Krugerrands and the silver ingots in it along with a fist full of my cartwheel dollars, handed it to her. "Yeah. What I understand it ain't a good idea. You put your foot in the wheel. If she wants to establish a numbered account in my Switzerland, that'll work just fine."

"You going try and go back across to recruit?"

"Depends." A guard with a pump shotgun slung across his back and a handful of leather ties with lead crimps came up.

"Alo Barb, new rules. We got to bind your side arms and seal them." I was beginning to pick up the language, or actually the creole, it being a mixture of a lot of languages.

"Lo Calvin. Whose idea this?"

"Hausmeister."

She grunted and allowed him to bind her Glock to her holster. I opened my duster and let him bind my Shansi as well.

Calvin clicked his tongue when he saw my gun, his eyes got round and his deference increased by about a ton. "Shansi armory, Chinese licensed Mauser?"

"Yeah. You've seen 'em before?"

"Not to touch. My grandma came across with a Bolo and this here shotgun I carry."

Checking out the trench shotgun slung across his back, I saw that there was a line of horsemen coming down from the hills. They had a guerdon at the head with a banner, just like the ones out front.

"What's with the bouquets out front?"

He glanced up from my pistol to Barbara's face. Looked to his right and left while rubbing the back of his neck. "All the Overlanders traveling to the west are under escort, it being a troubled time and all. The Flowers and House Mihaly are suppressing banditry. They've even hired in Medji from the Pacific Maritimes to better cover the foothill and passes. To the east, it's easygoing."

"So, we'd have a lot of Flowers accompanying us to the 'Springs?"

"Springs is under martial law, Miz Barb. Had a fuelcell farm blow up last week and the Confederated authorized the Mihaly to activate the local Militia and request aid from the Pika. The Overlanders are using a laager outside of the 'Springs and the Militia is vetting everyone bound for the 'ville."

I looked at Barbara and then flicked my eyes towards Alena who was standing in line outside of a rustic port-a-potty.

Barbara grimaced. "Well," She said. "just as well we're bound for the Big River."

Calvin clicked his tongue against his teeth and finished strapping down my Shansi. "Big River? Out of your home range a bit, hmm?"

"Taking mi Ahijada East to settle her a bit, get her away from you roughnecks."

He snorted and said something low and dirty in Spanglish. Barbara giggled. Kinda scary hearing her giggle.

I tugged at the peace bond, it'd hold for just long enough to slow a shooting. While Calvin and Barbara exchanged mild insults and occasional information, I thought about things.

They slope east, cross over somewhere in the Upper Missouri and engage the Bankers. Meanwhile I stir the pot. The bit about the fuelcell farm indicated that someone was playing Partisan games. But right now, the Koshitsu and their Quislings were busy screwing down the lid. The Partisans needed just a little help. And the Tao of partisan I could recite in my sleep.

"I'd better be on my way home Ms. Barbara." I nodded at the hills to the west. "Think it might blow up a storm and I'd like to get under cover sooner than later."

She looked to the west, saw the horsemen and nodded. "You best get moving then." Her eyes asked the question; if I'd followed the byplay with the guard. I laid a finger alongside my nose and winked. She smiled and turned away to look at the hills.

I gathered up the reins and led her horse and Alena's cripple towards the forge. Alena had been inside the outhouse, came out just about the time I got to the forge. I saw her, out of the corner of my eye, stop and speak to Barbara then take something from her pack and follow me over to the forge.

ALENA 36

He was standing in line with my horse and Barbara's. He'd left his horse and the pack animals under her eyes. I had a small pouch of gold.

"You will need this." I handed the leather bag to him.

He nodded and tucked it away in his long canvas coat. "She's poorly." He said rubbing his hand down the foreleg of my horse but flicking his eyes toward Barbara. "Best see to her quickly."

"What do you intend?"

He grinned at me tilting his head towards the teen idling on the sand-barrel by the door. "Get your horses boarded and all that, then slope off easterly."

"You going to doing any visiting?"

"I hear tell there is a traveling revival of 'Breaker of Houses' over in Sandoval territory. Thought I'd get a little culture."

I nodded, more to buy time while I decoded his allusive statement than to agree with him. "I will see you again?"

He sobered. "With luck, you will."

I stood on my toes and kissed his cheek, before I could lose my resolve, then I walked away from him.

Barbara was leaning against the rail of the fence watching a pack train come down from the hills. "Hire a groom to watch his critters?" She asked.

"Trust them?"

"Mostly, it's the Jaspers that don't sleep here regularly that I dislike. Right. Let's go in and see where that one Overlander is bound for and if we can get berths. We're going to Cantry Ford."

"That's East, on the Grand Pracht'e?"

"Kikuza are running the Overlanders west of here, you want to run your face past them?"

"Does he know?"

"Yup. Time we left." She motioned a young child over, sexless in its overalls and queue, tipped it a quarter and told it to hold the reins for "M'Tallen". Then she bent and whispered in the ears of the dogs, ran her hands over them and let them lick her hands. She looked about the station then, like she was leaving for good and wanted to remember and walked into the light of the back door. The dogs whined and danced in place, but they did not follow. I did.

TALLEN 37

The kid at the forge, not the smith but his helper I thought, took the saddles from the horses and listened while I told him about Alena's horse coming on lame. He looked up from the hoof, measuring me. He was older than I'd thought at first. "You're fresh from the States, aren't you?"

I smiled at him, my off hand palming a knife. "What makes you think that?"

He bent and rubbed his hand over the lame leg. "Boots and tack, plus you came in with Barbara LeRenard. How are the Cardinals doing?"

I blanked for a second and then connected. He was wearing a shirt with the name McGwire and the number 25 embroidered on the back. "I don't follow the game much, but I hear McGwire is on track to break the record."

"Yeah, but I'd rather see them get into the series.

Looks like she's got a bad bruise in the frog, but that's all."
He was shorter than me, but not by much. Burnt just about
as brown as Barbara was with black hair, light blue eyes and
the face of a Hitler Youth poster.

"You a horse doctor?"

"Almost. Put two years across the Veil in AngTerra,
Pre-Vet, and washed out. Came back here with a new copy
of the Merck manual, a bag of instruments and set myself
up with Uncle."

"Didn't stay?"

"Nope. I like the girls and loved baseball, tolerated the
music, but it was not what I needed." He just waved a hand
at the horizon to the north. "I need the Empty Grass."

I looked at the two riders complaining at the smith by
the forge, their hands waving at a half dozen horses in the
corral. They'd ridden in, after I'd lined up, on sore footed
nags, I wouldn't have fed to Barbara's dogs, let alone rode.
They were dressed in dirty brown tunics, wrapped puttees
from their short boots to their calves, with a very modern
looking battle rifle slung across their backs and a tanto at
the left hip.

Been a while since I'd seen Imperial Cavalry.

Although they were speaking Spanglish and not
Mandarin, they were a lot healthier than any of the Japanese
other ranks I'd ever saw, it still gave me a long moment of
confusion. That was then, but...

Suddenly one of them slapped the smith across the
face.

Everything froze for just that moment, then all hell
broke loose. The one who'd slapped the smith was punched
so hard as to knock him clean out of the forge and into the
corral, teeth flying and blood everywhere. The other one
tried to draw a sidearm, but the peace-bond held, long
enough for the smith to turn and grab him by the crotch
and throat and fling him over the fence and into a mat of
prickers. The rest of the troop tried to weigh in and were
proceeding to get the ever-loving shit stomped out of them
by the smith and the rest of the hostlers when a trio of
guards came on the run. One shucked two quick rounds

into the air while the other two leveled their guns at the troop.

I could see that this was going to get way too much attention. I tipped the baseball loving horse doc a gold piece, dropped the horse shoe I'd been using as a knuckleduster into the quenching barrel and drifted out of the forge. I stopped and looked fondly at a trooper choking to death on his teeth. I drifted on past and collected my horse and the dogs from the gate just as a slew of Koshitsu officers and the Hausmeister descended on the smithy.

Nobody likes Kikuza.

ALENA 38

Barbara succeeded in reserving us a place on the Eastbound Overlander, shaping northeast to the Grand Boulevard and to Cantry Ford. The 'lander was full. The aisles in the center of the coaches were crowded with standers and every single berth on the second tier was double booked. Everyone who had the means was leaving the sweetgrass and the foothills. Crossing the Empty Grass.

The Overlander took a day and a night to get to Cantry Ford, non-stop all the way through the lower Aansi Territory and to the west fork of the Grand Boulevard. I spent most of that time sitting at a window, watching the land go by. We were on the Jen Trace most of that time, a broad path worn into the prairie by oxen, steamers and now these Diesel turbines. No 'villes, few stations, but there were many camps. Most of the Pika were on the move, although it was coming late in the season. I asked the handlers if they knew why, they shrugged and spoke of bad times in the wintering valleys to the west. Raiding and such, way outside of the banns.

Twice I saw a column of light Confederated Armored Dragoons rumbling through the grass on the verge of the trace, buttoned up with their 25mm guns trailed forward and off to each side, ready for action. One had a bright smear of metal shining against the dark green camouflage on the turret, that smear had been a glancing shot and not from a small caliber round.

We did not see any Koshitsu. I did see some Medji who wore Rim livery, lightly armed and watchful. They were idling at one of the way stations that serviced an Overlander trace up from the Texas Gulf. They did not enter the Overlander, being more interested in who got off and where they went. At one of the stations where I knew there was a small transit through to AngTerra, there was a Koshitsu bannered Overlander stranded with its engine compartments open. Its complement of twenty Medji was more than balanced by thirty Dragoons tending to a sick scout car.

The danger came at Cantry, after we left the Overlander. Cantry Ford was a sink of soft spots, there was better than four hundred fords in the seven hundred or so square miles of river bottoms and wooded gorges that comprised the Cantry. It was the third largest constellation of fords in the 'Zeme', only Roma and the Yellow River held more in as limited an area. Only three crossed over into AngTerra. Most were Hanse or Middle Kingdom, with a sprinkling of Picardy-Normandy, Little Englanders and one very busy broad ford to Hindi-Imperial. Each ford had its own gallery built over the soft spot. Many were simply foamed concrete domes inset into the hillsides. The crossing esplanade was coiled typically around the interior of the dome. Incorporating a series of partitions that slowed the progress of anyone making the crossing, raid stoppers in other words. Usually the guide would take you through the stations of the crossing, walking or riding up or down the esplanade to the doors. At either door would be a concierge with a customs agent for the respective world, taxman and all that. Some of the destinations had no officials from that sheaf or world warding their entrances since they were innocent of the existence of the doors and the galleries but, the concierge served as guardian for those worlds. Keeping the contraband to a minimum tolerable by consensus and by the Eisenring. The Hanse had their own people warding the gates, with Eisenring and Confed 'Advisors' embedded in their offices. If the Hanse wanted something or someone banned from 'their' gates, it was banned. Conversely, if they wanted something to pass freely through the gates, the Eisenring moaned about it but stood aside.

Around the Ford a city grew up. Twenty-two hundred years old and well over a hundred thousand citizens. Romano-Britannic in its founding era, like most Dai cities now it was a pleasant mixture of styles and conveniences, except for rapid transportation. The trolleys were horse, the streetcleaners were motorized. The chairlifts up and down the walls of the gorges were expressly for the crippled or excessively pregnant, the broad staircases next to the lifts were for the rest of the population. There were escalators and elevators in the buildings that ran up the sides of the terraces of the gorge, but there were no public lifts. If you had business in Macy's-At-The-Ford, you could take the escalator for a quarter-bit. Got Macy's a lot of walk in traffic.

Only on the river running through the gorge were there motorized transports. It made for a slow pace and many self-contained neighborhoods. Nice place to live, maddening if you were in a hurry to traverse it.

I knew three galleries very close to the Overlander station where we could cross over to the Hanse. All were Hanse only, well-tended and busy. Each one had a contingent of Medji with Rim livery hanging about. They weren't openly harassing the customers, but they were closely watching anyone that came into the galleries. There were matching detachments of Hanse Milita, Eisenring Uniformed Officers and Confederated House Dragoons watching each other loitering. The street vendors were doing a landrush business keeping the various detachments hydrated and fed.

Barbara had insisted I dirty up, dragging me into the women's lounge at the Overlander station with the expressed intention of 'dusting the lily'. She tied a rag about my hair and after adding a few smuts declared herself satisfied, remarking that I was quite smudgy to begin with. Then she fished out of her black leather carry-sack an ultra-suede jumpsuit, a monogrammed purse with matching sandals, and a fine dark brown scarf. She stripped down to her underwear and quickly dressed while I blocked the door, wrapping the scarf about her dark red hair as a finishing touch. She produced a makeup kit from the same carry-sack, quickly darkened her eyes and with a deft touch drew a fine red line vertically between her eyebrows. She regarded her image in the mirror, opened the purse and checked its contents. When we left the lounge, she was the image of a Hindi-Imperial Matriarch, a Covert De Dai for we were unknown in that milieu.

She also loaded both of our carry-sacks onto me. I was to play the part of a local day porter. She was in route to a season of shopping in the elegant steelyards of the Hanse. Wealthy, chic and disinclined to break into a glow carrying her own bags.

Outside, the High Street was not busy, it being the hour after the second meal. Barbara stopped about a block from the station entrance and fiddled with her purse, allowing me to close with her. "We got a tail." She muttered. "Follow my lead."

I blinked and shifted the weight of the carry-sacks across the pack frame on my shoulders. She blatantly consulted a cheater and then marched off in the opposite direction from the Hanse galleries that I knew of. I made a face at her back and shifting the carry-sacks again followed after.

She headed away from the river, climbing a series of steps and short but steep alleys, her purse slung across her body and her right hand casually on the bag and the gun slit. I just kept laboring in her wake. Eventually I spotted the tail, two boys twice as dirty as I was and starvation gaunt. Barbara pulled them along, lingering just enough at some of the middle Trade shops to keep the tails ignorant that we had them.

I was beginning to think she was determined to walk to the Texan gulf when she took a sudden turn into a shop, dragging me through the door by the loop on my carry-sack. It was a coffee shop, crowded with Turkic customers. A path opened up and we made a beeline to the rear, through a heavy velvet curtain that fell closed behind us and down a long flight of stairs. No one had spoken to us and after the first startled glance from the barista when I came stumbling into the gloom at her heels, no one looked at us either. At the end of the stairs was a long tunnel, slanting down to a soft spot. I could feel it.

I looked down the ramp to the ford and shifted the carry-sacks again. Where they were clipped onto the suspenders ached. They were heavy as sin.

"Where?" I asked.

"A Madriguera. In the Hanse."

"An unregistered ford?"

"Masked as well as being off registry. It's well inside the interference radius of one of the bigger galleries."

"How long has it been operating?" I brushed my fingers over the wall. It was rammed earth between foot wide oak beams.

"I've known of it for fifty years, but..." She shrugged. "If we have the chance, you can come back and inspect the woodwork another time." She casually opened her purse and took a handgun out, pulled back the slide and chambered a round.

"We will need these?" I tugged at a strap on one of the carry-sacks and a flap drooped open revealing the 10mm pistol in a tearaway holster.

"Never know. The folks on the other side are just about as shady as you can be in the Hanse, which means nothing. The four times I'd come through here, it was to pick up a party and not be crossing over myself."

"Discard the sacks?"

"Not the leather one. Clean up just a little before you drop the other one, you know dirt sticks out in the Hanse, but keep the dinero and the guns."

"What dinero?"

She took the black leather pack from me and turned it inside out for a moment. Inside, flush against the back and tied into small pouches were coins.

"Tallen?"

"Half of what he was carrying, gold and silver. Handy fellow for a youngster. I rigged the packs while you were sleeping."

"Why didn't he..."

"We passed the coins under strange eyes and since when have we been alone to trade stories?"

I changed my outer gear. Wiped down my hands and face with a field wipe and settled the money we had into three wallets. I stripped and reassembled one of the carry-sacks into a slightly oversized purse. I strapped the 10mm's holster into the purse and threaded magazines for the gun.

"I am ready." I slung the other carry-sack into a corner.

"We get through this I'm going to be worthless for about two, maybe three days. Too many crossings too quickly. You ever have been on the Ha'strasse in the Hanse?"

"Mihaly keeps a Household there. I had the freedom of the Street for six years since I Manifested."

"You serious about doctoring me?"

"Tallen said, 'You ride for the House, the House provides.'"

"You offered more than that as well."

"Yes."

"I left my House out on the Coast, but I never renounced it."

I walked over to her, took her hand and began to walk down the slope. "Once we were allies."

"True."

At the bottom of the slope there would be the gallery. This was a crossing made to the oldest pattern. Before we started using mechanical crossing gantries, it was configured for a walking crossing.

Any raiders coming across the ford would first have to make the gallery their own. Then they would face attacking up the slope. In the old times there would have been murder holes above the incline and rock oil reservoirs at its head to feed fires. The ceiling of the transit was low, maybe two hands above my head, the better to hamper attackers surging up the incline. The width also varied, to disarray any attempt at a shield wall, incorporating fighting alcoves.

"You're a Fähremeister," she said, "aren't you?"

"I can open a Ford, Walk the Gallery and close the Rideau behind me but, I am not a Master." I saw the first manifestations of the Rideau before us; the standing wave of the river of worlds, bending the images traditionally painted on the walls of the Gallery, forming the invisible pool of the Ford. With each step the images wavered, changed as the standing wave reacted to us.

"Ferryman as well as Heart Binder." She said in English. "Do you see the critical path?"

"The light blue shadows?" The pool was waist deep now and I could rake my fingers through the path guides without stooping.

"Cobalt to my eyes, but yes."

"Lean on me." I said.

"I will, Mistress Alena, I will."

The pool lapped over our heads, it was just as dangerous to retreat now as go on. Out of the corner of my eye I could see the path behind flutter through the spectrum and then dissipate. The stronger the Ferryman, the longer the path stayed true and safe. "Shall I lead?"

"No. I know the Book for this Path to the Hanse. It...is complicated. There is a knot in the flow. It is why this was never exploited fully."

I could see echoes on either side of us now. Monochrome images of us. The Germanic traditions called them doppelgangers, after the ghosts common in the Hartz. In any tradition, to see echoes was big trouble. It was as bad for a Ferryman as icing on a wing was for a pilot. It meant that the Ferryman was losing the bubble, it was shrinking in around him and if it collapsed altogether, the best that could happen was a quick death.

I pushed at her, lending her the energies that I would have used to open the Ford. The hedge school had taught us to pool our energies, thus two or more 'weak' Ferrymen could open a Ford normally beyond their frequencies. It had its price. You spilled half of what you lent, and you could simply destabilize the Ferryman you were trying to help.

Her color improved and the echoes faded quickly. One pair stopped and turned their heads to regard us as we walked deeper into the gallery, their faces were pocked and scabbed and their hair falling out in patches. They vanished with a silent flash of light, in the manner of a bulb burning out. The other pair never wavered. They simply faded into the mists about us. I followed Barbara into the mists as well.

TALLEN 39

I figured I could make a dogleg towards the foothills to the south of Manitou Springs, where Alena had indicated there was a significant cluster of Mihaly ally hearths. One man, two dogs and three horses were not likely to make a big footprint on a three hundred square mile prairie, or so I thought. The second night out on the grass proved me wrong.

Barbara's terrier had taken to sleeping with his head on my shoulder, outside the blanket I used instead of a sleeping bag. The first night there had been some disagreement over where he was going to sleep and if I was going to get any sleep at all. After the third time he squatted on my face I flung the dog over the fire in the general direction of the horse lines and he got the message. The shepherd mix had settled down with the horses from the beginning. Bigdog and I had come to an agreement much earlier. I was the god-like Sergeant and he got the occasional strip of jerky, just like the army.

I tolerated the terrier. I think he, the terrier, regarded me as a necessary evil because he couldn't open a can of dog food and I had a can opener attached to my wrist. Bigdog hunted on the move, small things like mice or a slow rabbit. The terrier rode on the pack horse and regarded the world as having changed, and much for the worse. He moped so like a displaced nobleman I'd known in Shanghai that I named him Stosh.

So Bigdog was bedded under the horses. Stosh had his bony nose resting on my shoulder and I was asleep. Then I felt, more than heard, Stosh growl. I didn't open an eye, just shifted a bit under the blanket. A gun was in my hand and I had the blanket gathered in the other hand to clear for action. I stilled my breathing and listened.

Stosh got up and trotted off into the night. I silently swept the blanket back and rolled off the foam pad I was using for a bed, then walked around the fire pit in my socks using the hunter's stalk. Take a step. Listen. Take two steps. Turn slowly to contrast the dark earth against the lesser dark of the sky. Listen. Take three steps. Listen again. When I got near the horses, I knew we had a guest. I had four horses now.

The new horse was huddled up against the other three, still saddled and with his reins dragging in the dirt. Bigdog was lying on the reins. Stosh came trotting past us, heading no doubt for the blanket. I stuffed my gun in my shirtfront. Then I ran my hands over the newcomer. He was slick with sweat, nervous under my hands and wanting the reassurance of my smell. His nose kept butting up under my arm. The saddle was just like the ones I'd seen outside the smithy, basically a saddle fork covered by a light pad or horse blanket. Not much of a saddle horn, just a slight rise of a cantle at the rear, gun scabbard to the right and a lance pocket on the right stirrup. Light and easy on the horse, hell on the rider if they weren't hardened to it. Essentially a McClelland saddle. With blood on it.

I was pretty sure it was human blood. The horse wasn't

hurt. The blood was barely tacky, almost dry, soaked into the pad and scumming the stirrup leathers on the left side. The rifle was still in the scabbard, it was like one of those worthless drillings I seen when Alena and I had fallen through a soft spot. I could feel an embossed chop or brand in the leather of the scabbard as well as the saddle, but I couldn't make it out by touch. I could tell what it was not. It wasn't a double axe head or a fucking flower. The saddlebags yielded a couple of those bagel-like journey cakes, a pouch of pemmican and a half dozen strips of jerky. I tossed one of the cakes and the jerky to Bigdog and went to break camp.

When I was ready, I cut a bloody swatch off the saddle skirts of the stranger, held it to where Bigdog could get a good nose full of it. "Find."

He wuffed and circling the campsite trotted off towards the north. I followed with my Mini 14 out of the scabbard and resting on my lap, the Mauser in its shoulder holster, the Lesser Dragon awake and riding on my shoulders like a hawk.

We trotted due north for about forty-five minutes, then swung in a wide circle to the east. Maybe five miles total overland to where I found the first body.

The kid was face down on the grass, one arm tucked under him and the other flung wide. In the faint light of the predawn I could see two wounds low down on his back, the blood staining his light shirt and trousers black. I dismounted and looked him over with a red pinlight. I rolled him over, carefully, in case he had a surprise tucked under him. He'd been dead a while, better than a day. Before the blow flies and bloat had gotten to him, he was a good-looking kid, dark hair and the deep tan you get when you live outdoors year around. Much like the horse doc back at the Overlander station. He'd had a pistol in his left hand, some sort of revolver. In his right hand he had a rank badge, torn from a collar. Three silver pips on a black strip of leather. A Flower's equivalent to a second lieutenant. I turned his pockets out; knife, wallet on a chain, packet of rounds for the pistol, a Rubik's cube on a key ring, some jerky and a laminated photo of a girl.

I flipped the jerky to Bigdog again and stashed the rest into the wallet. It was a bigger version of what the bikers and truckers wore across the Veil, riding in a pouch in the back of his jacket much like the game pocket of a hunting jacket. The wallet had small pockets in it holding silver coins, a larger section for papers and the like. The kid had been across the Veil. Rubik should have told me that, but the California MVD Learners Permit with his picture on it made it very clear. Carl Federer, brown eyes, five foot nine, hundred and forty pounds, fifteen years old. I took my trench shovel out and cut a narrow grave in the sod, as deep as my arm could reach. I stripped the saddle from his pony, laid the boy in the grave, and covered him with the horse blanket. When I'd finished throwing the dirt back in, I laid the saddle and tack on top of the grave. I drove the drilling down at his head. It took all of twenty, maybe thirty minutes. I had sprinkled a layer of chili pepper onto the blanket, to try and keep the varmints off. I was surprised he wasn't splintered bone and rags already, I'd heard coyotes at sundown.

Then I cast about for tracks, knowing the boy's pony by this time. When I found them, the pony's tracks led off north east.

The real killing ground was a half day's ride to the northeast. I was coming up to a slight rise when I heard a chorus of coyotes singing and complaining. I stopped just short of the rise and stood in my stirrups, to get a sight on what they were going on about. On the other side of the rise was a waller, a small creek with a wide mud pan well suited for buffalo to drink and roll in. It was crowded with buffalo. Dead buffalo. I dismounted and dropped the reins of my horse to the ground. I motioned Bigdog to 'stay' and walked down into that waller.

The coyotes faded away as I walked through the dead buffalo, though never quite out of sight or hearing. They were all obscenely fat, their heads slicked with blood and offal, reminding me more of the big rats I'd seen in the Somme than the rail thin ghost dogs I'd always enjoyed watching back home. The hollow was carpeted with dead animals; buffalo, horse and men.

I counted ten horses, six riders. Most were boys, one was a girl and one I couldn't tell anything about. I found a couple of horses that might have carried a Flower chop. Someone had cut a six-inch square patch out of the dead animal's hide to confuse the issue. Up on the other side of the rise I found two blood signs that didn't end in a corpse, one by a dead horse with no brand. On that rise I found enough brass to fill a bucket, Russian 5.45mm. AK74 or something very close to it. That matched the glimpse I'd got of the Kikuza guns at the station.

I sorted through the gear and tack I could find in the waller. It didn't come to much. Most of the saddles had been cut away, bridles stripped from the horses. The bodies had their pockets turned out, some were naked, all had been shot to doll rags by the 5.45mm's. Two were mutilated extensively, after death I hoped. It looked like three of them had forted up behind an enormous bull, then dropped their horses around them to make a strong point. Held out until the Kikuza had to ride in close and grenade them. With luck they got a couple of the Flowers.

It was close to sunset when I mounted up and started down the Flowers' path. They'd been arrogant or battered enough to camp about two miles upstream of the waller, just above a brush pile in a bend of the stream. Three small fire pits, a big bonfire and a trash pit. The trash pit had field dressings and food wrappings, some horse tack and a couple of disposable handcuffs. The bonfire was an attempt to hide a grave. I broke out the shovel while the dogs went walkabout.

The kids at the waller got four of the sons-of-bitches, even with drillings against AK's. Two were bandaged up some. Two were laid in the dirt just as the buckshot took them. Nothing in their pockets, no ID, no lint. They had one-inch square scars on their right sides, just below the armpit. Like a burn scar hiding a tattoo. Their faces were shredded to hamburger and crawling with maggots, 'unknown but to God'. It seemed to me that their buddies were worried that someone would know them, so they helped nature along just a little.

The dogs started barking at something in the brush pile about the time I finished digging the last bastard up. I looked at the trash pit with the disposable hand cuffs and I got a little weary, but I went to see what they had found anyway,

What the coyotes had left was pitiable, but the piano wire in her neck told the story. Most of her nails were gone down to the quick, but she had skin under every nail she had left. The cloud of blowflies about her suddenly crisped away, caught in my backwash.

I pulled the brush pile down on her, stacked it high around. Then I cut four saplings into lance shafts about seven feet long. I set the shafts in a ring about the bush pile and then sharpened the ends I had hammered to set them in the ground.

I rode off about five hundred yards and cached most of the loads and tack from the pack horses under a rocky outcrop I thought I could find again. Then I took the pack horses and Carl's pony and went back to the waller.

Just after moonset I put a light pack on the horse I was riding and threw a saddle bag across the one that had come calling in the night. I had kept a weapons load-out on one of the pack horses. Four forty round banana magazines, a spare rifle, a bag of grenades, a pair of a Singapore knock-offs of a German recoilless grenade launcher, a half dozen mini-claymores and two kilos of C4. I stuffed Stosh into the saddlebag, tied off the horse with the weapons at the end of the string and lit out down the road. Behind us was a roaring fire witnessed by four heads, mounted on the stakes.

We rode all night at the wolf march; trot a quarter hour, walk the horses for a half hour, dismount and walk a quarter hour and then repeat. If you're in good condition and your horses are sound, you can almost make sixty miles a day. I stripped off my boots the first hour and ran barefoot over the sod alongside the horses and Bigdog. The tracks were confused. I lost them twice in the darkness but

Bigdog kept me in line. After a couple of hours, they settled down into a standard route march. Main body with a small scouting party ahead, outriders to ether flank and a pair of horses in the drag position. From the horse apples in the tracks, they were a good day ahead, maybe more depending how far they were willing to push their horses.

I pulled up just after sunup, fed the horses a handful of grain each and unsaddled them. I didn't want any of them pulling up lame or getting saddle sore. My horse was in good shape, better than I'd hoped for. It was one of those Prunty geldings that Barbara'd been so proud of. The pony was not quite as well off, it'd been hard ridden in the last two days or so and showed it but, it was still sound and willing. The two pack horses were in decent shape, though fractious when I tried to ride them bareback. I let them all roll in the grass with Bigdog supervising while I walked about counting the tracks.

I counted maybe thirty separate horses in total, give or take a half dozen. Two had thrown a shoe, one was unshod. One of them was pissing blood at every stop. I found some trash; spilled grain, a cartridge case, wadded up paper. Route march with damn little discipline. The paper was food wrappers, I think. From the smell it's had been a smoked fish.

I wiped my hands clean and ate some of my rations then re-saddled the horses. I guessed I come close to twenty miles since midnight. I was figuring on them being thirty or forty miles ahead of me right now. As slow as they'd been on the march, it was still going to take me three hard days of riding to catch up. Days that'd break down if not kill my horses. On the map they weren't making for any clear goal. Riding in a shallow arc towards the northeast. I could try and cut across the arc but, they could simply drift in another direction and leave me even farther out.

Then, about four hours after sunup, I came across more tracks. Horse and an ATV of some sort. Jeep sized but lighter than a Jeep by how shallow the tire marks were. They'd come out of the west and joined up with the batch I was trailing. The head count was up over fifty for horses, making the actual riders number about twenty plus whatever the ATV could carry. They also slowed the hell down. Not three miles after they joined up, they camped. Swung off their trace and into another small cottonwood stand. I came up on the stand slow and easy, just in case they'd left a trail guard. But there was nothing in the stand but a half dozen firepits, more trash, a slaughtered horse that was drawing flies and the buzzards that had clued me into the camp. To my surprise, the firepits were warm. That meant they were only half day ahead of me. Fifteen miles at best, more like ten or twelve.

This changed things.

If they made camp at sundown, they'd be a maximum thirty miles from where I stood, more likely twenty or twenty-five. I could hole up here, rest the horses and mount up again around five. I'd smell their fires around midnight, moonset would be just after that.

My time.

I moved northeast through the gullies until I hit another stand of cottonwoods upstream. I unsaddled, fed and watered the horses, then fed the dogs. I didn't feel the need for any sleep, but I was hungry and wanting a cup of coffee more than I wanted a platoon of mechanized infantry along for the fun. I made a small fire and set my only pot to boiling, then hunkered down with a map. Stosh clambered up on a half-downed tree and took lookout, gnawing on his ration of jerky, Bigdog trotted off to supervise the horses.

The pot was singing when I heard Stosh's alert, that low growl. I stood up and climbed on the tree trunk with my Mini 14 to hand. Probably should have kicked over the coffee pot but I was to the point of insanity over the chance of a good cup of java. I had a 4x32 pistol scope on the rail just over the fore stock, it would give me a nine-yard field of view at a thousand yards. I swept the quarter Stosh was focused on and found a rider seven hundred yards up wind. Riding up my trail from the other campsite, slow and obvious like.

I had the coffee ready when the rider was within

shouting distance, probably a hundred and fifty yards. He stopped and waved his long gun in the air, slowly. "Ehey-yah! The camp!"

I stood up, waved him in with my hat.

He rode closer, then dismounted and walked the last ten yards to the holler. He was a big man, big through the chest and carrying a substantial belly, the way a bear carries its belly. He had a long version of one of those drillings resting on his shoulder, cased in leather and ornamented with an eagle feather. The rest of his gear was western standard. Chambray shirt, jeans and a set of chaps, a flat-crowned drovers' hat. No boots, he wore mocs that laced up to his knees under the chaps. He was burned dark as the leather skirts of his saddle. His hair was white as salt. Meant he lived on the Grass. Traveling Pika.

When he had swung off the horse, the top of his shoulder cleared his saddle horn, a big man. He walked quietly through the grass, walking with the habitual toe and heel of the still hunter. His gun was still on his shoulder, butt to the rear, carrying it like an ax. He dropped his reins and stepped into the swept area around the fire. He looked down at the bare earth, brushed clean of twigs and debris, nodded.

"Long day," he said.

"That it has. Coffee?" I stepped back and waved at the pot singing on the small fire I'd allowed myself.

"Don't mind if I do." He reached round behind himself and produced a blue metal cup. He squatted at the fire, draped his gun across his knees and picked up the hot pot and poured a cup, put it back on the fire and sipped at his coffee. "Come far?" He grinned at me the way the dog grins at the treed coon.

I squatted across from him, poured myself a cup with a rag wrapped about the red-hot handle of the pot. "Maybe thirty miles sun up to sun up."

"Helluva lick, on the run?"

"You got a name?"

He blinked. Anyone else I'd said he was thinking about lying. This one was thinking over the reason behind the question. "Nate. Nate Dockens."

"Tallen." I nodded to him just like we'd been introduced over a poker table. "You cut my trail about three miles back. Where the small band joined up with the bigger pack?"

He nodded.

"I cut the small band's trail maybe twenty miles before that, at a buffalo waller." I held his eyes with mine. "They'd killed about two hundred buff, maybe ten kids. Took at least one alive, left her in a draw after they broke camp."

"Flowers?'

"Believe so. Found sign." I dug in a pocket and flipped the rank tabs I'd recovered across the fire to him. He snatched them out of the air with one hand.

"Flower."

"Thought I'd trail after them a bit. I figure I'm a day behind now. Rest a little, feed the stock, walk out the stiffness and then come moonset…"

"You catch up to them, what are you going to do?"

"They need killing."

"By your lonesome self?"

"They're hell on Buffalo, death on half-growed kids but, I'm a different order of pain." And I let a little of that pain show.

"Big talk."

He saw the dogs then. Stosh coming up from the creek and Bigdog loping in with a gopher right behind him. He dropped his cup and started to come to his feet, then froze when he was looking down the barrel of the Mauser. "I know those dogs. El Corredor."

Big dog dropped the gopher by the fire and waited for his commendation. Stosh was a bit more jaundiced, he trotted past us and settled on my saddle blanket. "So. You know the pair of them. And the Coyote."

"A good friend." He said.

"She wished them on me, while she takes care of some things for La Senora."

"I doubt…"

"You carry the favor of the Mihaly?"

"I spoke for them among the Pika."

"And now."

"I am unreliable. So much so that my head is required in atonement."

"Excellent." I fished in my shirt for the ring Alena had left me. "You would know this?" I snapped the leather thong I had it laced through and threw the ring to him.

His hand blurred as he swatted it out of the air. "A signet. Mihaly y'Mihaly?"

"The same."

"I know the name, not the person."

I repeated the chain of descent; the one Alena had enumerated to me to show her place in the critical path.

"Hildur's granddaughter?"

"So, I am told."

"You could have taken this…"

"Yes. I could simply shoot you now and avoid more complications. I have been bound." And in the back of my head I heard Alena say 'if ever so lightly'. "And my mission is to observe, contact and organize resistance to the Flowers and their allies."

He grunted and threw the ring back. "A likely tale. But good as a beginning as any, I should think. And your plan is?"

"To take them as I find them."

ALENA 40

Above the Hanse end of the Madriguera was a small shop that specialized in cleaning clothing. No one blinked an eye when we walked through the door by a rank of ionizing chests. I left four silver cartwheels on the counter and nodded then we walked on out the door. The door had not unlocked until the shop was empty of customers, which made for some worrying moments as the door behind us leading to the gallery was locked when we tried the latch.

Outside there was a floater stop and a bank point. I fed a gold 'rand in to the stop and ordered up a two place. After a hiccup while it assayed the coin, it gave me a half hour estimated wait and a flag. I sat Barbara on the bench with the flag, looping the lanyard of the little black box over her hand.

"Are you all right?"

"No."

"Would you like something-?"

"Something warm, to hold if not to drink." She gave in to my mothering.

I tucked my extra jacket over her knees, for the breeze was freshening. Then bought us both double mocha lattes.

The flag updated the wait time to forty-five minutes, indicated a problem with the load level and that there would be a credit for the inconvenience. It asked for a bank number, which reminded me that we were here without documents.

This was not a good thing. If we had come through an approved crossing point, we would have documents. If I presented them with nothing more than an adequate deposit of ready credit, gold or whatever, the Hanse Documentary Agency would have taken some biometrics and produced a temporary passport.

This would have made us visible to the Concierge and acceptable to the civil authorities of the Hanse. The Concierge programs tied into the security-cam and transport monitors were designed to observe but not violate what privacy the citizens had. Unless there was a crime, a disaster or an accident, no humans saw the records the cameras made. The records were retained for a variable period of time, one to ten years and then irretrievably wiped.

The Concierge expert system watched for things that it 'knew' were wrong. Gunfire, alarms, bodies scattered across the bricks, sudden blooms of heat. All of these incidents would trigger a human overseer along with a quick response. You could fool it. A popular form of amusement by some of the wilder young sets was producing incidents to attract the Concierge aegis. This was winked at as long as the incident did not mimic insurrection or arson.

The System did not particularly care what your ID was, as long as you were carrying an ID. Even if your ID was bogus, it allowed the system to follow you about. Someone without an existence in the Concierge Database would get flagged, tagged and quietly pulled aside for an inquiry.

Anyone carrying two ID through a wicket, a turnstile between two cantons, would be remarked as well and the anomaly resolved before any further travel. So, we needed two adult ID, locked to our biometrics. But, outside of an official entry point, obtaining such an ID was officially impossible.

It was not physically impossible. Simply expensive and worse yet, noticeable.

If I were concerned about the whereabouts of Mihaly scions, one of the first places I would set down Ferrets would be at the places where you could slide past the Concierge. Ratwickets, they called them. Some were actual unmonitored doorways where a cantonial border had moved to intersect a structure. Other were places you could buy an ID or arrange illegal transport. But if I had managed to slip across the Veil to the Hanse, I would need to turn up at one of those wickets sooner or later.

But I had another option, one I hoped my faithless cousins had not learned from their street walking mothers.

I went to the bank point and gingerly opened the interface. The little green light came on over the camera eye, informing me that I was under overt recording. I fed the bank point a silver. Then bypassed the b'metric pad and tapped in a long number with a code word. This woke my suitcase.

When I survived the cull a number of things were done. Samples were taken of my DNA for the stud book, they drew off and froze a half-dozen eggs from my ovaries, they took images of my retinas and my sinus cavities and they established a false flag identity in the Hanse.

The identity was kept fresh. It had enough credit for two years modest living and established me as a citizen, which would protect me from some of the rougher practices the Hanse had with sojourners.

I could have had one in any milieu that knew our kind, or even in Little England or Tallen's world where we stayed in the deep shadows. I chose the Hanse. This made the suitcase easier to carry, and more dangerous to use.

Several generations back we had become silent

partners, by marriage, with the Steelyard Technical that wrote and maintained the Concierge program. In Maria's dowry was a suite of artificial intelligence cores, several orders superior to what the Hanse Public Order Systems had then. Where we got them from is a mystery, it being well known that the Mihaly send all their accountancy to the House Dexter and are not above the need to count out change with their shoes off. Those cores were the fortune of that Steelyard, making them the preeminent Technicals of that era. And they were using black box code, which we owned the keys to.

You could not fiddle with the system blatantly. There were auditors and an internal police force that watched for corruption or other abuses. But the Concierge was tolerant within certain limits on how far protocols and procedures could bend.

The sponsored 'suitcase' was a practice mostly unknown to most of the Dai. Although their members often individually established a cover or a legend, the Houses usually regarded this with disfavor. Suitcases smacked of treason, or not being confident at the very least in the prowess of the House. For a House to set up and maintain these identities was very much out of character.

But we had returned once, from being a Footlocker lineage, long before. The saving grace had been that the Mothers of that line had intuited disaster and sent several dozen seedlings away before it burst about them. It took three generations of being a hidden House, living as Medji, before we rose again. The oral memories of that time drove our caution.

The suitcase was still intact. I queried the system again. The last time the identity had been trotted out for an airing was two months ago, not four cantons away. I placed my hand on the b'metric pad, took a deep breath, then commanded a scan.

I told it that I had lost my 'pass and needed to have a new one coded.

The system hung for a second, then fined me a thousand credits, printed a two-page lecture on

Communitarianism and our mutual need for security and order, and burned me a pass. I was legally here.

I sent a quick letter to a friend telling her I was having a fine time in Low Wiscon, be glad to see her soon. This told my suitcase and its minder that I was using the emergency identity and not to work it anymore. Then I quickly shuffled my accounts, passphrases and resident information, ordered a new comtel and checked my maildrop for any messages. There were thirty or so. Some blind solicitations for my custom. Some dummy conversations to keep any sniffers happy. And then there was a photo.

It was a picture of my cousins and me, the last season we were all on the Empty Grass although it was not identifiable to anyone as being in the 'Zeme. There was a note with it, some banality about finding the original file and hadn't been fun, signed "Trina". That was a flag. There was a message hidden in the coding of the digital photo.

I fed a silver into the pay slot and ran a program embedded in my suitcase. It abstracted the message from the photo.

Alena, it said, since you are reading this, Del got you clear. Events have moved too fast, but I think it is the Madgji lineage we face. Do not use the Kantonalbanc. I shifted every major asset to Terrilured Banc Chartered. It is not a front for House d'Mihaly. Our lineage owns it. I left enough at Kantonalbanc to keep the Ferrets attentive. I suspect hegemonic interests in the struggle. I have established safe holds at several hostels, their link numbers are at the end of this. You are the only free player on the dice board now. Use Del and her contacts in the Fain...more I have not the time they are at the stairways.

I love you.

Break them.

Doni.

31 (36) 136-1930 Standerdmolen 8 3995 AA Hugens

21 (80) 633-1931 Cedex 728   1145 FV Gunreel

44 (20) 591-2941 Foukston B   352 BD Treis

Doni had been sixth in line for the Holder, she was a

third cousin, once removed. The date stamp of the note was three days before Del appeared on my doorstep. Eight days ago.

At the end of the program another door opened in the teller and a data wand was extruded. It should hold the current numbers and passwords for the new bank.

"Some more coffee?" I touched Barbara's arm. I had thought she was dozing. She raised her head and looked about us. The Hanse had overrun their world ten centuries sooner than Tallen's folk had. What was wild still in mine and unruly in his was manicured parkland here. But it was still late fall. The trees dropping red and gold leaves to drift in heaps along the boulevard. The sky a bright blue with a spray of clouds catching the sunset's beginning.

"I thought to be ready, to take my leave of this." We watched a sudden rush of squirrels burst through the drifted leaves and swarm up a tree in headlong joy.

She said. "No. I am not ready." She stretched out her hands and flexed the knuckles, the bones showing gauntly under the thinning skin. She had aged in the hours I had known her. This day's effort had drained her. "I would stay longer at the dance, if I could."

I looked away, to watch the fallen leaves dance in the wind.

She touched me with her hand. "Shall I say it for you? That I freely and with forethought bind..."

"No. I will not accept." I could not look at her through my blurring eyes. "We will be allies, not bond and bondholder." I blinked away my sorrows and faced her. "I will need allies. Witting allies who know the ways and means of a Cousins war."

"You bound him."

I smiled. "It would be a mistake, I think, to make over much of that bond."

"You left him."

"We have had this conversation before."

"You never answered."

"He's older than he looks."

She started to say something, then bit it back, her eyes

considering me. "How old?"

"Perhaps... a cohort ahead of yours."

She blushed. "An Avar after all. And I was lecturing him about the Houses like he had just begun to shave." Then she blinked. "But he doesn't have the patois."

"There are Houses that shelter elsewhere than in the 'Zeme."

Her eyes lit up for the first time. "A House in shadow. How marvelous. Have you the badge? Surely not on AngTerra. I knew the badges of most of the Footlocker Houses west of the Kush- "

"I don't have the emblem," I lied, feeling the sudden weight of the pouch on my hip. "I think he has an altered version. His House went under while the Fords were dark."

"Even better, perhaps his House disappeared in the Breaking of Nations..."

I sighed, that was a cant term for the wars on AngTerra.

"Perhaps."

The jitney floater whirred to a stop in front of our seat. I helped her stand and step into the compartment.

"Tinroll Landing." I told the jitney and swiped my pass through the reader. I had a notion on how to make an honest Bonder of Barbara, but not a clue about how I was to keep reign on her romance.

TALLEN 41

The Flowers had doubled their numbers.
We'd come up the trail in the early dark, then when we got a sense of where they might be from lights highlighting low clouds, we swung wide and came towards them from the East. Nate had kept up with me, stolidly forking his horse all night while I kept up the ride a while, walk a while routine. I offered to spell him with one of mine, but he just shook his head. I worried that he'd ride his horse into the ground, but it didn't seem to mind the pace. The horse didn't seem over matched, it was seventeen hands high if a foot and likely weighed close to a ton. It made my string look like Shetland ponies.

We'd sat and jawed at each other into the evening. He'd produced a bag of bread dough wrapped in cheesecloth, a pot of grease and a small skillet. I contributed coffee, a fresh slab of horsemeat, a can of carrots and two handfuls of dried cranberries. The horsemeat was stringy as hell, but the pan bread seasoned with cranberries made up for it.

Nate had come across a Kikuza buffalo kill site. He didn't come out and say it, but I thought he had something more than dead buffalo on his mind. He had a shoulder pouch full of loose cartridges for his double rifle, a composite bow with a quiver full of arrows and a pouch of pemmican and rough-cut tobacco. After we finished off the food, with a quarter going to the dogs, he sat down and pulled a small tin from his pouch. It had seven small jars and a shiny piece of steel.

I puffed at the pipe of tobacco he'd prepared for me and watched him paint his face and hands. He was puffing away on his own pipe all the while, drawing patterns on his hands with a fine brush.

"What be you?" He asked, dabbing at his face with black and mud-brown paint on his fingertips, making rosette dapples on his skin. "You don't strike me to be Medji?"

"Not as I understand them. You are...?"

"Skrinner, most often. Judge upon occasion." He paused in his marking, his light blue eyes looking me up and down. "You're new caught. Don't know Judge from Skrinner."

"We didn't have the time."

"You're not Medji, don't have the stink."

"Thank you, I think." I pulled my haversack closer and began to collect what I was going to use later. Two smoke grenades, one flash bang. Three double magazines of .308 NATO for the carbine that I slipped into a rig that would ride under my right arm. The Mauser was in a balancing rig under my left arm, with six magazines of .45ACP to feed it. "What do they smell of?"

"Money. Dirty money. White metal."

"La Senora bought me with gold."

"You are bound, not bought." From the smallest pot in the kit he took a dab of bright green slime and rubbed into his nostrils like some of the patent chest rubs my stepmother had used on me as a child.

"Proper Houses hire Medji, they do not bind them." He inhaled sharply through his nose, exhaled with almost the force of a shout, but silently. He did this, three times, his eyes closed like a man tasting wine, to focus the taste.

I left him to it, knocked the dottle of my pipe into the fire and carried the haversack over to the horses. I left the claymores in it, along with the rest of the grenades and the C4. I looked through the barracks bag again, considering. I had a pair of rockets, a silenced .22 auto, an extra Mini-14, magazines for all of the iron and several packs of ammo.

I'd offered him one of the Mini14's, but he'd turned me down. His double was a shoulder breaking .50-120, throwing nearly an ounce of lead. "I stay with what I am used to, Medji-not."

He'd laughed, slowly rubbing each finger long cartridge, cleaning off any corrosion or travel dirt, looking them over for dings and imperfections. "This is the same gun my grandfather carried, new stock, but same gun. "Why should I change? You use that cannon-in-a-box?" And he pointed at the Shansi Mauser in my lap. I'd laughed along with him and kept field cleaning my Mauser.

What I kept coming back to was the little German rockets. They were small, rugged and had a two-hundred-meter range. They were also damn near silent, for a recoilless rocket launcher. Used a captive piston system with a plastic counterweight. It sounded like a .22 short and didn't light up the sky for a country mile.

I kept including one in the load out. Its warhead was just over a pound. Didn't frag worth a damn. I ought to be saving them for when it came to house-to-house or cracking armor. But the itch in the back of my head told me to sling one across my back when we sloped off.

"You should take it." Dockens had come up quiet behind me.

"Yeah?"

"You know when to listen."

"Maybe." I fished the tube out, checked the self-test

and slung it across my back for now. "It's time to get on the trail."

"Time and past time." He peered at me, cupping his hands about his eyes as if he was looking through a window. "Walking Knife, I see you." He slapped his hands on my shoulders and walked over to his horse. He mounted up, settled himself in his saddle, and then rode off in the direction of the Kikuza trail. He was singing, it was some country tune from the fifties about walking after midnight.

It took me and the dogs about ten minutes to get our act together; piss on the fire, finish rigging the horses and such. He was not too far ahead of us, just letting his horse amble along while he lay back on the rump and rumbled songs at the stars and the moon. I thought I knew the music, but the words were never quite right. He sang all the way, double rifle across his lap. Laying back and singing to the stars or sitting up and rumbling at Stosh, who'd jumped onto his saddle bow for the ride. All the music was old. Country and Western, pre-Urban Cowboy, or County Blues. But the words were about walking the warrior path or getting drunk with Coyote. He was higher than a kite.

"You, don't sing do you."

"Not much."

"Oh, that's a pity." He sat up and looked around him. The moon well under the horizon and the stars populating the sky from rim to rim. "Two alone against fifty. Hunting Skin Walkers who butcher the Grandmothers and Grandfathers of the Pika. There are songs for this night, songs to put Breaker of..."

"Light on the horizon!"

"Ayuh." He looked at the stars again, and then shifted his horse into a trot, heading for a gully off to our right. "Looks like an aircraft."

"Thought you didn't have 'planes?"

"Uncommon. Getting more common. Think the Kikuza been using them to scout concentrations of Buffalo."

We huddled against the north wall of the gully, until the light and the faint noise faded off to the north. "Maybe a re-supply run?"

"For our Flowers, mayhap. Best be going, softly-like now."

"No more singing,"

"Ayuh, not till the doing is done. What can I sing to the Walking Knife?" He trotted off, up over the rim of the gully and on a beeline for the sector of the sky where the aircraft disappeared.

They had a few pickets out, mostly lancer types glued to their horses. We walked ours through a two-hundred-yard gap. Bigdog leading off and Stosh keeping watch from the withers of Nate's horse. The breeze was from the north and none of their horses caught our scent. When we got within fifteen hundred yards of the camp, we hit another picket line. A little more professionally set this time. Again, they were mounted, riding in pairs in a roughly circular patrol. We left the horses in a depression maybe two hundred yards outside their circuit, with Bigdog on guard, to work our way in on foot.

The ground was flat on the maps but had more than enough rolling contours to hide troopers used to snooping and a pooping. I had the Mini-14, a night glass and the Armbrust rocket launcher. Nate brought his long gun but, he also carried the bow and a fist full of arrows. After we got inside the mounted patrols we slow-stalked to within a hundred yards of the outer gaggle of tents, within three hundred yards of the west end of the landing strip. The whole camp was maybe one hundred yards wide by one hundred fifty long, counting the horse lines but not the landing strip. Half the tents were strung between the horses and the north side of the camp. I could see guards walking slowly about the horses. They'd tucked the horses in close to the strip and well within their perimeter.

They'd used an old, graveled road for the plane. Marking off the landing strip with some chemical lights. They had three of the ATVs clustered around it, along with one of the big Overlanders parked about fifty yards off. The plane was still open at the rear and a cargo party was working at unsticking one of those ATVs where it had gotten crosswise on the ramp. It was a big four engine beast, slightly larger than a C130 across the Veil. The ATVs were boxy. Bigger than a Jeep but smaller than the rest of the SUV type vehicles I was used to. Their rear ends were squared off and stenciled to beat hell with arrows, lettering and 'do not mess with' in sign language. Other than the cargo party, the troopers night herding the horses and a very alert squad guarding a wire cage at the far northwest end, the camp was asleep.

I focused the night glass on the cage, though I knew what it had to be. There were four prisoners hunkered on their heels and another one lying on the ground wrapped up in a blanket. There were six guards, all carrying modern weapons. One of the guards had a distinctly bulky helmet, likely one with a radio headset.

I handed the night scope to Nate. Whispered in his ear. He nodded, watched the cage intently for a quarter hour or so and then handed it back.

"Just a cage." He whispered in my ear. "Fifteen yards from cover. I can be there in one and a half hours. It will take all horses. Attack then. Leave you afoot. Run south by east to the river."

"Go." Was all I said.

ALENA 42

The Hanse had an effective mix of transport modes. Jitneys, trains, airplane and orbital shuttles. Each mode had disincentives. You did not jitney if you could walk the distance in a quarter hour. If you were traveling a hundred kilometers you used a train. Two thousand kilometers might require an airplane. Orbital shuttles, they were not used so much for point to point rather than to access the high cities in synchronous orbits. If you used a mode unmindful of your Communitarian responsibility, it cost you. Not only did it cost money-credits but, there would always be a little article in the local single sheet taking you to task for unnecessary travel. Names, dates and places all in big type on the front page.

We were on the edge of respectability with the trip to Tinroll. It was at the far corner of the Low-Wiscon canton, more than three hundred kilometers from the Dels where we crossed over. Instead of a jitney, we should have embarked on a train, but we needed the time.

The bank point had delivered my comtel before I shut it down. With it I began to establish a reason for Barbara to come to the Hanse from AngTerra via the 'Zeme.

First, I booked an appointment for Barbara at a hospice on the Gulf coast, which caused no end of fuss with Barbara. After I convinced her that the Hanse 'hospice' was a synonym for the AngTerran hospital, I went on to book an overnight car for two to the hospice and to hire me as a guide.

A guide being one of the semi-respectable jobs I held. What my social index classified me was over educated, under socialized, and on the loose. A Maifliege or Mayfly. It made the rather Rootless and scantly recorded state of my illegal identity classifiable to the Hanse database keepers. If I had been legended as a Karrieremachers, this cultures equivalent to AngTerra's Salaryman, in a well-organized urbs, the Social Police Ferrets would have been running up my pantlegs. But a broken scholar, living off the common roll and what jobs she could eke out, while existing so delightfully irresponsibly? If my index did not exist, the database would have to have me invented as a cautionary tale to the rest of the urbs. Most of the penny dreadful sheets were full of wild Maifliege being socialized by earnest Karrieremachers, when they were not full of earnest Karrieremachers being seduced by wicked Maifliege. The truth was, many, if not most urban Hanse spent a season or two as mayflies. Only the rustic and the over coddled went straight from the university to the steelyard or the counting house.

At Tinroll, there was a major train nexus, an airway hub and a landing pool for an SSO shuttle. It was a very busy place, even by AngTerran standards. There was a Ford there as well, which was central to my plans. We rolled up to the concourse. I got Barbara out and into the high atrium. I had her go to the transients' lounge and change her clothes while I drew three sets of currency from three different bank points. Each time I stayed under the magic number that should attract the attention of a human teller, since I was drawing different local currencies the amounts did not add together even though they were all convertible into Unicredits. Then I purchased a suitable set of clothing for who I was and changed in a different lounge from where Barbara was.

After all this I had an hour to waste. On that hour a non-stop train from the western coast, a heavy aerodyne from Eurasia and an orbital drop would all arrive. In the forty minutes it would take to unload all of those arrivals, the local population of Tinroll would rise ten times over. That was the hurly-burly I intended to slip Barbara through.

I walked through the high bay, watching the Hanse idle away their time. Most of the sub-Karee were studying on mobile terminals or reading uplifting manysheets. The Kareemacher class, 'on whose backs the whole commons rested', were catching a bit of lunch or a nap between transports. I drifted through packs of Maifliege, some dressed in bright motley and some in acid washed greens, depending on their roles in the game. I wore the motley, face paint and all. By the rules, Motleys, were allowed a great deal of variance. In both how the fools behaved and how they were costumed; any mistakes I made as a Citizen would be written off to my social role. As a melancholic green I would have had less windage.

Twice I saw what had to be pairs of Ferrets, interrogating Sojourners. They were looking for something in particular, going through the identity fiche a Sojourner was required by law to carry. Each time I spotted them I casually changed my direction of drift. Even as a citizen, it was not a good idea to come to the notice of the SozPols. They had an off the wire data system that relied greatly on the human observer. And on human prejudices too. SozPols did not care much for Maifliege or Sojourners, considering both to be imperfections in the 'crystal' that was the Commons of the Hanse.

It was when I saw four Crows, KrimPol officers, frog marching Hutton Major through the concourse that I began to worry.

Hutton was one of the Madgji lineage, noted more for his ability to judge and blend coffee roasts than for any gift of intrigue. But he was a Madgji and in good standing within the critical path Madgji. To see him here, in the concourse and getting roughed up meant that there were more adept Madgji scions lurking under the eaves. I found an empty table at an alfresco restaurant, ordered a drink and a pastry and began to seriously count the Crows.

They were thick in the crowds waiting to embark on the aerodynes to the coasts, less thick at the holding lounges for the trains and not evident at all at the gate to the SSO shuttle. What the crows were doing was letting the SozPols flush quarry into their nets, or if the SozPols actually rolled up something interesting, then the Crows took over. In either case, what the Crows were looking for were Sojourners. Or Sojourners passing as Citizens. Interesting.

"A moment of your attention, Citizen."

I looked up to see a pair of Ferrets. I had sat too long over my pastry, an Maifliege still was an Maifliege up to no good. I decided to be arrogant. I looked them up and down, flicked a crumb in their general direction. Then I looked away. "You have had your moment, good day."

"We should like to…"

"Are you proposing an indiscreet act?"

"You misconstrue our intention..."

"I do, then why do you always speak in multiples? Or are you infested?"

One of them struck me, bless him. I saw the blow coming and let my head snap back with it. Then I stood and shrieked at the top of my lungs. Pointing at the one who'd slapped me, with my other hand covering my smeared face paint. Screaming for the Crows to aid me.

Other Maifliege and even some Citizens came to gawk. I was shortly standing on top of a table and begging the onlookers to summon the Kriminal Police to rescue me from these perverts and thugs. The Sozial Ferrets were trying to coax me down from the tabletop, to shut my yap and to shoo off the crowd. Then a quartet of Crows, in their matte black jumpers, trotted up.

I showed them my face, coloring quite nicely under the smeared face paint into a spectacular bruise. I proffered my biometric ID, my 'pass, my reason for being here and that I was sitting at coffee and a pastry, prepaid yet, when these...

The Crows regarded my bruise, marked the smear of paint on the knuckles of the taller ferret, ran the data through the bases. I came up feckless, but no felon. Spoiled perhaps, but no Sojourner Auslander. And they despised Ferrets more than anyone. It being the case that they usually had to back them in 'sanding down' the 'imperfections'. Both Ferrets were assessed demerits then and there and sent to present themselves to their committee of review. I was escorted to the nearest lounge to repair my face and make a complaint to the Concierge for further inquiry.

Which was the transient lounge where Barbara was.

When the system monitors flashed up that the trains had arrived, I ordered a lift chair to the lounge and escorted Dama Corredor to the nearest Documentary Agency cubical.

In forty minutes, under the bored eyes of three Crows, a SozPols Inspector and a quartet of Dai Crossing Wardens, Barbara posted bond. She was not on a watch list, she was obviously sick, a light wash of green face paint will work wonders, and she was being escorted to a known hospice. The Inspector was much more interested in me, since he had a full report of the late unpleasantness. I was kindness itself to Barbara, indignant that they would hold her up even a quarter hour and coldly contemptuous of the Inspector. Once they did a quick check for communicable diseases and sufficient hard money, she was given a wristband and an ID card.

On the way to the train, on the back of a Kriminal Police jitney as a courtesy to Barbara and a lagniappe to me for pissing in the SozPol tea, she leaned up against me. "If I had known I was going to be banded like some bleeding waterfowl..."

"Take heart. For a while there was a proposal to

implant a transponder in all of you" I empathized with a solid poke in her side. "Sojourners, but it was voted down at the Moot." And I tugged at my ear as a caution.

What she said after that was in a form of Spanish I could not begin to follow, but the neck and ears of one of the ever-so-helpful Crows turned a bright pink.

TALLEN 43

I was watching the cage when the first arrow dropped the trooper with the radio helmet. His mate stood up from the small fire he was nursing, took an arrow in his belly, staggered and fell on the fire. I dropped the night scope and picked up the Armbrust. I'd crawled to within a hundred and fifty yards of the transport, where I could be sure of lofting the rocket round into the cargo hold. They had finally unloaded the first ATV and a man-high stack of boxes. They were slowly backing another, bigger still, ATV down the ramp.

I lined the rear of the vehicle up in the sight of the launcher. The Greater Dragon flared to life within me, its aura swirling about me. I could sense the threads of some of the men in the camp before me, some waking, some still fast asleep. I swept my immediate area. The last pair of picket riders had passed behind me a quarter hour ago, the next were due. I was still clear and secure.

I fired the recoilless launcher at the squared off back of the ATV. Just like something kept drawing my hand to the Armbrust launcher, something drew my eye to the rear of the ATVs. I guess I figured anything with that much in the way of cautionary flags couldn't be happy about getting an anti-tank round up the skirt.

The Armbrust functioned as advertised. Not much more of a pop than a .22 short. Hit the back of the ATV with a helluva high whap-crack and the back of the aircraft filled with a white fog when the ATVs rear deck broke apart like a dropped china plate. Then a blue white fireball burst, burning through the side of the transport like hot coals through rice paper. The fuel tanks in the wings ripped open, spewing a black and orange curtain of smoke and fire, drenching the supplies stacked under the wings. The rest of the ATVs exploded with a single crushing blast, sending a shockwave of flame rolling up the hollow.

I buried my face behind the launcher, smelled its plastic starting to burn, smelled the grass burning all around me and my clothing smoldering. I rolled downhill away from the flames into a creek. The firestorm had rolled over my position, raining dribbles of flames and white-hot aluminum scraps. I had lost the night scope, the Mini-14 as well. I was deaf. My nose and ears were wet, likely bleeding from the concussion, and my pants were wet. Hopefully wet from dousing in the creek. The creek bed was a pool of darkness in a sea of smoke and crackling patches of flames that were starting to grow together. I looked towards the landing strip once, then made the rest of my escape from that small patch of hell with my eyes shut and using the perceptions the Greater Dragon brought me. The entire plane, the Overlander and all the ATVs were burning like magnesium in an oxygen blow. Blue white pillars of flame into the early morning dark. There were fires all over the campground, where the nylon tents had been. Like burning moth cocoons, glowing in the smoke.

I ran into a troop of Kikuza horsemen, racking over the high ridge to the south. The first one knocked me flying with his horse, then tried to follow up with a lance. I think he got in the way of someone else. I felt more than heard one of those damn drillings let off and the horse changed directions abruptly. I had a flash bang and a smoker left. I triggered both of them and hit the dirt. I let the Dragon take me then, dancing among the confusion with my eyes closed, in a game of blind man's death.

When I am the Dragon I have to be in reach of my enemies. At full force the Dragon's aura leaves deep slashes in flesh and a rapidly spreading burn through in the Subtle fields. The marks of an Imperial Dragon's Talons, in a poetic turn of phrase. Full force also burnt the hell out of my fingertips, leaving bone showing if I wasn't cautious. There is always a price.

I raked the horse first, every time. I'm fast and tough when I wear the Dragon's cowl but getting run over by a fifteen-hundred-pound horse is still beyond me. I drop the horse. Cripple it or kill it. Horse down, man down. I hunted for the auric bodies glowing with all the primary colors of fear and rage. The horses knew I was alien. An enemy and tried to attack me even in the blinding smoke or the after glare of the flash grenade. But they were hampered by their riders, caught in the crossfire or just plain confused. The Kikuza troopers were even more disoriented. Four of them were shot down by friendly fire. Out of the eight that had stumbled onto me, six were dead before the smoke grenade quit generating smoke. One tried to escape but, he ran directly past me. The other was tangled in the stirrups when his horse went down. He scrambled out and snatched a saber from his saddle bow, slashing around desperately in the middle of the smoke.

I busied myself with giving 'mercy' to the horses I'd crippled. Staying out the swordsman's reach. Then he staggered, turning his ankle on a drilling. I stepped in close behind him and poleaxed him down with a slash through his Subtle body. And I was careful with the Talons of the Dragon. My hands hurt, but they weren't shredded like they were in Canon City.

I dragged my prize over to one of the dead horses.

Draped him face down across the barrel of the horse to keep him from drowning on his own spit and settled in to wait for full daylight. I could hear again, though my ears were ringing. The grass fires had burnt out once they got outside of the shallow bowl the camp and landing strip had nestled in. Dark smoke rolled out of the bowl and swept southeast over the ridge. Smelling of plastics, metal, and burnt pork.

One of the horses provided me with a sack of rice cakes and an AK along with three magazines. I ate all the rice cakes and a raw chunk of horse rolled in the wasabi paste they all carried. My belt was loose again, and all my foodstuffs had gone off with Dockens. I looked over the sword my prisoner had been slashing about with and waited. Either the local commander would rally the survivors and mount a sweep with his remaining horses or, it was a total rout, and this had been the largest unit surviving. Either way this was as good a spot as any to await developments.

I got up and went through the pockets of the dead. Plundered the saddle bags. More rice cakes, some vacuum packed and irradiated fish, cartridges for both 5x45 Russian and local drillings, odd tools and the occasional newspaper were most of what I found. My prize was a nominal Major in the House military arm. If I read the kanji printing on his pay book right. He had a sidearm of 9mm caliber, extra magazines, a purse full of coins, tin of mints, a pocket knife, a first aid kit and a pack of cigarettes. When I rolled him over, to go through his blouse pockets, he was conscious.

I told him good morning, in gutter Japanese, and went on with my search.

"I am worth…much" He gasped out in what passed for English on this side of the Veil, one hand trying to pluck at my ragged sleeve.

I was impressed. I unsnapped his pockets. He shouldn't have been able to wiggle a finger, let alone grab at me. What I'd done to him with the auras was much like sticking a scalpel into his spine at C4. My version of paralysis ought to wear off in a month or so, unlike what you'd get with the scalpel, but still and all he should be as limp as a rag dolly. He had a map in the right-hand pocket, notebook in the left pocket.

I ripped open his tunic and checked him for a belly band. Back when I was hunting Kempetai and regular Imperial Officers through Manchuria I learned they kept a lot of contraband in the corset they wrapped about their lower abdomens. Money, documents, knives and even a few derringers were found strapped to them.

This one had a packet of photographs, instant photos. Trophies.

"Much white metal. Help me."

I looked up from the pictures and smiled. All around us the blowflies and face flies crisped out of the air and I could smell ozone so sharp it should have made your nose bleed. I held his eyes with mine until he knew. Until he began to cry. I reached out with my Subtle hands and cupped his Centers one by one. Peeling away the film most people live with.

When the Jurchen had no Dragons living among them, they called their war leaders Snakes. Don't ask why. I don't know. I don't know why the diplomats and spymasters were married women, the best cooks were single men, or all the horse doctors were women past child bearing age. It just was. The Snake was the name for the warrior who commanded the Household Horse. He did not initiate any plans. Strategy was not his role. Snakes did just what the Eldest Sister of the Eldest Brother told them to do, with no fuss, no hesitation and no scruples. Any person capable of acquiring the arts of the Lesser Dragon, and those arts were not beyond a healthy human with a bit of persistence, could become a Snake.

Dragons were more, much more.

They commanded the inner and the outer Yards. They could overrule the Sisters of the House of War and they held the High and the Low justice. On the robes I wore at formal occasions there was embroidered a rampant Manchu Dragon with a broadaxe in one clawed fist and a barbed whip in the other. There was a blue knob at the crest of the beanie I was supposed to wear when I was trotting about in my Dragon robes. This indicated I was of high rank, a gentleman and a judge. I was pulling my trousers on only one leg at a time but, I ranked up there with the Elect.

And the foremost reason for this rank was the thing I was about to do to the Major. It was not the killing, anyone can kill.

I gripped his shaven head in both my hands and summoned the Dragon up the shaft of my spine again. My breathing slowed. Deepened. My heartbeat slowed, as well, and beat in time with my breathing. Sounds became clearer. Louder. Then overwhelming. Until I willed my ears to cease hearing. I could see Northern Lights dancing faintly on the horizon. I looked down at the man between my knees. The pores of his skin were plain, and I saw his pulse beating in his neck. Auras became luminous to my sight, both his aura and mine. His was a volcanic red, veined with black channels and gray webs that faded in and out of focus. The gray showing the damage I'd done earlier. If I was concerned at all with his future, I'd be working at knitting up the gray webs. Instead, I slowly extended a hook fashioned out of my own auras, curling it about the index finger of my right hand. With a gesture, peeled another strip clean away from his Subtle body. It flashed to gray smoke and drifted away, like a puff of blood in moonlit water. It hurt much like being skinned with a dull knife and pliers, or so I was told.

I smelled piss. I leaned forward and looked into his eyes. His eyelids peeled back by my thumbs, tears slicking his cheeks and snot beginning to bubble in his nose. I let my aura coil about his head, filling the space between us, settling into the wounds I had exposed. The Dragon broke through the shell of his Subtle body, traveling down his spine and the glowing Kundalini paths to the seat of his being. While his auras crackled and burned through like film before an arc lamp, I sifted through his life. Like a miner sorting gravel with a screen. Looking for nuggets among the sand. His Subtle body vanished, the energies evaporating into the flow about us, or being sucked down by my own cobalt blue banners. But before he passed beyond whatever hell I could put him through, I had his memories as clear as if they were recorded on film. Clearer than the instant photos I'd found in his girdle.

I stepped away from the husk that had been Force Major Saburo, wiping the slickness from my hands with grass. I picked up the AK and walked up the slope of the ridge, forcing Saburo's images to the background. I'd liberated a fair set of binoculars and I started sweeping the horizon with them.

For the last month the Kikuza, according to the late Major, were engaged in search and suppress sweeps through the plains, looking for 'unreliable' Mihaly or allied folk. Ensuring that there was to be no refuge for the Mihaly among the irregular Houses of the plains by the simple method of killing off the irregulars.

Saburo had a vague notion that the Plains Houses were small, disorganized packs of nomads, that could be put down by a disciplined company. The four or five harvesting bands they had encountered had died hard, but not hard enough to make a difference in his opinion. The Kikuza were well armed, carried short range radios and could call for a very limited air support. The people of the high plains had those damned drillings, lived with their horses and worshiped the buffalo the Kikuza were killing.

The camp I'd burned off had been a three-horsetail rendezvous, two hundred troopers. The landing strip was one of only three safe supply points deep in the Empty Grass. Points that could accommodate the heavy cargo aircraft and that were isolated enough to avoid casual discovery by the Confederated Houses. The Koshitsu House Cavalry was using horses for the combat teams, the ATVs as mechanized pack mules and, by occasionally rendezvousing with the other teams for bulk re-supply, they could avoid the problems of fixed base operations.

The ATVs were experimental items. Made with mesh-reinforced composites and powered by a fuel cell arrangement. The mesh made them proof against anything under 12mm, fifty-caliber in my numbers. The fuel cells made them damn near as independent as the horses. The fuel cells fed off of a super-compressed magnesium alloy tank of gelled liquid hydrogen, wrapped in insulation and composite armor, also proof against anything under 20mm. The big tanker was supposed to be a milk cow, feeding the little ATVs and reducing the need for more frequent resupply operations.

I think my little anti-tank round ruptured the tanker's armor and the shock flash-vented the hydrogen to atmosphere while its shaped charge ignited the magnesium. Why the other ATVs went up so spectacularly, I couldn't rightly say. I've read liquid hydrogen is chancy stuff.

There had been other glitches in other operations. Radios that didn't work right, ammo mismatches and just plain getting lost. Once they had a transport go down in a thunderstorm. Clipped by a down burst, Saburo had thought. As their other light transport was laid up with an engine off line, they had to commandeer several Overlanders to make the less critical supply runs.

The 'other' transport. "Oh, my." I said to the dead Major.

I looked to the north and the dark pillar of smoke that still punched into the blue autumn sky. This was going to severely impact the plans of the House Koshitsu. And I wasn't half trying.

ALENA 44

The hospice had a jitney waiting for us at the station, which was thirty of their long miles away from the sea. The hospice itself was closer to the Gulf but, the high-speed trains were not well suited to enduring direct hurricanes. The jitney was piloted, and since I had suspected the train suite was bugged as well, we had not had a chance to get straight our stories before we arrived at the hospice.

"Dama Corredor, do you have the letter of credit I am to present to the Terrilured Banc Gmbh.

"In the black valise, outer pocket." She swayed and leaned on me. "I fear I may have waited too long..." She rested her head on my shoulder and whispered in my ear. "I just slipped you my last piece. If it all goes to hell, don't look back. Don't try to raise forces here. Get back to him and let him go a-helling through the borders."

I patted her hand. "I am sure they will see you right, Dama." I helped her out of the low contraption and walked her up the short path to the intaking foyer. It took twenty minutes of bureaucracy, coin changing and general chit chat before they took responsibility of Barbara. Her thumb and DNA on the contract, as the patient. My thumb and DNA, as agent of the guarantors, and their corporate thumb and DNA. Now if anything happened to her under their care, from breaking her fool neck on a wet patch of tile to a strike from orbit, they were responsible. Of course, if the guarantors defaulted on the remainder of the funds…

I left after another half hour of courtesies. She looked very fragile and very much alone in the suite. I got clear of the door and walked to a jitney stop a half-mile towards the ocean.

I had a shadow all the way there. She was not particularly clumsy about it, but I was waiting for one to appear. She was Madgji of course. Not of the lineage, she did not have the look, but she was from the 'Zeme and not bred in the Hanse commons. She walked to cover ground, ignoring any overtures from the idlers on the path. I, on the other hand, strolled down the paths to the jitney like any Hanse Boulevardier, gifted with all the time in the world. I flirted with some and coldly rebuffed others. Walked arm in arm with a Soldatmachen from the colonies who tried to enlist me in her company. Got on the jitney with the Soldatmachen just as a rain squall swept inland from the beach. Next stop was back at the railhead. The next step was to present myself at a bank. My shadow was a jitney back and very damp.

She followed me all the way to Gewinnville, sitting in the same commons on the train. At the nexus, the change all for the local rails or to uplink to a transcontinental rail, she was removed from the commons by the Crows. Some sort of document irregularity according to a Sozpol's running commentary as he gawked at the fuss. I shrugged and exited the train. Swept through the concourse shops and went into the women's lounge a proper Maifliege. Exited twenty minutes later a well-dressed person of mercantilism. I got on a transcontinental maglift, passing through two gauntlets of Sozpols sorting Maiflieges, then settled into my private compartment for the six-hour run to the Northern Lake Metropoles.

Once there, I simply walked into the regional office for the TBC and asked for an account manager. What should have taken only thirty minutes took better than two hours and a blood sacrifice but, at the end of that I was House Mihaly in presence.

My mistake was to use a Regional office, instead of a Cantonal office. There were maybe fifteen Regional offices for any major player in the Banking game but, within each Region there were between five and fifty Cantonal centers. Anyone trying to cover the lot would have had to deploy close to four thousand agents or teams of agents. They did what I would have done, and should have thought of, in their place. They set flags at the Cantonal offices and placed agents at the Regional offices.

It should not have made a difference. We supposedly owned the bank absolute. That meant that its security and management should have been mine to command from the time I identified myself. Instead there was a longish wait in the open foyer, a shorter wait with refreshments in a lounge of the TBC and then a short, armed, escort through a security wicket to the Names Account Manager's office. At each delay I wondered if things were happening behind the stage as it were.

When I was ushered into the presence of the account manager, I no longer wondered. I knew there was a problem. He was not one of the listed managers. "Good afternoon, Dama Mihaly, I am Dom Irby. How may we help you?" This was not the reaction of an employee. He was trying for distance and showing fear.

"Irby. And where is Dom Stiffelman? He was the manager we dealt with beforehand." I sat the chair where I could keep the edge of my vision on the door I had entered by. I slipped my weak hand into my carry sack's holster. I had obtained, in the six-hour run to this office, a legal Hanse milieu weapon. Sealed to my palms, tagged and monitored by the Concierge system. It was not a big gun. It would not penetrate Crow armor and its firing chip could be suppressed by Crow jammers. But, the existence of it would explain to the Concierge Expert Systems why I was carrying a weapon. Needless to say, the gun I had my hands on was not the Hanse milieu example.

"He is no longer at this office, I have assumed his portfolio."

I smiled. "How very odd. I shall have to call upon him later." I tapped on the glass table top with a data wand and his eyes grew big as saucers, not hearing the safety snap in the carry sack. "This needs to be swept and then linked to your systems. Please do so." I held it, just out of easy reach. As he stood to take it from my hand, I felt the air change slightly as the door opened.

I stood, dropping the wand into his hand, two stepped to my weak side and dropped to the floor. Kicking the chair over to mask me slightly. Two persons were trying to come through the door at the same time. Both armed and trying to get a clear shot at me. Their guns were proscribed needlers, smuggled from my milieu, lethally tipped and propelled by a captive cylinder. The needles would cut through ballistic cloth, most leather and a good half inch of soft wood but, they were no louder than a 35mm camera shutter.

They fired a hundred rounds, into the desk, into the wall behind the manager, shredding his binders in the book rack at the side of the desk and ripping open the chair he had been sitting in. Some exploded with hot, bright pops that sent tufts of stuffing or paper into the air. Others burned holes in their targets or left spreading stains.

Selai loads. I was so very honored.

My gun was not as elegant, nor as discreet. I took the nearside one first. Double tapping him in the upper chest. He went down but, more from surprise and fear than from any harm my bullets did. The body armor translated my bullets into blunt trauma, painful but not a killing stroke. His partner flinched back behind the door frame and thrust his hand around to spray the room blindly with more needles. He also exposed his knee. I put two rounds through it, then changed my position to gain a bit more cover from the desk. I also gained a sight on the manager, who was curled into a ball in the knee well clutching the data wand.

The gunman on the floor had back stroked through the door as well. His needler abandoned on the carpet. I heard more needles being fired outside, which implied Hanse involvement, which was distressing.

Then two more attempted to enter the room behind a spray of needles. I double tapped one in the groin, hoping for a bone break or a femoral artery hit and was rewarded by a heartfelt curse and a lot of blood. He spun on his good leg and fell back through the door. His partner was much faster and slightly better trained. Which was the cause of her death, I think. She shot up my empty chair, the corner I should have used to cover the door, then executed a perfect forward roll towards cover to the left of the door, while her partner and I were exchanging fire. She swung her gun to cover me, her eyes flashing over the small blue pistol and squeezed the trigger plate. Which beeped to signal empty.

I shot her in the face, twice. Ejected the magazine, hit the panic button under the desk top that slammed the door shut and locked down the room. Then I slipped a new magazine in my gun.

I pulled the manager out from under the desk, inserted the real data wand into the reader.

Five keystrokes with the wand in the reader and I was rooted in the computer systems. First, I locked down all the interior doors and called the Crows, reporting a major crime. I opened an unlimited draw to the benefit of Barbara. Keyed in a deadman clause, sending all of our resources to several allied Houses upon my death and sealed it. Then I took a deep breath, smelling blood, burnt wool and hot metal.

The manager was crouching by the door, holding a chair in front of his face. In my left hand was my pistol, pointed loosely in his direction. "Pity about your friend here." I carefully nudged the dead woman's gun within my reach, knelt and picked it up with my free hand. "Did you think you could pass her as me, or were you waiting for a closer match to the Path?"

She might have been a Mihaly cast off. She had the bones for it although the hair was not quite right. Outside I heard excitement and someone tried the door, first with a key and then with a kick. I triggered the internal defenses, tear gas and fire foam by the labels. Herr Irby tried to stand, and I cautioned him with my pistol.

The building shook. The lights above us flickered and dimmed then came back up. Outside I could hear a sudden chatter of light weapons then a bullhorn shouting orders. Another chatter overridden by heavy weapons fire. Then silence.

The communications panel chimed. I answered it. "Yes."

"This is the Kriminalpoliz, Kommander Garsia speaking. You are holding hostages?"

"A suspect. You will need to contact the Office of External Affairs, Kommander."

"And why?"

"I am Mihaly. The Mihaly niMihaly."

"You hold a Hanse citizen hostage."

"He is evidence that Hanse and transient forces were conspiring against the good order of the Commons, subverting the transfer of office, engaging in cross portal mercenary operations, attempting to murder the heir and holder of the House Mihaly, namely me, and conspiring to commit bank fraud." If nothing else, the bank fraud charge would get their attention.

"I see. And your situation is currently?"

"Awaiting developments. I trust you will presently secure the outer offices?"

"May I speak to Herr Irby?"

"Why not." I motioned to Irby to bring his chair and sit close by the communications panel. "He is here, feel free to converse."

"Herr Irby..." And the Crow Garsia launched into a torrent of high-status Hanse. I could have followed it, but I did not bother. Either I was shortly to become the problem of the Xternen de AngelegenheitenBüro, or I would shortly be dead at the hand of a domesticated Crow. In either case this ivory's pass was done. I let the hammer of the pistol down and waited, twirling the seal in my freehand. My eyes resolutely fixed on my victim. I wiped at my face with my sleeve, my eyes open.

I wondered if I could get a night's sleep in something that was not moving…

TALLEN 45

I moved off about a thousand yards from the hollow where I cracked open Major Saburo. Snuggled into a hide, just under the crest of a ridge overlooking that hollow and settled in for the day. If Nate had gotten away before I blew everything the hell up, he was going to make for a river south east of here. I did not like my prospects of trotting off cross country in the day, with a pillar of smoke drawing everyone's attention. Night would be better, even if they had infrared cameras. Cold Walking, an art the Rinpoche taught me as a moral exercise back when a Bakelite telephone was high tech. With practice, even with moderate exertion, I didn't show up in the IR scanners.

It had driven the techs crazy.

I wanted to do some thinking anyway. Lying in a shallow grave watching the scavengers gather was always conducive to mediation.

When you sift a mind, you have ghosts in your head for a while. The more radical the sifting, the sturdier the ghosts. There are several different ways to lay the ghost but, the way that always worked best for me was to talk to it. Debrief it in other words.

I settled in and began to talk to Matsui Saburo, late of the House Koshitsu.

Saburo was new come across the mountains, having spent the last five years as a Nachi on the West Coast.

On the coast you had five basic flavors.

You had the Jingai, who were basically all of the non-Koshitsu populations left over from the Settlement. The Settlement was when the House Koshitsu and allies came down the coast from what is British Columbia in my world and consolidated the minor Houses between the mountains and the sea. Sort of a land rush with the odd atrocity thrown in. From what I gathered the Settlement had occurred about 1930 our time. Saburo still kept time by the reign year and his Emperor was not the one in my world but, the numbers were close.

There were the Sansei, third generation of the settlers. All still 'pure' and unmixed with the Jingai, but rustic all the same. In Saburo's opinion the Sansei were beginning to have a worrying number of Anioko children, half Jingai, half Nipponese. The fourth generation.

You had Kibei. These were second generation settlers who had been enriched by spending most of their education in the Home Islands. Very reliable but somewhat colonial still.

Then there were the Issei and Nachi. Issei were first generational settlers, fresh come from the Homelands. Issei planned on staying, while the Nachi were here for a tour of duty before returning covered in glory to the Homelands. Both sets were extremely 'reliable'. Which meant to our Saburo that they could be relied on to do whatever the Koshitsu asked, without any sort of hesitation.

Matsui Saburo was a Nachi. Officially he was just another officer being rotated through the Imperial Army colonial forces, for training and seasoning. He was nominally a Shosa, equivalent to a Major in the western system, commanding a demi-battalion of mechanized infantry in the local Imperial Army establishment. Unofficially he and his half battalion were at the beck and call of the Kempeitai. Acting as a reliable back up to the paramilitary Police forces. Forming a quick reaction force against any incursion by the 'degenerate' Houses in the Sierras and finally, as coup arrestors inside the Imperial Army.

Then, just as his tour was nearly over and rotation back to the "pure land" beckoned, he got tapped to command a 'discreet' operation on the dry side of the Rockies.

Someone in the 'black' side of the Ministry of Information had acquired assets among one of the stronger Houses of the Degenerate Dai. If the current lineage could be removed and the assets 'restored to their rightful place' then there would be a door opened to the Southern Plains. So, it was proposed and so, it was done. Almost.

The lineage was not quite strong enough, so volunteers were rushed across the passes under the command of a Medji Force Leader. The Medji was found with his throat cut and three quarters of the volunteers, a ragbag mix of Jingai and Anioko, had vanished into the chaos of the dry side. So Eddiko-Tokyo, required that another force be volunteered, with a very 'reliable' Nachi officer in command. Since the operations were to be as low profile as possible, the officer had to have a firm grasp of horsemanship as well as Sanko-Sakusen operations. I recognized that term when it came floating up. It literally translated as three lights. It referred to the Chinese idiom of light equaling thoroughness. Thoroughness in killing, looting, and burning. They ran a company of Imperial light infantry through a quick course in staying on a horse and rounded up every Sansei Militia who had horses in their dossier and sent them over the passes as Medji auxiliaries to link up with the Mihaly Loyalist forces.

Saburo's first order of business, even before linking up with his Mihaly employers, had been to wipe out all the small stations and villages on the dry side of the Divide along with any visible remnants of the first Koshitsu force. Then, having suitably impressed the locals, he linked up with the Loyal Mihaly and proceeded to outline his vision of prosperity and a properly ordered society on the dry side.

Three quarters or better of the Loyal Mihaly decamped before the next dawn, along with their horses and families. The ones that didn't go north to the other Mountain Houses, rode east into the plains and settled among the Pika.

At great cost, with much howling about the expenses and more howling about who was in command, a trio of rare short-takeoff and landing cargo aircraft airlifted another mixed force of Imperials and Sansei troopers over the mountains. The passes being closed by a recent series of extraordinary out of season avalanches.

Induced by gelignite I would suspect.

Two of the aircraft landed safely at Manitou Springs. The third, with most of the command stick, never appeared. So Major Saburo was the senior commander of an over strength company of awkward but very reliable home island Naichi, three-week-wonder dragoons, leavening a reinforced battalion of West Coast Sansei Koshitsu, who were to stiffen Mihaly Medji and Loyalist cavalry.

I almost felt sorry for the bastard. Imagine having Coldstream Guardsmen reinforce Irish Wild Geese Dragoons to stiffen Indian Sepoys. Courts Martial every morning before breakfast and duels after supper in the mess.

No wonder the pickets had been jokes.

They were either Dragoons, who were doing well to stay on the horse, or they were Loyalist Mihaly, who weren't particularly loyal. The Sansei were more reliable than the Mihaly, but they were not as 'steady' as the troopers fresh come from the inner lands. Which meant that the Sansei were likely deserting like the Loyal Mihaly, just not as often.

Saburo had lost better than five percent of the Sansei

to unknown causes, and I didn't think that was all casual bloodletting in the alleys. Even though no one likes Flowers, a lot of the Sansei could blend right in among the Pika.

Though after the details of Sanko-Sakusen gets out I thought it would be unlikely that any one who couldn't pass as a dry sider would survive to desert.

I began to regret having killed the unesteemed Major, being as unsuited for his current posting as he was.

Saburo had been working the Near Rim for the last forty years or so. Helping the Dai Nihon's preeminent House 'rationalize' all the Dai Nihon Houses and Organizations, other than governmental. Sometimes he was a diplomat, sometimes a thug, and always 'faithful unto death' to the Chrysanthemum throne in its dust ups with the rest of the world. He had gotten very used to being backstopped by overwhelming force. He tended to see atrocity as simply a quick means to get the attention of a subject class or nation. Not as the way to wake a resistance movement.

Saburo, the ghost, began to fade about the time a propeller driven aircraft throbbed overhead. It circled the smoke, dropped some paras, then made some very low-level orbits about the landing strip and the burning cargo plane.

It spotted the little dell where I butchered Major Saburo's escort. Circled it several times. Then rotated its wings up to make a vertical landing on the hill to the south of the dell. Just before it would have touched down a fire-team jumped out of the rear door and dashed down the hill. Checking each of the bodies.

I'd figured that the Major had a GPS gadget on him somewhere and that the Kikuza high command would come looking for his ass, one way or the other. Between the massive loss of the big cargo airplane and almost all the troops, they would have had a serious come-a-part. Either Saburo was honorably dead or he was about to die at their hands. Either way they were going to come looking for him.

I had decided to ratchet things up a notch in the war for hearts and minds. I'd left the dishonorable Major arched over the horse but, I'd done a little embellishment of the scene. I'd stripped him to the buff and using my finger wrote the kanji for Dragon into his skin. The auras leaving a very dark welt deep in the flesh. Then I'd taken off his head the hard way, with a dulled knife and stuck it on a lance. Then left his broken sword beneath his grinning skinless head.

Judging from the excitement I could see around the dell, they had found the hapless Saburo right off. Also, from the constant strobing of camera flashes, they were going sparrow documenting what they found.

I snuggled back under my cover. Set the Lesser Dragon to overwatching and drifted off to sleep.

After midnight I slipped over the top of the ridge and started sloping off to the south. There was traffic in the air, but I was cold walking and keeping off the skyline as much as I could. Come false dawn I was about eighteen miles south and east of the landing strip. I found a coulee that had an undercut dirt bank sheltered from the north. I wrapped myself in one of the horse blankets I liberated and slept the day away at the base of the undercut. Late in the afternoon I woke up, ate more horsemeat and wasabi I had in my coat pocket, and then I got moving again.

Twice I heard a prop throb off in the distance. Once I could see lights just off the horizon to the northeast, moving fast. But other than those times, all I saw were stars from horizon to horizon, a perfect bowl. I kept at the wolf trot, faster now that I only had my hunger to carry.

Before morning I smelled smoke and coffee. My goddamn coffee. I walked up a crest and saw a small fire off in the distance.

When I walked up on the camp Bigdog came trotting up with a prairie dog in his mouth, dropped it at my feet.

"He's been looking for you."

"And the other one?"

"He's only along for the grub."

"Sounds right. Got any of the coffee left?"

"Pot's over there. Need a cup?"

"I'd like one, yes."

I walked into the camp ring. Counted seven more horses and my Prunty. There were a half dozen blanket rolls scattered about. One sentry on the ridge above the camp. One sitting with Nate.

"We 'bout gave you up."

"It got kind of entertaining there for a bit."

"We got four out of that cage. One was my sister's son." He slapped gently the head of the kid sitting with him. "I thank you, Walking Knife."

"That's thrice you've named me that."

"It's a medicine name." The kid spoke up. "Uncle saw an unsheathed long knife riding tall on a Prunty, with a blue haft and grip, Kikuza heads bound to the breastplate by their ponytails."

"Your turn on watch." Said Dockens.

The kid got up and left, limping slightly. I poured me a cup and waited until he was clear. "I saw five."

He shrugged. "One did not live." His auras belied his disinterest.

"You going to speak for Mihaly?"

"Nearest Tinkerhold is a day to the east. We go there, call in a few long riders and gossipers. A week, maybe three, we have all of the Pika on the warpath. But five weeks maybe ten, Old Man Winter comes to stay and not just visit. Not a lot of time."

"You see the fires?"

He nodded.

"Just about every swinging dick in that holler is burnt to cracklins. The aircraft is junked. All of their transport on the ground is either burnt up or run off. I cut off the head of the officer commanding that half brigade of horse and stuck it on a lance."

"Truly?"

I pitched him a pistol belt, Major Saburo's. "If I'd thought about it, I'd brought his head."

"You put a hell of a crimp in their dick."

"Said I was a different order of pain." I sipped at the

cup. "You going to bring all the Pika to the dance?"

"Said I would."

I unslung the AK I'd been carrying, for proof. "This is what you're going up against. Thirty round magazine, full auto, effective range between a hundred and a hundred fifty paces." I handed it to him.

"Seen 'em before." He turned it over in his hands, rubbing his thumb against the grey matte finish.

"Your drillings won't serve."

"Know that. We have other guns, but any standup fight we will lose. To these clumsy things."

"That long gun you carry, what's its reach?"

"On a good day, six-hundred paces. On a very good day, a thousand yards."

"Truly?" I asked.

He blinked, at first almost affronted, then smiled the slow laugh of a shared joke. "Truly."

"So, you hide well, your ponies trained to lie on their sides. One shot at three hundred paces, two at the most, on a good day of course."

"They leave their dead behind, you know."

"To be expected. And they will try to flank you while their fire teams probe with these toys." I waved my cup at the AK.

"And?"

"You are gone. Away on your ponies and flashing your white tails at them."

"And this is victory?"

"They mount up and rush after. Then your second team shoots from the flank."

"One shot, maybe two." He said thoughtfully. "More like hunting."

"More like being pecked to death by chickens."

"Nothing to sing about. Shooting from hides and running like coyote."

"Ten men holding down two hundred? And rubbing their noses in it? Better than telling stories in the lodges in the cold time."

"Winter can drag on so." He jacked the AK open,

released the magazine and rubbed his finger around the throat of the breech. "Dirty. Careless of their weapons, shameful." He placed the assault rifle on the blanket he was sitting on. "After Grandfather Winter comes to live with us and we sleep in snow camps, in the foothills? They will pull back into the cities out of our reach. Then the passes open in the spring or they lift more of their Flowers across the hills?"

"While you eat and belch away the winter, I'll be hunting in the shadows." And I let the Greater Dragon stir in his sleep. "Their commanders will be headless in their beds. Sentries with their lances run through them from appetite to Kikuza," Black lace began to drift through the air, like an early snow. "Dressed scalps hanging from windowsills. Reliable Mihaly missing their parts," Dockens slowly squirmed away from me, one hand on the long gun at his side and rubbing the other one through the naked earth, trying to rub off some of the lace that had settled on his skin. "Breathing through a tube in their throats because the fronts of their faces are burnt away." I smiled, steam rolling off me in the early evening chill. "And songs…oh there will be songs."

There was a long silence between us.

ALENA 46

It took three hours to get an external affairs functionary on site but after that, things went quickly. The dead woman in the office with me, as well as the three dead in the outer lobby, were determined to be non-citizens. Unregistered and unclaimed. I was fined two, fifty-credit coins each for their disposal. Herr Irby was a citizen, extremely repentant and in deep trouble. The best he could hope for was to find himself bonded to me for life. Other fates included being broken to the helot class, expelled from civil society, civil execution, or the true death.

Being tired of the man, I demanded that he become my indentured bondsman and then had him sent across the Ford to the 'Zeme as my personal banking representative. He actually lasted six local hours before the Madgji had him needled, but they were slow off the mark. Tallen had been a busy little legend on the EmptyGrass. An entire reinforced company and no friendly losses. My, my, my.

A month later the political jackals began to gather. Nathan, the House Mihaly Komornyik for the last three short generations, stuck his head through my office doorway. "The Twelfth Undersecretary to see you, Madam."

"I will have coffee in the solar. Discreetly record visual and sound." I closed my flat pad and tucked it under my arm. Patted my hip where my needle gun resided and took the hall to the solar. I'd had the House reopened, staffed for a long stay by thawing out all of the vetted retainers and hired three separate sticks of mercenaries as external security. Then I started working my way through catalogs.

We had money and agents, both here and abroad in the Sheaf of Worlds. I could not transfer weapons or weaponizing techniques into Tallen's hands but, I could send civilian aid. And authorize activities in other locations.

The Twelfth was a tall woman, ex-military according to the House books. M. Ledhrad. She stood up as I entered, shook my hand once, then sat back down. She was taller than I, by perhaps a foot, with her jet-black hair cut close in ringlets around her head. Her eyes were brown. One drooped slightly as if from a damaged nerve. I crossed the patio and curled up across from her in a double chair, with my pad by me and a fresh carafe of coffee on the table by the chair.

"And the day finds you well?"

"Well enough Madam Mihaly..."

"Mihaly. Mihaly alone is the proper usage."

"Yes. Well there is some question about that usage."

"No question. I have the Bloodseal, the codes and forces in being."

"Perhaps here, but across the line?"

"The last reports indicated that there was heavy fighting, on the plains and in and about Manitou Springs, between House Mihaly and the Madgji-paid agents of the House Koshitsu." I smiled. "A heavy lift craft, two ground transports and more than two hundred troopers killed or wounded? Do you have further news?"

"No. We have, of need, closed all the wickets between your milieu and ours. Someone tried to force the Wicket at Three Rivers, with heavy infantry."

"Not Mihaly," I hoped. That was a very drastic step, fighting in a gate has catastrophic. "we favor less obvious tactics."

"I see. Like your identity here?" That was a sore spot, both the XternBuro and the Crows suspected that we had been manipulating the Concierge.

"Madam Ledhrad, before the eruption on my home line, I had every intention of settling within the Commons." Ledhrad snorted. "Truly. Your cities are immaculate, your people are happy, your trains are reliable and the toilets work, winter or summer."

"Preserve that overripe sentiment for later. Our stud book does say that you were quite out of the running for Holder." She crossed her leg. "They sent me because I once went to the Gaiten, for the XternBuro, and being female I have bit of a resistance to suasion."

She was mistaken about the gender being an aid. "You came across. When, may I ask?" This wasn't in the briefing books. Nor was her association with the XternBuro.

"Two decades ago, in the European zones."

The Commonality of Europe. And they hadn't told us that the Hanse had sent a XternBuro resolution team among them. Pig buggers.

"There were instances of transits that were outside the agreements." She shrugged. "I succeeded in resolving and redressing those instances. Since then, the Greater Circles consider me their Gaiten expert." She made the wry face her culture used to express 'what a load o'shit'.

Gaiten. The Hanse name for the Dai, not quite a curse.

"And on one trip across. An impressive achievement."

She knew us just enough and worse yet knew that she really did not know us at all.

"Thank you. Now then. I have been given white gloves, Freehands. Your bank is restricted. Your links to the computer nets are being run through three sets of filters, two Enhanced Electronica's, one human, none of which involve the possibly compromised Concierge. After the unfortunate Herr Irby's example, none of your retainers or employees will be allowed to approach any of the approved gates."

"And Madam Corredor?"

"She is improving. A more detailed prospectus will arrive by the evening post. She arrived in time for the cancer to be stopped." She looked to her cup. Poured. "She is very vocal about seeing you." She smiled into her cup. "I have learned new exquisitely obscene constructs in several dialects."

"The last time I ventured abroad..."

She sighed. "We did not consider it a possibility that someone would suborn one of the uniformed police."

"Have you determined the hold they had on him?"

"He barely survived the attempt upon you, and then the Kriminalpoliz interrogation finished it. But we think it was one of the Hegemonic forces from the 'Zeme."

"My source indicates it was Koshitsu."

"Our sources lay the corpse at the feet of Koshitsu, the Commonality of Europe and the Southern Cross in equal and absurd portions." She looked up and met me, eye to eye. "If it were not for the biologicals, for the occasional artifacts and the ever-constant gold. I would press for a permanent closure of all the wickets to your milieu."

"We threaten you."

"You... disturb us. Each year the numbers grow. People choose to leave the Common Land. They never complete their gymnaos, or they agree to have their learning blocked, to stay within the boundaries. They leave and never return. Their lines end at the doors to your gates."

"Most do not stay with us."

"No," She made a crooked smile. "they are used to warm toilets. But they pass beyond. And the ones left behind, each year they linger a little longer as Mayflies or the Green Brethren before they become members of the Common Land. Some drift so far from us, they never become of the Common Land, only dwelling among us."

"You prosper from our trade."

"We could prosper as well without it. And before you raise the simile of gates as vents, we have six off world colonies for the more adventurous to emigrate to."

"There were seven once."

"Yes. Before your presence was known widely. The seventh colony failed after the legends of the Elf Hills were made true. I think you are a poisoned chalice, quite beautiful and thirst quenching, but poisoned nonetheless."

I sat back in my chair and looked at her, my mouth quite open. "And your opinion is well known throughout the Over-government?" I had visions of having to close two hundred Fords in the western hemisphere alone or mounting enormous covert crossings.

"My opinion is known only to my cat, to make it known to anyone else would send me straightaway to either a Waysmoother or a post in the Arctic Circle." She sat the cup and saucer down upon the table by her chair. "Although now having emptied my heart, in front of the Dieu knows how many recording devices, I might as well be shouting it on the corners every Sunday morning."

"Well, I certainly will not be passing this on to any of your fellows." I picked up my flat pad. "It might give them ideas." I keyed in an address and sent off a short message to someone I had been avoiding. I saw her start to stand out of the corner of my eye. "Please do not leave."

"I have..."

"Please. Stay. The Mihaly requests your attendance at lunch. Nathan!" I raised my voice to a horse stopping shout. I heard crockery smash in the next hall and his moon face came around the door jamb with a large gun barrel indiscreetly at the ready. "Three for lunch, two bottles and detail someone to spring Madam Corredor for an evening parole."

"Yes Mihaly"

I returned my attention to Ledhrad. "Sit. If I cannot go around you, then I will have to enlist you." I raised a hand to her indignation. "Not suborn you, nor will I offer a bribe. I need to get back to the 'Zeme. I need to move assets from the Common Land to other venues and send aid to my rear guard. You need to get me out of your hair. Let us explore possibilities."

She sat.

TALLEN 47

Flann was my minder, the second one I got issued. I had a minder since neither Nate nor the elders of the Pika really trusted me any further than a shotgun throws. Even though Nate had seen me in a bona fide medicine dream, and I had been responsible for killing close to a hundred Kikuza in a two-man raid, I was still a Greener from 'across'. They hem-hawed around for ten days as we shaped north on horseback and spoke to other rings of Pika.

There are Nineteen nations, each with a favorite Territory and we covered six of those Territories in those ten days. It went usually like this. We'd ride up on a camp, might be around and in a copse of woods on a good-sized creek. Or might be under the lee of a small butte where the wind was less. About two hundred yards from the camp, outliers would casually ride up. Guns on hips, across laps, or lances. They'd look us over. See Nate and greet him. See

Flann or one of the other hardcases and insult him, he insulted back. Much bobbing of heads. Then they'd see me and ask who I was, in front of me, like I was witless or deaf. Nate would pull out the AK and start the story. Making it last all the way into the camp, past the boiled Buffalo, past the whisky hour, and finish up in time for us to get bedded down.

For the big kick of the tale he'd kept back one of the kids, not his nephew, that we'd fished out of the Kikuza camp. She was a hard luck story to begin with, only had two uncles and a mother living to form the Ring. After the Kikuza snuffed out the meat packing vanagons she was an orphan.

At the right time, Nate always had her stand up in the firelight and drop her robe. That always tipped the paraffin into the fire. Not because she was nude. The Pika don't have much of a nudity issue, I kept walking around with a permanent blush.   And not because she was maybe thirteen. Pika often set up tents and fire rings around fourteen or fifteen. But because, in katakana ideograms, a notice that she was property of Troop B, Company A, 45th Imperial Cavalry was stenciled across her back.

Killing Buffalo and enslaving Pika was the two of the top three ways to get a Nation all worked up into a killing mill.

The third involved ploughs.

They never found out that Nate and I had worked up the stencil, or that the girl thought the ideograms were "on the wind" and wanted to get more as they seemed to draw a lot of the faster young men. She had her heart set on acquiring three visiting husbands, setting up a rest stop for Overlanders and restoring her lineage by the old-fashioned way. Babies every spring and occasionally adopting in a likely orphan. Nate came up with a scenario involving Kikuza, the girl and a plough…but I told him he was gilding the lily and to give it a rest.

After the sixth or seventh show Dockens tucked me away in one of the principal Te'sep, what I would have called a tribe in my yellow novel days and sloped off south with some real rough looking characters and a long string of fast horses. If I had to give an opinion, I'd said they were going to check my story. My watch kept stopping so I lost count of the days. From the cold rains we were getting every three or four days I'd said we were in late fall. But the Pika said it was an unusually wet Full Red Moon and started making up lots of buffalo hide for an early winter and smoking extra meat. I was in the way, so I scooped up my rucksack and sloped off from the encampment. Flann and the dogs were at my heels, followed casually by a Pika lancer at about fifty yards. I still had the Shansi Mauser, anything smaller than a shoulder busting drilling didn't count as a weapon. My Mini-14 had been stowed away into safekeeping right after we settled into the first Tinker's encampment, along with just about every other item I had packed along. But they left me the Mauser, a heavy knife and a couple of lock blades.

And the Dragon.

And so, I go off and find a bit of running water. I felt ripe. Not dirty. Just ripe. There is a difference, although I suppose you'd have to experience both conditions to know it. Ripe you can cure with a bit of sun or a bit of smoke over the clothes and a good dunk. Dirty involves burning the underclothes and burying the rest. I hadn't had a proper bath since I picked up Alena across the Veil, maybe two weeks gone by. And I think Flann hadn't had one since last spring. I asked him, straight out, if it was a good place to soap up.

"Here?"

I shrugged. "You got a YMCA?"

"Not closer than Little Cantry."

"Wisenheimer. Is it proper to use this water?" I knew some of the Indians on my grasslands were averse to bathing or contaminating running water.

"Won't be a problem." He gave me a big smile and I knew I was supposed to be in trouble. He turned to the mounted sentry, who was casually watering her horse a little downstream. "Okay if the Nopfler gets a dip?"

"Yah." Big grin on the sentry.

I turned my back on the pair of them, shucked my jeans and shirt, running my thumbs along the seams for the greybacks, although to be truthful I never found the one among the Pika. I laid the Mauser in the middle of my shirt along with the lock blade and did a few Tai-Chi movements in the sunlight. Then I stepped into the thigh deep creek.

It was cold. Cold enough to kill you in a short quarter hour, if you had nowhere to get dry and warm in a hurry. Or if you didn't carry the Dragon. I dipped under the wash and came up, running a brush over my shoulders and scraping under my arms. Scrubbing and murdering a song about short'nin bread. Flann was flabbergasted, the lancer was laughing fit to kill. She kicked her horse around and trotted about twenty more yards upstream.

"Y'll got a problem?" I ducked under again and came up shaking off the water like a dog. Then I climbed out and dried in the sun and the breeze, steam rolling off of me. "What's the matter, never seen a body take a bath?"

Flann just blinked, his mouth open. He was real quiet the rest of the night. And I got some seriously nervous looks from the rest of the Pika. Whispering in the quiet when they thought I couldn't hear.

Skinwalker.

I drifted through the camps, always with Flann or his designate trailing along with me. A Tinkerhold had three or more camps, each with a different stream of Pika calling them home. The kids and both sets of dogs moved through the camps in schools of noise and dust. They were mostly unsupervised although I saw times when someone culled out a handful of kids and set them to chores or sent them to a lodge with banners and emblems of the written Pika Creole. The men did men things and stayed out of the way if not the reach of the women. The women cooked and sewed and did all the early bronze age chores that they were accustomed to. It was informal and pleasant and about as authentic as a theme park.

Out on the rim of the Hold there were several camps of motorized caravans. Big, almost double wide, trailers on equally big and wide tracked bogie sets hauled by an eight

wheeled tractor that almost matched the Overlander
tractors. They had kids and dogs and horses as well, but
most of the adults wore jeans and wool shirts and they slept
in the caravans, the kids often sleeping in the Lodges of
their friends and cousins in the inner ring. Some of the
caravans had blacksmiths associated with them. Some coal
fired. Some LP gas fired. A lot of weapon tinkering and
horse farriering went on, along with brewing beer and skullpop. There was the traditional cluster of old farts around a
chimenea. I pulled up an empty spot on the ground,
ignoring the two empty lawn chairs, and just listened to the
conversations.

My minder, Flann as it was that day, pulled up and
squatted next to me, inquiring politely about a gourd of
beer for a couple of passing men.

"A Gourd. A flaming tub of beer and a pound of pig
cracklings is your usual tariff for not bothering the women,
you greasy Kit fox."

Flann nodded. "Now that you mention it, Uncle, that
does sound like a fine thing to be having at the end of a
long hard day." It was straight up noon.

One of them grunted. "Amiee, bring your worthless
nephew some beer and a tub of cracklings."

From inside the trailer. "Which worthless nephew, so I
know how to spice the cracklings?"

Flann leaned into me and stage whispered. "All of her
nephews are worthless, but we get the best cracklings
because..." And an empty can of beans spun past his ear.

Flann and I ate cracklings and listened to the older
men opinions on everything under the sky. One by one
they got up and ambled off to their own fire rings or BBQ
pits. Eventually it was just Flann, the owner of the
chimenea, who'd tipped his hat over his face and gone to
sleep, and me. An old man in traditional dress wandered by
and dropped onto the turf with me.

"And you would be the Mihaly's man?" He pulled a
clay pipe out of a fringed pouch at his side. His hands were
gnarled and scarred, the hand of a smith. He smelled of
coal and hot metal and Juicy Fruit chew.

"I am that."

"You are new to the Dai, but you are 'of' the Dai?"

I nodded.

"Well then." He lit the pipe. "You are come from the Bloodlands and wonder just what we are?" He didn't pause long. "We are a jackdaw people. Cuckoos in the nests. The Pika have been on the Empty Grass for fifty generations, in one form or another. The Dai have been on Mize for four times that."

"Unless your generations are as short as a mayfly..."

He grinned around his pipe stem. "The Pika took this path maybe three hundred years in your past. The Grass breeds with the Sky and their get are nomads. Here it is Uncle Horse and Grandmother Buffalo, there..." He waved off to the East, his pipe trailing a brief smear of light. "There it is Epona and cattle and sheep upon the steppes. But everywhere the Grass lies under Sky, Nomads spring up. The Plains tribes appealed to our wilder children and those cultures displaced an older Pika."

We sat for a while in mythic silence. "And so. We raid when we can, trade when we must and borrow what we will not return. The lineage you came from, the Gunpowder civilization. We have been drifting through the gates to that linage for perhaps five hundred years. Borrowing."

"Copying?"

"Sometimes we think we are rediscovering our own roots. Or improvising on a theme." He looked at me out of the corner of his eye. "We are orphans, you see. Adopted unwillingly by this world and her peoples, settled in and comfortable, but orphans. And deep inside we are looking for our history. Which is why, in another lifetime, I was an archeologist. "

I had wondered where this lecture was going. I looked to Flann, he was chatting up a daughter of the fire ring. Our host was snoring, and it was two hours or more before I might get properly fed. I settled myself in, asking politely for a new gourd, a plastic cup from a football stadium in truth, of watery beer and nodded.

"In another lifetime I was an archaeologist, perhaps

fifty years before you were born. For three generations before I joined the Dai Project, the Grand Universities of Europe had been researching the spread of the Dai. Documenting it. Measuring it. All of Humanity arose in the arms of Africa, but the Dai originated in Asia, a mutation, a very successful mutation. We are interfertile with homo sapiens. Our traits recessive. But we displaced the H. Sap populations in every arena. Like wine staining blotting paper. I was a very young academic, but I was also all-but-dissertation. The Project could trace the spread of the mutation by the bones. There were consistent differences in the jaws and the Paranasal sinuses."

My eyes began to glaze.

He accepted a cup from the girl Flann was romancing and after a long drink went on. "Every hunt has an end. We narrowed the mutation locus to the Indus River Valley. Then to the upper end of that valley. And we found that all of the Dai traits appeared over a long generation. Under a layer of charcoal was a prosperous clade of bronze age tribes in the valley. Above it was graves containing Dai jaw bones and early steel grave goods. Above them there were mixed remains of Dai and Homo.sapiens.sapiens in early iron age graves."

"I bet that dropped the torch into the gunpowder."

"Oh, my very word it did." His voice, his words had slowly shifted from plain talking Pika, to being even more of the 'quality' as Barbara Ann would have said. Nebraska to Boston in my milieu. "A long generation of academics ranted and demonstrated and dueled in papers and with cavalry sabers. Accusations of hoaxes and suppression of evidence flew through the air like sheaves of war arrows. And then your world offered us carbon dating."

He knocked out the dead dottle of his pipe and put it away. "The carbon dating process stabilized the likely dates for the strata we were dealing with. It established with little room for speculation that the Dai mutations sprang full blown upon this world within a long generation."

"A gate."

He smiled. "That insight brings death. An insightful

population was culled from the institutions of Europe and Asia. And archaeology is now a risky business. Even here, across the water, in the dark woods of the Confederated Houses, it is a risky business. One by one my colleagues have dropped out of sight or suddenly expired. Libraries have burned or been reorganized."

"Where..."

He shrugged. "I was junior at the department table. Perhaps the senior academics traced the gate, or perhaps it had drifted far enough away that none of the Walkers we had could Walk the path. I never knew. Suddenly the amiable cooperation between the Learned Houses of Europe and the Excellent Chrysanthemum Throne evaporated and the Kush Sub-Continent became at first a battle ground and then the tightly held prize of the Kizikua."

"And here?"

"Frankland became perilous in the extreme. I decamped for the Confederated Houses where I found no better prospects. Then I sold myself to a steam Overlander, and once deep in the Empty Grass dropped off the back of the wagon and became a Tinker. The Pika are mostly indifferent to what came before today or what comes the day after tomorrow. When investigators came trolling through the Tinker holds, they afforded them the same treatment as census takers. Indifference at best, the worst does not bear remembering."

We set for a while longer in a companionable silence, listening to the camp come to supper. "So, I remain. An all-but-dissertation scholar well versed in early bronze age archaeology, living as a bladesmith and a farrier. And I have outlived the majority of my fellow academics, in exile but alive." He stood, his joints crackling. "An amazing tale, is it not?" He turned and for the first time I realized he was missing his right eye. "But what is my tale, to Breaker of Houses, eh?" And he drifted off into the camp.

I didn't take any mind, just hung out with the rest of the extra males and tried to learn how to Hide the Sneaker, while not getting drunk on warm watery beer or thin whiskeys. Gambling. It being one of the eight traditional pastimes, Gambling, Bundling, Tending weapons and Making tack. Those were the things you did when you were not Killing enemies, Stealing horses, Hunting buffalo or Speculating on how fast a horse might go if that horse had the right parentage. You did other things too, but the eight pastimes where what Men did, and all the other stuff was just 'bother'.

Couldn't Hide the Sneaker worth a damn, but I did teach them how to roll dice on a blanket. Won most of my stuff back too, till we had to give back the dice so the women could play Monopoly.

They bedded me down in a ring, gave me a real old buffalo hide blanket and the honorable corner in a tipi of a headman. I ate buffalo or antelope three times a day, tried to learn the three-cornered language they used and sized up the Pika, while they sized up me. I found that they mostly used dressed pine poles for the tipi's, but I found about three quarters of the 'poles' in the ring I was staying in were a dark bamboo. Bamboo. Lighter than the pine and sealed with something that felt like polyurethane filler. I asked one of the Pika, the one who was following me around, why bamboo and where it came from.

"Lighter." You damn fool his expression said. As for where it came from. "We grow them down towards the gulf along the small streams south of the old road, once a year we send the juniors down to harvest some. They will grow to a good length in a wheel of the seasons, maybe two." It took seventeen for each tipi and the pine might take four or five years to grow to a useful length, they wore out faster than the bamboo as well. I found me a couple of castoff lengths of bamboo and fashioned a pair of bo staves and a pair of fencing staves. I'd gotten lax, twice one of the lancers at the airstrip melee had almost nailed me. One of the hard-bitten men Dockens had wished on me lit up at the sight of the bo staves, stripped to his breechclout, betting his tack and clothing but not his rifle or the over grown pony he rode, and laid into me with one of the staves.

It was a near run thing. I got three bright sets of bruises striped across my back and side. Each one being about three inches wide, from a wicked combination attack. I also got a loose tooth from an elbow I hadn't seen coming. But I say my prayers regular, I live a clean life and I cheat a lot. I feinted to his groin and windmilled the little bastard, sweeping his legs out from under him. On the way down, I hit him in the soft spot under the ear with the thick end of the stave.

When he woke up, the next day, I made sure to lose all his stuff back in his general direction at Sneaker. This made me a real gentleman among the swells. I took it, I dished it out and I wasn't pig greedy. My whiskeys got less watery and they tried to teach me how to drum.

Bigdog got fat, Stosh got fatter, both stayed close to me. Old Stosh had a new fondness for my company, being that I had a talk with him about the Pika and their occasional fondness for fat dogs as a change of pace from Buffalo. I don't think he understood me, but I do think he knew when the menu smelled like boiled corgis as opposed to antelope.

Flann was a tall one for a Traveler, not as tall as Nate, but tall. Long legs, short body, long arms. Face was flat, like he'd been hit with a shovel when he was a baby and tanned that dark outdoors color that every Pika had from about the time they were knee high to a coyote. He was a full-time traditional Kit Fox. Skin clothing, paint, braided hair, carbon steel knife, one shot carbine and a lance. Carried a bow too.

"I'm not too hot with that."

I was looking over the bow, sitting cross legged in the men's tent. It was a tipi, taken straight from the last century and smelled like it was that old. We had a pot simmering on the fire, most of the smoke was going out the smoke hole and it really was warm and cozy while outside it was cold enough to put a skim of ice on standing water.

I looked back down at the weapon in my lap. It was a traditional bow, although I had a thought that if I peeled off some of the rawhide wrapping, I'd find a bowyer's mark

from my California. Short, the limbs wide and thin, some
sort of leather bonded to the side away from the shooter.
"Yeah? Why do you carry it all the time?" I'd seen him
stalking through the camps every day with this bow either
hanging off his arm or slung across his back. "Some sort of
medicine?"

He huffed, puffing out the long Fu-Manchu mustache
he wore. It was odd seeing people who otherwise passed
for Hollywood Indians sporting luxuriant face hair or long
blond locks, but six hundred years of mixing up the gene
pool will do that. That huff was as far as he went, laughing.
"Might say that."

Most of the Pika would talk your legs off at any
excuse, Flann was one of the minority that liked to have
you pry. "Not medicine, then what?"

He grinned and leaned to whisper garlicky in my ear.
"Fillies."

Oh. "Mean to say the bigger the bow..."

Big grin and an even bigger nod. I'd noticed that he
slept close to the door and that there was a lot of traffic at
night. He was ever slipping out through the weather flaps
or someone was slipping in, but it wasn't the Mihaly's cause
he was advancing.

I just shook my head. This wasn't anything like any of
the American Indian cultures back across the Veil. Most of
the peoples I'd read about were very strait laced, with just
enough slack in their customs to let get things started
between their young folks. But over here there was little
notice and less shame in blanket hopping before or after
marriage. Most of the Pika, Traditional or Rahvee, passed
the linage through the women and the women set the
mores. I'd seen a couple of spectacular dust ups when the
women of a tipi or a fire ring decided that they'd had
enough of some feckless male. If he was lucky, he got out
with his hair still on his head and without a drilling load of
salt and dust in his ass. Children belonged to the mother or
her linage. The father was just a convenience for the
studbook. Having a child outside of the studbook was the
real scandal.

Now when white money or buffalo rights went with a bride...then things got serious. There were two clans we had to be real cautious about. More than a hundred years back they had plans for a strategic marriage, if the plans had proved out both would have been in the catbird seat for their particular basins. Instead they had a scandal, that could still draw blood today. Over buffalo and gold. Most of the scandal was that they were fighting over gold. Buffalo or horses, but never over white metal.

Flann. I handed him back his bow and its antelope leather case with its long fringes.

"However floats the stick. I'm going to turn in." And I went to my buffalo robe bed. Lot nicer than the saddle blanket I'd been using, even with both of the damned dogs bedding down with me. But I slept less well the longer I was under the tipi. We'd had urts once, felt tents drawn over wooden ribs...

That night the Kikuza stumbled over us. It was simpleminded buggery on both sides, as my Sergeant Major said about the Somme. We were camped just two thousand paces from an east west trace, running from where Greeley was sited across the Veil towards the Cantry. We had about three hundred head of horse, maybe thirty Recreation Vehicles or the like and a good two hundred Pika in about thirty lodges. Lots of fire pits, nothing in the way of light or radio discipline. People coming and going, no sentries or pickets to speak of. We stood out on the grass like cat shit on linoleum.

Somewhere west of us a half company of Kikuza Dragoons mounted up to do a road show down the trace and seeing our inviting campsite long about midnight, invited themselves to the party. Their Overlanders rumbling into the camp shooting anything horsey and beating up the boxy RVs as a way of saying "Hello". After the first moment of surprise, the camp doused the fire pits, killed the lanterns and swarmed the two Overlanders. Every loaded gun in the camp went off in the next mad minute, sweeping any gunners clear of their hatchways and smashing out every window.

First thing I did was get clear of the tipi. Big dog went
a-helling off towards the Kikuza that had made the error of
dismounting from their Overlander to mix it up with the
Tinkers. Between the Great Murdering Dogs, the enraged
horsemen and the berserk RV crews, the Kikuza were
melting like snow under blowtorches. The few that had any
sense ran for the shelter of the other Overlander, whose
crew and fire teams had profited from their partners lesson
and stayed buttoned up to rake the encampment from gun
ports or with their turret mounted guns. I suppressed two
of the gun ports with the Mauser and then got close
enough I was under the guns and among the hapless
Kikuza refugees.

I awoke the Dragon, carved the Kikuza outside of the
Overlander into a drift of dead men and liberated a satchel
charge from one of their sappers. A wee bit of prying and
one of the luggage bins on the bottom of the monster bus
banged open. I chucked the satchel charge in, tamped it
with a dead Flower and got my ass clear.

It went off and the Overlander popped smoke at every
seam. Hatchways and doors spanged open and Kikuza
came wiggling out like woodlice.

At the end of the night there wasn't a Kikuza whole
and breathing. And there were a good thirty dead with the
marks of the Dragon on them. If I had wanted to, I could
have made a cape from the scalps I was due.

And that was a problem.

We broke camp and scattered that Tinker's bend to the
four corners. Flann and a half dozen others mounted up
and escorted me towards the south. The atmosphere was
cold, colder than hell. And I am not talking about the
weather. I wasn't real sure if I was an honored guest or the
central figure at the next entertainment. The rest of the
team rode with their guns uncased. Flann rode beside me.
His gun and his bow cased.

I figured talking about it was against union rules, so I
just tucked my blanket parka a little tighter about me and
kept the Greater Dragon just dancing under the surface.
Everybody noticed that what little rain the wind was

carrying, wasn't sticking to me, steaming off like rain on hot pavement. Helluva drain, but I could keep it up for a while. I'd let them finesse me off the Prunty Gelding, put me on a remount of dubious character. That was copacetic, I dislike killing my horses.

There comes a time in every cavalryman's career when he has to kill his horse. Even if you are lucky enough to serve all your time between wars, there are always gopher holes and bob wire. And after you put down Hero or Traveler or Brute, with a pistol shot behind the ear or a razor to the throat, you were less inclined to name the next one. After a while it was 'that bay' or 'the nag over there' or just 'this one.' When you didn't know them by name, it was easier.

So, I was happy they had double shuffled me away from the Prunty. I was keeping the Greater Dragon at a simmer by tapping into the life of the horse I was riding. If you kept it to a minimal draw, pulling just a trickle from the horse, the horse was not harmed, and you could keep your reserves topped up and ready to go. This was a good tactic on a long pursuit, for example, when you didn't know when the prey might turn and offer resistance. Or if you were captured and the enemy did not know your calling, keeping well and ready until they were off balance, expecting you to be wounded, starving and helpless.

I hadn't realized just how ignorant the Pika were.

I later gathered that Selai, or the Dragon, was a semi-myth to the Pika. The rest of the suite of talents that made up the Manifested Dai; the Skrenners, Firebugs and the like, they knew and accepted. Selai were something else.

Something too close to witchcraft. Shape changing, soul eating, witches. Taboo. And like most things taboo to a mind that lived close to the earth, a Selai was best cured with the true death.

Unless you could cloak the taboo in a greater mystery.

"They plan to kill you with me?" I swung myself sidesaddle in the McClellan and grinned into the startled eyes of Flann. "Or are you just the Judas goat to be leading me into the kill chute."

"I am tainted..."

"Horseshit."

Flann shouldered his horse into mine or would have save mine was dead and fallen under his horse's hooves, while I jumped Flann. He dropped from the saddle with a grunt, stunned, and then I was among the escort. Two got off their shots, one even hit me though I'm thankful to say it simply clipped a teaspoon worth of hamburger from my hip. But when the flurry was done, all were down or reeling in their saddles, bringing up last month's supper like a freshman at a kegger. I held Flann across my saddle bow, my left hand buried in his hair and my right steaming slightly in the moonlight, inches from his face.

"Skinwalker" He whispered.

"I told Dockens I was a different order of pain." I dropped him to the ground again, a good deal more carefully than I had dropped the rest of them.

He staggered from his knees to his feet, a long knife glittering in his hand, more from reflex than any intent. He shuffled his feet in a slow circle, counting heads. Each one of the hunting party was moving, if only to throw up last midsummer's leftovers. All had been kissed by the Dragon, all were wearing clothes burnt to Polish lace where I had swept my hand across. Their skins sunburnt under the rags. All living. All tainted.

"You have rested enough, oh you pale and frightened children. Fearful of wind in treetops or small mice at play in the dry grass. Or, should I wait a while more?" I pitched my voice as my top sergeant did, on the drill grounds at the Plains of Abraham. Scorn and careless scorn, seasoned with a misplaced, mocking, concern.

I rode Flann's horse through them twice, at a slow walk. Steam trailed from me. I nearly glowed in the false dawn, with the energy rising up my spine. Even a spavined horse held more than enough energy to set me to boiling like a teakettle. And every step, every honey dripping insult, focused their anger and their fear on me. Me, not the taboo. Then I brought the horse about, having chivvied them into the crescent I wanted, with me at the focus.

"Now that I have your attention, here is the truth. I am Tallen, Royal Anton Tallen. I was born on Earth in the singularly blessed year of eighteen hundred and ninety-three. Which makes me close to one hundred and six years old. An extremely tough son of a bitch. I enlisted into the King's Canadian Rifles in the dark winter of nineteen and fifteen and the King in his wisdom…"

And I inducted them into the legend of the Breaker of Houses.

Like Preacher Dexter said when I taught the children's choir a drinking song, I have no shame.

By the time we got to the next Tinker gathering, a good day's ride to the northeast, I had bound them into a sacred band. Sworn to silence and sealed with a blood oath, right out of Beadle's Pocket Library, jack knives and candle flames and all. The secret held twice as long as I figured it would. All the way to the next sunrise.

Short Moon, Corbin to the moderns, was sitting cross legged outside my tipi in the morning, lightly shaking a rattle. Naked to the cold, eyes staring into the rising sun, fresh blood running down his chest from where he'd taken a razor-sharp curl of flint and cut four deep lines into his skin. Cut in the manner of a bear's slash. He was thin to the point of death, burnt black in the sun and blue from the cold, his skin puckered with scars and chilblains.

Corbin Watt was the nearest thing the Travelers had to a Bishop. He lived the tradition except for his sabbatical moon every year. Wore nothing but traditionally dressed skins, lived in a tipi, disdained rifle for lance and a broadaxe and refused to touch any of the medicine drinks the cornflower folk used. His nose ran constantly, he read letters at the end of his arm and suffered from the occasional toothache.

Each year, on his sabbatical, he moved into a spa up in the Cantry flats. Had his teeth worked on, caught up on the professional periodicals of the Vespucci Shaman Sodality, steamed the cold out of his head, had two martinis at supper and a toddy before bed. He wallowed in the seductive luxury of the spa for a month, then he rode back to the grasslands for another year of ironing out the kinks in his spirit. He was a tough old man, hoping to see sixty winters, likely to notch a hundred.

I crawled out of the tipi and settled in next to him, on accident as it were. I had a pipe of sweet tobacco in my ruling hand and I was wearing my last pair of jeans, going thread bare.

I offered the lit pipe to him and he took it with his off hand, shaking the gourd all the while with the other. He puffed a smoke ring to the rising sun and to the north and the south and to the dark mountains far to our rear. I did likewise.

"I see you Walking Knife."

"I see you Short Moon."

We sat there and enjoyed the morning calm. The kids working the horses. What families there were starting their daily rounds. Dressing hides, tending stock or wheels, cooking and carrying on a culture. A culture that had a broken link back to the eighth century after Christ. The Christ of my world.

The War Dogs came trotting in from their patrols, greeting each other with a rough shoulder and a flick of a tongue across an ear, one in every war pod watching me while his kin counted noses in a silent roll call. 'All present or accounted for.' Then breaking their hunger with the sound of crushing buffalo long bones. We saw the ground pickets sortie out on horse and trike, lancers and bowmen stiffened with the damned drillings. These Travelers. These Tinkers, weren't about to be caught off guard like the luckless ones at Hugens Knopp.

"It appears there is a sweat lodge, just to the north." Corbin wiped his nose with his free hand and then wiped his hand on his breechclout.

"Truly?"

"I have heard it so. It would be a good day to take a sweat. In my time I have seen few days as good as this one for such a thing."

And so, we did.

I crawled into the sweat lodge after the half-naked old

man, half naked as him in my ragged jeans and wishing the protocols would have allowed a mug of coffee at least before the honorable court was in session.

Which is what it was. A court.

I ignored the two dog soldiers in the corner with the odd guns, dye markers they used for tagging the free herds. Their faces were painted the white of ghosts and death and unclean things, meaning they were so unclean as to be invisible to everyone who was righteous. If I'd seen them, then I was patently unrighteous, and they'd be in the way of killing me. With paintballs? Something was wrong with that loadout, but I let the questions go.

Hot and dark, three men, three women and the ghosts all crammed into a hide covered wicker basket not nine feet across and maybe four high with a fire bucket in the center and a smoke hole at the apex letting out most of the smoke.

I sat in the prisoner's box, so to speak, my back to the entrance and to the ghosts. My face unpainted and my skin naked in the dark, my scars invisible.

Everyone else was painted in the liveries of their societies. The paint more remembered than seen. Dog Warriors, Horse Brotherhood, the Buffalo's Children, Stinky Box, Shamans and Broken Bow. Each of the major threads in the Traveler's world was represented here. Most adults had two or three sodalities they walked in, a major, say, and two minors. If you were a horse breeder, you would be a Horse Brother; usually you'd be a member in one of the militant societies as well. Horses tend to get stolen. If you were a Child of the Buffalo, someone whose life walked in step with the buffalo's year, you also carried a pouch of peyote buttons and a bone whistle so you could talk with Grandmother Thunderer at need. Stinky Box was where the Blacksmiths, Gunsmiths, Tinkers and Mechanics had settled out. And Broken Bow was where the happy wights that would have been politicians or rock stars flourished. Licensed liars all.

Everyone had a seat in at least two councils, even Broken Bow had an amateur circle for those with more soul than talent and every child spent a long season with the

Shamans. You specialized as you grew older, but you never lost touch with the rest of the Travelers.

Everyone had a place, but me.

"We see you. Tallen. Sometimes called Walking Knife." The tone was formal, the phrasing in the Creole insulting. Rey, the headman of the Horse Brothers.

I closed my eyes and let the silence stretch out. The white-faced ghosts were close. Close enough that I thought I could cut them down before they'd fire. But, outside I felt and heard a dozen ringing the sweat lodge. They'd blow the lodge to rags and offal, every one of us, if it came to killing. And there was the matter of my being bound, if ever so lightly.

I let the Dragon rise through my Chakras, seeing the darkness drop away with my inner vision. I let the swirls of my auras trail through the clouds pouring from the sextet facing me, reading their intentions. They feared and they marveled, and they quivered in horror at what death I might bring to them or what visions I might disclose.

I sat in silence and gathered my thoughts, letting their fears grow and then ebb.

"We see you, Tallen." A new voice. One of the women, The Mako'sae of the Night's Sisters society. She was clean and clear as snowmelt. Fearless because in her center there was nothing to fear death. The Night Sisters were Aknepteh. Orphans all, and almost as taboo as I was. But they killed with the blade or the rawhide thong and did not steal souls.

"We see you, Outlier." Warden, of the Stinky Box. He kept pushing at me. Outlier in the creole had several definitions, most of them warranting a blooding.

"We see you, Walking Knife." Corbin.

"We see you, Tallen n'Mihaly." A Child of the Buffalo. Her voice rough and raspy.

"We see you, Breaker of Houses." The last of my judges, the Broken Bow. And if I remember the whispered brief I'd gotten from Flann before I had crawled out of the tipi, my accuser.

I still let the silence speak for me. Let the heat from

the rocks seep into me. I drew the smoke deep into my lungs and exhaled slowly and calmly.

I opened my eyes, they were fixed straight ahead.

"I see no one." I said. They froze, insulted beyond reply. "I see naught but children. And should the Breaker of Houses waste his time upon frightened children?"

"Breaker of Houses."

"I am."

"Truly?" Broken Bow was squirming in delight and fear.

"Indeed. Who is oldest here, who has seen five score winters?" No answer. "I thought not, you play at Elders like children. I was the Young Dragon, Leader of a seven-horsetail banner, Judge of souls and Keeper of the Gate of Death when your grandparents were learning their letters."

An exaggeration, I had maybe forty years on the Broken Bow. "I was cutting Kikuza throats and bellies when your fathers were learning not to 'make' on the tipi floor. I took the last Koshitsu on AngTerra across the Veil, took his head off his shoulders fifty winters back and rode through a thousand miles of civil war and devastation to plant the rotting melon on a lance at the death gate of my clan House, a payment on a blood debt." I leaned forward and extended my hand, my fingers spread, to the six huddled in an arc before me, my ghost guards forgotten to either side. "You doubt?"

The Mako'sae, slashed her hand, unnecessary but dramatic, and placed it under mine with the bloody palm up. "I doubt. Your House." Her eyes locked in mine, fearless.

"Jurchen. I was Lijong, the Young Dragon. The lice I hunted, down a score of years and across half a world, were the pigdogs of the Chrysanthemum." I let hunger loose down my arm and into her, my auras rising from my skin to sheath me like chain mail.

Her blood dripped onto the hot rocks, cooking meat fresh cut from the prey. I didn't sift her, didn't tear at her. I let her come within me, if she dared. And she dared just enough. Just enough to learn, then fear. She closed her eyes and took back her hand with a long hiss of pain.

I was stunned to see her bloody palm, with a faint white line across the center of it. The slash healed. I was slow to realize that my hand hurt.

I looked down and saw a faint cut across the palm of my hand healing.

"Jurchen." Warden broke the silence in the sweat lodge, "but the House of the Breaker..."

The Broken Bow laughed, the sort of giggly laugh someone burps out just before they have a serious come-a-part. I think the Buffalo poked her, the laugh stopped abruptly.

I leaned back from the fire pit, watching my hand slowly heal. The auras of the judges before me swirled and rippled, fear and astonishment uppermost. I looked up from my hand to the Mako'sae. She was painted in day paint, bright red swaths under her cheekbones and a sky-blue line bisecting her chin. What it meant, she alone knew but, it was bright and flashy as was the body paint she wore. In the night, she would have worn a charcoal wash with random smears of black. Now she was just grey under the paint. She had read more than I knew, I realized. What I could do, what I had done, what I was going to do. She knew me.

"So, my children, what good will come of having Legend walk among you?" I casually wiped my hand clean on my knee.

"You are bound." Corbin rasped. "To La Senora."

I nodded. An ironic voice in my ears, If ever...

"What binds you to the Pika, to the Wandering peoples?" Child of the Buffalo.

"Many strands. You ride beside the Mihaly, the scalps of Kikuza dry on lances before your lodges, you live under the same sky as I do."

"You came from over the Veil." Warden.

"But I still live under the same sky. Your lances fit the calluses of my hand, do they not? I sleep well beneath the sky of the Pika and I do not repine for the soft beds of the Cousins, is this not true?"

"You are a Darkwalker, to hunt us you can become us." Warden again.

"Perhaps. You have truth readers? Let them read me."

"You would kill them if they read you, or you can defeat them." Again, the representative of the Stinky Box.

"So." I turned my head to either side, looking the ghost soldiers in the face. Then I leaned across the hot rocks. "How much white metal have the Kikuza bought you with? Truly? Warden?"

He started to scuttle backwards, then froze, the sharp acid stink of fear cutting through the smoky fug of the sweat lodge.

The Mako'sae, ever so lightly, held an obsidian needle to his neck, at the pulse just under the jaw line, its tip smeared with a paste that glowed in the dark. I reached out my hand.

"Have a care." Corbin said softly and I could hear the guards stirring at my back.

"Like milking rattlers." My hand, or rather the auras nesting about my hand glowed in the dark lodge. His aura was thinned almost to nothing, like very clear water flowing over a stone. Some folks naturally never showed much color in their auras. It was rare, like albinism. Made things interesting. I had to trail my fingertips through the ripples. Leaving long smears and smuts of color off my auras. Painting his skin in the darkness.

Warden pissed himself, snapped his head to the side to impale his neck on the needle the Mako'sae held, his eyes shut tight against the fear. The needle slipped beneath the skin and between one sharp breath and the next slower gasp he was past any formal inquiry. As the Greater Dragon, I could have dragged him back across the threshold, to face his cowardice and his treachery.

I didn't bother. They were already skittish.

The Mako'sae lowered the body to the floor of the sweat lodge.

She held each of the remaining honor court, held their eyes for a second and then tipped her head to face me. "Tallen, sometime Breaker of Houses, sometime warlord for the Mihaly linage, guest among the Pika; we have found you to be a known Darkwalker." She smiled and for the first time I had a shiver of fear, her eyes glittering in the shadows of the lodge and the deeper shadows under her hair. "You are now Aknepteh, of the thirty Snakes, until this season of war is done."

Gurkhas on ponies. "Until this season of war is over." I repeated.

The morning after the courts-martial was when Nate and the Pika Elders came to a plan of action. He just appeared in the tent they had me bivouacked at, eating boiled meat and sopping up the gravy with some flatbread.

"Hoy Tallen. Snakes can't sleep under cover."

I wiped the sleep out of my eyes, noted that Flann was hunched by the door flap chatting up one of the womenfolk the tipi belonged to, while two of the hard men that had rode off with Nate were curled up asleep at the side of the tent. "How do, Nate. I sleep where I want."

"You left one hell of a mess back yonder."

"Intended to." I rolled out of the bedding and got dressed. "Told you I was a whole 'nother world of pain." I was beginning to lose what nudity taboos I still had, tribal life is worse than being in a British barracks for lack of privacy.

"Scared half the Tinkers into peeing crouched when you went and sucked up all the Kikuza souls at Hugens Knopp."

"Only the men. The women still piss standing."

He laughed, throwing back his head till his fillings glinted in the firelight.

"Someone laid a stick on you, Walking Knife."

"Yeah." I stretched and crackled my back into place. "I damn near stuffed it up his ass. Flann tells me that Ottmar, you call him the Sidewinder, is still walking with his head on backwards." I nudged Stosh out of the way and sat down next to Nate. "Any coffee?"

He poured me a cup.

"Rode down to where that cackled up mess of Kikuza were camped." He freshened his own cup. "They had hauled off the Overlander, bulldozed the airplane and what was left of the rest of the gear into a big tangle and seeded it with booby traps."

"To discourage honest fellows like you?"

"To entertain the coyotes. I think they buried their dead under the junk."

"Wouldn't doubt it."

"Ordered a set of big blades out of Cantry Ford. Going to peel that junk back and see what is what."

"And why?"

"Like to know how many dead, whose dead, and why."

They formed up two fire teams. Gave me Flann, two cousins and a short-tempered woman who was a horse doctor. Flann, the Cooper twins and I were to get the attention of a Kikuza patrol, then the other fire team was to put a hurt on them. They had ten shooters, to my three. Nate and the Elders sent the girl, who called herself PaintedGajin by now, back to a safe encampment with three of his cousin's kids as escorts. Paint was mightily disappointed that all of the escort were initiates in the WalksFar Sorority, women lancers.

I left the dogs with Flann's band. Bigdog had accounted for three Kikuza, Stosh had hamstringed one and finished a couple of others, this gave them real status.

They got promoted from walking pantry to honored guests. Meant we'd only eat them if we got really hungry.

After a bit of painting, some odd smoky conversations in the Band Chief's RV, only the young and the seriously crackpot traditional fooled around with late stone age and early steam age technologies, the rest used four-wheel drive buses and fuel cell ATV trikes or snowcats in the winters. After talking over the portents of the raid, we mounted up and trotted off into a long march in a spitting, cold, rain. Behind us the Band broke the encampment and scattered. We'd heard that two new transports had flown through the Rockies, the local name was Western Rampart of the Sun, but I called them the Rockies and made do, through the Rockies. The Kikuza patrols picked up about ten days later and we set up for business.

The first five or six times we pulled the rolling
ambush, it worked slicker than sin.

Team one knocked down two or three riders, suckered
the rest into enfilade under the guns of team two. We killed
every trooper in the patrols, took their guns and most of
their horses. Big medicine, big prestige. And our numbers
swelled. Swelled enough that we started turning down
marginal forces, riders lacking in horseflesh or sense. Most
of the marginal types sortied out against the Kikuza, against
our advice, got promptly killed by the giddy Kikuza. This
meant that when the Flowers next ran up against a Pika
raiding party, they thought it was an easy kill. Likely it was
one of our teams and we left the Kikuza to fertilize the
grass.

We made the plains a No-Go area for anything less
than a company strength sortie with an armored car or one
of the armored Overlanders clattering in the rear. Once we
suckered a troop of armored cars into an occasional stream,
bogged them down and laid satchel charges against them.

Then there was the last time that we played at ambush.

Nate ran the first team, four shooters and two horse
holders. I had the second fire team, only two shooters and a
horse holder. We had three youngsters up on big, fast,
studs keeping a running tag on our chosen Kikuza troop.
When we had a good fix on their route, we set up just like
I'd planned. Running the double ambush.

There were fifteen heads in the Kikuza, twenty horses.
Snow had come with first light, dry and hissing through the
grass all day, but it was just a promise. Daylight was grey
and damn near shadowless, the light scattered about by the
clouds. When a sunset came it just changed from a light
grey to a dark grey to black, without a clear line between
any of them. The wind was cold and from the north. The
riders were muffled up to the ears, hunched over, enduring
the ride. Not watching as they walked their mounts through
the rolling prairie along Twin Butte creek. The shallow
bottoms gave them a bit of cover from the wind, but their
dark figures stood out against the dusting of snow on the
slopes behind them.

We were tucked in shallow scrapes waiting for them to enter the kill box, covered with low infrared drop cloths and wearing our ultra-thermals. Which beat shivering under a wool horse blanket dressed in leggings, a Holiday Inn towel and a jean jacket. I blew into my short-range FM mike and clicked my tongue to wake them up. Ghost riders.

Alena had started shipping supplies across from the Hanse in the first weeks of her September. Some short-range FM radios, thermal blankets, thermal underwear, winter survival items for horse and man. No weapons though. She said Barbara was on the mend, well enough that Barbara and she were thinking of slipping through to AngTerra and sending us some guns. I didn't like that much. I'd shoved a thumb in Brougham's pie, but I didn't know if he was off the board. I liked Barb, I thought she was hell on wheels once upon a time, but I wasn't too sure about putting her up against Brougham in the now.

There had been six shipments so far, five through Cantry and one through the smugglers ford to the south of us. The messages accompanying each shipment noted the specifications of the items and their intended uses. Drop cloth intended to protect outdoor hotbeds from early frost helped us reduce infrared traces from the horses and ourselves. Ultra-thermal underwear not only kept us from freezing our collective asses off, they reduced our heat signatures, even in combat. Long focus microphones, intended for the patient naturalists hunting data on prairie dogs, served us as early warning sensors for aircraft or ground vehicles. Static Snowrunners were for breaking bones in snow, the youngest cadets grabbed them up and became our courier force. She had failures. Foldaway beds, no stick lube sprays, hoods to match our thermal underwear.

To keep the customs happy, she tried to slip proscribed hardware through every so often. She got caught, paid the mordita or fine, and got pissed about it in public for the benefit of the Watchers. A little drama. A little tit for tat and everyone was happy.

The two serious things she did pull off made more of a

difference than any job lot of advanced weapons would have. She somehow killed the 'Zeme satellites and the GPS system with them. And she transferred a single pallet load of Warsaw Pac weapons to us. Sixty RPG anti-armor missiles. They weighed about fifteen pounds, had an effective range of about a hundred yards and punched right through the armor on most all of the Overlanders the Kikuza had acquired. Either feat would have been worth an OBE in the old days, but to pull off both. If I had a garter!

I sent her a bowling ball in a cooler lined with dry ice and stenciled with a biohazard trefoil along with the sword and the dispatch case. I'd brought the case and the sword across the Veil into the 'Zeme when we followed Barbara up that dry creek. I bet Hanse customs had a serious come apart when that shipment came through the gate at Cantry Ford.

The Overlander armor was cheap aluminum, sometimes with an overlay of 'slick' steel to help forestall the occasional armor piercing machine gun round. And usually with a liner of ballistic cloth to reduce interior spalling from a contact blast. Like Barbara said, they were armed just enough to discourage the casual bandits, anything more was a waste unless you intended to be in a real shooting war. The Overlanders were not military vehicles. They were trucks with odd equipment loadouts. The Kikuza seized them, under the thin guise of being agents for House Mihaly, and started retrofitting them with heavier weapons and add on armor. We had problems with them until the RPG's turned up.

The rocket grenades blasted a molten shaft of copper the size of my thumb through the armor and sprayed the engine volume, our usual aim point behind the thickest armor, with about a pound of white-hot copper drops. If it didn't catch fire, and usually it did, the Overlander would come to a rattle-bang halt. Then every hatch would pop open in a hapless attempt at escape, before we laid a satchel charge or two to finish the job. Hapless because the rules had become very simple. No quarter asked or given. Ants swarming over a dead snake was the image I associated with the end of those ambushes. The Flowers used the Overlanders like they were light tanks and lost them like pennies through a hole in their pocket.

.

Between not having much armor, real or wishful, and no GPS to guide any air assets they could keep, all the Koshitsu could do was shovel men and horses into the two airbases they held on the dry side of the mountains and try to win our minds and hearts with stirring propaganda and the occasional exemplary atrocity. The Travelers replied with filthy songs, filthy jokes and constant, merciless, guerilla war. And me, they gave me the few prisoners they did take. What was left of them?

I put my first round in the horse just in front of the guerdon bearer, I figured that might be the troop sergeant. I wasn't using one of Nate's shoulder busters, it takes a lifetime of using those things to make a marksman with them. I had my remaining .308 and we were a true three hundred yards from the Kikuza, a hard shot with them on the move but I was aiming at the horse not the man. Even so I think I hit the rider in the thigh with my first shot, my second shot took the horse at the base of the neck.

Three more were down. They were milling, trying to form up and locate the attack axis and tend to the downed all at the same time. I put a double tap on one carrying a long gun, might have been a light machine gun. Where the first round went, I got no clue, but the second one blew a pink mist into the air and the rider went down with that doll rag crumple of the quickly dead.

"Okay." I said and slithered out of my shooters hide. My partners fired their last rounds, backed out of their hides and opened their rifles to reload as they ran up the hill. I was a half-step behind them, hearing the crack of the Kikuza rounds flying wide overhead. Our hides were badly situated, purposefully. They had to see us, running or shooting at them, to fall into the ambush. We had stung them too often. We had to get their blood lust up. We ran up hill for a long twenty yards under their fire, then we were into the cover of a small stand of cottonwoods between us and the Kikuza. None of their aimed rounds came close but, they were emptying their guns at full auto and random chance favors no one. I was glad to be in the lee of the woods. I hauled myself on the Prunty, my Mini-14 slung across my back, and kicked off after Flann and the Cooper twins.

After we broke contact my team laid their horses down at the ridge line we'd picked earlier. They reloaded their long guns and checked that their damn back up drillings were loaded and ready. Then we waited. I had time to wish I'd pissed before I'd knelt down behind the gelding, before the Kikuza rode around the woods and finding our tracks came a-helling up the holler after us. They were maybe a quarter mile off and hadn't seen us where we were bedded down, just our tracks going off into the gloom. I wound the sling around my arm and snapped off the scope sights. The light was going quickly, and I was going to lose the optics in the gloom. Iron sights would have to do.

I setup on them and waited. The Dragon curling up my spine, warming my fingers, setting me up. It didn't make me into a walking night scope, but it gave me an edge. My eyes were fully dilated, my heartbeat slow, my breathing slow and deep.

When they saw us to their downhill flank, with our horses forted up in the snow drifts, about that time was when Nate cut drive on them from their uphill flank. With all of his team. Two shots each from a rest at two hundred yards by marksmen accustomed to shooting offhand at three times the range, with guns made to shoot accurately for nearly a thousand yards. Each round hit home. Blowing every rider out of the saddle or knocking down the horse and rider. One man had tumbled off his horse and hit the ground, to bounce back on his feet and volley a burst in Nate's general direction. I saw two more shots hit him, spin him around and drop him in the creek.

The rest of the troop was down on this side and that of the creek. I blew the check fire whistle and waited for a long minute. Watching the light snow starting to darken the Kikuza troop horse's coats, letting them mill about. Which saved our sorry asses.

Just as I was about to stand up, there were three flat cracks from behind Nate's fire line. Then grenade air bursts popped over the killing zone, knocking down all of the surviving horses. Two helicopter looking things wobbled over the ridge and swept down towards my team. All whirring blades and struts with no canopies and guns flashing from the cockpits.

"-be go to hell." Someone swore into an open mike. Might have been me. I swung the Mini-14 up and emptied the magazine into the aircraft that was tracking to pass directly over me. I saw flashes all along the bottom of the cockpit tub, then the blade at the rear of the tub froze into visibility with a screech of metal. The thing stopped flying and dropped like a lead leaf, towards me.

Nate's fire team chimed in then, long spears of flame in the dark. My helicopter lost a rotor and just came apart in mid-air, short of my position. Random chunks of metal and fiberglass falling all around on me and the gelding, with the motor landing short of us. The Prunty struggled to his feet and knocked me on my ass as he headed south, having had more than enough of this shit. The other helicopter half rolled and tried to evade to the west, up stream. White flashes registered all up and down the rear and side of the tub. It just flew into the streambed, tearing up the ice and gravel, then flipping end for end as its rotors clipped the brush at the edge of the stream.

I sent one of Nate's boys out to retrieve the horses that had bolted, while we counted heads and did a little recon.

I headed for the helicopter that had landed almost intact. It was belly up in the middle of the stream, leaking blood, av gas and steam. The gunner had tumbled clear of the thing with one arm missing at the elbow and his knees not bending the same way. But there was still life in the pilot by the way he kept trying to get his head clear of the water. I squatted down, stuck the Mauser in his ear and asked him his name in gutter Japanese.

"Fuck you, you sorry, dickless, son of a bitch." She spat at me in Billingsgate English. Then her head slipped back under the water. I put the Mauser away and began to de-bone the helicopter, like a chef preparing a squab. Only I was using a machete to chop away the composite skin and separate the tubing ribs. The heavy blade on the one side being grand for breaking and delaminating the composite while the diamond toothed saw on the back side of the blade made short work of the tubes. I counted the hacks under my breath and hauled her head clear of the water every sixth stroke so she could snatch a lungful of air. I had the pilot freed up in short order. Eased her out of the shoulder belts and stretched her on the ground. I ran my hands over her body, dipping into her auric streams and rearranging things before her Subtle body got any worse. Nothing broken, but her spine was bruised, and one arm was twisted out of its socket.

"Nobody killed. Gunther got shot in the ass and his pony's stew." Nate squatted beside me, his breath steaming slightly in the yellow lantern light.

"Lucky is better than professional. That's why Gunther keeps eating good." I rocked back on my heels and put away my multitool, sheathed the machete. "Nate," I said in English as I finished lacing her in. "meet Pauline Hendrix, late of Hendrix Flying Service Limited." I'd rigged up a spine board and used some expended Flower saddle leather to improvise a neck brace.

"Charmed. You going to take her hair, or am I?" He had two scalps in one of his hands and a long skinner blade in the other. Nate had his moments.

She opened her eyes to see him looming in the lantern light. "Gezzus, you got talking bears on your side?" I heard Nate cough down a laugh and the skinner disappeared.

"Pauline, I present to you, Nate Dockens. He sings as well. Nate, she'd like to defect."

"Yeah." She grunted. "Fooking pissant Yakuza hires me to Fooking well teach them to fly Hendrix Gossamer Gyros. They buy some kits and then shanghai's my ass into Looking-Fooking-Glass Land. Shoot my mechanic for not being respectful. Feed me fooking riceballs and raw fish. Make my gyros into gun-Fooking-ships and now they fly like lead pigs. Fooking-ay I defect. Give me half a chance, I'll shove a ten-inch spanner up their Yakuza noses…" She slipped off into a soft snore. A grain and a half of morphine will sidetrack the best snit.

"Doesn't say much, do she?" Nate rumbled at me in Trade Manche.

"Very delicate and retiring. What papers she has supports her story. The Dragon says she designed, built and sold these gyrocopters. On my northwest coast. They got about two hours range at fifty miles an hour, carry two smallish crew and light arms. She didn't mention the rape attempt, did she?"

Dockens hawked a curse and spat over his shoulder. "Why these flying trikes?"

"Mounted outriders just disappear, horse or trikes, but set these fliers to scouting at a clean five hundred feet off the grass and you are mostly safe from nasty horse boys. If they can stay up. That would explain the jerrycans of gas on the mules the boys found, back at the first ambush point. They're quieter than dirt bikes, they don't blow up like hydrogen fueled trikes and she says they're easier to learn than a horse."

"Flying outriders, !Cono! If they are using them for nuisance patrols, any Overlander convoy would have them."

"According to her, they got just three assembled. One is having problems with the carburetors, the other two are here. But there are three in crates at the Springs's airstrip and sixty more being fabricated across the Veil in the Hanse."

"She really wants to defect?"

"The Dragon says what she really wants to do is shove a monkey wrench up a Light Colonel Bukawa's fundament and change his sex from the inside. Can't do that on the Kikuza's nickel."

Dockens whistled. "Can they do that? Change the rigging from the inside?"

"Wouldn't know. Why, you in the market for that?"

"I'd pay a cartwheel to watch."

"Yeah, I bet you would. They had a radio link. We need to clear the area. She says they still got two functional conventional helicopters. Any other prisoners?"

"Other than the lady, no."

The bodies were completely covered in snow when we left the killing zone. Old Man Winter had come to visit.

ALENA 48

The meal was a qualified success.

Barbara being particularly congenial, if not merry, away from the hospital and Ledhrad enjoyed the exotic fare. But we did not come to terms about either my presence or my status in the Hanse. I sent her away in better spirits than when we met, but I was still under house arrest and hobbled financially. We were a rich House, richer than I had known before the Bloodseal came to me, but not rich enough. In the eyes of the Hanse we were of the mid-range.

That next month I received Savka Andreev Kochiurov, the Confederated Houses Emissary to the Common Land and First of the Elders of the Jurchen House Displaced. I would have seen him shortly after the Twelfth Undersecretary had made her appearance at my door but Tallen had sent me a gift. I had managed to divert a shipment of arms from one of the arms manufactories in

the Slavic states to Tallen. Tank killers. I had also, before
the Twelfth managed to compromise my back-channel
supply routes in the Hanse, dropped a constellation of
satellite killers. They homed on GPS signals in low orbit.
Any GPS signal at all.

Tallen was delighted. Awarded me the ears and the tail
of a mythic beast called the Boojum and sent me a large
box with a biohazard trefoil on it. Also, a small arms
shipping box. The biohazard item was never released, and I
was given a strong caution over shipping such items from
the 'Zeme.

In the small arms box were the sword and the dispatch
case from Koshitsu in shadow. The note suggested I hang
this from a peg over the fireplace and see who turned blue.

After things calmed down a bit, I invited Savka
Kochiurov for late meal, customarily a rye bread and sharp
cheese accompanied by a light beer or ale. I set the stage;
coal fire, the sword and the dispatch case over the mantle,
two chairs and two benches for the guards, inlaid
chessboard with the food. The leather sack was upon the
board.

Tallen had caught me stealing the emblems.

It was in the scurry as we were loading out the horses
at Barbara's ranch. He had left the barn to bring another
load of gear out and I riffled through his pack.

I had the leather pouch open and was about to
substitute a quartet of silver cartwheels when I felt a cold
touch at the back of my neck. The bright edge of a knife.

"As lightly as I am bound, is this wise?"

"You walk lightly."

"You grave rob."

"I gather power."

"These are long dead, although the Koshitsu are..."

I could smell ozone crackling about us. I saw a horse
fly crisp and bounce off the saddle bow in front of me. I
could not draw a full breath, feeling, seeing out of the
corners of my eyes black lace curling about. Then it
withdrew and the ozone grew faint.

His voice was harsh, choked. "My House was..."

"Jurchen in shadow. They lost a cousin's war around the time an AngTerra civil war was in contest. The one between the English Crown and Parliament. They were still strong enough to simply come across and claim a stake holding on AngTerra. After a century or so, cautious relations were opened across the Veil."

"Then?"

"Jurchen in Sunlight was one of the last of the old traditional houses to hold on on the mainland but, they were driven from the land or they swore to the Takamikura throne."

"A second sundering?"

"Yes. Now the House exists, but like a cut plant in water, Rootless."

"And the ones who took oath to the Flowers?"

"Their names were written in pools of water on a road of mud. Their children live on, but not the House."

"What will these four graves bring?"

"The Confederated trusts only those who cannot grow roots in the land."

"They are the Medji for the Confed?"

I laughed. "Should you meet them, or any of the other six Rootless Houses, please do not use that particular description. I should hate to pay the gold to lay to rest all of the blood feuds that would result."

"I don't know about this, Alena." He withdrew the knife from where it rested on the back of my neck. "I was well and truly bonded to the Jurchen. Jurchen in Shadow by your conventions. Now you hold my bindings but, would…"

"I do not know how it would go but, I have a great deal of trust. Trust in you as a man, as well as trust in you as a terribly cross-grained and contrary, bullheaded individual."

"Thank you," I could hear the smile in his voice. "I think. Take them with my permission. The bag as well." He left the barn as silently as he had entered it.

Now they sat in the center of the chessboard, in the

leather bag. I heard the door open and my House stirred about me as Savka niJurchen came within my walls.

I stood as he entered the room at the head of his people, it being our conceit that every Dai is a Warrior and the Medji are only reinforcements in the event of our foes being vulgar enough to outnumber us.

He paused at the threshold. To either side of the door was a Medji in the proscribed Jurchen Livery. Each bearing a great sword in the antique leaf pattern. I was dressed in mourning white and white was draped about the mantelpiece. My two guards were in Mihaly livery and armed only with the long knife. I wore a hideout needler.

He bowed, his eyes flicking to each side, marking the Medji at the doors. I made a leg, my eyes holding his, without knocking over the table or falling on my bum. Ilona would have been proud. Then I walked to him.

"Savka Andreev Kochiurov of the Jurchen, welcome to my table."

"Savka Kochiurov. Madam Mihaly. The House you mentioned is but a story." He took my hand. "I am a bonded functionary for the Confederated Houses."

"It is the House Jurchen I address now, not the functionary." I retained his hand, the offhand of old tradition and slowly escorted him into the room and to the chair. "Tomorrow I shall receive the emissaries of the Confederated Houses. Tonight, I must speak matters of blood and honor." Behind us I could hear small struggles as his guards were replaced by the liveried Medji. Struggles that ceased as his guards were convinced that the liveried ones would truly serve and protect. Or maybe the liveried ones were simply killing them. As we got to the chairs, I heard the doors close and the great bolts slide home. "Matters that touch both our Houses."

"Indeed?" He was sweating, although the room was pleasantly chilly. "What matters may I ask?"

"The clocks are striking eleven, shall we sup?" I sat. Cut a slice of cheese and poured a schooner of beer. Cut a slab of bread. Placed all upon a plain china plate. He wiped his hands on a napkin and did likewise, his eyes widening when I offered my cheese and beer to my guards. He carefully arranged his on the testing plate and watched as both my guards and his new Medji consumed the food. Then I cut myself a wedge of cheese and poured a great mug of beer.

"The beer is the last of last year's brew. The bread new baked in my ovens and I have no idea where they bought the cheese."

"I once was planning on coming here to offer you my good offices in settling the terms. Some thirty Mihaly displaced persons have sheltered in our 'yards since the start of the turnover."

"Coup."

"Yes. And I rather believed you had made quite the accomplishment to slip the identity tokens though the barricades, seize the banks and make a nuisance of yourself. That you would bargain and bargain hard but allow the turnover to proceed and accept exile."

"I think not."

"Yes. I have come to reassess my beliefs. Your 'stay-behind' forces have stirred all of the Nomadic remnants into war on Mihaly..."

"Madgji."

"Quite. And their Koshitsu volunteers. Even some of our less steady Confederated units have exceeded their orders, somewhat." He sipped at the beer. "This is quite good. From your cellars?"

"No. But I shall send you the name of the brewer." I pushed the food aside. "The Mihaly have no intention of letting a Madgji linage seize the critical path, nor of letting the Koshitsu gain a foothold over the Sunset Range." I drew a pen knife from my sleeve, slit the leather laces holding the pouch shut. "In fact, we intend to eradicate the Koshitsu from even the High Range and the Wet Slopes. Leaving only their heads nailed to boundary posts as a sign they were once fouling those grounds."

His eyes were watching my hand and the pouch. "Strong words for a middling House."

"Middling House or not, all of the Pika are beginning

to walk our path. Truly?"

"War such as that is outside the banns."

"So are Kikuza dragoons shitting on the Empty Grass." That brought a shocked pause.

I snipped the last lace holding the pouch shut. "But I will make my petitions tomorrow. Tonight, we shall lay ghosts."

I unfolded the pouch and gently revealed the four emblems.

He stared at them for a long time. Long enough that the beer grew warm. Then he touched them gently with his dominant hand's fingertips. "These are graves, Lady."

"I know."

"The Koshitsu have been accusing the Confederated of 'interference' in internal House affairs…" He rubbed the Chrysanthemum emblem, raggedly cut in two, and he picked up the emblem encased in lead. "Jurchen in Shadow." His face worked through frozen emotions.

"So, I have been told." I turned my head away to watch the coals flicker in the darkening room. One by one the lights faded to black, the timers the frugal Hanse required shutting them down after a suitable period.

In the dossiers the House kept on all the Confederated personnel in the Hanse, Savka Andreev Kochiurov was listed as a Psychometric. We called them Sniffers or Finders. They could take an item and follow its provenance, the history, of the item back into time. Some did better with organics, cloth soaked in blood or sweat was a classic. Some things required long, long usages to get any sort of readings, think of a bed handed down through four generations. And as they followed the item back in time, they could perceive the people around the item. Sometimes they could evoke phantoms of those persons most strongly associated with the item or, the events surrounding it. Violence usually was the strongest imprint, driving traces into steel and stone almost anytime it flared up.

"And he lives yet?" I turned about. The leather bag was folded shut the emblems tucked away.

"Yes."

"You have bound him?"

"In service to my House."

"I should kill you now and throw the Confederated Heavy Armor into the plains to rub him out." He was not angry. His voice had the bleak tone of the man condemned to death by cancer six months hence.

"You could kill me. I think you might be able to kill him but, the price would be heavy."

"The Koshitsu assured us that he, of all that House's retainers, that he was dead."

"And the truth was?"

"They were blocking the advance of the Koshitsu in shadow, grooming a Sekau to retake the Jurchen House-in-Sunlight. We were offered alliances, to maintain our independence in the North. If we turned our eyes away..."

"You still had contacts with AngTerra after the ban?"

"Always."

I nodded. "He hunted those emblems to extinction."

He nodded. "Koshitsu in Shadow rescued not one in a hundred of their Manifested Dai. Less than that of the Fain. The Chrysanthemum Throne sent a short regiment of Medji across the Veil, against the ban and with proscribed arms, and they disappeared. Swallowed by that dark and bloody world. A drop of ink into the sea."

"He wakes the Dragon for House Mihaly now. He considers it a lagniappe that his main foe is Koshitsu, but he is of my House now."

"And if we should demand him?"

"I do not know." Bound but lightly. "Do you ally with the Kikuza these days?"

He coughed deep in his throat. A tiger giving warning. "Betrayal beget treachery. We are landless, shorn of Fain, shorn of honors. My Uncles died on the Sichotealin coast covering the flota, only the Confederated would take us in. Koshitsu gave us the cut direct, We were no longer a House. We were not worthy of their notice."

"Then why borrow trouble? Let Mihaly and the Pika send the Chrysanthemum to beg water in hell."

"And the Dragon will know, sooner than later."

"The ones who turned their eyes away, where are they now."

"The fortunate are in hell, the others are slaves to the Chrysanthemum Throne."

"So."

I returned to watching the fire fade. Letting silence make my arguments.

"They will fill his ears with our treachery."

"I think, given a choice, he will forgive House Jurchen over the Flowers."

He never noticed the sword.

TALLEN 49

When the big storm system came swirling down the foothills and roared across the plains there were only a few places you could find free range Kikuza. Most on the sunrise side of the mountains were in cities or forted up Overlander stations out in the foothills. It was worth more than any Flower's life to venture out into the plains in less than battalion strength, and even then, it was a chancy prospect. The foothills and the rolling plains were crawling with Ho'ne pods, lobo killers and the occasional platoon of Confederated Mounted off on a holiday. And every mountaineer from the Gold rivers deep in the north, of what should have been the Canadian Rockies, to the dry canyons of the Novo Jura's in the south hunted Flowers for fun and profit. Mostly profit.

The Pika had posted bounties.

Five gold bits for a Kikuza head, in brine, with a true

and sworn provenance. Five bits being just about the price for a string of three Prunty geldings, meat rights to a dozen buffalo, or the bride price for some of the more traditional minded Pika. Caused a sensation, it did.

We had a hundred jugged Kikuza heads by the end of my October and about twenty heads that we were none too sure of. I caught out one happy little trio who were selling any head that even looked remotely Kikuza. Fed one of the three to the Dragon and gave the other two to the buffalo. Dryland keel hauling is the gentleman's description of what happened then.

We got into the lee of the Black Hills, an outcropping from the Wahatoya Mountains to the east, just north and west of where Trinidad was in my world. Redleg Woman kept the caravans on the move since the Travelers sent around the Bloodbanner and the Long Arrow Bundle. The Bundle meant "War against outsiders, so stop your usual feuds and horse thieving". What the Bloodbanner meant was "No Quarter.

Redleg Woman was older than dirt, swore she knew my lineage but kept mixing me up with her cousin's nephew three times removed. He was dead thirty years. But she knew where the grass still was good under the snow. She knew where the waterholes were. She knew when the storms were due and when they were going over. And she had an itch for Kikuza. Several times the Flowers had tried to drop a commando in on her. Each time she got the itch and pulled out for the next rendezvous. Leaving an ambush force behind. Hard on the Kikuza.

The outriders picked us up, scouts. In weather like this the Pika used big, mute, murdering, dogs for close in defense. They had a ring of riders inside of the dogs, the lancers escorted us in. In the shelter from the northwesterly wind we could see a whole fifteen yards through the snowfall. Big improvement.

I whistled up a medical team and what passed for MPs among the Pika. They knew we were coming back with wounded, but not Pauline.

"Make sure she is stabilized, then east and north to the

Tinker Flats. She is under the hand of the Thirty Snakes." I took the hand of the leading Striker and emphasized. "Under the hand of the Snakes." He nodded. Met my eyes and nodded again. The first MP Striker we had at the camp thought prisoners, particularly Kikuza, were walking chew toys for his dog pack. When I got in his face about this practice, he challenged my authority, questioned my tactics, basic loyalties and probable parentage.

He died better than I had thought he would.

This impressed the hell out his Second. I gave the torc to him still slick with his former commander's blood and informed him he was now the First Striker of the police sodality and 'did he have any problem with me?' Not a bit.

I got off the sore backed nag and walked it to the horse lines. One of the cadets trotted up and helped me unsaddle the nag, clean its hooves and work some hot liniment into the sores I was raising under the saddle tree. Then I surprised the ex-Flower remount with some grain mixed with a dollop of bear tallow, draped a thermal tarp over its back and carried my saddle to the tipi circles.

The ring holder's oldest daughter took the saddle and my guns, handed me a mug of tea and a berry laden chunk of bread. I walked back towards the horse lines, gulping the tea and dipping the bread in it so I could eat the bread.

In the 1860's we put the transcontinental railway across our plains from the east to the west. Alena's people had put one in from Hudson Bay to the Gulf three centuries earlier, about CE 1500. It wasn't a railway precisely, being they hadn't stolen the idea of rails yet, it was more like a Roman road. Foundations set deep into the ground, built wide, horse high and defensible, and intended for a lower slung version of an Overlander.

The road had no real bridges, just fords. Even the fastest Overlanders took about three months; from Hudson Bay to the Gulf. It was a toll road too. With off ramps at the fortified toll booths and its own police-cum-militia to enforce the tolls. It coined money like a treasury stamping die, began to open up the Sunset Range like nobody's business. A string of cities sprang up along its route and things looked rosy.

Until the Commonality decided that the North American Continent was in dire need of rationalizing, and taxing. One of the places they landed the Invasion fleet was at the Gulf terminus of the road.

The first two hundred miles of that road are a long washboard of trenches and strong points now, some still full of skeletons. That was the war Alena had sketched, in my truck, on the way south. The war where the militias and Household irregulars delayed the Commonality Armies, until the Confederated Houses could arrive from the East and cut them up at the southern end of the plains while the Pelagic mercenaries wiped the Commonality Navy from the sea.

The cities that road had pupped grew up orphaned but grew up they did, serving the back-country settlements and the agricultural valleys to the west. They also served the city less plains, treating the Pika better than the Knobbers or the Cantry Ford people did. The Drysider city folk, the nominal Houses and single branches, intermarried into the Travelers as well as the greater Houses. They were all kindred, if ever so distantly.

Now they had two over strength brigades of Kikuza quartered among sixteen thousand Drysiders and Settled Pika. Occupation troops taking out their frustrations on the Mihaly and all the other Houses, real and notional, in the cities. All the Kikuza supplies on this side of the Sunset Range came from two airstrips; one at the foot of Fisher's Peak, the other just north of Manitou Springs. There was a smaller airstrip in Long Valley, the Mihaly home stake, maybe a thousand-foot long that might take a useful transport but, from what Alena told me, it would be an iffy proposition.

Airports were fords. Choke points and kill zones when the dice rolled right. I could take the two major airfields on this side of the front range, if I wanted to. Take one; dig small trenches across it the tarmarc, or park heavy equipment on it, and entrench a reinforced platoon covering it. If the defenders were motivated, it might cost the attackers most of a battalion to retake it and the rest of the brigade would be reduced to holding the airfield open. Take both of the airfields on the Front Range and all of the Kikuza on the grass would die or surrender by spring. But it'd be a slow fall for the Kikuza, butchery for butchery. The folk in the Drysider cities were kin to the Pika and the Pika would not stand and watch the Kikuza butcher them. They'd force their way into those cities with all the attending brutality of house to house fighting. There were maybe five hundred mixed Madgji and Kikuza holding the Mihaly Hundred, the lands around the airstrip in Long Valley, with their hands on the collective throats of six thousand Mihaly Fain.

Then I remembered the late Saburo and the problems he had trying to cold wield that mix of half-breed and tainted Nihon with the superior strains fresh from the home islands. I realized that, maybe, we had been using a hammer to dig holes.

The Bloodbanner promised no quarter. That meant even the most reluctant warriors fought like heroes out of yellow novels, because there wasn't a choice. But two thirds of the forgotten 45th Imperial Cavalry Regiment had deserted. Fled east over the grass and into the lower 'Zarks before Major Saburo's replacement had established a coherent hold over the unit.

They left before we raised the Bloodbanner, what deserters we had seen since then you could stuff in a small Overlander.

Two thirds of a regiment, two full cavalry battalions, scattered and turned their coats up and down the Front Range. And we hadn't really lifted a hand. Since then we had broken three battalions and massacred one, at the cost of a hundred Pika warriors and an uncounted trickle of freelancers. Not many more Pika than they would lose in the course of a season of war between the lineages but, the looting was better, and the head bounty was just honey on the flat cake. But we were seeing more and more motorized Kikuza. Trikes and four wheelers, better armored Overlanders and then Pauline's tinker-toy flyers. Soon enough, if we gave them time, they'd find a mix of technology and brutality that'd give us a very bloody nose. But to not give them time to catch their breath, we would have to assault. Butchery in the dark.

They had three working 'heavy' transports that could make the jump over the mountains in the winter. If those three transports failed there would be no resupply until spring or until the Home Islands sent more transports. Without the slow trickle of light mechanized troops, or the attendant supplies, they would have to hole up and wait for spring. We take down the transports and force them back upon the cities, where the Kikuza would begin to …back to butchery in the dark of winter.

I realized I was chasing my tail when I found a skim of ice in my tea. I threw it out and stumped off to bed.

ALENA 50

Ten days later I received Savka Andreev Kochiurov again. This time there was little ceremony and slightly less stage setting. I was in the solar where I had entertained the Twelfth Undersecretary.

The day after he read the emblems from Tallen's bag I had officially placed my complaints and requests before the Confederated. I held the Bloodseal. I controlled all the bank levers on 'Zeme, AngTerra and the Hanse. I had forces in being on 'Zeme that were contesting Madgji and the Flowers. I had allies, the Pika. And there were a double handful of traditional Houses up and down the eastern rampart uninterested in having Flowers, or their tokens, for neighbors.

Like most bureaucracies, being presented with a reality outside of their walls disconcerted them. It took ten days and the easing of the Hanse embargo before they had formulated a response. It, the response, had no connection with the facts on the ground in 'Zeme. It did have a connection with the facts in Brandann Haven and Hudson House.

They decided to have a consultation.

This was decided under the auspices of the local embassies of Confederated House and Southern Cross, with the observer and guarantor being our Twelfth Undersecretary. I objected in that nothing needed to be consulted about, I held the Bloodseal. I held the purse strings, and if the Confederated would simply perform their agreed upon role and confine the double damned Koshitsu to the Western lowlands, all would be well.

The response to that intimated that I was an adolescent female with pre-menstrual delusions of grandeur. I hinted that the apparat confronting with me had been gelded at birth with a dirty shard of glass in order not to pass his incestuous and quite damaged germplasm to future generations. I was quite certain of his inference. He was still parsing my insult when I swept out of his office. It should be needless to say he was not of the Jurchen gens.

I let them, the Confederated, organize a consultation in the House Mihaly.

Savka attended as the representative of Croton House, first among equals of the Confederated Houses. The Twelfth Undersecretary and a pair of high-ranking Crows were there. There was Adai of the Southern Cross who also stood consul for the Pelagic Houses. Cala whose House straddled the great river that fed Brandaan Haven on the Texas gulf, Randal Walker who was fed by the Six Houses of the Lakes and two factors who held briefs for about eight other Woodland Houses. All in all, the usual gaggle of orators and time servers.

And they had brought a Madgji, some cousin who had left 'Zeme a long generation ago. He looked the part, silver hair and strawberry nose. He was now propped up as an embassy. His minder was a Koshitsu, one of the main lineages from the way he carried himself and the way he dressed. Mon embroidered on the left lapel of his

Kareemacher tunic and an impressive imperial Chrysanthemum screen printed across the back of that tunic. His face was not quite right, coarser than his clothing. Mainland Korean I wondered. That was a killing insult, to be hoarded at need.

I gave the Madgji and the Flower the cut direct, a grave but diplomatic insult, and only addressed the Confed bureaucrats or the Hanse functionaries. When Koshitsu or the Madgji tried to direct a comment or a question to me. I did not hear them. Oddly enough it was not the Madgji that offered violence to me, but the ever so elegant Koshitsu.

The Flower had become more agitated as the morning went past. His chair was a low campstool at the left edge of my mahogany desk, his refreshment a piss-warm canned drink served without ceremony or glass. And he faced a carefully devised display of trophies, 'brought' from the 'Zeme before and after the direct gates were embargoed by Tallen's jape with the bowling ball. A buffalo hide cloak fringed with what appeared to be Flower scalps, several broken swords of the officer caste and a badly mutilated and suspiciously stained iconic image, supposedly of the current Emperor. And of course, the Norikuni Tachi, along with the battered canvas dispatch bag.

The only authentic items were the Tachi and the dispatch bag. The rest had been improvised by several of the 'Breaker of Nations' enthusiasts on my long-term staff. One of the local feuilleton channels had picked up the story. Someone having made available to them three different imported packages, a very bad cinema play, one excellent televised series and an excellently terrible opera.

I had lifted more than the emblems before we crossed over from AngTerra to 'Zeme, I don't think Barbara noticed. Or if she had, she had not yet commented.

The discussions had become a tiresome round of 'you must yield to the logic of the situation' opposed to 'we intend to prevail. Would you care for more tea?' When the Flower crushed his canned drink, kicked over his chair, and drawing the only weapon, a short tanto, left to him by an intimate and insulting search, lunged at me across the desk.

The Twelfth Undersecretary had the honors, putting a 10mm round into his face and knocking him down before anyone else had put hand to weapon. But close and firmly behind her was the Madgji. He used a full magazine, thirty Selai rounds from a very well-hidden pocket needle gun. (Upon reflection perhaps passed to him by one of the other attending functionaries.) All of which he emptied into the thrashing Flower. He proceeded to drop the needle gun on the floor, spread his arms and beg asylum. From the Mihaly.

"Well." I said. "This is rather a disconcerting turn of affairs." I was spattered in blood. The desk was spattered in blood, tea, and a cheap diet drink, which were doing no good to the elegant position papers now scattered to the winds. The Flower was thrashing less but burning more, with thin tendrils of smoke curling up from the needle point wounds. "Cousin," I said. "whose bread do you eat?"

He nodded at the corpse on the flagstones. "Not gelded Selai. The fools in 'Zeme have welcomed the very devil into their hearth room."

"And what would you have of me."

"A rescue and a forgiveness."

I sighed. "Do all the Madgji with sense emigrate?"

He smiled. "It would appear so."

I nodded.

I looked up to see Nathan at the double doors with a very indiscreet short double gun hidden behind his leg. "Nathan, do escort our cousin to the Walnut suite. And have this cleaned up. Send the carrion on the floor to the cycler." I did not want an autopsy on that carrion. The Hanse were very uneasy with us as it was. Gelded Selai. Meg save us.

I led the remainder of the consultation out into the secure garden.

"I must thank you, Madam Ledhrad, and compliment you on your deftness with a heavy pistol."

"He was still alive." She was looking at the blocky pistol still cradled in her strong hand. She was dotted with blood as well.

"Mm, yes. That is why our cousin, whose name I have unforgivably been remiss in remembering, touched him up with a magazine of needles. Training, conditioning and the odd rearrangement of genes at an early stage in the zygote. They make quite formidable soldiers. Useless diplomats of course, but the Koshitsu do tend to confuse the two."

I turned to regard the Confederated. "I would cite this as a further instance of faithlessness, on the part of the Koshitsu."

Savka nodded. "Unfortunately, he was not representing the Chrysanthemum Throne but simply aiding the representatives of the House Madgji."

I did the head bob that passed for a shrug among the Hanse. "Ah well. I feel disinclined to continue the meeting. You will excuse me, my friends, if I retire. Upon another day."

And I shooed them out the door.

The cousin was standing in the Walnut suite, with a sworn Medji covering him with a machine pistol.

"Mihaly." He nodded to me, his eyes downcast and his hands behind his back.

"And you are?"

"Gian Arkwright. Late of the Shortrun linage."

"And..."

"As you said, most of the sharp knives of the Madgji went for an Avar. You did not ever use us gently, Mihaly." His eyes were bleak, when he looked me in the face. "Cannon fodder at the best of times, less than that when the guns were quiet."

"The hand changes, but the blade remains the same. Your new-found friends..."

"Never my friends. Never before this and less now that we have heard of the killings among the Fain."

"And what do you bring to the table?"

"Treachery. And allies."

"Mm?"

"The Flowers have their own uneasy folk."

"Truly?"

"For every blooded Koshitsu, eager to give his life for

the god emperor, there are four low life troopers eager to
desert. My Madgji embassy is blessed with a secure back
channel and a gate."

"What price?"

He looked away. "Amnesty. For the fain who are
Madgji, for the Dai who fled the Kikuza, for the troops
who will turn their coats and strike. Exile for the children
whose hands will be innocent of blood, exile to somewhere
blood feud won't follow."

"Amnesty. For the Fain, for the Dai who never rode
with the Kikuza. Yes. For those who rode against the Fain,
no. Not even if they turn coat and ride the Kikuza down.
They may buy time. I will grant them ten days leave before
I loose the hunt. Ten days through the Gates and I loose
Pika and any other hunter. Agreed?"

"And for the Madgji lineages?"

"The ones who squat in my House, who pulled my
mothers down like wolves set loose upon Grandmother
Buffalo, who strut about with my heirlooms? I will flay
their skins to make dance drums, break their bones to feed
my flower beds, mount their skulls as spittoons and their
jaws to scrape boots. I will feed their souls to my Selai, my
Dragon. And we will draw a line through their name, dam
and sire and get."

Arkwright nodded slowly, his face gone parchment
white and suddenly old.

Suddenly much like the Jurchen.

"Forgive me, Cousin. I spoke in heat and not
necessarily in wisdom. We shall, consider, your offer." I
looked to the Medji. "Feed him, let him make his contacts."

And I left the room.

TALLEN 51

Things stayed quiet after we brought down the two gyrocopters. Another good storm system came down from what was Canada on my Earth, fine snow and high winds and then a day or two of bright cold. Rinse and repeat. The Kikuza brought two more big transports over the mountains, and then a storm system angled into the mountain interior and made things very chancy for low flying transports. If they wanted to, they could have got up above the weather and landed at the two airstrips on the dry side of the Front Range. But the Confederated were already rumbling about the increasing number of Koshitsu volunteers, advisors and Medji. By flying low, they literally stayed off the radars. Adding 'inappropriate' technology to a culture that did not welcome such technology was inviting official notice. Official notice meant that the Confederated would throw their fast armor into the Grass and drop mountain troops into the interior.

I asked Flann what was the difference between a Winnebago with six-wheel drive and a jet transport.

"RahVees don't spook the buffalo."

I smoked a bit more and let the coffee cool a little. "You keep going on how you'd like to learn to fly a gyro."

"Kinda like when I saw Grandpa on his first Harley. In the wind they are."

"Hmm."

That night they brought me a madman to sift.

I woke up with a hand on my throat. Mako'sae was kneeling by me, cold flowing off her clothing and her soul. I glanced to the door way and saw Flann starting to get dressed for a winter hunt. Someone had squatted in front of the door and sheltered it from the wind with a buffalo robe, a courtesy for the rest of the lodge's sleepers.

"I see you." I whispered to her. She was painted for night work and her eyes glittered in the faint light of the lodge fire.

She smiled. "That is good. We have a problem for you to solve."

I sat up slowly, her hand gone from my throat but not from my mind. "Raiders?"

"Selai."

I slithered into my winter togs and began to wake the Greater Dragon. "Close or reported."

"Close. We have a survivor, perhaps."

"Mhh. Marks of the Dragon?" The light in the lodge slowly came up, growing brighter in my eyes as the Dragon wakes.

"Very much akin to the marks you left at Huygens Kop."

I strapped on the Mauser and slipped my feet into a set of boots and shouldered my way out of the lodge.

They had the survivor at the edge of the encampment, under a quick shelter with halogen lights and a fuel cell heater running full blast. The shelter was another gift from Alena. It looked like a tin can tipped on its side and sliced in half lengthwise, much like the Quonset hut of my misspent middle age. It had air cells and shape changing soft plastic ribs in a folded-up kit. You laid the kit out on the ground and then inflated the air ribs to raise the hut, either with a carbon dioxide cartridge or a tire pump. Then you ran a twelve-volt current through the plastic ribs, setting them. Very sturdy and damn near self-warming. The material was highly insulated. Didn't break down half as easy as it went up but, there you go.

They had the ends wide open and our survivor was lying on a stretcher in the middle of the shelter. Guarded by six Aknepteh and Short Moon.

The Aknepteh were very stoic and their guns were focused on the bloody rags. Short Moon was not stoic at all. His eyes wide in a hasty paint job, three used hypodermics and an empty bag of saline solution. "Not good." Was all he had to say.

"Yeah, get out." I said dropping to my knees by the stretcher. "Bring a nag. Get the Snakes out and keep everyone away." I looked at the Mako'sae. "You game?"

"I stay." Her face was pale under the paint and the halogens.

"Let's see what we see." I peeled the rags away, my body steaming in the halogen lights. My auras were already skinning my hands and drifting through the air. The Snakes sealed the end to the south and making haste slowly, left. I could smell the blood, blood and piss and six-day old death. "How long?" I asked.

She stepped closer to the gurney. "A day, maybe, before he was found and two days to here."

The face was yellow and drawn, gashed here and there to the bone, the edges of the gashes dry but pus glittered in the deeps of the wounds. His breath whistled through his nostrils and fluttered one of the deeper cuts on his left cheek. Short Moon had a drip forcing saline solution and a broad, broad spectrum antibiotic in the drip by the hype hanging off the side.

His auras were cobwebs, fading. I slid lacy black auras in through his cobwebby grays to try and stabilize him, while I dragged the auric gauntlets on my hands across his

wounds. They sealed shut and then opened again as my
hands passed.

"The wound that will not heal." Mako'sae whispered.

"Yeah. The Dragon." I shifted position and knelt in
the melting snow at the head of the stretcher, my hands
cupping the dying man's skull. Then I started peeling what
was left of him. Like peeling an onion with your
thumbnails.

He was far down the road. So far that he had no name
and few memories.

A horse in sunlight. Hands plaiting grass into a rope.
Holding a smoking cigar. Polishing leather in firelight. Light
and dark. Rain, snow and warm sunlight against his face.
There were faces, there were voices, but there was nothing
more than that.

Then I came upon the Dragon. Young and hard faced
in a cold sunlit room, killing something small and pink and
helpless. Killing with the slow delight of a child licking a
candy stick. Behind the Dragon was a pair of killers in snow
camouflage and behind them something burning. The
Dragon finished and began again in a stuttering loop of
memory. The nightmare you could not wake from.

More threads led from this one memory. Kikuza
springing from snow graves with guns and long knives.
Flickering images of fighting, then capture and then back to
the Dragon.

And back to the Dragon.

I looked hard, if you can call what I did when I sifted a
man Looking, at the Dragon. This poor thing I held
between my hands could not see the auras but, I could see
the 'tells' of the Dragon as he toyed with his prey. I
watched him through the blood dimmed eyes of his victim
until I was sure I should know this Dragon when I found
him. Then my auras swept through the mind and body of
the man on the stretcher, like fire to cleanse a plague, and
he was released to what might come.

I opened my eyes and looked at the withered corpse.
The Mako'sae had not fled, but she openly held a knapped
obsidian knife. Like a child might hold a comforting doll.

"Two days by horse?" I asked her.

She blinked and the knife vanished. "Yes."

I gently wrapped him in the thermal blankets, tucking him in like you would tuck a child in for the night. I wiped my hands clean in the snow and dried them on the blankets.

"Six horses for each of us. We will likely kill the lot. Light counter-armor load out in case we run up against Panhards. Bring your Dark blades and your ball guns. Sing your death songs. Send to Herself that it is no longer a Cousin's spat but a Monster's ball. We ride against Takamatsu, a Miyake."

"We raise the whole of the Pika?"

"Why no." I stood in the warmth of the shelter, weak but still strong enough. I walked past her to the south door. "No. Twenty of the Snakes, you and Breaker of Houses will be enough to put down the dog of a Kikuza." I stepped through the membrane and there was a familiar horse shivering in the morning light. The loot I had ridden before. I really didn't need it. If I could have knitted up the 'wounds that will not heal' I'd been about as knackered as…well, I'd been fair knackered. As it was, it was an embarrassment. I stepped up to it and let it get a good nose full of my scent to calm it, huffed in its ear and it dropped dead. I turned to face the Aknepteh. "They did not leave him a knife, a blanket or a horse. Head and hocks and a good length of steel, agreed?"

They nodded. I turned and stalked off through the snow, Flann at my elbow.

"You know," He whispered in that sly way non-coms and old lags have, audible but untraceable. "You know, you would have made a helluva shaman."

"It's all Santa Claus. You believe so they will believe, and they believe so you will still believe. And then you all get tangled up and lost and end up believing absolutely. Get my kit together; I need to be gone from this knocking shop an hour ago."

I was gone within two hours. I left Flann, the Prunty; who for all its virtues was not much of a winter horse, and

the dogs with Redleg Woman. Much to all their mutual
dismay. Mako'sae and twenty-one Snakes all draped in
winter camouflage and gray paint came with me.

In that two hours I'd had a look at a topographic map,
a quick tea with Redleg Woman and culled twenty-one out
of forty-five volunteers. I packed; a couple of bricks of C4,
a pair of frags and four flashbangs. I also added twenty
disposable mortars to the unit loadout. Almost one for each
of us. They were more like a grenade launcher on steroids,
30mm. You set them up, rigged the firing sequence and got
away. Not too accurate. Not much range, seven hundred
yards being about the absolute maximum with a following
wind. But they had a five-shot magazine that fed the tube
on the recoil, so you did not have to man it after you set the
base and the bipod. There was provision for timed fire,
tripwires and other remote triggers, and their ammo was
preset to burst at five feet above any solid surface. They'd
penetrate any reasonable brush or tree canopy and they had
a kill radius of about ten yards. The best thing about the
vicious little things was that they were free. We'd recovered
six cases from a Kikuza Overlander. Force multipliers.

I let Mako'sae set the pace. I just forked a horse, tried
to catch a little sleep and figure out if and when and where
the ambush was going to occur. Someone had worked very
hard to set the stage and I did not intend to let his work go
to waste. I also did not intend for his plans to survive
contact with me. I let us get a half day clear of the
encampment and I called a long halt.

I hunkered down in the lee of my horse and had a hot
cup of something out of a thermos. I motioned Mako'sae
to join me. She hunkered down as well, her eyes glittering
in the depths of her paint.

"We ride to a trap." The first words out of her mouth.

I smiled at her. "Oh, very good. When did you come to
this knowledge?"

"An hour after my ass froze."

"You know, I am afraid my rude ways are corrupting
your language something terrible."

"You just wish you were corrupting me."

Yes. I stamped that thought down. Yes. "You never had a name for the one they left us?"

"No. And the dead were beyond anyone knowing."

"Tell me again how he was found."

"A scouting pod got downwind of smoke, tainted smoke. They got a line on it, circled to come from up wind and found a razed harvesting station. Sod hut just upgraded with adobe walls and a shelter with three walls for horses and the like. They'd thrown the dead into the hut and fired it and fired the horse shed. Took the horses and killed the rest of the critters, dogs mostly, as an entertainment. They'd staked him about ten feet from the hut, head tied back so he could watch."

"Watch what?"

She spat. "They were all dead before the Kikuza started the fire."

"Yeah. A stay behind team was likely watching your pod as they made the rescue."

I let her walk through the event chain.

"They didn't follow the pod."

"You get on the balloon phone and I'll bet horse, gun and saddle that there have been three or four such rescues in the last week. None of them ending well for the survivor, but none ending like this one. What would have happened to him if the pod hadn't recognized the nature of his wounds?"

"They'd given him the mercy stroke. Why?"

"Ah Kikuza just naturally like to commit atrocities, nobody would have thought much about it, just reciprocated when they got a chance. But those who'd been at Huygens Kopp, they'd see something special about the wounds."

"And trot off to consult Breaker of Nations."

"Right."

She said a breathtaking phrase in trade Manche.

"I don't think that is possible, given human anatomy."

"I need to send a runner..."

"I had a cup of tea with Redleg Woman while you were chivvying Snakes into line. By now there is a bare spot where the encampment was and a wistful reinforced company waiting for a Kikuza strike force to appear."

"You don't think they will come down upon the camp?"

"They are running out of seriously stupid commanders. Besides this trap was crafted for me and not thee." I finished my cup, stood and all my joints crackled like peanut hulls on bar floors. "Saddle up." I swung onto my horse and we started off again.

Every stop we made I stood in the stirrups and gave a quick look around with every sense the Dragon bore, and some high-tech optics lashed to a tip less lance. What I was looking for I couldn't have told you but, I knew I'd find it sooner than later. We stopped for a quick meal where the harvesting station had been. I could still smell the dead and the fire. We 'found' faint tracks leading us away and towards the Road. I didn't point out that they were not as 'faint' as five days in drifting snow should have left them. I just let Mako'sae and the Snakes have their head.

Later:

"You up for another 'Breaker of Houses' story?"

"I think I liked you better as a brave but simple Avar."

"Houses are wary of keeping monsters such as me."

She snorted in agreement, a small puff of fog trickling out of her daytime white camouflage suit.

"Judging from my experience," I said. "they would like to have the talents without the disrupting side effects."

"Side effects?"

"What the Chrysanthemum Throne wanted was domesticated Selai."

"What did they receive?"

"Oh, they got that. But at a price." I swung off the horse and trotted alongside of it, giving it a rest, stretching my legs and giving my ass a rest. "There are many ways to make a Selai, most of them killing nine out of ten of the candidates. The Kikuza found a fairly foolproof path of invoking those particular talents. Physical stress and drugs along with auric conditioning." I winced behind my snow mask, remembering sessions in a kitchen long gone. "They also devised a method of retaining a semblance of control. They stunted the candidate's brain."

"To what end?"

"Keeping the candidate at the mental age of three or four."

"Keeping?"

I swung back on the horse. "Yeah, the ideal candidate for the Kikuza short course Selai is about three years old. Just verbal enough to understand orders and instructions. Just rational enough to understand punishment and reward. And they bond very well with their creators."

She said something that I did not catch but I surely understood. Her aura blossomed in all the primary colors of killing before she got her emotions under control.

"Yeah. I had put three of them down before I caught on. They looked a lot older than they were, physically or mentally. They had a way of forcing maturity using infusions of hormones they'd harvested from the Anu-or so the story went. I found the dojo for making stunted Selai, at the end of that war. An old manor up in the very north of the Home Islands."

"And for the staff of the dojo?"

"They did not die well. Not well at all. The Dragon can be a very slow path to the next world."

I took a smugglers boat across the Yellow sea to Manchuria. Tipping four lacquered chests of drugs, herbs and thousand-year-old scrolls into the winter sea as we crossed. I thought that was the end of the Kikuza, between China and the swath I cut through Hokkaido. I had half a dozen heads and three dozen right hands salted down in the fifth chest that I buried at home. I thought I'd lost my last illusions as well. But all is illusion.

We cantered for an about a quarter hour then settled into a slow walk. I got off the horse again.

"This was to draw you out." She said.

"I think so. With luck and a bit of misdirection we might evade their ambush. But even if we counter-ambush them successfully, they will have gained their primary objective."

"To pull you out in the open."

"Yes."

"And your plan is..."

"To stick your head in the noose."

"That is reassuring."

"They are being cack-handed about it, no doubts there. Your hunter pod got snookered. The harvesting camp was a stage setting. But I think something happened. If we'd stayed at the ruined camp long enough, I think we'd found traces of a landing zone for something more than those light helicopters we've been knocking down."

"That story again." Mako'sae shifted uneasily on her saddle. She'd spent three years living a legend over on my side of the Gate. Enlisted in the American Army sometime in the late sixties and kept her light under a dark bushel. Mainly working as a logistics analyst. She had a good grasp of air mobile theory, from the time when the best thing out there was the Huey. She also had a professional disbelief in technology as a form of magic.

We'd heard tales of fixed wing aircraft scouting the Buffalo road, but they never landed, and they never lingered. I remembered the small aircraft that had dropped the commando stick at the Landing Strip Fight. I had not seen the like since. Its wings rotated up to allow it to hover. I'd debriefed Pauline before we sent her away about what aerial assets the Kikuza had beside the gyrocopters. She'd seen the C-130 knock-off transports and the light helicopters the Kikuza had ferried in the transports over the mountains. She had not been impressed with the quality of either the aircraft nor the establishment flying and maintaining them.

"One A-and-P mechanic to every four jumpsuits and that was being charitable and kind. They did maintenance strictly by the book. Engine replacement at 1700 hours of flight time, not before and not after. Check the hydraulic fluids for contaminates every 500 hours and not consider it might be a good idea to dip a stick every time you turned over a prop."

"And if it wasn't in the book?"

"It didn't get done. You've been around the block with these gomers before, ain't ya?"

"Yeah." Although it was horses and not flying contraptions I was keeping well.

"Uh-hunh. The pilots were all very low hours in anything, let alone type. All male and all from 'the pure land'. No Gaijin need apply."

"Helicopters and transports, any strike aircraft other than your gyrocopters?"

"Funny man. No, I didn't see anything that would even reconfigure as a fixed wing strike craft. They hung guns and rockets off the helos, but their own pilots were banging up the birds faster than they could modify them to carry weapons. One baka had only soloed in a taildragger when they stuffed him in an Alouette with three hours of simulation training. He got about two meters up when he lost it and scattered parts all over the tarmac."

Then I asked her about a tilt-rotor aircraft. Her eyes brightened even through the extra grain of morphine. "Sounds like a Boeing Osprey. You saw one?" Pauline was as crazy about flying iron as Herself was about horseflesh.

"Dropping Kikuza paratroops once. Any information on a Kikuza Osprey?"

"No. How big were the props?"

"Maybe forty-foot diameter, lots of down blast and they dropped the stick from the rear ramp."

"Osprey knock-off I'd say. That bird will make maybe three hundred knots on the flat and about four hundred nautical miles combat radius. They could carry twenty to thirty troopers, mount some hardpoints under the fuselage, light machine guns on the ramp."

"How rugged are they?"

"No idea, but three of the Boeing Prototypes fell out of the air with wiring and software problems."

"Think bad thoughts at it and it crashes?"

"They had a hard time making it pilot friendly. Can I go to sleep now?"

I told her I'd see her come spring. She drifted off and that night we sent her on her way to Tinker's Flats.

"Yeah, that story. Been wondering why we haven't seen that aircraft, now I know. They were saving it for an auspicious day. But something's wrong. They used it to insert the bait, but they didn't use it to recover."

"Maybe they wanted to make a trail?"

"They did make a trail but, they didn't drop the blocking force or the ambush team. I think the operation didn't occur. I wonder why." Bad thoughts and it crashes, I hoped.

It was the morning of the seventh day after the kill. We'd rode hard through the day and through the night, leaving a dribble of dead or dying horses across the ground. I kept a steady tap on every horse I rode. Not enough to kill them, enough that I was the Greater Dragon every step of the way. It would not do to stumble into an ambush without the Dragon riding me like a cloak.

The snow was dry and drifting in the wind. There were places where there was no more than a dusting of snow trapped in the late season's withered grass. There were stretches where there were sculpted drifts three or four inches high and ten yards long. For a horse in good condition it was not dangerous, if you did not force the pace.

We forced the pace.

It was almost twilight, the sun sliding down into the mountains, when the tracks we were trailing curved to the west. They'd lost one of the horses they had taken at the harvesting camp. Stripped it and did a quick job of butchery. Then they swung to the west. The horse was more and less than it appeared. It hadn't been that close to foundering when the Kikuza took it down. I had one of the troopers do a quick field autopsy.

"Sucker's bugged!" He was holding up a small black box, about two inches on a side, with a trailing wire and a blood crusted lens.

"Looks that way, don't it? Somebody's idea of clever." The blood had frozen solid around and over the exposed lens after they had stuffed it in the butchered horse.

"Blood done up and froze around the thing."

"Well don't clean it off, put it back where you found it, as you found it." I had no doubt there was an alert flashing on someone's flat pad. We'd been made. I didn't tear the trooper a new asshole. We'd rumbled them too.

I stood in the stirrups and gave a quick look around with the lance optics. Maybe four miles away there was a smudge nestled in the hills near where the old north-south road had run. Smoke, not from an open fire.

"What'd be that way?"

"Used to be a toll station. Flat place in the hills. Most of them are still standing, sort of. Adobe walls and fired tile roofs will last centuries."

"Flat place about fifty yards long?"

"Maybe, depending on what might you call a flat place."

A landing zone.

I gave the order to the guderon. "Open order, skirmish line, advance to the west."

I turned the troop towards the smoke and kicked it into a brisk trot. I was rolling dice again. We'd seen nothing of a rear guard or drag the entire time we'd been on their trail. So, I was betting they were still fat and stupid. I could have been wrong, but I wasn't. We got within a mile of the smoke before I decided enough was enough. We were on the eastern side of a slow rise, a rise tall enough to hide the troop but shallow enough that I still could use the lance and optics trick. I signaled a halt, threw out pickets and pulled Mako'sae and her Striker into a huddle with our backs to the north wind. The rest of the Snakes drifted out into a line just shy of the crest of the rise.

"What you got in your pouches?"

"Half and half, armor piercing and Selai loads." Nasty things, Selai loads. Mixed toxins bound to silver oxides in olive oil with a speck or two of white phosphorus, the rounds burst open on impact.

"Kill the handlers, leave me the Dragon."

"Why not stand off and shoot them to doll rags?"

"Light's going. You don't want to fight a Dragon in the dark. Even an Iting telung, 'Broken Dragon' would cut you up in the dark."

I dismounted. Pulled my rucksack, a pouch of grenades, and a thermal blanket off the saddle. I sketched out what I could see through the optics, let her take a look.

"Give me about an hour, then engage from that ridge line as you see fit, set up the mortars to cover the ridge line and the defilade. Then fall back when they rush you. I'll get myself out of the fur ball." I scooped a handful of dried meat and cookie dough from my pouch and ate it. Then I killed the horse. It collapsed in a tangle of bones and skin in thirty seconds. Mako'sae and her horse crow-hopped to about ten yards away. I think she was more bothered than the horse. Dead horses had become a commonplace in its universe.

"Don't shoot me, by mistake or on purpose, it will just piss me off. Understand?"

Then I went cold. Dropping my skin temperature close to ambient as I could, shrugging on my rucksack. I could hear one of the Snakes singing a ghost song under his breath as I faded from his IR goggles.

I wrapped myself in the thermal blanket and trotted towards the Buffalo road, angling to pick it up just south of the old toll station. Between the fading light and occasional snow flurries I figured I could just about stroll up on their positions. With luck I wouldn't have to pop a cap or break a neck until I was well inside their perimeter.

They were getting ready to up the ante, I was thinking. Maybe going to commit a full reinforced regiment of regulars to the glorious cause. Some happy spook boulevardier decided to drop a Dragon into the Grass, letting him or her have a good, noisy, time. Then disinformation would be planted hinting at Breaker of Houses having slipped his leash. Hoop-la, the resistance would fade away. Or if they got lucky, Breaker of Houses would come looking for their domesticated Dragon and Hoop-la! Honors all around. They'd had a standing offer of a patent of nobility as a reward for my head back in Manchukuo. I suspect the offer still stood.

But it looked like the first time they sortied into the

grass they seriously screwed the pooch. I think someone didn't have a clue about winter flying in the Sunset Range. Or like Pauline said, they knew fuck all about flying in general. The Osprey knock-off was flipped over. One nacelle ripped clean off and the tail crumpled like a giant had twisted it with his hand. No fire, no big jet fuel fire I mean. They had a little smoke coming out of a mostly ruined building. Lots of traffic in and out and around the building. Crew served gun positions on top of the building, a couple of quick graves scraped in frozen earth in the lee of the crash and six horses freezing to death in a wreck of a corral. The building looked like a stagecoach station from my early nineteenth century. Adobe walls, deep set windows and doors, and river rock foundation. The walls were slowly melting from centuries of neglect, deeply cracked from weather and deeply scarred from bullets, blackened from fires.

When I got close, I could See the troopers moving about in the building, their auras leeching through the walls. I could not sense the Other. The Gelded.

We had a name for such a thing. A name other than abomination. Alena referred to any crippled Talent as a Gelding; Selai, Skrinner or Gate Walker. Any crippled Talent was a Gelded one. Which practice, I thought, spoke volumes on how the Houses saw the Manifested. The Ächtet Zirkus, in the inner school, had more terms for how Manifested Dai appeared than words for rice. What Mihaly named Gelded we called Iting telung, Broken Dragon, and it was something shameful and cruel when it was a forced thing. It happened naturally, as well as being shaped. If it happened naturally it was a great sorrow. There wasn't a cure and you couldn't let them live, no matter how young they were when they rose to the form. Tsui lao te chieh mei, the Dragon that had formed me in the hearth room of the Three-Legged House; her first and only child Manifested as an Iting telung, a Broken Dragon, when she was ten. This was maybe sixty years before I came to the House. Tsu had kept a festival robe, that they had made for the girl, in a cedar lined box under her bed.

Hunting Dragons was chancy at best. None of the ones I had rubbed up against since I was coaxed into Manifesting had much of an auric trace when they were passing for human. And each one was unique in how the auras formed around him when he manifested the Dragon. Every Dragon manifested weapons but one might favor expressing his auric weapon as a cobra, another one favored flames. Oldest Sister said I manifested oddly. Not favoring any particular school. A Dragon at rest, when the talent had not been invoked, had almost no aura at all. One of the disciplines the Ächtet Zirkus taught me was to wear the Greater Dragon but not reveal it. I could trail an aura just as I could suppress it, very useful when you were hunting Dragons and their support teams. Broken Dragons rarely had the discipline to suppress their auras. But, if they were in a light trance, asleep on their feet, they were easy to miss. Their handlers liked to keep the Iting Telung in that trance, made it less likely that It would take issue with their leash and rip into them. Another reason the Kikuza favored the Iting Telung was that their auras barely reached a hand's width away. And so, the Broken Dragon had to be close to be effective. Safer for their handlers.

I made an assumption that might have ennobled the local command structure if I was mistaken, the assumption that our Broken Dragon was here but suppressed.

The Kikuza troop had an overwatch, using IR and what have you. Three machine gun positions placed on top of the station, three or four sensor clusters on extendable masts that were whipping in the winds. I was snaking up to the upwind side of the ruin, from the general direction of the wreck. I figured, or hoped, that my Snakes would spot the gomers on the roof, suss out the matching gun pits near the corral and pop caps whenever they got comfy. I'd rigged a drape with the thermal blanket and I just kept drifting a little closer every time the wind picked up.

I'd snaked through the outer pickets, mostly single riflemen in shallow firepits and winter camo, not bothering to pinch off their heads as I went by. Half of 'em had pulled all of their cover over them, shivering in the cold and not keeping watch worth a damn. Piss poor planning leads to piss poor performance. I figured the outer pickets were more for punishment detail, with the added bonus of alerting the unit if someone killed them. I left them alone and snuck up on the inner rings, IR, motion sensors and radar.

But overwatch is worthless without tucking a human into the loop. Air cans of nitrogen and insulated coveralls could approximate my trick of cold walking, at least for a while. And radar or sonic motion detectors would be foxed by the snow swirling about in the wind. But humans could tell that the IR ghost on the screen was not just a swirl of snow, snow does not leopard crawl into the wind. I tried to keep to shadows even in the snow.

When I got a little closer, I tumbled to their trap. Then I knew that they had ran through all of their useful idiots and put the professionals in play. A Miyake like I had told Mako'sae.

Someone hadn't been a careful little rigger, pushed by cold or by just being sloppy, he'd scanted the camo and backfilling the dirt. Three feet away, under the scant snow drift I was cuddling, I saw a directional mine. And not just any mine, but a directional anti-tank mine. A box of plastic explosive and shaped copper that would self-forge a billet, a billet that could easily punch through light armor, or disperse a Selai into a pink cloud. Overkill, but I was an Operatic Plot Device. It was focused on the front of the ruined station. Down their own throat as it were. I was not particularly happy with it being pointed away from me as the back blast would be a bitch.

I quickly, more quickly than I should have, crawled away from that mine. The light was failing fast and I knew that Mako'sae would have to engage soon or break contact. The dead horse telltale had let the Kikuza know someone was on their doorstep, breaking contact might be more of a problem than she realized. I back slid a little more, looking for angular forms in the dusk. The three I saw were in a loose arc about fifty yards from the front of the station. I figured there were at least another three in an arc to the west, because there was a gun pit on the west side that hadn't been manned. And if I was laying these things, I'd put a couple more with a wire mesh screen in the front of the mine close to the Osprey knock-off.

I thought about it a little more. They had to be command detonated. Someone was waiting for me to come knocking at the south door or to the west and they would send a spark down the line.

And blow their own positions to hell and gone to get me.

I fished the FM transmitter out of the rucksack, pried off the battery pack and stripped out some of the not-quite superconductor wiring that was laced through the antenna. Tied a frag to the wire and estimated I had ten yards of usable wire. I bent the wire around the terminals to the battery pack. Then I stood up.

I don't know if the Mako'sae saw me stand or if one of the gomers on the roof line saw motion and reacted, but I could hear a round hit the rooftop with a meat-ax thump about the time I had the frag whirring through the air like a bullroarer. I let it fly in the general direction of the first mine I'd spotted and as it paid out, I dropped flat on the ground and triggered the on switch, dumping the battery into the wire. It didn't short until the frag hit the ground at the end of the wires reach. And being more lucky than good, it triggered the cap in the mine.

I think whoever was commanding the mines got spooked and set them all off, or maybe they'd gotten dumb and set them in series and not individual. Later on, I counted eight mines, all but six focused on the station. I just dug myself deep into the frozen ground as things went shrieking overhead. My rucksack ripped away, and I got one hell of a bruise from the straps as it went. Lost the last .308 with the rucksack. I couldn't hear much at first, but I could feel shockwaves through the dirt I was mindlessly digging into. Those automatic mortars, maybe. I quit digging and standing up, ran north. To the east and slightly south of me the defilade of the ridgeline was covered in bright flashes as the mortars stonked where a surge of white camouflaged troopers assaulted the ridgeline through the dusk. I forced myself to look to my front and made my own charge. My favored shovel in my left hand and the Mauser in my right.

The station was a wreck. Its roof dropped into its middle and the entire South wall smashed into smoking rubble no bigger than my two fists. Broken heavy machine gun barrels and a light pack cannon were sticking out of the smashed roof, along with one of those light armor recon cars they liked. It was burning with lots of smoke and secondary poppings. I stumbled over several corpses in the foreyard, recognizably human so they hadn't stood up to the penetrators. I swung wide to the west.

Behind the station, under a collapsed awning there was a wheeled APC, like the one burning in the station. This one hadn't been hit by any of the penetrators, all buttoned up and with a light machine gun in a turret shooting at ghosts in the light of the burning station. It was pinned fast to its hide by a heavy beam upended over the hull back of the turret. The driver was making the six by six wheels smoke in the frozen dirt.

I flicked the Mauser to full auto, jumped up on the hull of the APC and bent the hell out of the light mg with the shovel. Then I shoved the Mauser through the slit in the mantlet and emptied the magazine. Ten rounds of .45 caliber armor piercing ball ammo, bouncing around in the compartment, produced a lot of screaming that I could barely hear through the ringing in my ears. I banged on the turret, once with the shovel, like I was priming a grenade. The back hatch flew open and three survivors rolled out with their guns on spray and pray.

I dropped down the front of the stalled carrier, I changed my magazine then holstered the Mauser. When I crept around the flank, two of the survivors were down and dying. Friendly fire. The third one was pressed against the open hatch and trying to load a fresh magazine into his gun. I knelt in the lee of the hatch and grabbed his ankles, pulling his legs from under him and pulled him through the churned-up dirt. I flipped him over and went to work debriefing him.

One of the two Gelded Selai had died in the crash, a day ago. The other one was at the rear of the waystation, tucked into a bomb proof along with his handlers and a Major in the Kempetai. The waystation was the trap we were supposed to be led to. When the Osprey knock-off crashed, the Kempetai crawled inside and made it into a strong point.

I don't think everyone knew about the directional mines. At least Joachim didn't have a clue. There was a vague notion that the Kempetai and their wet team had purged the Nachi command file of the half company of Sansei that had been tasked to hold the waystation. I had a brief hope that the mines had done for the Gelding and his handlers. Then I felt it wake up and strip the Chakras from one of its handlers.

Not a lot of self-control in an Iting telung. It was awake, hungry and indifferent who knew it or who might serve as dinner.

I looked down at the fool weeping between my knees. Just a tanker, Joachim Stahl. Nothing really special, good with diesels and light armor. Lately seconded out of the Commonality Dai. A European Commonality Gaijin.

What a Gaijin was doing working for the Kikuza bore further examination. And a Gaijin who was a non-commissioned officer no less. One who worked for a living, not some cashiered Staff Embezzler from a ceremonial light regiment. I knitted up some of the tears in his Subtle body and sent him into a light coma. If I didn't come back, he'd freeze in his sleep, which would be a mercy, really.

I got to the back door of the waystation just as the surviving Kikuza Sansei boiled out of the wreckage. They knew what had laired there with them and they were more than willing to take the risk of freezing in the dark or dying under the knife of a Pika. If they had known I was out there, the calculations would have changed.

As it was, they scuttled away. Then three of the handlers in grey and white camo staggered out, pot shooting with their dress pistols at the poor bastards running into the dark. Right on their heels came the Gelding, dragging something by an arm and waving a swagger stick about. I back shot the three handlers with my Mauser, one round dead center each, between the shoulder blades. The Gelding shied from the muzzle blasts, dropped his dead man and his swagger stick and shouted to the burning doorway behind him. Then he drew something that gleamed in the firelight and charged me in a crouch like a football nose guard.

I pumped four rounds into one of his knees, dropped the empty gun and pulled my shovel out of the back of my belt. It flattened his nose on the fore stroke. The back stroke took his ear off on the way to breaking his collar bone. Not dead but certainly down for a bit. Two more minders came out of the smoke, one with his hair smoldering and the other one favoring an arm with pink bone gleaming in the firelight. Neither one got more than a step out in the fresh air. I axed them down and then threw the corpses over the top of the armored car. I waited to see who else would come out. I snuggled myself into a corner, watching the Gelding thrash and wiggle in the middle of the patio at the back of the waystation.

Someone fired off a burst of paintballs from inside the waystation, raking them across the open door of the armored car and through the shadows where three of the dead minders lay. Nothing moved. Trash on the winds, but nothing moved. I could hear guns, deep booms and light crack-crack-cracks, the crumps of mortars or grenades. But nothing cooked off near me. I could hear the fire, feel the heat. And I began to see a drift of auras, standing out from the smoke like colored firework smoke at night.

Something sidled out of the smoky doorway, paintball gun in one hand and a dark glass blade in the other. He was crouched, bent almost double, his head swiveling constantly but gracefully, slowly. Quick movements, graceless movements, they draw the eye. He was graceful like a Tai Chi Master, his movements flowing through the flickering dark. When he was just within reach, I swept a curl of my aura through his Subtle body. Kempetai.

I broke the arm with the blade, dislocated the gun hand with a sudden brutal twist. Then I dropped him to the packed and filthy earth. The Dragon had stunned him, much like a shot bag to the back of the head. He was someone else I wanted to take a little time with. Get to know.

I picked up a bent length of rebar and dragged the Gelding around to the lee side of the armored car. I dropped him a good twenty feet from Joachim and drove the rebar through his belly, sticking the Gelding to the frozen dirt under the snow. He was starting to knit up his wounds, so I took a brick and pulverized his joints; knees, elbows, hands. Then I sealed the crippled joints with a smear of the true Dragon, a lick of fire to cauterize a wound. He kept trying to throw auric probes, looking for someone to drain, someone to ease his pain. I took a moment to cauterize the charka centers that generated and received the auras.

Then I went back for the Juni Kempetai. The graceful one with the glass knife.

By true dark it was quiet. I'd put the Gelding down, when I knew he had nothing of interest for me. Even with his Charkas cauterized and joints crushed, he was still as dangerous as a gaffed shark. I used the glass knife of the Juni to take the head. Joachim wasn't much better off than the Gelding, but his existence had a purpose, I wanted him for an exhibit. I spent a little more time and energy knitting up his injuries. If they let him live, after the inquiries were done, he might walk with a lurch the rest of his shortened life. Joints heal oddly at the best of times.

And graceful Juni Kiba, he had been a reluctant wealth of knowledge. The order of battle for the next wave of 'volunteers'. The fact that they were losing three out of every four aircraft they put across the mountains. The lamentable truth that they were not getting sufficient aid from the more rational factions in the Confederated in 'rationalizing' the Pika and the Mihaly. And only slightly more support from their likeminded cohorts in the European Commonality.

This explained Joachim's presence. And the presence of a short troop of Gaijin armored cars. They'd snuck through the Confed cordon a light scout troop of armor. It also explained why the Confederated were not getting more involved as the Kikuza ramped up their presence.

I rather wished I could have kept the Juni. But he had a hideout capsule. Unusual for a non-commissioned officer but maybe standard for a minder. Even the Dragon could only delay that death. He was shamed that he had failed the Emperor but, he was oddly reassured at how he failed. They would welcome him at the shrine, at Shōkonsha. So many of his comrades had fallen to the "Breaker of Houses", there would be no shame.

I waited until I picked up a skein of auras to whistle a recognition pattern. Not Shave-And-A-Haircut, but something like that. They paused, right inside my limits and someone whistled back.

"Hoy! Snakes!" I yelled.

"Ay-up."

"Come on in."

Two of the raiders slipped through the wreckage and subtly covering me and my prize, took a knee. "You Okay?"

"Yeah. Lost my head set again."

"Uncle Dockens said you lead with your forehead. Catch." He threw me a handset. I slipped it over my head and worked the earbud into place.

I pushed the talk button. "Five."

"We setting up here?" Mako'sae asked.

"Weather closing in?"

"Think so, and we got walking wounded and prisoners."

"You do? Prisoners?"

"Well they back shot half of the Flowers for us and then put their helmets on their rifle butts and called quarter." Dry surprise came through the FM link. "I thought to let a higher authority sort it out."

Meaning me. "Thanks." I stood and looked over what was left of the buildings. We had minimal cover to the west and nothing at all to the south. But we could pull down the rest of the roof and make a lean-to to keep the snow showers and wind out from the north and east. The fires were mostly out. I looked to the scouts. "Any out buildings worth looking at?" The older one shook his head. "Might have been a tack barn once but between us and whatever you let fly it is just kindling wood."

I winced. I 'let fly'. Another episode in "Breaker of Nations Part II". I gave the scout a dirty look, mostly wasted in the gloom. "How many are we going to cram in here?"

"Fifteen of us, less than ten of them."

I clicked the talk button. "Okay, bring them in."

She double clicked back at me.

"Go find the balloon set up." I told the younger scout. He nodded, sidled out of the corner I'd snuggled into next to the armored car and the adobe wall, and disappeared into the gloom. I had a suspicion we were down to a horse for every other man and we needed to get a little back up.

I shoved my chin at the older scout. "Grab a couple of 'em and start getting a perimeter set up, might be some guns in all this mess that still work."

"You think they may be back?'

"This is the only place to get out of the weather, cozy up to a fire and get a bit to eat. They'll be thinking about coming back while they are still warm."

"Fuckin A." And he grabbed two of the first in through the gaps in the wall and was gone.

It took about a half hour to make the place survivable. Cooking horse steaks over an open fire in a very old steel drum, drinking water laced with a small tot of sake and getting a half hour sleep before standing to guard. We had canvas nailed up over the worse holes in the north wall and draped over the six-wheel scout car. Tucked our walking wounded in close to the wall and sat a guard over the prisoners with a full auto shotgun.

I duckwalked over to the prisoners, looked them over like I was picking Sunday dinner. They gave me the same wall-eyed look I once got from bull calves I was about to promote to steers. Everyone was wearing snow camouflage, so I had no fucking idea of who was senior. I just reached out and snagged one out of the huddle.

"Lowlife. Your rank and the name of the donkey that your whore mother accused as father."

I shook him until his jaw wobbled and snot flew. I back handed him and then let them see that I was not the ever so frightening Pika Snake leader. I was worse. I was smoking in the dim light of the chem sticks.

"Talk to me. All I will do is strip the meat from your bones and scatter your soul to the dark. She," and I waved at the Mako'sae who had stripped to the waist to let the horse doctor dress a knife wound across her back. "She likes to play with her food for a long while."

She gave me a considering glare, then turned and smiled broadly for the audience, opened her obscenely pink mouth in her corpse gray face and licked her black lips with a red tongue. The huddle drew tighter, almost like mice trapped in a corner.

"We begged quarter." The prisoner I had in my hand was squealing, like I had docked him with a dull knife. Not quite pissing himself. But a smaller, more coherent Flower in the middle of the huddle raised his head and glared at me. "No honor..."

I dropped the hapless Nachi and kicked my way into the huddle to kneel with my shoulder pressed up against the speaker. "I have no honor. You know what I am. Why did you think to turn your coat?"

He nodded with his chin. "They fed us to that thing. The Pika couldn't be any worse."

"And then you found me at the end of that path."

He nodded.

"You are one lucky baka. I lied. I have honor. Of a sort." I held up a hand and it slowly became gloved with black lace, crawling up and down the hand like ants. "There are things I need to know, and I will know them, one way or another. There are things that once done, once seen, cannot be unseen. If I find them within your heart, you pay the forfeit. Understand?"

He nodded and closed his eyes to what I was about to

do. I swept the black lace dripping off of my hand and over his head and then drew it back into my hand with a twist and a flurry.

I had already sifted him when I knelt next to him, but stagecraft is always in order. I nodded in a dumb show and stood. Then I walked through the huddle, trailing my hand over each of the Turncoats.

One had been with the Iting telung, he looked me in the eyes, his rimmed with shadows like kohl. "Shall I sleep?" He asked. "Shall I sleep well?"

I nodded. "You will sleep at Shōkonsha with your fellows." I took him by the back of the neck and quickly flipped through his memories then peeled his auras away like a magician pulling a tablecloth. He had not hunted with the Iting Telung but, he had stood guard while it fed. He was dying in any event, of fear and shame and a horror that was eating him alive. I scattered his auras to the night.

He drooped into my arms and I lowered him to the ground. His eyes were shut, and the dark shadows were fading into gray. "Wrap him in a ground cloth, lay him straight out in the snow." One of my Strikers nodded, and I turned away.

We got the balloon up and bounced a signal off of it. Dockens replied and said that he'd have Flann and a remount troop to us in three days, weather permitting. Herself was coming.

Joy.

I made a turnabout the camp. We had two working machine guns and three broken machine guns that one of the Tinkers was trying to cobble into one working gun. Lots of the Flower AK knock-offs. Two of the anti-armor mines still existed. In their crates. I left them there. We had just enough fire teams to make a nuisance of ourselves if a Boy Scout troop from my world should come calling. But we were only cold and not freezing. We were fed and the Strikers were cautiously fraternizing with the Flowers. Three days or a week before things might get chancy. And if a mob of Flowers came looking for their tilt wing, I might have to think about signing on the Turncoats.

That was not going to set at all well with either side, but they were edging towards that mindset all on their own.

The Pika were a lot like the Irish were supposed to be. "All their wars were merry, and all their songs were sad." Which wasn't really true for the Irish, but it almost captured the Pika's attitude. Think Samurai with a sense of humor that was about twelve years old. Puns and practical jokes, mostly involving buffalo chips and the random snake. If you didn't cheat at dice, fought well, and died well if you had to. Hoy! You were an honorable foe. And if you ran away if you got the chance well then; when the season of war was over, sit down, tell lies and drink with us.

Killing Grandfather Buffalo or wantonly killing Brother Horse, that was a different thing. War outside the banns. And you might burn out lodges in the summer, that being more of a nuisance than a killing stroke. But you did not burn in the winter or kill Fain. Or anyone not armed.

And seven times never kill the Buffalo.

We won't even mention ploughs.

The Flowers were a dime novel version of Samurai Yakuza from what I could figure out. The further away you got from the Throne, the more corrupt. But that was propaganda from both me and their yellow press. My Grandfather on my Father's side once told me that, "The best soldiers make the worst neighbors."

I didn't believe him, being full of 'honor' and 'Boys Own' novels. But he was right about it, he being a 'dammed' Horse Soldier in the Civil War.

My wars were darker than the Pika's. It was always a surprise, not always a pleasant surprise, to encounter someone who fought with some attention to the 'rules'. Often this just muddied the tactics, on both sides. When you expect the opposing force to help you recruit irregular forces by the 'exemplary' atrocity and they instead insisted on community building…

In my war, in China, I could almost always count on the IJA, and later the Reds, to recruit for me. I tried to avoid recruiting for their forces, but I will admit that I didn't always have the control I desired. Once or twice I had to resort to exemplary atrocities in my own units to get the attention of my troops.

I bedded down between the Flowers and the bulk of my Pikas. Wrapped a ground cloth about me and began to drop into a light sleep, with the Dragon drifting just under the surface. Then Mako'sae slid into my ground cloth. Her hands under my parka.

I wasn't too surprised. We had been dancing about since the courts martial in the sweat lodge. She knew me better than anyone since Li Na had died under the knives of the Kikuza. But there were restrictions and conditions and forbiddings. She was my executive officer. And my keeper. And the executioner, if I got out of hand.

Then in a cold camp, at the end of a long day of killing, she came to my bed. Her face scrubbed clean of paint, her hands clean.

Halfway through the night I asked her. "And what will I call you in the quiet?"

She smiled into my chest. "Dael." She raised her head, smiled again into my eyes but her smile did not reach her eyes. "Until this season of war is over, Dael."

I smiled back and I hoped my smile did reach my eyes. My auras strengthened and wrapped about us enfolding her Subtle and Overt body. "Well met, Dael."

ALENA 52

I interviewed Arkwright several more times, gaining details about what he offered. The Embassy Gate opened into a roadhouse in the passes to the west of the House proper. A 'quiet' Gate, large enough for at most, three at a time. He had names and contact points for the Turncoat Kikuza, names for the few Sleepers within the House proper working for the Kikuza or the Europeans. Lists of Fain that had escaped the grasp of the 'turn'. All helpful, nothing un-looked for.

Then he casually dropped a lit match in a bucket of gunpowder.

We were at dinner. I was getting to know him. He was not particularly talented beyond a firm grasp of trade and a dab hand with a needle gun. But he was educating me in just what had transpired in 'Zeme.

"And Reiten said that the Tokumua was very unhappy

at the way the Madgji and the Kikuza action teams had taken the Elders in the House. All went down fighting. None were captured. Tokumaua had two Kempetai action teams culled for incompetence." He sipped at a cup of tea. "They wrung out all of the aides to the Elders, demanding information on bizarre operational programs."

"Oh?"

"Yes, programs with names from potboiler suspense policiers. 'Iron Fledgling', 'Lakewood Gnome', 'Buttermilk Sky'..."

I stopped listening, my own cup half way to my lips. When I had gotten past the mindless paperwork of opening the Townhouse and took my keys to the office and its computer, I received a very short overview of everything. Everything. Everything since the House Mihaly on 'Zeme fell. Information had been percolating in to every major consulate and Household we held through the fifty Worlds, overt and covert. Piling up like mail in a corner. If I had gone to the Hindi Imperium I would have opened and inhabited a dwelling suited to my apparent wealth and standing, the same with Little Englander or any of the other 'comfortable' covert milieus. This assumed I lived to open that House. But, if I had lived, I would have found a suitable residence ready, with servants and an appropriate Legend in the covert milieus.

Much of the information was mundane; costs and solicitors and taxes and bribes. But some things were not so mundane. Hidden from the casual place holder and referenced under code names.

All three of the operational names Arkwright was prattling about over the tea at the end of the lunch were secured under three levels of warding. I knew the names, not the information under them. And he knew the names because the pig buggering Kikuza were trying to pry them out of the dead.

I shuffled the poor man off to his pleasant but confining suite, set the guards to condition one and passed myself into the Mihaly's office. It took an hour to get past the paranoid security systems for our version of the

Concierge. It ran my fingerprints, my iris, my blood type and it listened to my voice as I sang a simple children's song.

Then I had a ghost appear…

Marta niMihaly, my mother's aunt. She was dressed in a dress that was fashionable a long generation before I was born. The system displayed her image on a large screen monitor but, the image was grainy and dark. First generation film? The room behind her was the library in Adobe House, the oldest residency. But it was not the library I knew. Differences crept into my awareness. Trophies, art, silver service. All were slightly different than what I knew.

She blinked. "I am Marta niMihaly, warden of the Mihaly House. I will not insult you by elaborating on how closely held the knowledge I am about to impart to you is. If you have any reservations about your right to this knowledge, stop the replay now. If you continue on it is on your head alone." Her eyes wandered to the desk top. She was dark haired still and her face only had a hint of the lines I remembered. And there was no tremor in her head. "Then," She said. "let us begin."

And in twenty breathless minutes I had the reason why the Chrysanthemum Throne wanted my lineage broken and my House overthrown.

And the way to break their hold on Mihaly, on 'Zeme.

It took three days for the idea to flesh itself out in my mind. Then I called in all the major players, except one.

I had my Komornyik set up a very high coffee service and called in Savka, Barbara and the Madgji ambassador. After coffee and the pierogi were rationed out, I leaned back in the winged chair and cleared my throat.

The boys quit discussing trout killing and turned their fascination upon me. "If taunte Marta was still alive she would be stunned by what I was about to say and then promptly issue death sentences for all of us." I sipped at the coffee and weighed the expressions on the three facing me. "This truly is a case of 'I can tell you, but then I have to kill you.' "

"Good coffee, 'Lena." Barbara said, balancing three pierogis on her knees. "So, quit teasing the boys and tell them."

"Mihaly has a bolt hole." Three bolt holes, but let's not be technical.

Silent consternation.

"And should I be hearing this?" Said Savka.

"Of a certainty since I intend to suborn you and your House."

"That House is a fiction."

"Of the three cadets about to Manifest, two will be Fain and thus cast out, no?"

I received a growl and nearly a face full of excellent coffee. "How many of the Cotswolds live as retainers to the Confederated Houses?" I asked.

"They live..."

"How many? I know of four, all in their last decade if not their last months of life, with no successors. Truly?"

"Your sources are mistaken, Mihaly. There are but two Cotswolds left. And your point is..." And the card turned over in his mind.

"Yes. We would shelter your Fain. All of the abandoned you can reclaim, behind our bolt hole."

I turned my gaze upon Arkwright, who was sitting with his mouth open. A bright man, for a Madgji, but more capable of a set piece intrigue than improvising a conspiracy from the whole cloth.

"Beside you there is a box. Within it you will find a presentation tile." He looked to his left with the stunned horror of someone sitting next to a terrarium full of cobras. He glanced at Savka, who was still turning the card I had offered him over in his mind. Arkwright reached for the box, snatched his hand back as if the cobra had struck. Then slowly took the box and opened it.

Nestled in white satin was a six by six tile of obsidian with the chop for the House Madgji sandblasted in it. Much as a hiltless knife is emblematic of leaving a House, such a tile is the mark of a Footlocker House. Sable on sable. His face went dead white. I spoke.

"Now turn over the tile, Madgji." He blinked at me. Just as I was Mihaly, I had addressed him as Madgji, in the form that indicated head of the House.

He paused for a breath, then he turned over the tile. The obverse was white ceramic with a House chop in red and gold, a chop that indicated an independent House. Madgji, in the old Nagi script.

"This is what I offer both of you. Rebirth. A true beginning."

"A bolt hole?"

I turned to Savka.

"Yes. A Gate unknown to the Confederated Houses, un-sanctioned and uncontrolled."

The Madgji stroked his hand over the white tile and laughed. "They know no law but their own, Jurchen. They are unregenerate Dai. No mercy outside the House, but...why Mihaly? Why?"

"This cast of the ivory by the Kikuza, it is the first move in the end of the game. Europe is all but domesticated, Asia is enslaved, and the Pelagic Houses are fading against the Kikuza. Soon the Confederated Houses must take on the attributes of their opponents if they are to stand." I sipped at the coffee. "I would not care to live under those regimes. Eisenring at every table, sitting with a clipboard and a red marker documenting every slight and every failing. Keeping a stud book and culling the crèches, domesticating the Pika and plowing the grass."

"So, we flee." Barbara finished her pastry and set the plate on the floor. "That galls me."

"We cheat the hangmen. Leave stay behind teams that only know twisted ways into the bolt hole. Let them harry and recruit."

"They could force them...suborn them, slip ringers into the recruits?" Ventured Savka.

"Has anyone ever forced a Gate, successfully, without a betrayal within the defenders? And as for doubled recruits, there will be methods to limit exposure."

"This has not been done before."

I turned to Savka. "Are we sure? If it prospers, none

dare remember it happening."

"What of the Gates here, to AngTerra, Little England and all the rest?"

"First, we stop-thrust the Kikuza. Then purge the collaborationists in the Confederated Militia Office." Savka sputtered a protest. "Peace, the Pika are killing Kikuza fresh from the Pure Lands. Someone is turning a blind eye to the Chrysanthemum Throne's intentions. Or are the Confederated breeding for stupidity now, successfully? And as for our links to AngTerra and the Hanse; we walk between the Worlds because we can, not because we must. There will be other Gates."

TALLEN 53

By the time Flann got to us, we had all settled into a cautious sort of truce. None of the prisoners were Issei, few were Kibei, the over educated third generation. Most were descendants of the Flowers that had overrun the Coastal Houses and started to marry into the local peoples. The Issei and other interlopers from the Pure Lands had abused them as much as they abused the Pika and their cousins.

Only the vague hope of getting to lord it over the Pika had kept the rank and file conscripts with the program. When they found that they had become meat on the hoof for the Iting, that soured them on the prospects. The Nachi in their wisdom had sorted out the 'reliable' from the 'suspect' and intended to use the 'suspect' to screen the rest of the unit. As well as feed the Iting telung.

Calvin Kita, who was the Ainoko, a half breed trooper,

who'd lipped off to me, had suborned his half company. The first volley from the ridge line and they hit the dirt and let the 'reliable' pass over and through them. Then they popped up and expressed their resentment at being Iting chow. They still lost about a third, between the Pika and their own forces. But the 'reliable' troops melted away and then Calvin cried quarter.

The other amazing thing was that the Pika gave quarter. Mostly gave quarter. But the Mako'sae had given the command and nobody really wanted to risk getting on her bad side.

Flann came through the snow squalls leading my Prunty and dragging a train of sleds for the wounded. He was agog at seeing close to fifty prisoners, we had picked up more survivors as they began to freeze in the dark, and kept his mouth shut. Mostly.

Then the long-legged galoot somehow sussed out the change in Mako'sae and just about lost his hair from contempt of Snake. He did lose a couple of teeth. But she'd pulled that elbow strike.

"Heh!" One of the Strikers, I think it was the surviving observer of the sniper team, laughed into his armpit. Drank some of the fresh coffee and grinned at me through the dirt, paint and dried blood on his face. "You never guessed they were siblings."

I was chewing some buffalo jerky, which was the only reason I hadn't dropped my teeth. "Mnh. Thought siblings couldn't See each other?"

"Ah that is just something we lie to the nosy parker-birds about. Maybe Grandmother's Great-grandmother walked that line. We don't. Besides, she's a Snake and they do what they please."

"I got a toothache." I said. Flann was kin to Dael. Kin. To. The. Mako'sae.

This took some solid considering. He passed me a steel flask with paint stripper in it. For the toothache. And he nodded. "I can understand that, Breaker."

Four days of changing weather dogged us to the next camp. The Ainoko and the Pika rode pillion and every one of them carried arms. In case. Just in case. Dael told me I was out of my ever-loving mind.

"If we run across Kikuza, those Flowers going to fight?" She was huddled with me, one hand on my heart, her breath steaming around my ear. Snow hissing against the tarp I'd draped around us. The rest of our troop were huddling over spirit lamps or dried buffalo chips. I was just at a steady glow. An undervalued benefit to being an Operatic Plot Device bundler, steam heat.

"Yeah. They already did. Most of them. They try and cry quarter to Imperial troops and they'd shoot them to doll rags."

She huffed. Angry.

"They are close to being Pika," I said. "more than the Pika are close to being..."

Her elbows were sharp, she didn't pull her strike like she did with her brother. I didn't finish the insult. "What are the Tinkers going to think when we bring Kikuza..."

"They are Ainoko. And they are sworn to me, no?"

"Yes."

"And I am of the Thirty Snakes, until this season of war is past?"

Long silence. "Yes."

"Then they are Snakes. And we all know that Snakes..."

"Are outside the banns."

"So, they tell me. Think the Tinkers want to get up in Aknepteh business?"

"Not now." She grinned. I felt her auras light up. "Not ever, if they can help it."

"Not since the Greeks counted time by the Kalends."

"What?"

"Sleep. Worry about tomorrow later."

She huffed again.

Flann was the ramrod. He kept his best men at the drag and to either flank of the column covering against pursuit. Ahead of us were placed four-man troops, laid up about a half day's travel apart. They'd have pickets out and joined the head of our column every time we came in sight. If they got wind of anything, their orders were to ride in our general direction lances up and each rider barely in sight of the ribbons on the lance tips. Four riders could quietly sweep a path better than twenty miles wide when the dice rolled right.

The snow squalls were turning into showers, into proper storms. This time Old Man Winter had come to stay. We heard light aircraft once, off in the distance and in the first day of the trek before the weather really started to turn.

The last night, before we could expect to hit Tinker outriders, I asked her about Flann.

"Thought you Snakes were supposed to be orphans?"

"Flann? Well..." She huffed. "You know there are nineteen nations?"

"Mnnh."

"Eight here in the middle of the Empty Grass. Four more to the south of the Empty Grass in the Big Bend ranges."

"That's twelve."

"Yeah. Pika been known to count all the way to fifty on occasion."

"I stand reproved."

"Seven more. North of here, along the Sunset Range..."

"Front Range."

"Who's telling this, you or me?"

I huffed in imitation.

"Along the range up to the Saka river and East to the headwaters of the Big River, there are seven nations. My lodges were from the Arathak Nation."

"Were."

"We backed the wrong side in a power struggle. Not a fatal error; but a raid and a season of the White Death while we were trying to recover from the ill-advised allegiance. Then we were two alone."

"So?"

"We came south. Flann was young enough to be adopted into a Lodge with little fuss. I was older, once of a warrior sorority, once a mother. I would have been an uncomfortable presence."

We lay in silence a while.

"The Aknepteh." She said. "They take those of us who do not have a Lodge and cannot find or hold a place. And we have a place then."

"And..."

"They are outside the banns." She shifted to huddle closer. "Most of us die under the stars, some leave the Grass and disappear into mist, and some find a place under a Lodge."

"Hmph. What does Flann think of you and I?"

"He is amused. I think I shall have to commission one of the more respected Contraries to entertain him." And she huffed something under her breath. If I had the construct right, Flann should sleep with one eye open.

Red Leg Woman met us at the edge of the Tinkers' camp, snow dusting her shoulders. She counted the horses, noted the riders and then catching my eyes in the falling light nodded slow approval. We rode into the encampment. The Murdering Dogs thoughtfully marking the Ainoko and the Pika, my Wolvers, and giving me their usual hard glare. I guess they resented non-union predators. Then we had the required round of boiled buffalo jerky, flatbread, canned potatoes, hot tea, boiling coffee and the occasional tot of harsh skullpop. No one mentioned the Ainoko as they slowly morphed into Wolvers. They traded their parkas for buffalo hide coats and the thermal tarps cut into long hooded serapes. The Pika latched onto the Imperial off casts and embellished them with embroideries, studs and bright paint. Soon enough they blended into one swaggering stand of troublemakers.

After a heavy snowstorm skirted us to the north, Red Leg Woman moved the camp twice. Then we settled in, right off a major track to the east.

"This wise?" I asked Dockens.

"Things are changing." He poked at a winter's potato buried in coals in a chimenea. "You take notice of all the Pika drifting in?"

"No."

"Not the ones that can barely sit a horse or know how to lace a snowshoe?"

I blinked at him. "No."

He fished the hot potato out of the coals. Broke it open and scooped the steaming pith out with a small spoon made from horn. "A lot of new comers."

"Red Leg..."

"She is bedding them down, finding 'cousins' to show them around and feed them. Three long trains have come through since you came back, food and sundries." He looked up from his food. "The weather over the Sunset Ranges is especially bad this winter."

"Herself?"

"Detained we hear. But a convoy of Confederation Blacklegs, infantry and armor, and Eisenring lice is due."

The Blacklegs, infantry and armor were tolerated. They were no more corrupt or abusive than any standing army, a lot of them were kin to the Pika. The Eisenring were not kin, nor tolerated.

Eisenring.

Generations back the Dai had come to the unpleasant realization that allowing or encouraging crossing over Gates higgledy-piggledy had opportunities for blowback.

So, they formed a paramilitary order much like the Templars to police and oversee the Gates. Seizures and 'fines' paid the Order's expenses and the 'Iron Ring' consulted closely with the powers that controlled the Dai. Except for the Kikuza, that is. And with little fuss and not a lot of attention, the Eisenring got a fat portion of the wealth flowing through the gates. And they got to be the bogey men that policed the Gates, corrupt bogey men.

Most of the Houses came to a reluctant accommodation with the Eisenring. Houses and their allied constellations that had extensive trade across the Gates used the Eisenring as an independent customs 'House'.

The Eisenring was tasked to stop epidemics and pandemics propagating across the worlds the Dai touched. The Spanish Flu of 1918 being a good example, although I was told that it came from one of the Muscovy worlds and not from a military camp in Kansas. In addition to disease control, drugs and 'inappropriate' tech transfer were heavily taxed, prohibited or sanctioned. Inappropriate tech can discomfort ruling elites, recreational drugs can offend the sensibilities of the dominant culture, the Eisenring helped to suppress such unpleasant outcomes.

Barbara had rubbed up against a tech sanction team. She still held a grudge.

The Pika liked Eisenring. They considered them a cheap live fire exercise. Only fifty years ago they quit putting Eisenring heads on lances around the Overlander Stations as a common practice. They still killed them on sight but, they stripped the bodies and left them to the coyotes and the birds. The Confederation could pretend to not know, the Eisenring would pretend to be baffled at their missing personnel and the Pika were just happy little savages following the Buffalo in the time-honored fashion.

Occasionally someone in the Eisenring directorate decided there was a need to investigate and rationalize the Pika. They might outfit a small expeditionary force to overawe the simple horse loving Pika and then send them off into the Empty Grass. And the expeditionary force just faded away. The Confederation Armored Cavalry would occasionally find burnt out hulls down in the Gulf coast badlands with matching serial numbers to the missing units. Or an Eisenring gun might be sold at Cantry Ford as a 'genuine' Pika War Band trophy, with unit patches stiff with blood and a finger in a jar of skull pop. The gun might be genuine. The finger was most certainly not. And that would be the end of that effort at rationalization.

"Lice, eh?"

"Hmhmm."

"What does Red Leg Woman intend to do about it?"

"Dunno. She told me you were going to take care of it."

"Truly?"

"That's what she said."

I dug in my pouch of pemmican, took a pinch and ate it. "You got any suggestions?"

"You being 'Breaker of Houses' and all, I was just going to sit back and watch."

"Okay. Be that way. I'll just dress the Wolvers up as Pika Warriors, set them on the Confeds when they roll into the lagger all fat and stupid. Then roll back up the trace to Cantry Ford, scalps and other trinkets a flutter from the radio masts. Ainoko and Aknepteh leading the way into the Ford for a bit of R&R?"

Dockens got real pale under the fifty-summers tan. "That is against the..."

"I am far outside of the banns, being a Snake in good standing and a Skinwalker to boot. I have been just about as well behaved as I can stand to be." I leaned in closer and looked him in the eyes. "So, if we are going to play silly bugger games, we are going to play for keeps."

"And..."

I hawked up a ball of disgust and spat between his feet. "I am going to collar the first Eisenring I come across and I am going to turn him inside out, like skinning a rabbit. I'll roll his hide in snow and give to one of the women to make mocs out of it. Then I shall ask the fortunate Eisenring what it feels like encountering a noted monster like myself."

Dockens grunted. "And if we entertain the Eisenring outside the camp?"

I kicked at the snow. Looked up at the sky. "Ah hell. Let them in. Set me up a demonstration. Say I have to drop a horse occasionally for the balance of it. Make sure they see me. No Selai loads, if you please." I smiled at the sky. "I'll give them a show."

He grunted again and gathered up a fist full of Pika and hustled to the horse lines.

As it happened, he got to the Eisenring before they came to call upon me. Didn't kill them but Dockens got them diverted out into the snow. Let the Confederate regulars in. The Eisenring were in very light armor, not well suited for winter operations. Lost, orphans in the storm. The Eisenring Directorate sent more out to us after that troop quit filing reports.

A day later Herself arrived. I heard the ruckus, waking

up alone, and slipped out into the night. Horse troopers, light armor and a handful of snowcats. The 'cats had the Mihaly crest in dark red against mottled grey.

Her Household.

One of the Confed Officers trotted his horse into the ring of Chimineas, dismounted with a flourish and handed his horse off to me as he ran off to open the doors to one of the 'cats. I took the horse to the lines, pulled the saddle off and rubbed the beast down. I gave the horse to one of the hostlers.

And I walked away. There were four pallets around the inside of the lodge. Two by the door and two across the fire ring from the door. I remember hanging up the Mauser and taking off my snow moccasins, but that was about it.

I remembered Dael later shivering in my arms, ice cold and painted for a sweat lodge.

Morning and nobody said one god damn thing about Dael to me, or about Calvin or about Joachim. One of the Great Murdering Dogs came up to play the dominance game with me. I thought about just leaving his picked bones in the lodge doorway. I guess that thought got across the species barrier. He quietly tucked his tail under his nuts and went off to take care of urgent business elsewhere.

I was in a mood.

Dael had gone before I woke. I changed clothes from the skin out and flaked off several layers of skin in lieu of a bath, one of the many benefits of being an Operatic Plot Device. And went out to breakfast.

I was finishing my coffee when Short Moon came strolling by. He was wearing more clothing than normal, a wool poncho and hood. He dropped down beside me and scooped a tin cup full of mush out of the communal pot. Started eating it with his fingers.

"Herself is in need of our counsel. Walking Knife."

"Truly?" I swirled the coffee. Drank down the dregs.

"Events, she says, are moving apace."

I looked at him out of the corner of my eye. He was staring off at the western horizon, or where the horizon would be when the sun came up in the spring. Face fixed in that solemn 'lard won't melt on my tongue' gaze. "I bet you've waited all your livelong days to say 'apace', eh?"

He flicked a glance at me, started to break up and then mastering his solemnity again, went back to searching the horizon for signs of spring. "Truly, you are a corrupting influence."

"You don't know the half of it."

A corrupting influence. I'd known that even before Kludge Willm had bought me. I hadn't just manifested my talent for casual mayhem when I arrived at the Western Front. From the time I was ten I used to regularly beat the living shit out anyone who slighted my late mother or my two living sisters. That included the step-family on my step-mother's side. They learned that I had no fear, a high tolerance for pain and little shame. And if I couldn't fight fair, I fought dirty. They were glad to see the back of me when I went off to the college. I was glad to see the back of them. Except for Da, who loved me but did not know what the hell to do with me. My sisters were gone by then, one to Oregon and one to Chicago and a TB sanitarium and then to her grave. My half-sisters were bitches and my half-brother was a worthless, toothless, piece of shit. I smiled at that long-buried memory, toothless to his grave he was.

I stood up and popped my back. I'd remarked on several new faces in the camp, with tidy new winter outfits and spiffy government issued iron hanging off of them. I marked them for Confederated force cadre, Clerks on horseback. And there were several ass kissers trotting along behind the Clerks, scared of their own shadows on the dirty snow. Expecting any moment to be the honored guest at a scalp dance. Madgji. And Madgji not acclimated to the Empty Grass or used to sniffing armpits with the giddy Pika. So, she had cut a deal. With both the damned Confederated REMFs and the back stabbing Madgji.

Joy.

I kind of preferred the Juni Kiba. You knew where he stood and all. He didn't want to make friends with you, just kill you. What I'd gleaned from Joachim and the occasional Madgji that I'd 'made' an acquaintance with made me want to turn them all, Confederated and Commonality, out on the snow field buck naked with raw meat tied around their necks. Then turn the Great Murdering Dogs loose for a rodeo.

Maybe I could encourage that outcome.

I walked over to Herself's lodge, stiff legged and spoiling for a fight. The Pika shied away from me as I crouched to enter, the Dragon at full spread just in case they were thinking of protocol.

Inside was different than I had imagined. They had grafted the lodge onto one of those inflatable Quonset huts. Then set up a conference table and a dammed white board and they were taking high tea with Herself and Barbara Ann. Or maybe it was low coffee. But it was less of an audience and more of a debriefing. Dael was wearing paint, just a light sketch of her 'daylight' face. She was reporting to Herself from a campstool by the table, with one of the eternal metal coffee cups steaming in Dael's hand. All the places on the table were full. I was loath to elbow my way into the select, at least without shedding blood, so I found a bench up against the wall.

Joachim was in a far corner of the hut, under guard by Snakes in their full dress, artfully dirtied skins and leggings over thermals, and he was holding hands with a slight man in a black turtleneck. A Truthfinder, I guessed. Joachim looked better than he did when I dropped him off at the medical station. One arm was strapped to his side and his face had fresh butterfly bandages over the lacerations. Someone had scrounged a Confederated Mechanized Unit battledress for him. No rank tabs or unit flashes but, the uniform gave him a little dignity. He was a bit glazed over, I had been rough on him at the waystation.

Dockens appeared and handed me one of the robin's egg blue tin coffee cups and settled in beside me on the bench.

"Been a long morning already?" He asked.

"Yeah. You want to give me the skinny on the players around the table?"

He nodded. "You know all the Pika except that Elvis

there, he is the new Stinky Box warden. Then there are the Confed representatives, those three jaspers off to the weak side in the matte black jumpers."

"Huh."

"On the strong side are the Madgji, a new allied House to the Mihaly."

I grunted. "Allied."

"Yes, and they bring to the alliance some interesting assets."

"I'll bet." The last I'd heard the Madgji were assets of the Mihaly, wholly owned assets. And likely to be liquidated assets for their attempt at supplanting the lineage. To rise to the status of 'Ally' they would have to have brought something significant to the bargain.

I almost dropped my cup when I figured it out. They were rolling over. Rolling over on their former patrons. They had to be. And giving us some sort of backdoor into the cities the Flower detachments were squatting on. This was significant and my dislike of the weasels abated. I'd kill them if they got in my way, but I wouldn't go looking for them.

Maybe.

And how did Alana and Barbara Ann cross over into the 'Zeme anyway.

"When did Herself come across?

"The day or so after you left. Came down the trace from Tinroll with a reinforced troop of Mechanized Cavalry and scooped up and organized a company of Dragoon Horse out of the waystation guards to come out into the Empty. Every Flower that the Mechanized Cavalry unit encountered bit the dirt and was seeded in a potato patch. Alena's Own Dragoon Horse felt slighted that they didn't get to plant Flowers."

"Thought the ground was too hard for digging?"

"They make an excellent digging charge now. Everything is all up to date with the People." He grinned with fake tribal bumpkin enthusiasm. "Hoy. Here comes the Mako'sae." And elbowed me in the time-honored fashion of friends commenting on sleeping arrangements.

Fuck.

ALENA 54

I saw Tallen enter the lodge. He had on the winter camo, knee high moccasins and his gun. He also had a large chip on his shoulder. I wondered if he was stressing over my sudden appearance or the company I kept. Mako'sae of the Thirty Snakes had brought me up to speed on the involvement of the Commonality hegemon and the surprising turning of the Ainoko. The even more surprising acceptance of their surrender was not mentioned in the debriefing.

Then I realized that there was an added complication. I could scent it through the paint and medicine sachets the Mako'sae wore. I could see his eyes track until he found the Aknepteh. Dockens had alluded that things were suddenly changed. For the better in his estimation.

I touched Barbara on the hand, but she was already watching the play.

"You want him here?"

She meant at the high table. "No. He is bound, if ever so lightly."

"Have I mentioned that I resent you letting me make a damned fool out of myself?"

"Obviously. He was more bemused than amused." I moved a sheaf of papers to give my hands something to do. "Late tea, in the Little Englander fashion. You, me, and the dogs."

"Going to freeze out the Snake?"

"No. But…I need to know what he intends."

TALLEN 55

She sent a flunky around to ask me to tea. And Bigdog with a mussel-shell collar came to escort the invitation. I was mostly over my snit then.

And it was a snit. I was relieved that she showed up. I had about run out of hats to pull rabbits from. I was happy she had not gone 'home' with Barbara just in case Braugham had evaded the double dutch I had arranged for him before we'd come over the Veil. I was interested to know just what the hell she was doing with the Madgji and the REMF Confederated. And I had a bad feeling about the linkages between us.

And I wanted advice.

They had a small lodge set for Barbara Ann and the dogs. Stosh stood up, regarded me and then turned his back and lay down again. Bigdog waited until I settled onto the rugs and then dropped his head in my lap.

"That one missed you." Said Barbara.

"Yeah. Lots of cold camps, I missed him."

"Mhn."

"Tea or Coffee, or...?" Alena settled in on a cushion to my left.

"Coffee." I looked her over. Her hair had grown out. Been tended to, lighter streaks through it. She'd changed and I wondered if there was a real mismatch in the flow of time between Hanse and here. Or if it had been a lot rougher than she'd let on. "Cushion?"

She darkened. "I…got clipped by a hit team just as we came across the Veil to 'Zeme."

"In the ass." Drawled Barbara. "Wasn't a Selai load, Oh Breaker of Houses, but it knocked her down. She was being obstinate about letting her escorts lead."

"Let your people do their job. Rule 127."

"I shall make a note of that. You have noticed the Madgji." She changed slightly, then changed again. Presence. Command presence.

I nodded. "Yes. I take it they have rolled over on the Flowers."

She nodded. "They provided me a backchannel gate to the 'Zeme."

"And the price?"

"It was acceptable. And your tame Flowers?"

"Mihaly by spilt blood. Wolvers of the Breaker of Houses." I challenged her. I settled back against the seat. "To business then. The Madgji have an advantage to provide us."

Her phernomes filled the lodge. Barbara Ann got that cross-eyed look I have seen before, much like when someone broke wind in an elevator.

"You are bound..."

"But lightly, if at all." I sipped at my cooling coffee, ignoring the gentile whine from the dog nestled in my lap. "Agreed?"

"And your price is?"

"I have none. I wish to break the Koshitsu, but I have grown very fond of the Pika and my Wolvers, who are neither fish nor fowl nor good red meat. I would not easily countenance spending either to throw the Flowers back across the mountains."

Or anywhere else. I hid behind the cup and considered this. Once I would have spent Flann and all his kin to grind the Koshitsu into bone meal. Once. Now, breaking the Flowers and confounding their plans for the plains and the cities at the edge of the mountain ranges was enough. And not worth the bloodbath I once considered fair trade. I had changed as well.

"And I would." She stirred with anger on her cushion.

I shrugged. "If not, you need to counsel your Confederated cadre. Or teach them to dissemble their disdain."

Her phernomes faded into the air. "I did not know."

"Save for the Mako'sae, who have you been briefed by."

"And she mentioned none of this."

"The Confederated were exceedingly wary of her. And exceedingly respectful. She is one of the Aknepteh, a credible and well-remembered threat. If she took umbrage at someone, his bones would certainly entertain the coyotes."

"And of you?" Asked Barbara.

I grinned. "I am but a superstition from the dark ages, I do not exist. Yet."

ALENA 56

I opened the portfolio and handed him the operational orders. "The Confederated Regulars are currently distracted cleaning house. We do have a reinforced company of mechanized Regulars and I have the command of the company. Ten Snowtigers and ten light troop carriers."

"Snowtiger?"

"Medium wheeled armor, optimized for snow operations in the Empty. Organic mortars and three-inch, quick firing, cannon."

He whistled. "Since when have you been to Armor school?"

"Since it took us about a solid week running down the trace to here." Barbara chipped in. "First Colonel Gephart was oh so eager to impart his experience and wisdom to an inexperienced..."

"I thought we were through with the pissing match." I said to them.

"Right." Tallen flipped through the orders. "Lots of boilerplate. Comes down to the Madgji lets us in the door and we take the Flowers apart like a cook deboning a chicken. And the Colonel will tell us how to hold the knife."

"And the tame Koshitsu?"

"The Wolvers." He shrugged. "If troopers surrender, and I am betting there will be more than a few, we should take them. We don't have a way to sort out quickly the hard core from the conscript infantry. So, infantry who surrender we give the benefit to, but strip their weapons and isolate them. Few of the noncoms and none of the officers will give up."

"Any other ideas?"

"Anyone ever mention that some Pika look like Flowers in the right light?"

I know I blanched. "No, that idea has not been broached." And please The Lady not in the hearing of the Pika.

He laughed. "The Wolvers talk about that a lot. Laying bets on just whose grandfather slept with whose grandmother. Not much more than broken ribs and the occasional concussion." He sipped at his cup. "The Wolvers are recruiting to beat the band, by the way."

I could feel the conversation escaping my slippery grip. "Which brings up what we are do with your…"

"Dress them up, teach the Pika some broken Japanese and the Ainoko trade Manche and let them follow me in."

"I hadn't planned on…"

"Horseshit, Alena. The only way this will work is if I get a crowbar in the back door while you are shooting the hell out of the front door."

"Who has been…"

"No one in particular. But we need to take the House back and decisively so. Heads on lances before the doors, that sort of thing. I got that bit of received wisdom from Dockens."

"We have a Gate into the back of the settlement around the House proper, midway between it and the ridges to the east."

"Madgji."

I nodded.

"And you trust them?"

"Not yet," I smiled. "but after they have tea with Breaker of Houses, I will."

TALLEN 57

It took a day to thumb through the Madgji. Two were Ringers or would be ringers. Both of them had the screaming conniptions when they found out I was going to be 'having a little chat' with them. Neither one of them were anything to worry about.   Alena and her 'Tame' Madgji had cleaned out the real Sleepers in the ranks.

Then it was time for me to sort out the Confederated. Four, two-man teams had hide out needlers with Selai loads and a deep background from the Commonality-The Unity-External Directorate. Two solo operatives were Stringers for the Flowers and they were carrying shellfish toxin crystals in their molars. The entertaining thing was that none of the four teams from the Euros knew about the others. Different buros in the Directorate. The Flowers were better organized.

One of the Flowers died too quickly. Even after I had

locked him up with an auric swarm, he managed to crush a molar. I was ready for the next Flower and held him on the edge of death just long enough to strip out his recent memories. The memories had been hard to find. He had been trained by people who knew full well the Selai form and its abilities and limitations.

The Europeans were more interested in killing Alena. A simple solution to a complex question, since all the rest of the potential players were dead or locked away. And when one set of operatives saw that simple solution would cause much more problems than 'guiding' her, that set changed their focus. The others hadn't gotten the word I suppose. One set tried to draw down on her at a dog and pony show. One of the Aknepteh hit the shooter with a beanbag gun. Busted hell out his jaw, all but broke his neck. But he lived to explain himself. Repeatedly. The spotter caught a spray of needles from Alena and was stiff when he hit the floor. She paused long enough to cycle her magazine and went on with the briefing. The other two teams rolled over.

The team leader that had changed his focus, he got closer than I liked to killing Dael. Only missing her by piss-poor planning and sloppy execution. He was trying for me. One of the Great Murdering Dogs took the needles instead, and bit the shooters arm off before the dog died. We just managed to keep the pack mates from eating the spotter alive. Dael let me do the honors of peeling his head open, in front of the Confederated elites and the surviving Unity operatives.

Gephart liked to shit himself after I let the thing die. If you fiddle with the auric fields just so, you can speed up cellular death and decay tenfold. The man was already dead, all of his cells just hadn't got the message; 'he' was gone, and I had all the relevant memories. I could run him through a log chipper, and it didn't mean shit to him or me. But letting everyone watch the flesh liquefy and slide off the skull like melting butter; that got their undivided fascination. Had to scrub the Quonset hut floor with carbolic acid after everyone revisited lunch.

I could tell after that bit of inspired grandstanding every one of the attending organizations, but the Aknepteh, wanted me dead. Beheaded, dismembered, burned and the ashes sifted into running water.

And even if I had been just a bog-standard Avar with some odd traits, they didn't want me loose upon the Empty Grass. The Confederated did not appreciate the concept of loosely bonded. As a matter of Progressive faith, they had discounted the legends of the 'true' Selai. Something that could not be safely controlled by a loose leafed binder full of operational protocols was way outside their comfort zone. They carried needle loads tailored for Selai but didn't expect the legends to be true. Now too many knew that Breaker of Nations walked among them. Drank whisky next to them and ate buffalo stew, just like a natural man.

The Pika were greatly entertained. But they loved the idea of slipping laxatives into tea, tripwires on the path to the privy and slow curing fletching glue on the toilet seats. Low humor at the best of times. Someone else's drawer wetting terror was their amusement. I did not remind them that two months earlier they were all huddled under the buffalo robes and singing medicine songs to ward off that noted Skinwalker. Me.

None of the Euros we turned over had been high up in Colonel Gephart's table of organization. One was an aide to an aide to an aide-de-camp for someone. But, Gephart was suitably embarrassed. Not that the Confed Houses were over supplied with useless officer drones, that was a given. He was embarrassed that a dirty assed Pika had caught the moles. Then after his Intelligence section got their hands-on Joachim, Gephart nearly popped a vein. Not only had the be-damned, pig buggering, Euros slipped in a Ringer into his beloved Corps, they stole four Tiger armored vehicles. And worse yet, they lost them to the dirty assed, horse buggering, Pika!

Then we got briefed. I think I slept through most of it. They tell me I snored.

The Ainoko were much more useful than anyone, other than I, thought they would be. They didn't just look like Flowers, they were Flowers. The roving mounted patrols out where the Empty Grass butted up against the Sunset Range were augmented with small penny packets of replacements escorting supplies every two weeks. It was easy to slip a half dozen of my 'tame' Wolvers into a patrol as a reinforcement packet. Every one of the troops they were reinforcing were bundled to the eyes against the winter. My Ainoko were just another muffled pack of dragoons riding through the snow and the murk. They had a dozen brother Wolvers ghosting along behind them, just out of sight but not out of reach, wearing the same sort of winter camouflage and load out. When the relieved Kikuza rode off for their barracks and a warmish bed, they were intercepted with dispatch and little fuss. No more big, noisy drillings. Just suppressed machine guns. Courtesy of the Confederated.

In the targeted patrol, the likely deserters were picked out and recruited. The hard core Kikuza were tagged. When the patrol slipped out farther, out into the Empty Grass, the hard core were iced down, the deserters inducted into the ranks of the Wolver-by-Bloodshed sodality and the wobblies were sent east to ponder their choices. The patrol continued on with new personnel and new commanders. Radio communications continued but, the quality of the links degraded with the weather. Imagine that. We had aerostats holding station at sixty thousand feet, interfering with all radio communications, including the communications links at the airfields and the big tower at House Mihaly. The SatComs were still down for the count so everyone had to make do with technology older than dirt. There was a lot of hate and discontent aimed at Herself for having the gall to knock down the GPS and the cellular satellites.

I asked one of the Confederated drones how come suddenly we had all sorts of wonderful toys to bugger the Kikuza with. He was inclined to be dismissive of my interest, after all I was but an illiterate, dirty assed Pika and not capable of understanding the high concept of strategy. Then he remembered the inspired grandstanding of the week before. I had someone come and pick him up from the dirty snowdrift he'd fainted into, before one of the Great Murdering Dogs had him for a light snack.

We took out sixteen patrols in and out of the foothills in less than a week. Some were less a reconnaissance patrol than a punishment detail of ten troopers and a corporal sent out to freeze their worthless asses in the snowfields. Others were the standard cavalry recon of thirty or forty troopers and an officer with a radio link. A link that didn't work so much anymore.

We left the double platoon or reinforced company sized hunter-killer patrols alone. The Confederated had plans for them involving Snowtigers and drones with cluster mines and stealth, ultra-light strikes missions, but that would be after we took the airstrips. I figured that the Snowtigers and drones would be as useful as tits on a boar, but they would keep the Confed out of our hair and entertained.

I dealt myself in on taking the southern strip. It had fresh troops from the pure land. Brought in by some of the last heavy transports in captivity.

Heavy infantry, not hobbled by pretending to be Horse Dragoons, carrying the latest and the greatest weapons loadout. Three reinforced Imperial Fudai platoons and a Kempetai action section. They were making life miserable for the Gaijin and the sadly inferior Ainoko bridge sweepings guarding the strip in Fielding. I knew there was another god-awful storm sweeping in and there were two more transport sorties scheduled to augment the Imperial's on the ground.

Gephart, who wasn't a bad sort once you got him drunk and occasionally laid, slipped three of his anti-air teams into the Front Range along likely flight corridors for the transports. The storm should force the transports lower and if they didn't want to fly into the unforgiving rocks, they'd have to thread through some valleys.

Shame about the storm knocking down those transports.

We formed up with the Wolver Anioko leading the

column along about dusk heading for the wire around the city just to the east of the strip. Three of them could pass for Kibei, wearing officer's kit and arrogant as hell, enough to get past the outer ring of guard posts. We had the current challenge and response from our Madgji, or as current as they could come up with. The guards at the gates were not mounted, they had what I called snowmobiles and a singlewide trailer with hay-bales to keep out the cold. They didn't venture more than twenty yards from the post. And each post was a good quarter mile away from the next one. I asked one of our Ainoko 'what the hell' and he said that they didn't need to patrol, they had sensors.

Sensors? And these were the elite Fudai?

I discouraged the Wolvers from thinning out the guards. Told them to just drape themselves with cold tarps and wait for the shit to hit the fan. Then they could raise as much hell as they wanted. Then I drifted to the rear of the column, leading a pony with a snowball in the frog of one of its off hooves. Kept my head down, just radiating dead tired old horse soldier, and gently tapping into the pony's life. As we moved up the road towards the town proper the Pika dropped off two by two and became one with the plowed-up snow drifts. When we did get in town, we didn't get a glance from the Military police in their Class One field uniforms who were stalking up and down the slushy streets. They were stylishly freezing their worthless asses off, half tunics with summer weight khakis and red berets. Their focus was on the despised Gaijin and the occasional solitary ordinary trooper. The Gaijin got shoved around indifferently, the trooper got a close inspection of his winter uniform for slackness.

The farther we got inside their zone, the slacker they became. No strong points, some light wheeled armor buttoned up tight against the cold. I began to be a little ashamed that we hadn't hit them earlier. The actual Fudai infantry I could see were only carrying side arms, not a battle rifle among them, and the Red Hats-the MPs-were stripping the rifles from regulars they intercepted entering the zone. Stacking the guns under guard.

When we hit the edge of the military compound, a cluster of warehouses and offices just off the air strip, they moved towards us to secure our weapons and one of the Wolver Shosa tore strips off of all of them, in excruciatingly formal High Nihon. Had them doing punishment katas for committing the offense of disrespecting an officer. One of the Fudai Strikers tried to slip off, intending to get some help in dealing with an officer of a lesser breed and I knew we had just run out of time.

I blew into a bone whistle and we herringboned. Every other man changed facing and gunned down any Flower in sight, then rushed into the compound shooting up the buildings with abandon. I dropped three in my sector and flipped a frag through a window. Then I dropped the pony and brought the Dragon all the way up. I went through the door and four Wolver Strikers damn near knocked themselves silly trying to be on my boot heels.

I didn't bother with the auric knives, just kept punching holes with my rifle. I could See through walls and in the dark and knew for example when a pair of Fudai troopers were trying to mousetrap the doors we were assaulting through. Modern rifles will punch right through engine blocks, let alone cinderblock exterior and lath and plaster interior walls but, you have to know where you are shooting. I just kept throwing three round bursts into the center of what I saw as blobs of light on the walls. Blobs that flared and winked out like broken light bulbs. My cover team made sure no one came around a corner behind me and left me to my housekeeping.

I had an idea where I was going, I'd marked where the Fudai runner had headed for and I figured he was after a Chusa at least, what we unwashed called a Light Colonel. I wanted badly to talk to the Chusa.

And I found him, two buildings over, shouting into a dead mike while fumbling with an unfamiliar assault rifle. I dropped him and I peeled him like a tangerine, back to his tasking briefing in the Pure Land. And I saw the hand behind the Cousin's war and what they wanted.

I shouted for the Wolvers and I ordered a courier on a

snowboard to dash to Alena. "The word is: No meetings for the Mihaly until I appear." And I flung her through a doorway into the gathering dark.

ALENA 58

I had a stream of would be conferees arriving at my fire ring every day. Consultative meetings with the Confederated, inquiries from buros without standing from the Commonality, offers of time limited liaisons, deals on time shares on the Southern Gulf. Barbara thinned them out with judicious applications of intimidation and outright violence, particularly the time share offers.

Savka had sent me a brace of trustworthy aides, aides closely bound to him and not the Confederated, to try and keep the blood feuds to a minimum. Between the three of them I had begun to construct the House apparat that would allow me to administer the House after we regained it.

We had inquiries from Houses remotely connected to Mihaly. Houses that had 'extras' that were interested in changing Tables. Wasn't uncommon. Houses always had more of one Talent than another. The Lesser Houses out west of Big River often passed around 'extras' instead of forcing them out of the 'Zeme. The Greater Houses in the East had a more jaundiced view. Their extras were lucky to get a hiltless knife and a barracks bag with an issue of clothing.

Of a necessity I was going to adopt more outliers than normal for a generation. The Fain and any Dai survivors would take at least that long to rebuild their clades.

It was late in the afternoon and I was about to close down my desk when I received two compelling requests. One was from a House once associated with Mihaly, up on the freshwater seas. We had not had over much to do with them in the last long generation, but my Aunt Marta of the Terrifying Memory came from them. One of their Gate Walkers had taken leave of the House to try and improve her position. She came scratching at my portal. I was a moment from admitting her for an interview when a breathless, raggedy, Wolver came through a fresh slit in the back of my lodge.

"A message Mihaly."

"And it could not come through the front?"

"One would not let me through, even though I held the Breaker's Token."

I slid open my camp desk's drawer and checked for my heavy needler. "Who disregarded the Dragon's token?"

The girl crouched at my feet, a long knife glinting darkly. "They wore Confederated battledress."

"So. The word?" I heard a commotion at the door.

"No meetings until I appear."

"Late the word I fear, gather the Pika and swiftly."

And she darted for the slit. I waited until she slipped through and then quietly spoke. "Enter."

I did not know the aide that slid the door aside, nor did I know the three robed travelers he admitted. But I knew. A Turncoat, two killers and a Binder.

I shot down the Turncoat, the heavy needles slicing through his tunic and dappling the lodge hangings with blood. The killers turned their backs to me, dropped their traveling cloaks and covered the door with their guns. The Binder dropped her robe as well, naked, sending a wave front of phenomes across the lodge towards me. I missed her with my last shots, though I killed one of her supports by happy accident.

Then it was a Binders' duel.

Her cloud of scent billowed towards me and I back stepped to gain time, clothes mask phenomes, I needed to shed mine. As I shrugged out of my tunic and t-shirt, I palmed two knives. One knife to shed my own blood if I got within range and one to finish me if I was lost. She did not rush to close and I heard even more commotion at the door. Then her cloud enveloped me, and the world collapsed around us. I dropped my last shred of clothing and opened a cut on my off hand, then bit through my lip as I jumped through the cloud to embrace her.

She fended off my bleeding hand with a pad, scrabbling at my knife hand with mesh gloves. I sprayed her face and eyes with blood from my mouth, and in the shock that brought I kissed her, exhaling my last breath into her lungs. Still the room began to turn beneath me, and her eyes expanded to take my will away.

Then black lace grew across her face and her eyes, like frost on a glass ball. I knew that lace. Her body convulsed and her Binder's surge collapsed back into her with my Hunger following through the lace. The lace that let my will pass and strengthened me.

The Hunger took her. I kept the lace at bay for a moment longer and then it faded slowly away, receding as my will commanded. She lived, her eyes a pinpoint pupil in a deep blue iris. She inhaled the laden air from my lungs and drank from my bleeding mouth. She convulsed again as poisons poured into her blood stream, into both of our blood streams. But the black lace returned, and I saw blisters on her face. I felt the blisters on mine, open and purge our blood. My Sister's blood and mine.

Then her eyes closed.

Still breathing.

Still alive.

A sister.

TALLEN 59

I purely hate helicopters. They rattle and clatter and bang like a badly maintained Model T and then they fall out of the sky. Like a lead pig. They only pretend to fly.

I'd sent the courier off and I knew I had to be hot on her heels. The Chusa had sent a ringer to where they thought Alena might be and they were closer on the location than I liked. This was four days before the night we took the airfield. That gave them time to get there, even on horseback. And I knew that it was not your usual incompetent wet work team in matte black and with the Golden Chrysanthemum emblem stenciled across the back of the armor.

A Binder, from the House Nihon stable. Six bloodsworn troopers with a Miyake cadet to cover her. All dressed in Confederated winter tunics and all carved into semblances of what passed for Gentry among the degenerate Dai by the best sculptors the Kikuza could muster. If Barbara or Dockens did not catch them, the dammed fool Confed would welcome them with open arms as a civilizing influence on the entirely too malleable Mihaly, hopefully to shuffle me off into the obscurity that I sorely deserved.

And I had to be there yesterday. Not that I am an indispensable monster, but in matters among the Talented I had an advantage. I simply killed them all and let the historians sort it out.

But the only magic carpet was a Bell. A fifty-year-old Bell; a goddamned, fifty-year-old terminally tired bird. With the doors gone, the canopy sand blasted to translucence and not clarity, oil piddling under the engine and the rear rotor covered in ninety knot tape. And above all else, a red tag hanging from the cockpit overhead warning in three languages and labels that it was down checked for flight operations.

I had been eating a burrito I had liberated from a benighted lunch wagon when they brought me to this zombie of a helicopter. "You are shitting me Striker Logan. This is what we have available after all the lovely iron on the airfield?"

Striker Logan, distant kin it would seem to P. Hendrix as evidenced by his love of flying ironmongery, gulped and nodded. "Your Wolvers shot up most of the other flyable craft something shameful, Breaker." My Wolvers. I began to consider adopting them out.

"And who is to fly this tinkertoy?"

He blinked at this. Then soldiered on. "We have a pilot sir. An Anioko ralllier. "

"I take it, Striker, that you mean a deserter who now wears our colors?"

"Sir."

"Produce this pilot, prep this piece of junk, address that" I pointed with my burrito at the red tag. "and get me in the air. Forthwith, at your peril. Which means I will skin you alive in front of God and Everybody if you do not complete the task. Understood?"

We got up in three hours. No working navigation electronics, no doors and I had them spray paint my chop in phosphorescent paint all over what intact surfaces it had left. "And your name is?"

"Jio, but you can call me Jake." He stuck his hand out to shake mine. This was not starting well. I did not see the hand, for he would surely need both of them to fly this piece of shit.

"Well that's right friendly of you." I began to wonder how he lived long enough to end up on my turf, with that sort of jaunty attitude among the Kikuza. "But I will call you Pilot, and you will call me Sir and we are going to fly that vibrating collection of scrap straight to the Tinker camp south and east of Corral Bluffs. And if we fall out of the sky, I will take you apart like cleaning a fish BEFORE we can hit the ground. And it will be a short but excruciatingly painful experience, for you. Is this clear?"

"Sir." He pulled his hand back and came to a facsimile of attention.

I nodded and levered my ass into the bubble, wrapped a buffalo robe about me and commended my soul to Eldest Sister, dead these seventy years but surely still haunting me. I closed my eyes as the rotor started beating at the air and thought good thoughts at the airframe.

He was a good pilot and he had a talent for slipping the damned thing through the air with the least amount of wild gyrations. We were a hundred and ten miles from the last place I knew Alena had settled in. The courier could make thirty miles an hour across powder snow, less across granular and goddamn fast when it was mostly ice. It also killed you going that fast on an ice field. The courier had three hours lead on us. We had fifty miles an hour on her best speed, saving the ice madness.

It would be a close-run thing.

A quarter hour after we got off ground, we broke through low hanging clouds and saw the moon to our west. Off north was another reef of snow clouds building and lighted by the moon. Below us were intermittent clouds and bright snowfields. It was almost pleasant. If you discounted a seventy-knot wind, cold and tooth rattling vibration. I remembered there was a reason I usually inserted on foot.

Our light discipline had certainly improved after the clusterfuck at Huygens Kopp. The fires were in chimeneas, banked and hooded. We had observers on every high point watching the four directions and quartering the sky. And there was a firefight going on in front of Alena's lodge.

I smacked him with the hand that was not welded to the airframe and pointed at the ground, behind the Lodge and close to the horse corral. He fucking near looped the helicopter, ignoring the tracers floating up at us and dove the banging, rattling Model T pig straight down. I will admit I was unhappy; I bent the airframe so badly that plexiglass panels on my side of the bubble popped out and vanished in the night.

I closed my eyes, felt the airframe twist and give, and the skids hit the frozen snow. And plunge beneath them to the frozen dirt. The engine quit and the copter blades came off. I could hear them crashing through the camp.

I flung myself out and opened my eyes. I ran to the back of Her lodge, shedding my robe and parka. Pulling a long knife out. The back of the lodge had a slit already cut in it and I just bulled through it, followed by two of the Great Murdering Dogs.

I ripped down the inner liner, kicked a bed and a suite of camp furniture out of my way and the Dragon burst fully into being about me. I felt both of the Dogs shy away and attack someone on the other side of the Lodge, while in the middle by a cold firepit two naked women embraced in a swirling cloud of pale smoke and blood drops. I flung myself into the cloud, cloaked in black lace.

Both Binders reached for me. The stranger was stronger than Alena. I let my aura entwine and surge down the stranger's binding smoke. Draining her life, ripping holes in her Subtle body and generally playing merry hell with her Overt body. I vaguely heard the Dogs rip into someone and felt a burst of gunfire pass over head. I knocked down the women and then threw myself on them, filling the room with the Dragon and killing everyone but us.

Alena surfaced long enough to lock her eyes with me and smile through bloody lips. "I have a Sister now." She said, cuddling the other woman closer to her. "A Sister, my Dragon, a Sister." And they both were out, like snuffed candles.

I sat with the two women snuggled in my lap, facing the door and watching my auras swirl through the room like birds of prey. I should have stayed in Missouri and been a farmer.

The Third Day:

Any other time I would have given Alena a week to get over whatever the hell she had happen to her. She was falling over seams in the lodge floor, knocking down valet stands, missing her mouth with spoon, fork or cup. She spoke in a scattered dialect of High Japanese, Creole, Spanglish and something that resembled French. She did respond to her name now. Right after the melt down she just gave me a thousand-yard stare whenever I tried to get her attention. Now she would perk up slightly and smile at me if I said her name.

The other woman was in worse shape. She didn't walk and eating was problematic. But when I gently asked Alena if we should give the woman the mercy stroke, I got belted across my ear and yelled at for a good ten minutes in a Dukes mixture of trade Cheyenne and something like an atonal Mandarin. Didn't understand a word. The gestures were enough.

I knew she had been poisoned. When the Kikuza operative, and we needed to give her a name, when the Operative had realized that she had failed, she suicided. It was a slug of fast acting venom mixed with a stimulant to force the poisons through the blood system. Nerve agents I supposed.

But I was in the mix and the quiet little secret about us Operatic Plot Devices is not only can we kill spectacularly we can heal spectacularly. I managed to keep them both going while I got their liver and kidneys purging the toxins, then I knitted up the Chakras that supported those organs.

But it was daybreak on the third day, and I needed her coherent and on parade.

The situation was getting antsy. I knew from my conversation with the Light Colonel that the Kikuza, and the Madgji dug into the House Mihaly, were getting the idea that all was not well with the Emperor's forces out on the Empty Grass. Sooner than later they were going to send out troops to make contact. And they had hostages. A quarter of the Fain that had clustered in the home valley were under guard. Most of these were Madgji linages, but they were on the whole innocent.

But that was not the problem. Our 'allies' were.

The Pika were supportive. More than supportive, bloody enthusiastic. I suspected with a creeping horror that Barbara had introduced them all to the Breaker of Houses saga. But the Confederated Political Officers saw this as a Meg-given chance to place a 'friendly' regime in place.

 Rationalize the regressive establishments of the Sunset Range Houses and settle the issue of the Pika. Their plans had to do with introducing Plows. Plows and a benevolent bureaucracy to guide the reordering of the Pika to a more settled, more civilized modality.

I'd blamed this on Savka. I had avoided him since he and the rest of the Confederated Political Office Clerks had turned up at the table. He was Jurchen and I was uneasy in his presence. I felt nothing. No tug at my allegiances.

The Confederated Military wanted nothing to do with any of this and immediately mounted up and decamped to hunt Kikuza on the Empty Grass in their bright shiny armor. When they got out of line of sight, they started having communications issues, just like the Kikuza. They knew just what sort of hellzapoppin' fur ball the political idiots were about to start, and they wanted to be four or five days away when the blood began to spray.

I noticed that there was a lot of Confederated Security Force Regulars, every time you let Clerks carry guns, they get stupid, loitering around Herself's lodge and the Confed Houses had gone from offering medical help to 'insisting' on taking over the 'burden' of her medical care.

Dockens did not take to this, nor did any of the other Pika. Which explained why gradually each of the Ferrets, we took to calling them that for their resemblance to the Black European Ferret, acquired three Pika shadows. Which is also why the Night's Sisters had set up housekeeping in Herself's lodge.

I sat down on a buffalo robe and snagged her as she drifted past, wrapping her up in my arms and enfolded her in the Dragon's aura. She tried to wiggle out, popped me a couple of times in my jaw with an elbow. Then she settled in as the auras began to knit up her Subtle body and reflect that in her Overt.

I was very worried about the holes I had perceived in the Chakras of the higher-level mindfulness. Alena's burn through spots, like the holes burned in 35mm film when the film projector jammed, were knitting up. Just not as fast or as clean as I'd like.

I had an idea. But she had to be cooperative. I sang very old songs to her while I smoothed away the kinks in her auras. I got horrified looks from the Night's Sisters and Short Moon came at the trot. He settled in at my elbow with a hot cup of tea and observed closely, so closely he got an elbow across his cheekbone when she got restless.

Long ago, when I spent all of a year in a German Kitchen embedded in a Chinese compound, I became the Young Dragon. Part of this was mushrooms and exotic toxins in dark rye bread, some was discipline imparted by Masters of the Way. But the main part was being enfolded in the auric robe of Old Dragon and learning as she shaped my auras, my Chakras and my thoughts. You can make a Dragon, a Selai, or a Skinwalker. You have to be of the linage that might carry that Talent. You have to be willing and there is enormous risk to the shaper as well as to the shaped. Shortcuts produce Broken Dragons and other obscenities. From what I knew, the main issue was that the shaper did not guide the candidate but forced the change. That and how young the candidate was.

I was of a linage, although the Jurchen had no idea which linage that might have been. Kluge Willm 'knew' I was of a linage and capable of wearing the Dragon. Once he asked me of my people and when he heard that my mother died in birthing me, he nodded slowly. "And her people?"

"We never knew. I never knew. Gypsies. That was the insult my stepmother flung at me and my sisters. Gypsy trash."

"Wiser than she knew." He sucked at his clay pipe. "No matter. You are Jurchen now and she is much the lesser for it."

I knew Alena. Three times now, maybe four, I had held her deep within my auras and enveloped her. Didn't plan this. It was reflex. I knew her on a deep level. On the same level I knew myself and the Greater Dragon. I could not copy her, not into my Subtle body nor into a stranger's. But I could hold an image up and let her auras flow into it and knit themselves whole. I held an image of Alena folded up into my auras like a map folded into a pouch.

And I held the Image of Dael as well, folded into my auras.

ALENA 60

I was asleep. It was spring on the Empty Grass. The sky bowl was filled with stars, the fire banked, and my robe wrapped closed about me. I was asleep. My head was pillowed on a great dog that grumbled in his dreams, dreams I strolled through. A woman sat drinking black tea, in a warm hearth kitchen. Drinking from translucent porcelain cups while her shadow knitted shapes from stray beams of light. The kitchen was lined with red ceramic tiles, mustard scorched my nose and my eyes wept tears of ink. I was asleep. I felt soft thumbs with long sharp nails gently etch ideograms across my skin, papery voices singing songs that I hummed. I heard drums and strings and a soft tin whistle. As I walked, I was handed my cloak, my sickle knife, my white staff, and my name.

Alena Constance Ni Mihaly. Mihaly of that House. And I am at war.

TALLEN 61

It would have been the big scene of the excellently terrible opera soon to come, if Alena had sprung up fully recovered from death's door. Was not going to happen. She was worn thin as washed out muslin, her finger bones lightly covered with skin. She opened her eyes and tracked the clouds that orbited us. Sighed. She was back from where she had gone, back and a long generation older still.

"My Dragon."

"Lightly bound but still."

"Bring me the Nagel and the Madgji. You have not killed all of the Confederated rat putz's I trust?"

"Soon, I would hope."

"Not this season. We must bind our 'allies' closer. I cannot follow you to the House. Barbara shall be my surrogate. Madgji to keep an eye on Barbara and Barbara to keep a very close eye on Madgji. There are always ways into a great House, some we put watchers on others we put traps."

"And some are only known to certain factions."

"Truth." She plucked at my arm. "My Sister?"

"I will give her to the Night's Sisters as their charge and their responsibility." I smoothed back her hair, threaded with silver now. "What happened?"

She laughed, softly. "I have no damn idea. One moment she is trying to Bind me, and I am trying to Bind her and the next moment you come in and throw paraffin on the bonfire.

Then I discover I have a Sister, born in Mino province, formed by the Tokumu Ki and nameless in the shadow of the throne."

"You know," I said. "they are going to have a great deal of fun with this in the next Breaker of Houses series."

"I dread the thought of it." Two of Dael's Aknepteh came and gingerly took Alena from my arms. "Go now and bring me the Nagel and the Madgji."

I watched them bundle her away and slipped out the lodge entrance. The dead were still there, the Kikuza dead that is. Ours were cleanly given to the Empty Grass or wrapped for the pyre. I ordered the Kikuza dead, in their Confederated uniforms, left untouched. Left for the crows. The six escorts that passed the Kikuza and the Demon Miyake through the Pika and into a lodge circle, with sworn assurances that they were conveying friends to her fire ring, Murdering Dogs and ravening Pika with short axes and large guns had butchered them.

It was all Dockens and the Elders could do to stop the Pika from dressing out every Confederated trooper in the camp and hunting down the ones out on the Empty Grass.

Now I was off and running to bring Barbara Ann and Gian, Nagel and Madgji, to attend Herself. It was going to get even more interesting. The Nagel. I didn't know Barbara Ann had a House all of her lonesome own. I don't think she knew either. I grinned in spite of the mess we were rolling in. She had been laying it on rather thick about my status as an Operatic Plot Device, now the worm turns.

I sent a double hand of Breaker's Wolvers to gather in
the Madgji. Told them not to kill his coterie, but to impress
upon them that Herself was in command again. I gave
Dockens the nod and he corralled all of the Clerks with
guns, with nothing more than broken bones, and produced
their nominal bosses at the door to her Lodge.

I got Barbara Ann.

She had a corporal's guard of Pika and orphaned Fain
at her lodge with the idea that they were guarding the door
and gaining merit. I came up out of the east with the
Wolvers and just went through them. She was sitting at
breakfast when I slid aside the inner curtains. She had a
sawed off shot gun across her lap. The dogs stood to, ready
to fight and then hesitated.

"You've damn near ruint my dogs, Breaker!" She
kicked at Big Dog. "They should be tearing you a new
asshole right now instead of rolling over."

"Nah, I just taught them the wisdom of not getting up
into the Real Big Dog's shit. Herself requires you. You want
to walk or have me carry your poor old carcass across the
camp?"

"You and whose army?" Six Wolvers came in the lodge
and dropped her corporal's guard in tidy groaning piles
around the ring. She thought about the gun across her lap.

"Now let's not be hasty, it's time for the next
installment in the saga you know so well." And I gave her
my best shit eating grin.

"I'll walk, thank you. May I arm?"

"Armed and in your best Sunday Go-to-Greet-the-
Gentry togs." I waved at the ring holders and looked
significantly at her valet stand with guns, blade and
embroidered jacket. They jumped and started fussing with
her Class A's and dress guns.

She smiled. "You are such a cheerful asshole. This had
better be good."

"Oh, but it will be, Nagel."

And she didn't notice the title in my voice.

It was a clear two hundred yards across the center of
the camp to Herself. The snow had been beaten down or

scraped away, as tidy as a barracks square. There was not a Ferret to be seen. Just a mill of Pika, orphaned Fain, undervalued Dai and 'my' Anioko. The Great Murdering Dogs were off guarding the disarmed Clerks. In front of Herself's lodge there was Savka Kochiurov, who was Jurchen as well as one of the exalted Clerks for Croton on the Hudson. There were all of the Pika Elders elbowing each other for the best place at the show. Madgji with a sable trimmed robe wrapped around him and a new bruise coming up on his cheek. Dael and three others of the Aknepteh, in dress paint, held the flaps.

Barbara kept her mad on until she got close enough to mark all the players on the field. Then she began to slow her steps. "What the ever-loving hell is this?"

"Just a council of war, Nagel."

And she stumbled over a shadow on the snow.

Alena came through the door to her lodge, standing by herself. Her robe was black, and it made her face even more pale, her hair pulled back and her face gaunt in the morning light. Someone had the wit to drag off the dead before we all had made our appearances, I think some of the giddier Pika were using them as step stools. She opened her arms, throwing back the cloak, and held out a hand to the Madgji. Gian started like a horse seeing a leaf for the first time then, with more grace than I had credited him with, bowed and took her hand. Then she turned to Barbara Ann, the Nagel, and held out her free hand.

We all waited. Then Barbara nodded slightly, bowed with her eyes fixed on Alena and took the offered hand.

"Cousin Madgji, honored observers of the Confederated Houses, my Pika friends; I present to you the Nagel of that House." Alena swept us all with her dark eyes. "The Nagel shall lead my War Band to take My House back from the Kikuza, the Madgji shall guide and advise and my Dragon shall clean the halls of the Eldest House."

Which meant that Barbara Ann stood deputy for Alena, Madgji was of sufficient rank to have respect among the snooty Clerks and bobbin counters and I was just fucking scary. I gave my best I-am-the-very-image-of-alegendary-monster grin. It was early morning and I intended to have my arm up to the elbow in the bowels of the Kikuza by this time tomorrow.

ALENA 62

I sleepwalked through the establishment. Tallen had not told Barbara what we were about and so it came to a complete and stunning surprise. She rose to the need, but I knew he'd pay dearly for his coup.

Afterwards they bundled me out of the cold and arranged me on a pallet at the back of the lodge. My Sister was still in sad shape, sleeping at the threshold of death. Why she was my Sister was a mystery. A Binders' duel ends with the lesser being bound by the stronger, a simple enough outcome. Often the lesser chooses to die, usually within moments of the end of the duel. She didn't die. Nor did I. I stared at the sun wheel over the door. There was an ache deep in me that I could not address, restless, angry. I wanted to be on my feet with the sworn Medji at my back. I stared at the sun wheel until it faded into the dark.

We were in a hurry. Most if not all the Kikuza forces

on the Empty Grass were accounted for, but we had to slip into the home valley and take House Mihaly before they could recover their communications links. Our allies from the Tidewater Houses wanted to bring up the heavy units still rolling through the hills and watersheds of the front range. I supposed images of armored battle danced in their heads like sugar plums.

I wanted the House intact. An armored assault would not leave one stone upon another and the House's dead would carpet the valley. I had hoped for the Madgji to give us leverage, I was heartened by the turning of the Anioko, but I read the intent in the mind of a Kikuza Light Colonel.

And how did I know the Colonel's mind.

A stir of cold air and I looked up from the buffalo robe across my lap. Tallen duck walked in, two of his shadows ghosting in with him. The Night's Sisters rearranged their posts along the lodge walls, pointedly ignoring his Wolvers. Tallen swept the Sisters with a dismissive glance, then sniffed. He had let his hair grow long, braided it tightly. His face was greased and painted against the snow glare and windchill, his winter pattern smock was stiff with blood and dirt and smuts. Over his left shoulder the blade of an entrenching shovel glinted, its edge sharper than a razor.

"How now, Dragon."

"Mihaly." He nodded to me. Than he sat cross legged, my pallet within his arm's reach. "It is after noon. We send the forerunners into the valley soon."

"I have lost time."

"Barbara and the Madgji will run with the Pika main force, the Anioko will go before them and clean out the outlying posts. Then they hammer the Kikuza at sunset."

"And you."

"I follow a hand of Madgji leavened with Aknepteh through the tunnel to the southeast of the main house."

"It is a well-known adit."

"Sold to us by the Madgji." He smiled under the dirt. "I do so trust them, now."

"We come to the end of the road." I waved him closer

until I could scent his essence. "I have questions."

He sat, his tunic open and his dammed antique Shansi tucked under his arm. He smelled. Horse and gun smoke, blood and that damned actinic pong he gave off when he was carrying the Dragon on his shoulders. The sleeves of the winter smock were dark and stiff with blood. His hands were clean, Meg help me, clean and the nails cleaner than mine.

"Questions?"

"Should I bind you, properly, strongly. Should I have you put down, quietly, discreetly. Should I bed thee or have Dael killed and then seduce thee."

He sat straight, light thickening about him and my nose burning with the ozone. "You have changed greatly." He said. "Some of this I had expected. The Binding. The gentle suggestion that the world would be so much brighter without my presence. But not my sudden popularity with Dai womenfolk."

"Oh?"

He stroked the air with his off hand. "Two more Pika have made, 'inquiries', as to my availably for the stud book. I was amused by the audacity of the first child. She made her request in front of the Mako'sae and every Pika in the lodge. My ears burned but I enjoyed the joke."

"She likely was not joking."

"I found this out, later." He paused for a long moment. "You think Dael is...?"

"No." I lied. "You read people with your black webs, I scent their hearts. Meg help her, the woman loves you. And she fears you and she mourns you and she may die with you."

He blinked. I could feel invisible legions of walkers questing over my skin. "Let us stop with the oracle pronouncements. It encourages my tendency to shake you until your teeth rattle. She mourns me, and I am still among the quick?"

"When this season of war is over the Aknepteh should kill you, and she would be the one tasked for this."

He grunted, like a fighter hit with a body blow. His

eyes grew distant and auras coated his face and his hands like chain mail forged from ebony. " 'Tallen, sometime Breaker of Houses, sometime Warlord for the Mihaly linage, guest among the Pika, we have found you to be a known Darkwalker.' And thou shalt not suffer a skinwalker..."

"Quite so." I folded my hands. "It is certain that you would kill her, but the Aknepteh would make a ritual out of hunting you from the Empty Grass and as far as they may reach into the Morning Ramparts." I leaned against my hard seatback and closed my eyes. "Likely they would cull their cadets by flinging them against you."

I felt air harden around me, smelled the sharp. sudden, fear of the Sisters arrayed along the lodge walls. "The Aknepteh would not long enjoy their hunt." A line of pain etched my cheekbone and I felt blood drip down my cheek. "They might spend the rest of their generations huddling in the dark, their yellowing bones breaking under the buffalo's hooves." Things broke in the lodge, fragile things. "The Chrysanthemum Throne has nightmares about what I did in China and Northern Hokkaido. I was young and clumsy, then..."

I waited. Things ghosted past my face and tugged at my hair. Then the air stilled about me.

"And if you had well and truly bound me?" He asked.

"As I am closely allied with the Pika, as long as they fear you, I would be fielding off subtle attempts at regime change or outright attacks. Encouraged no doubt by progressive elements in several cliques in several governments." I let the blood run down my face into my robe. "As long as you walk the Empty Grass."

"And if I am gone."

"They will sing songs, elaborate tales, send young men and young women to find you and learn the Tao of partisan from you. Away from the Empty Grass, you are someone else's curse."

"And Dael?"

"I do not know."

He looked away from me, the air shimmering about his

head. "It was a long time ago and I was a younger fool. But I cared for a woman..."

"Yes." My tone stopped the memory.

His head snapped around and I was transfixed by his eyes. For a long, long moment. "Well, perhaps I am well and truly bound at last, except for signing the writ in blood."

"I believe so, oh Dragon." I said in appalling mandarin. "Bound to me and to my new born Sister."

He blinked. "We really need to name that chit, before someone culls a name out of the telenovela and inflicts it on her. Tell Short Moon, then, that I am tightly bound to the Mihaly and thus to her Pika as well. That should put the wind up the rest of them." He stood. "Lightly caution them, Alena."

I raised my voice to carry through the lodge and to the Nights' Sisters sitting around the sleeping platforms. "And well bound. In the dark old fashion." I held out my hand, slicked with my tainted, blessed, blood. "By blood I bind thee to war and peace, life and death, honor and shame, to my blood and my House. Tallen called Ray, henceforth be known as the Wolf of Mihaly in Shadow. Carry Justice and Honor on your shoulders. Let Terror and Vengeance run at your stirrups and bear the Silver Spear of Mihaly Herself before you, in disdain of my foes."

He paused for a second, slit his left hand open with a thumbnail suddenly sharper than a razor and clasped our bloody hands together, looking around the lodge with a fierce grin. Black mail swarmed down his arm to lap around my neck and face. "The shilling' he took, and he kissed the book." He rumbled. He bent his head closer to whisper. "But I get first pick of the litter."

I blushed through the mail, and I wondered if I needed to tell him she carried.

TALLEN 63

House Mihaly was a big compound in a valley west of a mountain ridge on the front range of the Rockies. It was close to where Buena Vista was in my Rockies. Butted up against the eastern foothills, shading up into the mountains. Farms and small ranches bordered the compound to the west. The compound was about a mile wide and maybe a mile and a half long. The maps Alena had did not use meters or feet and I had to do the conversions on the fly. There was a well graveled road, snow packed now, from the gates past the steadings of the Fain to the small airstrip in the center of the valley. A two-horse town near the airstrip and straddling an intermittently snow-plowed road that ran north and south. There were light defensive positions at the edge of the compound and up into the foothills behind them, intended to discourage casual raiding and the like. Then there was the compound itself.

One sprawling two story adobe and stone ranch house with narrow shuttered windows and gun ports on the second story. A hundred yards away, a three-story Tudor with a tower of stone and slate butted up against it. And a quarter mile off to the west, next to an artificial lake, was a French Chateau. Half sized, with vinyl siding and a satellite dish facing south. Gnomes in a grotto off to the side. Madgji.

The side yards were full of light recon cars, knock-offs of Hummers and other SUV's mostly, and beefed up Overlanders. The recon cars were covered in snow, since the last storm had overwhelmed their snow tires from my reality. If you wanted more transportation than horse back or cross-country skis you whistled up an Overlander with dually snow tires on the rear double axels. If there were any drivable Overlanders left. There was a light helicopter parked out front of the adobe house, but all of its access panels were open and one of the blades was missing. I could see it was down. Maybe make it into a planter in the spring, right next to my damned Bell.

I slowly backed off from the ridgeline. We were about three quarters of a mile to the south and east of their perimeter.

"They are full of Kikuza, Madgji and some gomers in a light grey camouflage battledress." I handed Dael the long binoculars.

She slid up and took a slow sweep of the area, then slid back down. "The ones in grey are mercenaries. Likely hired with Her money before She got Her hands on the banker's throat in the Hanse."

"Any good?"

"The mercenaries?" I nodded. She cased the optics and shrugged. "They could be very good, or they could be worthless as nipples on a boar. I could see no unit patches." She sat there rubbing at her eyes with her ungloved hands. It was snowing again, lightly and with little wind. But we knew a big storm front was coming over the mountains again. "Most of the small holders are burned out, or displaced."

"Fain?"

"Yes." She pulled a linen handkerchief from somewhere in her parka and wiped her watering eyes, then blew her nose most ladylike. I refrained from noticing.

"According to our trusted Madgji the holdings closest to the adobe house have access tunnels to the food cellars of the house. The Nagel proposes to secure these holdings and demonstrate against the Kikuza."

"Basically, tease them until we can pry open the main house."

"Yes."

"Escape tunnels?"

"Escape, reinforcements, winter pathways, play grounds." She shrugged. "Diggers play in the dirt."

"Any of Her people survive?"

"Of the ones that stayed, I would venture not a one."

"Your hands are turning blue, put your gloves back on."

"She made a bargain with the Madgji."

"I know. And the Madgji who bedded down with the Kikuza stand outside of that bargain." I patted her shoulder. "And it may bear reminding to the Madgji I have a history of butchering Kikuza and any of their allies."

"I shall."

I stood up in the lee of the ridge and popped my back. Even though I was a noted monster and an infamous Plot Device, lying on the snow-covered rock was hell on my joints. "How far to this tunnel?"

She pointed over to our east. There was a battered old-line shack, an artfully, battered old line shack with a lot of Wolvers becoming one with the snowdrifts and a ragged fireteam of Madgji being miserable in the wind.

I looked up to the sky. Then I looked at my watch. "No time like the present. Barbara Ann is likely to start the dance without us."

"I have something to say."

I touched her gently on the arm and spun auras about us in the late afternoon light on the ridgeline. "I know." I pulled her close and drew a breath through the hood of her anorak. "Sufficient to the day is the danger thereof."

"Which means?"

"Let's go kill some Flowers."

ALENA 64

I was better. The soup the Sisters was forcing down me and my Sister seemed to be doing much good. My hands had plumped up quickly and I was beginning to have a healthy appetite. I wondered what besides the knowledge of the Light Colonel's mind I gained from Tallen. I avoided considering just what the meats they were boiling in the broth were. Savka, Jurchen in Shadow, came calling with several Clerks-With-A-Gun as escorts, or keepers. One of the Clerks became arrogant with the Aknepteh.

Savka did not turn around at the sounds of arrogance being refuted. The other Clerk asked politely for a cup of tea and a piece of flatbread. I sipped at my broth and regarded Savka closely over the steaming cup.

"You have come, perhaps I might know why?"

"Mihaly," His voice was low and studied. "certain factions see this time as another auspicious moment for change. They do not want to miss this opportunity."

Well. I owed Uncle Dockens a stick of bear-sign. He said the weasels would try for me again.

"A caution, Savka. If they agitate the Tinkers' women, I will do nothing to preserve their skins." I caught the eye of one of the Sisters and nodded slightly. She disappeared through the back of the lodge.

He smiled and asked in sign for a cup of broth and a piece of flat bread, maintaining a fiction of having only a limited facility with the Creole. "I understand full well, which is why I am taking the lesser meal with you. If I am breaking bread in your presence, I only have to guard against the Security Service and not the Warrior Sororities."

"You would hide behind my skirts?"

"But of course, any wise man would."

I smiled. "Well then, I have a price for your shelter."

His eyes widened slightly. "Name it, Mihaly."

"What names you find appealing? For girls." I thought he was going to drop his cup.

TALLEN 65

The tunnel was more than I expected. We descended to it through the line shack by a spiral staircase, thirty feet down. There was a substantial door at the bottom with a guard post, then through the door to the tunnel proper. Ten feet wide at the base, the roof seven feet above the floor and the shape of the adit was a truncated triangle. Not much light and the air was still, damp and cold. There were a couple of dead men in Madgji livery bundled off to the side along with three prisoners huddling in their ski coats.

Our tame Madgji had taken up positions about fifteen feet down the tunnel, flanking the narrow-gauge rails. On the rails was a trolley about twenty foot long. Its bed maybe two and a half feet off the floor. Dael's Striker was handing out body armor, flashbangs and night vision headsets. Others in the assault group were shortening their carbines and checking the unfamiliar weapons. I was not well for giving them modern weapons, not without training but, sawed off shotguns and autoloading revolvers were thin gruel against the Kikuza. So, I had stripped the Clerks of their guns. Anyone that gives a desk knobber a submachine gun is a bleeding idiot anyway. Of course, having my happy little band of brothers at my back with modern weapons made me just a little anxious. I saw blue on blue and 'simpleminded buggery' in my future. And every bleeding fool carried a short, well sharpened, trench shovel.

Dael pulled me over to the carriage. "First wave, Madgji at the front. Then you and the pick of the Wolvers."

"The pick?"

"The ones I think won't shoot you in the back, on purpose." She pointed at another carriage on a shunt. "Then me and everybody I can squeeze on that."

"How fast?"

"I have no idea. Old motors and, Meg help us, the batteries are crusty at the seams."

"Com links?"

"We are out of touch down here, that's why they have those..." She nodded her head at a box bolted to one of the beams. Black box, black handset with a crank and wires disappearing into the gloom of the tunnel. "Pick up the handset and crank..."

"I remember when that was the latest thing. Leave a pair of Strikers here and when we carry the other end, they can play relay."

She blushed. I could see it under the paint and in the gloom. The Dragon was waking without my conscious urging. "I forget you're older than dirt."

"Yeah. I forget it too. Sometimes." I got on the carriage, sitting just behind the operator and his tiller. "Let's go, we're wasting dark." Half the lot of us clambered on the skeletal carriage. It started off smooth and we were swaying along in the dark. The operator flicked on a catseye lamp but, his right seat man backhanded him gently and he turned it off. Habit will kill you, worse yet, it will kill your mates.

One of the Madgji, one that came with Herself, knelt

next to me.

"At the other end there will be a slight rise forcing the cart to slow. Guards to either side. No working alarms."

"And you know this?"

"Loyal Madgji. But the Flowers are watching them closely. And we have no way of knowing who is on shift and the last thirty feet are lit by red lamps."

Staging on the fly. "Stop maybe forty feet short of the kill zone. If we are living right the shit hasn't hit the fan up above and the gomers will be zoned out."

He didn't look at me. I could see him very well in the dark without the aid of modern magic. He was just focused straight ahead and keeping a very tight hold on his fear. But his auras swirled around him, trailing behind like a banner along with everyone else on the wagon. He was terrified and not of the gomers at the end of the track.

"You got a name?"

He started like I had stuck him with a hat pin. "Jether."

"I am going to clear the wagon when we get to the stopping point. Then, after I have secured the guard posts, you bring the rest up to end of track. Stairwell up?"

He nodded and caught himself. "Yes. Strongpoint at the top."

"Very good. Pass the word, no guns. Not even suppressed ones. Shovels, knives or just put the boot in. Anyone lets off a round without my express order will regret their birth."

"Sir." And he slid back to whisper loudly to the Strikers behind me.

I wondered how and when I had started channeling the shade of Staff Sargent Rukin. I first noticed Staff when I was bashing the Anioko pilot, now here.

I snapped the stock off my rifle, slung the shortened weapon over my back and brought the iconic shovel around to where I had it to hand. Then I let the Dragon loose. We were slowing down as we took the rise. I flowed off the wagon and ran up the slope to the strong point. There were four on this side of the door, more on the other side. I ran up, letting my auras thicken in the dim light, like a smoke candle.

Before they could quite believe that something was running in the middle of the smoke, I had dropped them all. Kikuza, Madgji and thin gomers in a grey field uniform. The door was not secured, and I went through it as meek as a lamb.

Four more, all Kikuza. Another two off in an alcove. Desk knobbers. Like drowning ducklings, nothing dramatic. My Wolvers filtered in and dragged the dead out of the way. I picked up the crank telephone handset in the alcove. There was a modern, well late 1960's at any rate, phone set with buttons next to it. But I cranked the phone.

A Pika answered, I could tell by the creole.

"Situation?" I asked.

"They just lit up the compound."

"Pass the word, we're in the Adobe House." And I hung up. I was stretching the bow a bit, we were three stories under the house; but what is that to an Operatic Plot Device anyway? "Okay Wolvers, Ladies and Gentlemen. Up we go." I felt Dael come into the choke point, inside the cloud of my auras. I let two of the Madgji catfoot up the stairs. I followed tight on their heels. They were my bird dogs and I was going to kill anything they flushed.

One of the Madgji hollered at the secured door that he had wounded to pass through, and the gomers unlatched and swung it out. I grabbed the edge and pulled hard, knocking two of my Wolvers down while the Madgji dumped their shotguns into the secure space behind the door. Then I led the way. Madgji, Wolvers, Pika and all at my heels. We were into the house.

It was hot work. Adobe House had grown randomly. I would have said like Topsy where Alena's contemporaries would have muttered about 'organic, self-organizing chaos' and meant that the house grew like Topsy. Each generation added rooms and halls, sealed up doors and windows as the outer walls became embedded in the interior of the house.

And the Kikuza were scattered through the rooms like raisins in a very tough loaf of bread.

I had a vague idea of where we were going, the Kikuza

had a murky idea of where we were coming from. Radios were crackling with static, the intercoms hadn't worked in thirty years and the inter-house telephones were hand cranked antiques or Bell knock-offs that passed through a central switchboard.

We started working our way through the house. You pass a stick of troopers down the hall until you had a door or a bend to deal with, scope it out, throw a frag around the curve or try a breaching round to unbolt the door. Most of the doors were solid wood with a steel or iron panel, fitted with a Judas door and a gun slit. Wasn't quite a pillbox, but it was damned close. And they had improvised defensive positions in the halls; sandbags, cinderblocks and four by fours.

The halls were wide. A good twelve feet wide. Even lined with cupboards and bench seats they were wide. And their rounds cut right through what cover we could drag up. Our rounds cut through their sandbags and cinderblocks too but, we had to know where they were behind the emplacements. They could see us coming. Even when we rolled smoke grenades ahead of us and rattled flashbang or frags off the high ceilings into the dead zones behind the sandbags, they still could see us coming. One thing that gave us an edge was that the halls had dog legs giving us a little cover once we had the nearest strong point suppressed. And my knack for looking around corners and through walls. None of their jack-in-the-box teams had a chance in hell. Before they could get the door opened, we pumped a grenade into the room they were staging out of.

But we were losing four or five men every time we took out a strong point. And we had to spread out as we fought our way into the house. We didn't know where their flanks were but, they sure as hell knew ours. Every time we got past an office or residency suite, we had to leave a holding force there to keep the gomers off our backs. We were running low on troops.

Then we cut our way into a dry courtyard. It was the backside of a carriage house that the Adobe had grown around, like a tree growing around a barbwire fence. There was a dead tree in a planter in the middle of the yard, a rusty ladder was bolted to the wall of the carriage house between the bricked-up windows and doors. It led to the roof. I had two of the Madgji at my back take their sledgehammers and open the door to the building and I flipped a frag in through the broken bricks.

Then the Madgji cleaned out the door so we could get in. The builders had made the ground floor of the carriage house into a kitchen, around the early jazz age on my side of the Veil I guessed. White porcelain appliances, gas refrigerators, a walk-in pantry. There was a dumb waiter leading up and another set of bricked up doors that would have led into the stables, I guessed from the horseshoes nailed over the doors. At the back of the kitchen was a narrow stairway leading up. At the top of the stairs was a hallway that led into the house again, along the edge of a fossil balcony embedded into the bricks and mortar of the house. At the end of that fossil balcony was a ladder to a trap door.

The rooftop. I had someone go and check the ladder in the courtyard. When I heard the guns rattle, I popped the trap door, surprising the fire team. After they were well and truly suppressed, I raised a rifle with a snooper clamped to the barrel and scanned the local roof. It reminded me like nothing more than a complex of rice paddies or terraces. A series of rectangular, flat rooftops, brick or adobe walls being two to three-foot high, ringing each roof square. Sometimes sharing a wall between two rooftops, sometimes there was a three or four-foot gap between the walls going down to the ground. Or a six-inch gap that went down about the length of my arm with a drain pipe leading to god knows.

And across the roof tops lay our target. The main courtyard. I could see mortar rounds lofting out of the courtyard against our people. I could see heavy weapons fire from rooftop strong points lashing down and out of sight. Tracer rounds came in from our people across the valley. Glancing off the roof or exploding in bright flashes on the plate reinforced strong points, tumbling over our heads.

I took a knee and pointed at one of the last Pika left to me, one of the Night's Sisters. She had a rack of breaching charges hanging off her back and a SatCom. We didn't have satellites, but we did have the aerostats hanging sixty thousand feet up.

"Opera Six actual Texas actual."

"Texas Overwatch Go."

"Blue on Blue! We are on the roof. Drop your fire."

"Flash."

I had a directional bullseye strobe on a folding rod, usually we would use that to guide an aviation asset in at night. It was shielded and there would be little leakage to either side of a fifteen-degree arc. In daylight and in a firefight, there would be little notice taken of it from the gomers.

"Illuminating."

"Texas Overwatch Illuminating green."

"Confirmed."

And the fire dropped off of the rooftop strong points. I handed off the SatCom to the Pika. "Ditch your charges. Let one of the Black Ribbon take 'em."

"Ah-yuh."

She shrugged off the rack and slammed it into the arms of the Madgji crouching next to her, said something in the creole that I didn't quite catch and duckwalked back to the end of the stick.

Black Ribbon Madgji. Turncoat Madgji. Oath breakers twice over. They were piss poor troopers, the dregs of the lot but, when you take and shove your sidearm into the armpit of the Flower beside you, you'll do just fine. They would frag the Kikuza to get our attention, then they'd lead us around the back side of any hard point and lead the way down the throat of the gomers holding the hard point.

They took to wearing black ribbons on their battledress, looped through a d-ring on their chest. The second or third time we picked up a cluster of Turncoats they suddenly sprouted black ribbons. The Madgji with the ribbons led the way. And they died leading the way, leaning into the gunfire like someone leaning into a wind and hard rain.

I looked around and I didn't have much left of the Wolvers I'd come up the tunnel with. Jether was nowhere to be seen. In fact, just about all I had with me were Black Ribbon. Madgji in Kikuza battle dress with black ribbons fluttering at their chests. Or soaking in their blood. I looked the one next to me in the eye. She didn't flinch or look away. She had a smear of blood and brick dust across her face and matted in her hair. Her eyes had the thousand-yard stare, but her hands were sure, and her auras were flat calm.

She scared me.

"You got a name?"

She just stared me down and shook her head.

"Okay then, stay with me and when I want a hole in the roof you use one of those charges." I turned my head to look at the Striker on my left. "Then you take a hand of Black Ribbons and drop through. Rock and roll. Got that?"

He nodded.

"Let's do this."

It wasn't that simple. Never is. They had more weapons teams on the roofs, light machine guns mostly, in sandbag faced railroad tie revetments. They were oriented to cover the approaches to the house and its surroundings and support the heavy weapon bunkers. They were not particularly oriented to cover the rest of the roof top. We maneuvered, pinned their attention and popped up to take them in the flank. Knock a hole in a roof, rip a door off a stairwell head, fall through a skylight, cut three rooms over and then come up again. Behind the gomers, or under them. They had made the mistake of setting the heavy weapons, the heavy machine guns and the light cannon, to only cover the approaches to the house and to its central courtyards.

We still lost men. Black Ribbon Madgji, but men and women. My men and women. I got shot up some but, between the body armor wished on me and the gift of the Dragon, it didn't amount to much. The Madgji at my elbow watched the auras stich up a six-inch slice through my arm, saw the scar form and then fade. Then she turned and faced forward.

I'd dropped a horse just before we came down the tunnel and that let me shrug off the damage. I dropped the horse in front of the troopers. Damn. That was just flaming stupidity.

No wonder Jether was so spooked. I'd gotten used to my hardcore Wolvers and didn't think to suppress some of the more disturbing perks of being an Operatic Plot Device. And the Black Ribbons knew all about the Dragon, every single lie in the telenovelas. She was not scared. She had already sold her soul to one devil. What's one more?

It took us a hot fifteen minutes from the time we broke through the roof top to when we spilled over the walls into the main courtyard. Where they had dug in two armored cars, a battery of mortars and the hardcore Flowers and Madgji. We rolled over the hard points on the rooftop and then just depressed the light cannons and opened the armored cars up like tin cans.

I dropped over the edge and waded into the mortars and their crews. I felt more bodies pouring over the wall, following me into the courtyard. I shot my gun empty and took to swinging the shovel around while a Dragon of black auras mantled around and behind me. That broke the back of every thought of resistance. I even saw a long service Kikuza NCO take off his cover and hold it up on his reversed gun for quarter. Dael got to him before I did. Cut his throat with a backhand slice of one of her black glass knives. Before she could get to the officer lying next to the dead NCO, I hip checked her.

"Stop that." I knelt and had my Dragon sieve the officer. He was young, fresh from the pure lands and knew just where the Miyake was forted up.

"Holder's suite?"

She pointed with her bloody hand.

"Link up with the Nagel. Tell her I am heading for the Miyake."

I picked up my shovel and loped into the doors on the other side of the courtyard. The radios weren't suppressed anymore. The Madgji were hitting their house, the one with the gnomes in the wee little grotto. The Flowers were dying in carloads, hit from both sides and hit harder than they expected from second rate troops. The astute planners of the Kikuza had put all the surviving Fain in the French provincial monstrosity, the Madgji Fain on the most part, and the Madgji were punching way above their weight class to rescue them. Barbara and her Nagles were swarming the Kikuza holdouts in the house and the surrounding holdings with dash, élan and bloody-minded close quarter murder.

Someone gave an alert that Kikuza troopers were falling back on the airstrip and they had a pair of jets warming up. And that the Troopers were killing anything not a Kikuza in the warrens leading to the airstrip and at the airstrip.

The Prince was going to bug out. I changed my mind and found a way up onto the roof again. I headed at a dead run for the airstrip.

I knew which way the airplanes were. North and West of the house proper and then about five hundred yards from that door to the hard stand. I did not want to get stuck into the Kikuza on the flight line. The only cover would be baggage carts and fuel trucks. We had to get to the back door as they fell back through the house. Their rear guard would make a last stand someplace inside the halls and then the Miyake and his close guard would make for the jets.

"Texas Overwatch, Opera Six actual." I gasped into my mike as I legged it across the roofs. Up and down, jumping walls and clambering over AC units and under duct work. "Mortars. Fire mission, secondary airstrip, flight line."

"Texas Four. Four tubes available. Shot out."

Two of the troopers pacing me disappeared, falling through the roof. One of the following Strikers sank his leg into a rotten spot. I kept running. I could hear incoming mortar rounds. I saw one hit the roof of a hangar just on the other side of the flight line. Dust and debris belched through the skylights. Clouds of black smoke shot through with flames rose over the berms that lined the flight line

and the airstrip, protecting the house from the noise of the
spooling up jets. I saw part of a wing loft up and then twirl
back out of sight. The high whine of the jets stopped.

I jumped across an alleyway and body checked two
Kikuza troopers back down an access stairwell. Behind me
I heard someone let fly two shotgun rounds. I was facing a
tall firewall at the north edge of a rooftop. Beyond it was a
drifting bank of smoke, laced with occasional tracers. I
jumped up and vaulted over the firewall.

I fell a good story and a half, flattening a knot of
Kikuza trying to set up a light machine gun to cover the
doorways to my left. The Dragon had come up full as I fell.
The Kikuza fell away from me like wheat under the scythe.
I grabbed one of their weapons and charged the doors. Just
in time to greet the close protection detail and the Miyake
as they came through.

It was close quarters buggery. I never got to use the
gun I lifted. Not as a precision weapon. I clubbed right and
left with it and my shovel. I felt the concussion of shots,
powder stung my cheek and I was knocked back by trip
hammer blows to my armor. But I broke the gun. Broke
the shovel. Stripped a long knife from one of the Kikuza
and spun through the middle of them. They ripped at me.
Pulled my snow smock to rags and I felt, rather than heard,
blades scrape on the armor, catching on where the
gunshots had splintered it. Guns hammered to either side
of me and blood splashed on me as my troopers caught up.
I just focused on the Miyake being dragged towards the
burning flight line. A Katana sheathed and in his left hand.

I flung my knife at them, letting it cartwheel through
the air like a billy club. One stumbled, his knee blowing out
as someone shot past me. The Miyake passed his long
sword to one of his guards and turned to face me with a
short sword held with its gleaming edge up. The blade
shimmering in the halogen lights.

I had not noticed the sun had set. It didn't matter.
From the corner of my eye. as I closed with the Miyake and
his short sword, I could see the guardian with the Katana
stripping the sheath away and stepping to the side to cut me

down. He cut down one of the Black Ribbon troopers between me and him. On the recovery from that stroke the swordsman thrust for me, to take me in the gap under the arm. A trooper stepped in front of me, took the sword through his chest and pulled the guardian close, inching his way up the blade, his own knife ripping out the swordsman's throat.

The Miyake dropped his smock. Dropped almost to his knee and tried to come up under my guard. Into the cloud of my aura. In the halogens I could see his face, crisping like tooled leather thrown into a fire. See him stagger, his grace broken into stop motion and I stepped past his knife and let my hand trail across his face and neck.

She fell. She.

Her free hand locking on my armor and the y-harness, pulling me off balance and down with her. One eye was smeared shut, the Dragon's kiss. The other was bright and tears ran down the un-ravaged side of her face. She tried. She tried, so very hard, to rotate that short black bladed sword around and shove it into me. Her breath bubbled in her throat and I felt her start to convulse. I wrapped the auras about her center and took her memories. Then I let her die, at once, like a broken bulb.

Her.

I gingerly took the sword, a long, black bladed tanto, from her lax hand. It came into my left like it had always been there.

The fighting died away.

Long crackles of gunfire dying away into single shots at intervals.

More troopers poured over the edge of the roof, on ropes and not in head long leaps. Others came out of the shattered FBO offices, some were Black Ribbon, some Wolvers, the rest were Pika.

I carefully slipped the tanto into a sheath I took from the Prince... The Princess. Then I turned to the Black Ribbon that had pulled her way up a sword blade to cut a throat. She was dead.

The nameless Black Ribbon.

402   Selai

I pulled the elaborate katana from her body and placed it on her chest. I slid the sheathed tanto into my rig.

"Opera Six."

"Opera Six actual."

"Mihaly is sending an escort."

"Opera Six, say again?"

"Mihaly requires your presence, Opera Six."

I looked around. Dead Kikuza in their winter camouflage, Wolvers in the night gray smocks and Black Ribbons in their white and gray. Pika dead in motley with emblems and tokens denoting their fire ring.

Pika troopers were moving through the standing troops. They were stripping weapons from the Black Ribbons, slapping them down. The Wolvers were about to get involved as well. On the Black Ribbon side. I saw one of the Pika late comers to the party get sucker punched, disarmed and tumbled into a waste can by two of my Wolvers.

As I walked to meet my escort, I glowered at one of the Wolver Strikers. "Ribbons and Wolvers with me. Condition One." And I walked through a cluster of Pika with the Dragon's wings rippling in the halogen lights.

One of them thought to detain me. A Pika with emblems I did not know. His eyebrows might grow back, though I doubted that the rest of his hair would. Behind me I heard someone order 'guns up and follow the Breaker'. I might have to kill every one of the Black Ribbons, but I would do the killing. Not some officious Pika or pissant Clerk. Besides which, I was under a death sentence just as much as they were.

Going back through the house and compound, to wherever Mihaly wanted me, was hard. I'd burned a lot of my reserves away. Shrugging off wounds and dealing with people who didn't have the good sense to stay the hell away from me. Now I was making a display of the Dragon and it was dragging me down. We hadn't thought to bring rations for me. The ever-popular cookie dough and raw hamburger diet. My knees were a little wobbly under my snow fatigues.

In the hallways I dropped the penumbra. I left the

Dragon bubbling just under my skin in case we hit any hold outs. The power was out so all we had to see by were emergency lights or the occasional bank of halogen work lights running off generators. The work lights were for the casualty stations scattered through the buildings and for prisoner collection stations.

One of the collection stations was where I found an Eisenring enjoying summary justice. With a trio of Clerks backing him up. He had three dead Black Ribbons sprawled over in the corner, two Kikuza and a wide eyed Pika kneeling in front of him. And he was loading another magazine of needles into his favorite toy.

We swept through the courtyard and things got ugly real fast. Three of my thugs butted heads with his gun bunnies and in the confusion, nobody noticed me coming through the door. Mateo shot one of my people in the face, using the standard toxin needles. Then he swung to cover me, and his face froze in a fearful grin.

I didn't flinch. Two needles hissed past my ear and then I had him by the throat with his needle gun clattering to the floor. "Well met, Eisenring." I whispered in his ear. Then my auras sucked him dry. His memories flashed through my nets. The only thing he could have given me I already knew. That there were wet teams moving through the confusion to rationalize House Mihaly and its allies. What I wanted was life, the glow running down my arm and coiling around my center.

I dropped the desiccated corpse in Eisenring black, kicked the rattling bones out of my pathway and stood over the trio kneeling on the paving stones. "What say you?" I asked them.

They looked at Mateo's bones and then as one swore to me.

The two surviving Clerks cowered in a corner. I drained a hundred years from them in a heartbeat and then motioned the rest of my entourage on. I grabbed one of my Black Ribbon Wolvers. "Any fucking Battle Police you see, any fucking Checkered Hats, fucking KILL them." He nodded, poker faced.

I let the lives I had just ripped away settle, memories draining away, then I followed. Pink bones crunching under my boots. My face was wet with tears. I did not know why. My hands trembling, the palms burnt to lace in my leather gloves. The black tanto back in my left hand.

Killing the Prince had...distressed me. Princess. Her memories, her gifts, were arrayed in my deepest mind and her terror still ran up and down my nerves like jolts of electricity. Add to that the fucking Checkered Hat thugs I'd just sucked down. Brain freeze, like eating an Italian Ice Grande in one bite.   Mateo, that Eisenring, had truly enjoyed hunting in my wake like the scavenger he was. He never knew just what he was risking. And the time he had to know, just what was consuming him, was sadly limited.

I could feel the gust front of my people, carving through the chaos of the aftermath.

My Wolvers.

Black Ribbons?

My people.

The Ächtet Zirkus. Let's name it plainly.

I could feel the Bindings fraying as the Wolvers recruited. This was really going to set the weasels in the hen house. A Selai unbound and gathering forces. Building a House.

We came through the last set of doors, guarded by Pika I knew by name and Mihaly Fain. Clustered in the middle of a courtyard, the courtyard that had held the mortar crews and light armor of the Kikuza, was an aid station. Dead Pika in their flash overalls, dead Kikuza and dead Confederate Clerks were scattered about the courtyard. The Clerks were very dead. Someone had worked them over with blades and a need for vengeance. A half dozen living Clerks were pinned against an armored car by Pika and half-pika, backed up by a dozen mute Dogs. Dogs watching prey at bay.

The Pika saw us come through the doors, nodded and went back to the Clerks. In the middle of the damned Clerks was that tame Jurchen, Savka. He still had a gun in his hand, standing between the Dogs and the Confederated.

He did not break his focus. The Clerks behind him were unarmed and hard used. He was the only thing keeping their skins whole.

He'd die before he let the Pika have his Clerks. Useful thing to know.

I stepped to the front of the Pika, shoving one of the mute Dogs aside.

"I was ordered here, by Herself, Jurchen."

"You took your time, Tallen."

I looked over my shoulder and nodded one of the Black Ribbons forward. He carried a head in one hand and a princely sword in the other. It wasn't the head of the princess. But who among the living would know?

"I was detained." I said, holding the head up by its hair, the sword displayed in my other hand. "The Dogs seem eager. I should wonder why?"

Savka gestured with his chin to the center of the aid station and the frantic medical personnel.

I did not look away. I held his eyes. "Have a care, Jurchen. I have already ended one princely line this day." He did not blink but, there was a hopeless grief in his face.

"Fuck me." I whispered. "The Mihaly." I dropped the head and the sword. And I turned my back on them; Pika, Dogs, Clerks and all. And shouldered my way through the medics.

In the middle, facing away from me, were two women. One cuddling the other. Both wore Pika battledress with Mihaly flashes on their sleeves. I shoved my way around to kneel before them.

It was Barbara Ann.

She looked like hell. Face blotched and her eyes swollen near shut. Blood seeped from under one lid, running down her face like mascara in a light rain. Thumb sized blisters ran across her face and down her neck. Dael sat behind her, holding her up so she could breath and an EMT knelt at Barbara's left hand, aspirating her lungs through a tube at the base of her throat. Foamy blood drained through the clear tube into the suction device.

"What happened."

"A hold out, with a needle gun." Savka was at my elbow. "A Turncoat Confederate. She was wearing Mihaly's torc about her neck."

"She's holding on."

"Not long, Tallen." Savka said "She wanted you and Herself here, to witness."

"Witness what?"

One light blue eye opened. Tracked towards me. Blinked and her hand tore the intubation away. She coughed, spat foam and blood, and gobs of mucus. "Tallen?"

"Here."

"Honored me they did. Selai loads." She was whispering. Gargling through the fluids filling her lungs. "Herself here?"

"Not yet."

"You'll do." She let her head fall back on Dael's shoulder. Her blood smearing Dael's cheek.

"Cut my hand, girl." She was holding out her left hand across her body, palm down. Dael paled under her grease, produced a small, knapped obsidian knife from somewhere and slit Barbara Ann's hand with an upward flick. "Now Tallen, cut her hand and hold them together."

I hesitated. Her blue eye glared at me, demanding. "Do it." I lightly cut Dael's hand with a ring knife and blood pooled in it. Then they clasped hands tightly, with my hand over wrapping them both. Bonded children jumping into a deep pool. "No time to pretty it up." She said. "I am the Nagel. I Claim and Adopt Dael, once of the Aknepteh, once of the Sisters of the Night, now Dael n'Nagel and Heir to that linage. And I call..." She choked. A gout of blood came through her throat and spilled down her front, half coagulated from the Selai poisons. I felt Alena step into my auras.

"Mihaly stands Witness and Guarantor and Ally to Dael n'Nagel, the Name of that House." And Alena's hand laid over mine.

Barbara coughed twice more. Then she stilled. Her auras burned away. I felt Alena move away from me where

I held Nagel that was and Nagel that is.

"Contest this passage at your peril." She quietly said, meeting each eye of the encircling audience. "Deny this heir at your peril. Confront my House and House Nagel at your peril."

I looked up at the encircling Pika, prisoners, Clerks with guns, mercenaries, Houseless wanderers and Footlocker dwellers. "And remember." I said. "Well remember. That Tallen, lately Breaker of Houses, and Nightmare of the Chrysanthemum Court, stands behind both Houses with the Ächtet Zirkus."

Savka winced and swallowed. Confederacy House was not going to be pleased. I smiled in his direction, the way the wolf smiles.

The End

###

ABOUT THE AUTHOR – THE REST OF THE STORY.

Like his characters, JD Bell is a big persona living in a world that is too small for his personality. An early reader of SF and fantasy, Bell's stories have captivated many listeners for years – but he rarely wrote them down. The few exceptions are still out there: early sales to The Space Gamer magazine with stories that perfectly linked the Ogre and GEV game universe. These short stories were too good to disappear, and in an era of disposable electrons, his work has resurfaced in reprints from Steve Jackson Games anthologies.

JD's presence at decades of SF conventions in the Kansas and Oklahoma region is also the stuff of legend. (But as the statute of limitations has not expired on some of those exploits, it is best we do not speak of these finer moments.)

His work is a remembrance of SF and Fantasy as it was, with ringing swords and phasers that are rarely set to stun. His characters are the perfect combination of larger than life skill set coupled with a world-weary point of view, caught up in the action of the moment. With no time to consider the finer points of etiquette, they rarely choose discretion, opting for a full-tilt fight though the outcome may be in doubt.

Add to that their ability to miscalculate the passions involved, and you have a character that is larger than life and extremely competent – sometimes tripped up by matters of heart and emotion.

In other words, a person much like his readers – and the author.

JD lives in Kansas with an adorable wife and with four daughters that take strongly after the cats he raised over the years: Fiercely independent, strong willed, extremely resourceful – and of course, beautiful.

JD currently has a second book in the Hidden Worlds fantasy universe in the publication chain. There is also a Space Opera under production – and it appears a direct sequel to Selai, in the Hidden Worlds milieu. Who knew retirement could be so productive?

www.ingramcontent.com/pod-product-compliance
Lightning Source LLC
Chambersburg PA
CBHW070903260626
47162CB00007B/2546